I AM LIVIA

PHYLLIS T. SMITH

This is a work of historical fiction. Apart from the well-known people, events, and locales that figure in the narrative, all incidents are the products of the author's imagination or are used fictitiously. Any resemblance to current events or locales, or to living persons, is entirely coincidental.

Published by Lake Union Publishing, Seattle

www.apub.com

ISBN-13: 9781477848821
ISBN-10: 1477848827

Cover design by Cyanotype Book Architects

Library of Congress Control Number: 2013914534

Printed in the United States of America

In memory of my mother

A woman preeminent among women,
and who in all things resembled the gods
more than mankind, whose power no one
felt except for the alleviation of trouble . . .

—Velleius Paterculus

Leading Characters

Livia Drusilla

Marcus Livius Drusus Claudianus, her father

Alfidia, her mother

Secunda, her sister

Marcus Brutus, leader of the assassins of Julius Caesar

Marcus Cicero, Rome's elder statesman, allied with the assassins

Caesar Octavianus, Julius Caesar's posthumously adopted son

Tiberius Claudius Nero, a prominent military officer who marries Livia

Little Tiberius and Drusus, Livia's sons

Julia, Caesar Octavianus's daughter

Rubria, wet nurse in Livia Drusilla's household

Mark Antony, Julius Caesar's right-hand man

Octavia, Caesar Octavianus's sister

Cleopatra, queen of Egypt

Sextus Pompey, ruler of Sicily

Marcus Agrippa, Caesar Octavianus's friend and leading general

Caecilia, Agrippa's wife

Gaius Maecenas, Caesar Octavianus's friend and advisor, patron of the arts

Chapter 1

I wonder sometimes how I will be remembered. As mother of my country, as men call me to my face, or as a monster? I know the rumors none dare speak aloud. Some believe I am a murderess many times over. They envy me, and they hate my power. In Rome, a woman's power, however circumspectly exercised, arouses revulsion.

Every death in my family circle has been laid at my door. People claim I am adept in the use of poisons. Oh, I have transgressed. But not in the way they think. It is when I remember my youth that I find myself recoiling. Do I recoil when I think of him, my beloved? No. But I paid a price in my soul, for loving him.

Old age can be a deceiver. My knees ache when I walk, but if I sit still, I do not feel so different from the girl I was. I tell myself I am the same. Then I glance down at my hands resting on the saffron folds of my stola, and I see blue veins under skin that is almost translucent. I cannot evade physical reality. And yet I believe I remain, in some essential way, the person I was at fifteen or twenty.

Today I am called by the honorific Julia Augusta, but inside of me the girl Livia Drusilla still lives. Certainly, the decisions that girl made long ago shaped who I am now.

The time is approaching when I must move aside to make room for other guests at the banquet of life. It is necessary that I prepare to explain myself before the gods. Above all, I must be ready to account for the young woman I was.

My beloved wrote a record of his deeds for others to read. Of course he obscured distasteful truths. But I will write the story of my youth in a cipher only I know. I will be honest. There is no point in lying to the gods.

It will take courage to remember the days when I was Livia Drusilla. I wonder if I can do it without flinching.

⋙⋙⋙⋙

The murder that shook the ground on which we walked, the murder all Rome remembers—I knew about it days before it happened.

I saw three men disappear into my father's study, and then I heard nothing, not even a bee buzz of conversation. What could they be doing in there if not talking?

I was borne forward by burning curiosity. Not the random inquisitiveness of a child; I had passed my fourteenth birthday. I wanted to learn every bit I could about the world in which my father moved, that of men who wielded power. I knew I could never enter that world, but it drew me as the sky draws a young bird.

Father's study was separated from the atrium by only a long curtain of heavy wool, dyed the color of raspberries. I tiptoed toward the curtain, so close that my face almost touched the rough fabric. I stood still, listening, and to my amazement heard not a sound.

I was used to hearing men's boisterous conversations coming from the study. Why would they be so quiet now? Were they telling secrets inside? My sister and I would whisper to each other. Our servants often whispered too. Whispering was something girls and slaves did, not men like my father.

I stood still, straining my ears to hear. At first, there was silence. Then a voice came, low but audible. "Not just him."

Another voice: "How many deaths would satisfy you, Tiberius Nero?"

The first voice, again: "As many as it takes to make us safe. I assure you I'm not bloodthirsty, but we're staking our lives here. Let's not behave like fools."

"Proscriptions again?"

Proscriptions. Before I was born, in the dictator Sulla's time, men's names had been posted on a wall—names of those who opposed him, or whose relatives or friends did, as well as those who had amassed enough wealth to arouse envy, or did anything else to draw suspicion or hostility from Sulla and his circle. Once their names went on the wall, these men were hunted down like wild beasts.

Father's voice rose, full of resolve and so much distaste he forgot to speak softly. "I won't have it. And Brutus won't have it. It's bad enough that we must put one man to death without trial." The voices dropped again.

A shiver ran through me. Because already I knew almost everything. I knew there was to be an assassination, and who was to die, and that my father was part of the plot.

Father lacked a son, and I was the elder of his two daughters. He had always shared much more of his mind with me than might have been expected with a girl child. He would speak about distant wars and kingdoms, and I would see the farthest reaches of the empire through his eyes. Or he would tell me his assessment of one public figure or another. He often voiced his discontent.

He had been born into one wealthy and powerful noble family, adopted into another, and had always expected to serve in public office. In the past he had held important military and governmental posts. But under Julius Caesar's rule, he could play no role in Rome's government, at least none in accord with his principles.

When I was small, he spoke to me of political matters just to ease himself, I think. Sometimes when I asked him a question, he would give me a surprised smile, as if he was astonished that I absorbed everything he said. As I grew older, he came to expect my questions.

Father talked often of liberty and the right form of government. Caesar, he said, was not just a dictator—that was an honorable office, circumscribed by law—but a tyrant. Five years ago he had ignited a civil war, and seized power. He had overturned the supremacy of the Senate and done just as he pleased. In his arrogance, Caesar had even renamed one of the months of the year—the most beautiful summer month—Julius, after himself. Lately his supporters, at his instigation, had begun demanding he don a crown and call himself king. I knew that Father believed that the Republic was being destroyed by this one man. He had not, however, intimated to me that he and his friends intended to act.

I see myself staring at the curtain, straining to hear more, a slender, red-haired girl with dark eyes too large for my face—a face now drained of color. The fact that Caesar was to die did not appall me. I had been taught to regard him as Rome's enemy, and I had never met him. I had only watched him from a distance as he rode down the Sacred Way in triumph, wearing a faint, ironic smile as he listened to the people's cheers. But I understood my father's danger. Caesar would not forgive an attempt on his life.

Perhaps I made some small noise without realizing it, or touched the curtain and caused it to move. One of the men in the study sensed my presence and ripped the curtain aside. My heart jumped. Father's friends stared at me with horrified expressions.

Father looked startled and embarrassed but said hastily, "Don't be concerned about the child. She will tell no one."

"Gods above!" This from Tiberius Nero, the youngest man present. "We're babbling to too many people. Now your daughter knows? This is absurd."

Another of the men, a white-haired senator, his toga trimmed with purple, gazed into my eyes. "Child, what did you hear?"

The gravity with which he spoke terrified me. I could not swallow and barely managed to whisper, "I think . . . you are going to kill Caesar."

The senator's face hardened. He looked as if he wished to strike me dead to assure my silence.

"Be easy, my friends," my father said. "It will go no further. Will it, Livia Drusilla?"

I stood hunched with fear and shame, but his addressing me so formally, by my full name, made me straighten my spine. "I will say nothing," I said.

"If she should talk—" Tiberius Nero began.

"But she won't," Father said. "She has given us her word. I assure you my daughter is neither a liar nor a fool."

Tiberius Nero looked at me the way men do at slaves offered for sale. "Is this—?"

"Yes, my firstborn," Father said.

"Ah," Tiberius Nero said.

I disliked his eyes on me. I stared back, my chin raised. After a moment, he glanced away.

He was a tall man with a sharp nose and watery eyes. At that time he was thirty-eight years old. I had never seen him before. The other two men present were longtime friends of my father.

They gazed at me searchingly, trying, I suppose, to guess if I had sense enough to keep their secret.

All three left with uneasy expressions. When they were gone, my father put an arm around me. "Now, daughter, it's wrong to eavesdrop on men's conversations. Haven't your mother and I raised you better than that?"

Close to tears, I turned my head and pressed my face against his shoulder. I hated it when he rebuked me, though he always did it gently. "Oh, Father—"

"Shhh."

I lowered my voice. "I'm afraid for you."

"You needn't be." Father spoke in a whisper. "I won't strike a blow. Only senators will take part. I merely stand ready, as several others do, to assume a post of official authority when the way is cleared. That's not very heroic or dangerous, is it?"

I whispered back, "But you're part of a plot to kill the most powerful man in Rome. If it fails, you'll be in great danger." Horrible imaginings filled my mind: Caesar ordering Father's execution or, because our family was a noble one, sending him a dagger and a note, *Salvage your honor.*

"The plot won't fail," Father said.

"I think you will be in danger even if it doesn't fail. Haven't I heard you say the people love Caesar? Surely he has friends who will want to avenge him?"

"Just see that you don't speak of this, and all will be well." He squeezed my shoulder. "Tiberius Nero . . ."

"Yes, Father?"

"He was Caesar's officer. But he has come over to our side. A fine fellow, of excellent birth. He is actually a second cousin of mine."

I said nothing.

"You will marry him."

In the course of things, Father was bound to find me a husband in the next year or two, so an announcement of this kind was to be expected. Yet a wave of dismay swept over me. I blurted out my first thought. "You are giving me to him to induce him to turn traitor to Caesar?"

"Of course not. What a thing to say!" Father avoided meeting my gaze.

I knew what I surmised was true, at least to a degree. I was part of the inducement—that is, my dowry was, and the privilege of an alliance with my father. But to say outright that he would wed me to a man as a bribe for abandoning his loyalty—that was wrong. It was crude and stupid of me to speak of such a matter with blunt honesty.

In those days, I often uttered foolish truths. My mother struggled in vain to break me of this habit, with a birch rod. Father was far more lenient. He would chuckle sometimes at what I said and suggest that I give a matter more thought. He even seemed delighted when some words of mine could make him pause and think.

The study was a special place for me; it was where Father and I had our best talks. It always smelled faintly of the preservative oil used on the parchment scrolls. Two of the walls held shelves of Father's favorite books—volumes of history and political philosophy and accounts of the lives of men who had fought for the Republic. On another wall was a magnificent mural, depicting the Battle of Zama. A corner niche held a bust of Cincinnatus, that selfless patriot who saved Rome from invaders, then immediately gave up power. In this study, I always felt so valued, so close to my father.

My stomach tightened because I had displeased him, the one person in the world I most wanted to please. "Are you angry at me?" I asked.

For answer, he kissed me on the forehead. "Run along, child."

I started out of the study, but another thought came to me. I turned. Father was leaning over his writing table, looking down at some document—a muscular man with iron-gray hair, our family's rock.

I knew I ought to keep silent. I had already given him cause to reproach me. Fear gnawed at me, though, and I ached for reassurance, so I walked back and whispered in his ear, "Father, who will govern Rome when Caesar is dead?"

"The Senate. Who else?"

"But you always say the Senate has failed to govern. We have had bloodshed for nearly a hundred years. Won't there be more of that if Caesar dies?"

"The Senate will govern justly now and command the people's loyalty. Marcus Brutus is an able and upright man. He will lead us."

Brutus was an important figure in the Senate. Moreover, he was directly descended from the man who, centuries ago, had led the successful revolt against Rome's evil king, Tarquin. His ancestor had, more than anyone, been responsible for the founding of the Republic. It was natural that Caesar's opponents looked to him for leadership now.

"No more talk of this. Now run along, Livia."

I started to go, but then turned. The more personal meaning of the day had just begun to seem real. "Tiberius Nero—is it absolutely necessary that I marry him?"

"Why, I've promised you to him, child."

"You could tell him you changed your mind. Couldn't you?"

"I've given him my word."

"Father, I don't like him."

"Don't like him? You don't even know him. You're beginning to make me truly angry, Livia. Now—" He made a shooing motion with his hands.

⋙⋙

I ran out to the garden. Tears burned my eyes. How could Father give me to Tiberius Nero? I'd felt an immediate distaste for the man. He had gazed at me as if he were inspecting a slave, and when I had returned his stare, he glanced away, giving me no personal acknowledgment at all.

What did Father mean by saying Tiberius Nero was a fine fellow? Father's exact words were *A fine fellow, of excellent birth.* As far as I could tell, if his birth was excellent, nothing else about him was. Not his looks, not his manner. I remembered the snatch of conversation I had overheard. The man had been advocating proscriptions, hadn't he? He would condemn men for their associations and opinions, just to protect himself. *How many killings would satisfy you, Tiberius Nero?* he had been asked. His answer: *As many as it takes to make us safe.* Was that how a fine fellow spoke?

Our garden was like a huge courtyard, the heart and focal point of the house, which surrounded it on four sides. Here, where no street noises penetrated, one could almost believe one was not in Rome but in some bucolic setting. Now, early in March, a few flowers had begun to bud, hinting at the garden's coming springtime glory. I had sought this place as a refuge. At least for a few moments, I could be by myself and sort out my feelings.

Nothing that had happened before to me had prepared me for the blow I had just suffered. It seemed Father had told me I did not matter to him. He had bartered me away, and then dismissed me. The only worse fate than finding out that Father did not care about me was losing him entirely—and I risked that if the plot against Caesar was discovered.

A statue of Diana stood by the little pool near the garden's north side. The sculptor had depicted the goddess as a huntress and had painted her in lifelike colors, with hair the shade of wheat and eyes the gray of storm clouds. She looked like a girl of my age graced with divine freedom. Wearing a tunic that stopped above her knees, she stepped forward, holding a bow in her hand.

People said that of all the Olympians, Diana had the most tender love for the people of Rome. She never seemed as remote and out of reach to me as other gods and goddesses.

I glanced around to make sure that I was alone in the garden, then approached Diana's statue and held out my hands, palms up in supplication. I whispered, "Goddess, I have no sacrifice to give you. But I promise you a gift—soon, very soon. I beg you, whatever happens to Caesar, please, please keep my father safe from harm. And please make it so I don't have to marry Tiberius Nero."

A moment later, a slave came looking for me, sent by my mother to fetch me to dinner. I knew Mother would be angry if I did not hurry, and so I went inside and paused only to wash my hands in the copper bowl at the entrance to the dining room. The first course had been set on the central table. My mother and father reclined on couches, already eating. My eleven-year-old sister, Secunda, perched on the dining room's third couch. I sat down beside her.

Mother, as always, was impeccably dressed for dinner. She wore an emerald necklace that my father had bought her at great cost, and she had her flame-colored hair piled on her head in a crown of ringlets. She possessed a natural poise and a gift for always arranging her body in an attractive way when she reclined, so her stola fell in elegant folds. People said I looked like her, though only our coloring was the same. I certainly had not inherited her grace.

"Well, daughter," she said, "your father says he has told you the news."

I glanced at Father. His jaw tightened, and he gave me a meaningful look. I felt he was silently reminding me of my promise not to speak of the plot to kill Caesar.

I understood that Mother referred to my coming betrothal, nothing else. Returning her gaze, I said, "Father has told me that I must marry." I could not keep myself from adding, "But I hope he will change his mind." I spoke in a mild voice and looked down at my plate, into which a slave was ladling fish stew.

"And why do you hope he will change his mind?" Mother asked.

"Because I do not like Tiberius Nero," I said.

Beside me, my sister gave an uneasy giggle.

"Alfidia," my father began, addressing Mother.

"No, please, Marcus, why not let Livia talk? Usually her chatter pleases you. Livia, I'm sorry to hear that you do not like your future husband. Can you tell me how he has fallen short?"

"I don't think he is a man of character," I said. "He switched sides, and that doesn't speak well for his loyalty. And he talks like a coward."

"You misjudge him," Father said. "To see one's error and come to follow better counsel in politics is not disloyalty but wisdom. You are right that Tiberius Nero is cautious, but who can blame him in these times? He is a courageous man, a fine soldier."

"I don't believe it." I kept my eyes lowered, but I was contradicting Father on the basis of no knowledge at all.

"Why, Caesar has repeatedly commended him for his bravery in battle. And Caesar—whatever else we might say of him—knows how to judge men."

"Does he?" I raised my eyes. "Is that why he keeps Brutus at his right hand?"

Father looked stricken. Probably for an instant he thought I was about to speak of Brutus's involvement in the plan to kill Caesar. Mother saw his dismay but did not understand its cause. "You see?" she said to my father. "This is what comes of spoiling her. Forgive me, but you have only yourself to blame. You talk to her of great matters and puff up her pride. And you make excuses when she disobeys me. Is it any wonder that she feels she can even speak rudely to her father at the dinner table?"

"Father," I said, "you taught me that without honesty there can be no honor. I'm only speaking the truth." I added, with more humility, "What seems to me to be the truth."

"Go to bed," Mother said. "You don't deserve dinner."

I looked at my father in appeal. I didn't care about dinner. Food would have sat in my stomach like a stone. But I wanted him to defend me.

He said nothing.

"Go," Mother said.

I rose and ran to my bedchamber, where I threw myself across my sleeping couch and wept.

Gradually, the sunlight entering from the small window in my chamber faded. By the time night came, I had stopped crying. I sat on my bed and looked out the window at the crescent moon, wondering how long I would be able to live at home before I had to marry Tiberius Nero. I hoped our betrothal would be lengthy, but I doubted that it would be. Many girls married at just my age.

The idea of marriage was not in itself frightening. But nothing about Tiberius Nero appealed to me, and I dreaded marrying him.

I asked myself if there was a way for me to escape. What if at the wedding I raved like a madwoman or fell to the ground and began frothing at the mouth as if I had the falling sickness? Surely Tiberius Nero would not want to marry me then. Or suppose I refused to say the words of consent at the ceremony, or spat the consecrated cake out of my mouth? Then there could be no marriage. I thought of these possibilities to comfort myself, and tried to convince myself that the marriage was not inevitable. Then I lay down and cried myself to sleep.

I had a very strange dream.

I climbed up steps of polished red stone and heard, of all things, a chicken clucking. At my feet was a hen that gazed up at me with bright, curious eyes. Though she had blood on her feathers, she seemed unhurt. She disappeared, and I found myself walking down a curving path into an enormous, lush garden filled with flowers in full bloom. In the center of the garden stood a huge statue of Diana. As I watched, the statue turned into a being of flesh and blood and leaped down from its pedestal, moving with the grace and strength of a lioness.

Diana's living face was far more beautiful than any sculpture, and it shone like a lantern. "I am the protector of the Roman people," the goddess said. "You promised me a gift. Do you know what it will be?"

I shook my head. "Perhaps a lamb?"

She stroked my hair. "Wait. In time you will know."

⋙⋙

The next evening my parents attended a dinner party at the home of friends, and my sister and I ate alone. I picked at my food. Even the oysters I ordinarily loved had lost all flavor. Seeing how miserable I was, Secunda said, "Think, when you marry you'll be in charge of your own house just as Mother is. You'll like that."

"I won't like being married to Tiberius Nero," I said.

Later in my bedchamber, I reviewed part of Aristotle's *Politics,* which I had begun to study with my tutor. I lay down the parchment scroll on my little writing table only after I heard Mother and Father arrive home. Mother always scolded me if I stayed up late reading by the light of an oil lamp. Thinking of what Secunda had said, I imagined being a married woman, able to read until dawn if I wanted. But no, I would have to go to bed with my husband, wouldn't I?

I was not ignorant about the physical part of marriage. In fact, I had once walked in on our steward and one of the slave girls as they copulated standing up in the kitchen, their clothes bunched up to their waists. I remembered how their legs looked, hers pale and slim, his dark and hairy. The girl had been bent over a table, and the man grunted with pleasure. I was repelled. What I saw was like the coupling of two animals. I did not want to believe it had anything to do with me, that I could ever be in the girl's place.

My own longings were different, shrouded in a dreamy mist. I imagined a young man's face, beautiful as if sculpted by Phidias, the outward sign of spiritual perfection. He and I would share the union of two pure souls, the kind of virtuous love Plato wrote about.

Foolishly, I had imagined one day marrying a paragon and experiencing an exalted love. Now I knew I never would. Instead I would marry Tiberius Nero.

Just as I was about to blow out the lamp's small flame and get into bed, I heard a knock on my bedchamber door. Father entered. "Come to the atrium with me," he said.

I draped a shawl over my sleeping tunica and obeyed him. Only one tiny lamp illuminated the atrium. It was set on the altar near the entranceway, before the statuette of the Lar, the god protector of our family.

Father walked to the tall, wide cabinet next to the altar and threw open its door. Shelves held wax portrait masks—rows of stern male faces.

"You know whose portraits these are, don't you, Livia?"

"They're of your ancestors."

"And yours," Father said. "Generation after generation, they held high office. Some even led armies that fought for Rome. Their blood flows in your veins."

Father often spoke to me of the history of Rome and the roles our own forebears had played in it. His stories always stirred me and made me feel as if I knew the men who had come before us and shaped our destiny. I would wish it were possible for me to join the line of heroes he told me about. But how could a female perform great deeds for Rome?

"Livia, ever since you were small, I have known you were unusual." Father touched my head, and I could see the glint of his teeth in the lamplight as, for a moment, he smiled. "Some people would say I have given you a rather odd upbringing, but it never seemed wrong to treat you as a reasonable being like myself, or to encourage you to think. It is possible that one day you will be a very wise woman. See that you are good as well as wise, will you?"

"Yes, Father," I said, warmed by his words.

"Perhaps Tiberius Nero is not the man you deserve," he said.

"Then—" I was about to throw my arms around Father, to shower him with thanks for setting me free.

"I do not say he is not a good man. I say it is possible—possible—he is not the man I would pick for you if my hands were untied. Listen to me, my daughter. I will not command you but talk to you as if you were my equal. These are not normal times.

We must strike for liberty now. Nothing less than Rome's future is at stake. It's necessary to bind Tiberius Nero close. He is one of Caesar's most admired officers, with many friends among the soldiers. His allegiance matters. Do you understand?"

I pressed my lips together and, looking down, nodded.

"If you were my son, and I asked you to pick up a sword and fight for Rome even if it might cost you your life, would you say no to me?"

I shook my head.

Father put his hand under my chin and raised my face. He stroked a lock of my hair back from my forehead where it had tumbled. "I think you would ride off to battle very bravely. Wouldn't you?"

"Yes."

"What you can do for our cause is marry this man."

"I would rather die in battle," I said.

As soon as I had spoken those words, I knew they were a lie. Fight in battle? I would do that willingly. But die? Even a heroic death did not appeal to me.

Father smiled sadly.

A thought pierced me: I would never die in battle, but he might. Young as I was, I perceived that the death of Caesar, the man who held the state together, might unleash chaos. All sorts of unknown perils lay ahead. If marrying Tiberius Nero could help keep the ground firm under Father's feet, I would do it.

"I will marry Tiberius Nero," I said. I made myself add, "If it's for the liberty of Rome, I'll do it gladly."

Father bent and kissed me. After a moment, he said, "You must not only marry him but be a good influence on him. His allegiance has been doubtful in the past. But if he cares for you—if you serve him and are a loving wife to him and bind him to you with ties of true affection—he may ask your opinion at a moment when it matters. Never be overbearing, but be his confidante and friend. Gently, gently. Do you understand what I am saying?"

"Yes, Father."

Father gazed at me with pride and tenderness. "You will be the mother of noble sons."

Chapter 2

On the morning of the Ides of March, my sister and I sat reading a Greek play with Xeno, our tutor. Antigone was about to be sealed alive inside her tomb. On the fourth finger of my left hand I wore a gold band—the betrothal ring that Tiberius Nero had sent me, in token of our coming marriage.

A slave entered the schoolroom and said that our father wished to speak to us at once, that an event of great importance had taken place. He added that our tutor was free to leave for the day. Xeno looked amazed to be dismissed in this abrupt fashion by a slave. Secunda, too, was astonished. Father never called us away from our lessons.

I felt sure that the event could only be an attempt to assassinate Caesar. My mouth went dry. Was Caesar dead? Or could the plot have failed? Might he still be alive, and ready to avenge himself on his enemies, including my father?

Mother stood with Father in his study. Father's hand rested on her shoulder. Mother looked as if the earth had split open beneath her feet.

"This is a great day, my daughters," Father said. "Word has come that Caesar is dead. The tyrant—the man who would be *king*—" Father's lip curled as he spoke that last word, anathema to Romans. "He has been put to death by members of the Senate." Dispassionately, he told us some of the details of Caesar's death, then glanced round at my mother, my sister, and me. "You three must stay inside. There may be upheaval. I'll go down to the Forum and see how matters stand."

"You should stay inside too," Mother said.

Father shook his head. "My place is at Marcus Brutus's side." Without another word, he left us.

Mother said there was no point in being idle while we waited for news, and she led my sister and me into the spinning room. All three of us got busy spinning wool. Even as I worked, fear gripped me. "I wish Father hadn't gone out," I said. "There will surely be uproar. The common people loved Caesar." They admired him, I knew, for his military victories, and he had wooed them with public games and festivals and with largesse. In particular, he was the hero of the poor. By contrast, the Senate—six hundred men appointed for life, mostly aristocrats—had little claim on the people's love.

"If the rabble riot, I hope the Senate will deal firmly with them," Mother said. "They require an iron hand."

"If they riot, will they come up the Palatine?" Secunda asked.

"I don't know," Mother said.

We lived on the Palatine Hill, the premier dwelling of Rome's aristocratic families, and our house was on the north side, overlooking the Forum. If the common people sought to avenge Caesar, they might surge up the Palatine's slope, into our neighborhood. I imagined them breaking into the house to vent their fury on us.

"Mother," I said, "if I go outside and stand on the doorstep and look down the hill, maybe I'll see something. I won't be in danger if I just slip out for a moment and look."

"Didn't you hear your father say we must all stay inside?"

"But if only we could know what is happening!"

Mother forbade me to go out, but she dispatched our steward, Statius, to go to the Forum and gather news. After he had gone, she said, "Livia, your father's friends killed no one but Caesar. They did not harm Mark Antony. Why do you think they let him live?"

"They did it to show that they are just and not vengeful."

"But Antony was Caesar's right-hand man, was he not?"

"Yes."

"Your father is a wise and learned man," Mother said, "but he can be too noble for his own good." Her face tightened. "Gods above, the rest of them—the leaders—what if they are all too noble?"

I knew—as all Rome did—that Caesar had carried on a love affair and fathered a son by the queen of Egypt, Cleopatra. He continued to live with his Roman wife, Calpurnia, a plump matron I had seen carried through the streets in her litter. On the eve of his assassination, Calpurnia had a nightmare. She awoke in terror, convinced that her husband would not return from the next day's Senate session alive. She begged Caesar to stay home, and he agreed. But the next morning Decimus Brutus—Marcus Brutus's co-conspirator and distant cousin—arrived to escort Caesar to the Senate meeting. The assassins planned to strike that day, and Decimus feared that the plot would be discovered if there was a delay. So he pricked Caesar's pride. How, he asked, could the ruler of Rome cower in his house because his wife had a bad dream?

In the end, Caesar went to the Senate session, held in Pompey's theater. Inside the theater, a senator fell at Caesar's feet and clutched at the folds of his toga like a desperate supplicant. Caesar tried to pull away, but before he could, the other conspirators set upon him. More than fifty men stabbed him, wounding each other in their frenzy. Many of them had fought against him in the last civil war and afterward received his mercy.

When Caesar lay dead, the assassins raced to the Forum. They held up their bloody knives and shouted, "Rome is free! Rome is free!"

People fled from them. Fear, not rejoicing, was the reaction of most of Rome's citizens. And we—my mother, sister, and I—felt fear, too.

"Oh, Mistress, Pompey's theater was set afire, and there are looters all over the market district," Statius told my mother when he returned home. "They are smashing their way into houses and shops."

"Board up our windows and nail the door shut!" Mother cried.

For a long time, the whole house reverberated with hammer blows. Mother, Secunda, and I stood near the entranceway. Four of the slaves nailed planks over the windows. I looked at Secunda. My sister's face had turned a milky white.

Anything could happen to us. The savage rabble might break into our home, and Father was not there to protect us. Who would? The slaves? They would flee. Law and order had broken down. We might be raped, murdered.

When the house was boarded up, the sudden silence seemed eerie. I felt like some small helpless beast in a hunter's snare. The sensation was new to me. Whatever Rome's political troubles, I had never before had cause to fear. We could do nothing but wait. Mother, Secunda, and I had no heart for spinning wool. We sat in Father's study and spoke little. Then, suddenly, we heard a tremendous banging on the front door.

Mother pulled Secunda and me into her arms and pressed our faces into her bosom, as if she wanted to shield us from the sight of what was coming, a crowd of killers bursting into our house. My nostrils filled with the scent of her perfume, and I could hear her racing heart.

I had an awareness of my own soft flesh, my vulnerable body. In my imagination, savage hands dragged me away from my mother. Enemies surrounded me on all sides, as Caesar had been surrounded. They violated me, and then stabbed me again and again with knives, just as Caesar had been stabbed. A well of fear swallowed me up.

Then I heard a familiar voice that almost sang with relief. "It's the master!" Statius called from the entranceway. "Take the nails out of the door! He's shouting to be let in!"

Mother released Secunda and me, rose, and smoothed her stola.

Soon Father was with us, saying that there had been some looting, rioting, and deaths, but the city was by and large peaceful now. The horrors we had conjured up seemed ridiculous. Secunda and I looked at each other and giggled. Even Mother laughed. But we were wrong to imagine that we were safe.

\>>>>>>>

Caesar's funeral was strictly a political event; my mother, sister, and I did not go, but Father did. So did Marcus Brutus and Caesar's other assassins. "Will there be a funeral address?" I asked Father as we stood in the entranceway before he took leave of us. He wore a toga, its folds carefully arranged.

"Of course," Father said. "That's customary. Caesar served Rome well in some respects. We will honor him for that."

"Who will the speaker be?"

"Antony."

I heard Mother draw in a sharp breath. "Are you saying, husband, that Antony will be allowed to give a speech to people in the Forum?"

An uneasy expression flickered across Father's face. "That was Brutus's decision. He put all the arrangements for the funeral in Antony's hands."

"But why?" Mother asked.

"To conciliate Antony." Father spoke in a clipped voice. "Alfidia, Antony is no Caesar. He is a pleasure-loving fool, drunk half the time. He can be appeased. Brutus is right to smooth his ruffled feathers."

Father always spoke Marcus Brutus's name with deep respect. He had a reputation for integrity, and by some alchemy of personality, he inspired confidence in others much as Caesar had—though Brutus's magic worked within a narrower, more select group.

After Father left for the Forum, Mother looked at me and said, "I met Antony once. He has small eyes, like a pig. My father used to say pigs are more cunning than dogs, but without a dog's loyalty."

"Mother, on Grandfather's farm—" my sister began.

"Be quiet," Mother said. "I'm not talking to you, you foolish child, I am talking to your sister. Go inside to your tutor." She glanced at me. "You come into my sitting room."

We went into the small alcove that Mother kept for her own private use. Like Father's study, it was divided from the atrium by a curtain. There was a couch, and wall shelves holding rare Greek pottery, very old pieces that had come down to her from her own family. "Sit," Mother commanded me.

I sat.

Mother sat on the couch beside me. "I have often thought," she said, "that women are the only true adults in the world, and men are a species of children. When babies are born, when the sick are struggling for life, when the old die, you will see women about, but rarely men. Women carry the burden of the family's survival on their backs. Do you understand what I am saying?"

"Yes," I said, though I didn't really. To me, it seemed all the world's great matters were in men's hands.

Mother brushed a loose lock of hair back from my face, no tenderness in the gesture. "Just look how messy your hair is. Do you even bother to glance in the mirror? And you almost a wife." She grimaced. "I've never liked it that your father talks about politics with you. It's a man's game. Why you want to fill your head with it, I can't imagine."

"It's important," I said. When I talked to Father it was as if I were brought up to a mountaintop and looked out at an endless vista. By contrast, Mother oversaw the cooking of meals, the spinning of wool, and the sweeping of floors. Where was the excitement and the challenge in any of that? "Politics matters."

"Does it? I think it's mostly fools' posturing." Mother shifted her shoulders. "I'm sure Caesar was a terrible man, just as your father says. He wanted all the power in his own hands. Imagine, noblemen having to bow to another man, as if they were his slaves. Still—for him to have been slaughtered at a Senate session was very strange and unsettling. And now—why would Brutus let his main henchman address the people?" Her face tensed. "What is he thinking of?" She looked at me as if she expected me to pierce Brutus's mind for her.

Father rarely discussed politics with Mother. She had never much wanted him to, as far as I could tell. Yet I think it rankled that I, not she, should share a part of her husband's mind. Now feeling a threat coming toward her family from this sphere, she turned to me.

"Mother, there are men in politics whose greatest aim is to look exalted in their own eyes. It could be that Brutus is like that. To let Antony speak in public, with Caesar's blood still wet, makes no sense. I think a man who cared for Rome's good, rather than his own reputation, would at least exile Antony. Allowing Antony to speak makes Brutus look magnanimous, but I am afraid it is reckless."

Mother sat listening with her hands gripping her knees.

"There has already been rioting over Caesar's death," I said. "I'm afraid Antony, if he is at all clever, will excite more and worse."

Mother gave an almost imperceptible nod of her head. She had been looking to me for comfort, but I had only confirmed her fears.

⋙⋙

The whole world knows what happened that day in the Forum. Antony held up Caesar's bloody toga and moved the crowd to pity. He read Caesar's will, which contained a bequest to each and every Roman citizen, moving the people to gratitude. He aroused in the multitude a fierce hatred for Caesar's assassins.

My father came home, grim-faced. He gave terse orders. An hour later, he, Mother, Secunda, and I, with a few of our most trusty servants, left Rome. We traveled by cart until the sun sank in the west. Father wanted us as far from the city as possible before night fell. We stayed in a roadside inn that night—Secunda and I shared a cramped bedchamber overrun with mice—and the next morning traveled on. We eventually reached Father's estate in Tuscany.

We learned later that the common people searched for Caesar's assassins all through the city that night, carrying torches, vowing to burn them alive. They came upon a man who had the same name as one of the assassins. Disbelieving his protestations of innocence, they tore him limb from limb. They found none of the actual plotters. Marcus Brutus, Decimus Brutus, and the rest had fled the city. So had my betrothed, Tiberius Nero, who like Father had played no part in the actual assassination but was rumored to be allied with the killers.

In our country villa, we waited to see what would happen next in Rome. I had always loved our Tuscan estate—being able to breathe sweet country air, wander among the olive groves, and watch ponies gambol in the fields. Now, with fear as my companion, I took pleasure in little. A month passed. Then Caesar's killers reached an agreement with Antony. The men who had stabbed Caesar would be left unmolested. Antony would be named consul. He and the assassins would share in the government of Rome.

As part of the accommodation, my father was made a senator. His birth and the governmental offices he had held would have qualified him for the Senate in ordinary times. Tiberius Nero—who, like my father, could claim descent from one of Rome's noblest families, the Claudians—became a senator too.

All would be well, Father assured us, as we ate dinner together in the villa's well-appointed dining room.

"I think we should stay in Tuscany," Mother said.

Father shook his head. "There will be a political struggle in the Forum and in the Senate for the fate of the Republic. I must be part of it."

"But Marcus—"

"If things go badly, don't you think they will hunt me down here?"

Mother winced and said nothing.

Father looked at me. "Livia, when we return to Rome, you will be married immediately."

I didn't need to ask why. With matters in flux as they were, and danger all around, it had become doubly important for Father to bind Tiberius Nero to him.

As we rode the cart back into Rome, I tried to gather my courage. I would become Tiberius Nero's wife in a matter of days. After the wedding, if my father's and husband's political fortunes dipped . . . well, perhaps this unwanted marriage would not last very long.

What had the plebeians wanted to do to Caesar's killers? Immolate them. I prayed we were not going back to Rome to be murdered.

Chapter 3

My wedding took place soon after we returned to the city. It was early summer, the month of Junius. I remember the sticky heat. The atrium was crowded with dining couches and packed with friends of my father and of my husband-to-be.

On awakening that morning, I had removed my bulla, the lucky amulet meant to keep me safe through my childhood, for from today on I was accounted a grown woman. I had bathed in rose water. For the first time in my life, my lips were rouged and my eyelids touched with kohl. My hair had been arranged in six locks tied with ribbons in the manner of a Vestal Virgin. My long tunica was of fine white muslin, my sandals of soft white leather trimmed with gold. I had on ruby earrings and a heavy gold necklace, gifts sent to me by my betrothed. I wore a diaphanous red silk veil and saw everything tinted scarlet.

As I waited for Tiberius Nero's arrival, I sat on a couch beside my mother and father, accepting good wishes from guests.

Meanwhile, I could not keep from hoping Tiberius Nero would trip on his way to me and break his neck. I pictured this vividly: his toe catching on a paving stone, his cry as he fell, his friends looking sadly down at him as he lay stretched out dead. More kindly, I wished for him to simply decide he did not want to marry me after all.

But there were boisterous shouts of "*Feliciter!*" at the entranceway, and Father rose to greet his future son-in-law.

Gazing at Tiberius Nero through the red film of my veil, I tried with all my heart to find something to like about the man. His toga was carefully draped. His black hair showed no strands of gray. He had the weathered skin soldiers often do, but I told myself that he looked the part of a high-ranking military officer, and that ought to please me.

I would have liked him to have a proud military bearing. But his manner was that of a happy shopkeeper who had negotiated a good deal.

A priest of Ceres carried forward a pig, which did not have the sense to struggle. However, when the priest put it on the floor, it gave a startled squeal. That was not a good sign—the sacrifice had come protesting. I glanced hopefully at Father. Might the wedding be postponed?

He looked away.

The priest bent down and swiftly cut the pig's throat before it could squeal again. It weaved like a drunken man, then its legs buckled. The puddle of its blood that formed on the floor looked black to me as I peered through my veil. The priest cut the pig's belly open with one practiced move. A sickening stench filled the air, as he bent over and studied the animal's guts.

I hoped he would find some awful anomaly and temporarily call off the wedding. I clenched my fists, bit my lip, and inwardly prayed. But the priest straightened up and cried, "The signs are good!"

Slaves mopped up the blood and carried away the pig carcass. Father and Tiberius Nero exchanged copies of the wedding contract. I knew that it mainly concerned my dowry—land holdings outside Rome, worth a substantial sum.

I stood between the two men. Again, my eyes sought Father's. Again, he refused to look at me. He took my hand and placed it in Tiberius Nero's tight, warm grip. He had given me away.

A desperate voice in my mind told me I still had the power to escape. *Do not say the words of consent. What can they do to you? Kill you? Only Father has the right to kill you, and he won't.*

"Where thou art Gaius, I am Gaia," I said to Tiberius Nero, proclaiming we were one person. Everyone cried, "*Feliciter!*"

During the wedding feast, my bridegroom and I reclined together on a dining couch. I felt a tickling on my forearm, looked down, and saw Tiberius's hand, a square hand with stubby fingers, lightly stroking me from my wrist to my elbow. He gave me a small smile. I quickly pulled my arm away, then wondered if I had offended him and glanced at his face to see. He looked approving. I was a well-brought-up virgin, exactly the kind of bride he wanted.

The wedding feast ended too quickly. I stood entwined in my mother's arms, and Tiberius Nero made the traditional show of dragging me away. Then he led me outside. Children threw nuts that fell around us like a shower of hail. We watched as the wedding torch was lit. I was led to my new husband's house by two little boys who each had two living parents—walking symbols of good fortune and fruitfulness. People in the roadway sang old songs with obscene lyrics as overhead the sky darkened and stars appeared. A smoke-colored cloud devoured the moon.

When we reached Tiberius Nero's house, a maidservant came forward with a bowl of sheep fat. As I had been coached to do, I took a piece of it in my hands and rubbed it on each of the two doorposts. Two husky young men lifted me over the doorstep with great care. No one stumbled; there was no ill omen.

The house had colorful murals on the walls and artfully done floor mosaics. It was the house of a wealthy nobleman, though smaller than the house I had grown up in.

The sounds of merrymakers outside faded as a servant led me to a room off the atrium. Soon my husband and I were alone. Garlands of flowers bedecked our bedchamber. The wedding couch was covered in red silk. A candle flickered.

I turned my head and gazed at the pale yellow wall as Tiberius Nero undressed me. Then I felt his greedy mouth, sucking my breast. I reminded myself that he was my husband and I must endeavor to please him. Heat filled the room. I touched his neck with my fingertips. His skin felt moist, and I could smell his sweat.

He pushed me back on the bed and pawed at my thighs. I thought of what my father had said as we stood before our ancestors' portrait masks; this was like laying down one's life in battle. I wanted to push Tiberius Nero away, but I forced myself to go limp. I could feel a battering, but then he withdrew and cursed under his breath.

"What is wrong?"

He laughed. "Nothing. It's because you're young and small, and so innocent."

He shoved a pillow under my buttocks. I looked up at him for a moment, saw his wide shoulders and his hairy chest. I turned my head and watched the shadows on the wall. His shadow rose and fell, rose and fell.

Tiberius Nero gasped. I felt a sharp pain and clenched my teeth. He heaved himself down beside me, his head on the pillow. I stared up at the ceiling. There was a tiny crack, barely visible in the dim light of the candle, shaped like a bird in flight.

"How beautiful you are." He gave a low chuckle. "Wife."

"Husband," I murmured.

After a while, he said, "Turn over on your belly."

I remembered seeing the steward and the maid in the kitchen, and understood. I didn't look at the shadows on the wall this time. I kept my eyes closed. I told myself that there was a part of me Tiberius Nero could not touch, that my mind was safe from him.

»»»»»»»

So I became a married woman. I was mistress of a mansion on the Palatine Hill, attended by well-trained and obedient servants, and given every material thing I asked for. I asked for books—a great many. I asked for a huge oil lamp with gold fittings, so that I could sit up late at night and read sometimes, while Tiberius Nero snored. I asked for some expensive jewelry too, just to prove my power.

In bed, I early developed the knack of removing mind and spirit, while my body mimed passion. I, who had been prone to blurt out uncomfortable truths, learned to playact adroitly. I think that Tiberius Nero believed that every night he held a loving wife in his arms, a creature of mind and spirit as well as flesh.

Frequently, in the throes of passion, my husband told me I was beautiful. This did not warm me so much as perplex me. No one had ever called me beautiful before. As my maid dressed my hair in the morning, I sometimes would gaze in the mirror and wonder if there was any truth in what my husband said. My eyes were big and a lustrous dark brown, my hair the color of flame. Perhaps there was something arresting about my features. The stola, which I as a married woman wore, flattered me. Belted beneath my breasts, it made me look more voluptuous and mature than my girl's tunica had. I was not particularly tall, but the long, straight linen folds falling to my ankles gave me some added height. I looked more like a woman now, less like a mere child.

At times, when my husband took me, my flesh responded and I felt the beginnings of pleasure. But my mind soon drifted away, and the sensation faded. I suppose the trouble was that deep down I rebelled against the use my body was put to. And yet, because it was my duty as a wife and as my father's daughter, I gave myself to Tiberius Nero whenever he wanted me, always with pleasant words and outward warmth. I pretended that his desire was a source of joy to me. He was, I believe, perfectly content. "I can't keep my hands off you," he said more than once when he pulled me to him. I would smile.

I began to take a perverse pleasure in pretense. If I could not be truthful, then I would be the best liar in the world. If I couldn't banish Tiberius Nero from my bed, I would try to make him completely besotted with me. It was a kind of game, really, and deep at the core of it was anger and mockery.

Compared to many others, my lot was enviable. But some part of me cried out that what happened in our marriage bed was a violation. There were times when I lay there, as he spent his passion, and I wanted to scream. I did not want him. *I did not want him.*

Once he bought me a pretty silver bracelet when I had not even asked for it. "It is beautiful," I said as I put it on, and I kissed him.

The happiness in his face hurt me. It made me despise myself because I was deceiving him. If I could have made myself truly care for him by an act of will, I would have done it. But that was beyond me.

When we had been married a couple of months, he said, "I call you 'dearest' and 'darling,' but you always call me 'husband,' or else by my name. Why are you so formal, my little dove?"

"Love is so new to me," I said. "You must forgive me."

He laughed at what he took to be my innocence.

"What do you wish me to call you?" I asked.

"In our bedchamber, when we're alone? Call me 'my love.'"

Afterward, that was what I called him, when we lay together. And that, more than anything, did something to my soul.

>>>>>>>>

The summer of my marriage was the time of Julius Caesar's funeral games. It was a rare thing to hold funeral games—a way of honoring an extremely prominent person, and a way for the giver to ingratiate himself with the common people, who loved to be entertained. These games were given by Caesar's great-nephew, whom he had adopted in his will as his son and heir.

This young man had been studying in Rhodes. He arrived in Rome to claim his inheritance. Mark Antony, now consul, had found some excuse to keep back part of the money that he held in trust for him, and the two squabbled over this. There was a bequest to the soldiers of Caesar's army that had also not been paid. The boy—he had been called Gaius Octavius at birth but now bore the name Gaius Julius Caesar Octavianus—paid the soldiers out of his own funds. Some people found this disturbing. My father, for one, did not like it that as a result the boy stood high with the army. But my husband saw no harm in young Caesar's gesture. "So what if he wastes his money, behaving like a show-off and a fool?"

"Is that how he struck you when you knew him before?" I asked. He had met young Caesar several times when the boy was fourteen or so and he, Tiberius Nero, was an officer in Caesar's army. "Did he seem foolish or arrogant?"

"No," Tiberius Nero said. "He was quiet and studious. No athlete, though, and no budding soldier. Pale and skinny, with a constant cough. And he had to be careful what he ate, or he'd throw up." He grinned. "Really, I never saw a more pitiful specimen."

We were eating dinner alone, informally, at a small table at the edge of the garden. "You find nothing strange about him giving all that money to Caesar's soldiers?" I said.

"Well, it's owed them," my husband said. "And he was a rich young man even before Caesar died. Now he's rich as Croesus. I suppose he'll get reimbursed by Antony eventually."

"You think that? I heard Antony has insulted young Caesar to his face. They loathe each other."

"Do they? Where do you hear all this, hmmm?"

"From my father," I said. "He is glad that young Caesar and Antony don't get along."

Tiberius Nero chewed a piece of fish. "Really? Why does he care?"

I was amazed that my husband did not know the answer to this question. In the two months we had been married, we had only occasionally discussed politics. He was often at the military training grounds at the Field of Mars or the Forum with his friends. I kept to my womanly sphere, learning to oversee the house and supervise our servants, which presented little difficulty but was a new role for me. In the evenings, Tiberius Nero's friends and their wives sometimes invited us to dinner parties, but these were not places for much serious talk. I had heard my husband speak knowledgeably of military matters and had seen other men bow to his expertise, and I had imagined he was politically knowledgeable, too.

"The last thing Father would want, or Brutus would want either," I said, "is for Antony and young Caesar to be united. Cicero himself has said that the more Caesar's adherents flock to this boy, instead of rallying to Antony, the better it is for us all." Cicero, the Senate's great elder statesman, had not been asked to participate in Caesar's assassination, because he was physically timorous. After the fact, though, he offered fervent support to the killers.

My husband chuckled. "You mean to say you've been seeing Cicero behind my back? And he's been confiding in you?" Tiberius Nero considered my interest in politics a great joke. He reached over, twined his hand in my hair, and kissed me. "Do you want to come tomorrow to watch the gladiators?" he asked. "Young Caesar Octavianus is putting on a grand show."

I shook my head.

"You don't want to go at all? It will be five days running."

"I'd rather not, if you don't mind. It's not as if we could sit together anyway."

"That's true. Well, I understand if you can't stand to see blood."

"It's not that," I said. "It's just that women have to sit so far back, it's impossible to see a thing." Tiberius Nero already had taken me to one gladiator exhibition. I had been terribly bored, sitting back among the women as custom demanded, looking down over rows of men's heads at the small, distant figures hacking at each other. Men said it was unseemly for women to sit up close to watch such bloody spectacles. But then why allow us in at all? The truth was, when it came to this one form of entertainment they loved the most, they had grasped at an excuse to hog the good seats.

⋙⋙

Two years before, in memory of his one legitimate child, a daughter who had died in childbirth, Julius Caesar had presented not only the usual fights between pairs of gladiators but battles between whole detachments of infantry and between squadrons of cavalry, some mounted on horses, others on elephants. His great-nephew wished to outdo him—and he did, pouring out vast sums of money for wolves, bears, and lions for the gladiators to battle, hundreds of horses and elephants, and cohorts of fighting men.

While avoiding the gladiator shows, I did attend a lesser event, also part of Caesar's funeral games—chariot races at the Circus Maximus. Tiberius Nero and I had excellent seats near the finish line, in the front tier reserved for senators and their wives. Even my father had spoken with grudging respect of how Julius Caesar had expanded seating at the racecourse, building tiers of seats along the track's whole perimeter so there was room for a hundred and fifty thousand spectators. Glancing around, I saw tiers packed with people, the well-dressed in good seats, ragged denizens of the city slums high up in the bleachers. The smell of horse manure mingled with that of close-packed human bodies and of sausages sold by vendors who walked along the tiers.

My husband and I had a wager on the first race, he on the Greens, I on the Reds. I watched the drivers leaning forward tautly, clutching the reins with both hands, each controlling four horses with practiced ease. They circled the long track seven times. When the charioteer dressed in red crossed the finish line first, cheers came from thousands of throats. Tiberius Nero paid his bet good-naturedly.

We waited for the second race. Young Caesar sat not far from us, surrounded by a retinue. Courteously, he came over to greet us. "I hope you're enjoying the games," he said.

I had never met him before. From Tiberius Nero's description, I expected Caesar's heir to appear frail. He did not. If his face had a certain pallor, it only made him look like someone who had spent more time in a library than outdoors. Nothing else about him hinted at sickness. He wore a light summer tunic. Though he was barely of medium height, his body was as perfectly proportioned as a Greek statue. He had unusual coloring for a Roman, eyes the blue of the sky on a bright day, hair falling on his forehead in careless golden curls. His features were fine-cut, and he was startlingly handsome.

Everyone was already speculating about whether he would try to take a political role soon. I gazed at him and thought, *No, that's impossible, he is much too young.* I had heard he was still a month or two short of his nineteenth birthday. My husband talked to him the way a man talks to a boy—a fabulously wealthy, well-connected boy, but a boy just the same. "What am I to call you now?" Tiberius Nero asked. "I understand you've assumed your adoptive father's name."

The boy moved his shoulders negligently. "You may call me whatever you like."

Tiberius Nero persisted. "No, I'm asking what you prefer. What do your friends call you?" He was smiling, the tone of his voice almost avuncular.

"My friends? Nowadays they call me Caesar."

"And you prefer that?"

Young Caesar moved his shoulders again, not quite in a shrug, as if to say, *Why not?* "Actually, I do."

Did young Caesar know that Tiberius Nero had allied himself with those who had killed his adoptive father? He showed no sign of it if he did. He sat down on the bench next to my husband, and for a while they talked amiably of inconsequential things. It was not politics but something else that caused the atmosphere to change between them.

"You're looking very well," Tiberius Nero said. "I was happy to hear your health is better these days."

Young Caesar stiffened, and his eyes went cold. "Yes, much better."

Tiberius Nero frowned. I was sure he had not meant to speak of an unpleasant subject, still less to wound, but the boy's instant reaction suggested his health was an enormously sensitive matter. Young Caesar's features still betrayed tension as he leaned forward, elbows on knees, looked past Tiberius Nero, and spoke directly to me for the first time. "Who do you like in the next race?"

"The Whites," I said.

"They won't win."

"No?"

"No," he said. "Do you want to make a bet?"

I shook my head. "You sound too sure."

He smiled, at ease again. He had a charming smile. "I know the Reds' charioteer—my family used to own him. You're wise not to bet against me."

For some reason, these words echoed in my mind: *You're wise not to bet against me.*

My husband excused himself. Perhaps he went to relieve himself; perhaps he saw a friend to whom he wished to speak. In any case, he said a couple of conventionally polite words and left me with this boy—this beautiful boy. We watched the next race together.

The Reds bumped the Whites, who went colliding into a wall near where we sat. Spectators gasped. I pressed my fist against my teeth. The driver had been thrown clear and lay twisting in the sand. He began to drum his fingers on the ground in agony. A horse also lay on its back, kicking its legs and screaming. Another horse tried to stay on its feet but sank on broken legs.

Slaves came to cart away the broken chariot, the broken horses, and the injured charioteer, while the Reds raced on to victory.

"Aren't you glad you didn't bet?" young Caesar said.

"Very. I'm sure the Reds' driver bumped them deliberately. He is a complete ruffian."

"All the best charioteers are."

I looked into young Caesar's eyes and felt a tightness in my chest. Surely every woman carries an image in her mind of what perfect masculine beauty is. For me, this boy epitomized it. And yet I had seen other handsome men and felt little. Now there was a prickling in my skin. I was aware of the sun beating down, of how the fabric of my stola clung to my body, of how my hair felt, warm on the back of my neck. I wanted to reach out and stroke young Caesar's cheek, very gently, to see if it felt as smooth as it looked. I wished I had an amusing story to tell him, so I could watch him laugh.

He was Julius Caesar's heir. Maybe somewhere in the city, even now, there were men who were threatened enough by that to try to kill him.

If I were someone who loved him, I would have advised him to stay in Rhodes and never claim his inheritance, to keep his head down and hope people forget he exists. No one important is on his side. Antony cannot be, for he wants Caesar's mantle for himself. Those like my father who follow Brutus can only see him as a potential enemy. Yet he walks in here like a shepherd boy striding unarmed into a den of wolves. He smiles at men who betrayed his adoptive father, and his eyes are peaceful.

"Did you know that you were Caesar's heir, before he . . . died?" It surprised me that I was bold enough to ask this question, but curiosity consumed me.

Young Caesar did not seem disconcerted. He answered me in a serious tone, "It was a complete surprise."

"Were you pleased?"

He glanced away, and then looked back at me, a smile playing around the corners of his mouth. "Overjoyed."

"You felt no trepidation?"

"Only an idiot would feel no trepidation," he said, his voice serious again.

"These games are winning you the people's love. You can have a great political career if you wish to," I said.

"You think the people's love is the key nowadays to a great political career?" he asked in a neutral tone.

"No, the key is the army's love. But of course you are buying that too."

He looked sharply at me. But he did not blurt out a lie, did not say that he had no intention of ingratiating himself with the army. We gazed at each other with a kind of understanding, odd between strangers. Yes, he would try for power. Soon. I knew it at that moment as if he had told me.

"I am sorry for you," I said. It was true. But the words slipped out against my will. I did not intend to speak them.

"Really? I'm surprised you're so softhearted."

"I'm not the least bit softhearted."

"I didn't mean it as an insult," he said.

I was silent. We sat looking at each other for a long time. He tilted his head and studied me. Then all at once he smiled.

I was a married woman. And my father had helped plot Caesar's assassination, as had my husband. This boy who sat happily gazing at me was Caesar's adopted son. We were enemies. Yet I could not keep from smiling back at him.

I looked down and smoothed the folds of my stola, which did not need smoothing. When I raised my eyes, I asked, "Did you love Caesar?"

"Very much. And I admired him more than any other man I ever met."

And so you will want to avenge him, I thought.

"He had the falling sickness, you know," young Caesar said. "He used to speak to me about that, and about the power of a man's will to overcome physical obstacles."

"And he wanted you for his son," I said. "I can imagine how much that means to you."

"Can you? Most people can't begin to, but I somehow believe you can." Young Caesar ran his hand through his hair. "I don't usually talk so openly with people I've just met." He gave an uneasy laugh.

"Neither do I," I said.

He looked puzzled. "What do you mean? I've told you a great deal, and you haven't said much about yourself at all."

Haven't I? I thought. *When a married woman looks at another man the way I look at you, hasn't she said far, far more than she should?*

My husband returned then, and young Caesar and I spoke no more private words.

That night, I said to Tiberius Nero, as we prepared for bed, "Young Caesar—will someone kill him?"

"Not unless he does something to ask for it." He gave a small, contemptuous grimace. "He's young and has always been a weakling." Tiberius Nero drew me to him. "What are you looking so worried about, my little dove?"

No longer affected by the charm of Caesar Octavianus's presence, I did a calculation in my mind. I added up his popularity with the people and especially the army, his vast wealth, and his love for his adoptive father, which surely implied hatred for his killers. I recalled the sense I'd had that he would soon reach for great power. A malign spirit possessed me. I imagined my father, my mother, and all I loved, trod into bloody pulp under young Caesar's boots. In terror, I said, "I'm afraid he's dangerous, very dangerous. Perhaps you *should* kill him."

My husband just laughed.

As summer became autumn, I walked with quick strides through my house, supervising servants who needed little supervision. I would reach for a book, take the scroll from its leather cover, read a few sentences, then roll the parchment up again. What I had felt when I was with Caesar Octavianus was well buried. But I would look at the birds and wish I could rise up into the sky as they did, or else become a nymph or a goddess and be lifted far beyond the claims of marriage and duty. Day after day I brimmed over with energy for which no one had any use.

Since my husband and father were both senators, I found it easy to keep informed about politics. I learned that every one of the senators who had stabbed Caesar had, in their fear of the common people, abandoned the city of Rome. Marcus Brutus took ship to Athens, there to await events and, of all things, study philosophy. Decimus Brutus went to govern the province of Cisalpine Gaul.

Meanwhile, Mark Antony took up command of Rome's legions in Brundisium. The soldiers mocked him for not avenging Julius Caesar. Antony tried to sweeten their mood by offering them a bonus, but they shouted that it was too little, so he had some of the malcontents beaten to death. This reduced the rest to gloomy silence.

Young Caesar remained in Rome, living with his mother, an ailing widow. He offered much more generous bonuses than Antony had, and raised a private army of three thousand men.

Antony came back to the city, intending to give a speech to the Senate denouncing young Caesar. But he got drunk and forgot about it. Then he announced that he would avenge Julius Caesar after all. He intended to attack Decimus Brutus in Gaul. He went marching off at the head of his legions. I wondered—was this the beginning of a civil war?

Shortly after Antony's departure, my father hosted a small dinner party, the first I ever attended at my parents' home. I had a pleasant sense of my new status as an adult, as I reclined on a dining couch as a married woman should, instead of sitting, as I had always done before I was wed.

Marcus Cicero came to this dinner. He was sixty-two years old, a plump, red-faced man with a wonderful, stentorian voice. He arrived alone. Everyone knew he had divorced the mother of his children to marry a fifteen-year-old heiress. Then he divorced this girl for quarreling with his beloved daughter Tullia, and for failing to mourn Tullia when she died in childbirth.

Also at the dinner was young Caesar. He and I were next to each other at the table, he reclining alone, I sharing a couch with my husband. He smiled at me and said, "It's good to see you again, Livia Drusilla." He had a sheen about him, the look of a young man pleased with where life was taking him.

"I've been hearing how you and Cicero have become wonderful friends," I said. Everyone in Rome knew that these days they were often seen in each other's company.

"He's become like a second father to me," young Caesar said.

That sounded as likely as pigs flying.

"A third father," I said. "Surely your great-uncle who adopted you was your second father."

He grinned. "Of course."

"You and Cicero have so much in common," I said. "Naturally you would be friends."

"You flatter me."

I shook my head and sipped some wine.

Young Caesar said in a low voice, not meant to be overheard by anyone, "Tell me, what exactly do you think Cicero and I have in common?"

I had the impression he was testing me. If I simpered and spoke about admirable qualities they shared, he would be disappointed. I said, "What you and Cicero have in common is that you both hate Antony."

He asked in the same quiet voice, "And do you think that is sufficient basis for a friendship?"

I considered the question. "Certainly. For a while."

The conversation became general, dominated by Cicero. He spoke about how the consuls who would be coming into office in the new year would go about raising legions to relieve Decimus Brutus. Young Caesar nodded at what Cicero said. I had the feeling the two of them had discussed this already.

The strangeness of the situation struck me. *Antony has gone to wreak revenge on Decimus, one of Caesar's assassins. Caesar's adopted son sits here, listening sympathetically to plans to protect Decimus from Antony's wrath. Here he is with Cicero, who publicly lauded the assassins. With my father, the assassins' ally. With my husband, who was Caesar's officer but turned on him. Young Caesar smiles at them all, full of good cheer.*

What is he doing?

"We have one other important matter to decide," Cicero said. "An official office for our young friend."

"Is consul an option?" young Caesar asked.

The law reserved the consulship, the most honored office in the Republic, to men at least forty-two years old with distinguished public careers behind them. Other than a dictator, no officeholder approached a consul in power. My father, when he heard this nineteen-year-old suggest he might become consul, looked as if he were about to choke.

Father had invited Cicero and young Caesar to dinner because he had wished to sound them both out in a general way, and in particular to get a sense of the young man's mind. Unfortunately, the conversation had already gone in a direction he did not like.

"I must have the legal right to lead an army," young Caesar said. "That is necessary."

"The idea of a private army is repugnant," Father said.

"I absolutely agree," young Caesar said. "That's why I want lawful authority. Surely Cicero has told you that I plan to put myself and my army at the Senate's disposal. I am honored to be able to help protect the Republic from the likes of Antony. If I were at least a praetor—"

"This is not the place to discuss this," Father said. Striving for a pleasant tone, he glanced round at my mother and me and added, "We mustn't bore my wife and daughter."

"I don't think your honored wife, the lady Alfidia, looks bored," young Caesar said. "And as for your daughter . . . I suspect Livia Drusilla finds this discussion quite interesting."

"Please forgive me, but you're wrong," I said. I was a loyal daughter. But I smiled at young Caesar to take some of the sting out of my words. "I'm afraid all this talk of offices and armies makes my head ache."

"Yes, please, do you think we might change the subject?" said Mother. Her apologetic smile looked painted on her face.

"We'll have to discuss this further, at a more appropriate time," Father said.

"I'm sorry to seem impetuous," young Caesar said with gentle courtesy. "I hope you'll at least give what I've said some thought."

"Of course," Father said.

All the life drained out of the dinner party. Young Caesar left as soon as he politely could. But in saying his farewells, he smiled at me as if we shared a private joke.

As soon as young Caesar was out the door, Cicero said, "I suggest we make him propraetor."

Praetors ranked second to consuls; propraetors, of course, were praetors whose time in office had been extended. Propraetor as a title for a youth who had never held public office was, on the face of it, absurd.

I felt a sudden, deep uneasiness. I sipped some wine. It went down my throat, cool and sweet, but did not soothe me.

Father was staring at Cicero. "You can't be serious."

"He would not, formally speaking, be a sitting magistrate." Cicero leaned forward on his elbow. He was across from me at the table, his face turned toward my father. "We need young Caesar—or rather, we need the troops whose loyalty he can command—to protect us from Antony."

My husband spoke. "I'm not sure that Antony is the only threat."

Cicero turned his fierce eyes—wide, round eyes like an old owl's—on Tiberius Nero. "Have you noticed who is marching at this moment to attack our friend Decimus Brutus? Antony should have died on the Ides of March. Antony! Antony! Antony!" Cicero slapped the table three times for emphasis. "Antony is the threat. All young Caesar wants from us is empty honors. Call him propraetor. Call him offspring of the god Apollo, for all I care."

"Call him propraetor, and you give him the legal authority to continue to enroll troops under his own banner and raise an even larger army," Father said. "I don't like it." But he did not speak vehemently. I sensed he would go along with Cicero in the end, and I felt a cold tingle down my spine.

"His army will be firmly under my control," Cicero said. "That child was in a schoolroom in Rhodes a few months ago. He trails after me like a puppy. And he comes to us with purses full of money, and with that name Caesar, ready to rally Caesar's soldiers and give us an army as a gift."

"One day he'll no longer be nineteen," Tiberius Nero said. "Give some thought to the long term." Like my father he sounded only doubtful, not as if he were prepared to oppose Cicero.

"Long term," Cicero said. A grin settled on his face. It was not a pleasant grin. It made one aware of his yellowed teeth, of his sharp incisors. "Long term, young Caesar does not concern me."

I found myself remembering who this man Cicero was. Many saw him as the great champion of the Republic, but during his consulship he had executed a number of citizens. He said they were conspiring to overthrow Republican rule, but some thought they were merely desperate men, agitating for debt relief. This took place before I was born, but I had heard about it from my father, who harbored some doubts about the rightness of Cicero's action.

"Long term, do you think I fear a sickly boy?" Cicero demanded. "We must use him for now. If one day he turns on us, we will know how to deal with him. Do you doubt whether you and I and all of us together are a match for him?"

I doubt it. He is Julius Caesar's adopted son, and the people and the army love him. They don't love you. My heart pounded. The room seemed too warm. Maybe I had drunk more wine than I realized. I felt a compulsion to speak.

It was frightening to feel sure I was seeing something my elders did not see, though it was right before their eyes. I knew—*knew*—they were miscalculating and that their miscalculation could spell disaster. The knowledge seemed too big for me to hold within myself. I could not contain it.

Incredibly, I did not even soften my words with polite phrases. "You think because Caesar is young, he is a fool. But he's no fool," I said. Cicero looked at me, astonished. I stared into his owl eyes and went on, "My husband is an accomplished man twice his age, and he aspires to the praetorship and has yet to hold it. He is expected to wait patiently; it's a great prize. Yet you'll give Caesar the powers of a praetor. What is he giving you in return? Only promises to be guided by you. And you think you're the one using him? You believe he has forgotten his adoptive father. You assume he doesn't imagine avenging him. Do you think he is not capable of smiling and hiding his thoughts from you? Don't you realize any little slave girl can do that much?"

It was a longish speech, but no one interrupted me. I think everyone was too stunned, as if one of the vases on the side tables had started talking. I fell silent, realizing how far I had trespassed. I flushed.

Before my marriage, if I had spoken to Cicero in this way in my mother's presence, she would have dragged me off and beaten me. Now what I saw in her face was not anger so much as disbelief. She said nothing. The only person at the table who had the right to rebuke me before others was my husband. But he chuckled as if I had made some endearing youthful gaffe, took my hand, and kissed my palm.

Cicero and my father did not respond to what I had said. Father was surely embarrassed into silence. For Cicero, it was as if I had not spoken at all.

I was fifteen years old. I was a woman. Was it surprising that not one man at the table, not even my beloved father, truly heard a word I said? I had no grounds for surprise, but I felt humiliated. I went hot and cold. And then, I saw my fate. I would not be fifteen forever, but I always would be a woman. I imagined spending all my years having my words discounted.

Father, Tiberius Nero, and Cicero continued to discuss giving young Caesar the title propraetor just as if I had not spoken. I could hardly bear to listen to them; I tried to withdraw to a place within my own mind. Then something that Cicero said jolted me and brought all my attention back to the conversation.

"I tell you, the boy must be praised, honored, and"—Cicero made a little waving motion with his hand, pointing at the ceiling, and raising his eyes piously upward—"elevated!"

Tiberius Nero laughed. My father had the grace to look repelled.

Maybe Cicero only meant that Caesar was to be first flattered and utilized, and then in due time stripped of power. But reclining across from the man, taking in his smug and predatory smile, I felt he intended something far worse. I flinched at the thought of young Caesar someday finding himself at the mercy of this duplicitous old man.

The girl who heard Cicero's famous jibe was not made of ice. Rather, my sympathies went every which way. I was still so tender, I wanted to protect everyone. I wanted to protect Father and his friends from young Caesar's betrayal. I wanted to protect that handsome boy, Caesar Octavianus, from the savagery I heard in Cicero's jest. If Mark Antony had made an appearance at dinner, perhaps my sympathy would have flowed even in his direction, and I would have wanted to protect him too.

When Tiberius Nero and I went home that evening, he commented on what I had said to Cicero. "You're perfectly right," he said. "I ought to be praetor by now. If they think they can give praetorian powers to a mere adolescent and go on passing me over, they're wrong. The next time I see Cicero I'm going to tell him so." He nuzzled my neck and carried me off to bed.

⋙⋙

The next morning, I went to visit a dressmaker in the market district. I traveled by litter, my personal maid Pelia, a Greek girl, sitting beside me. The litter was roomy, the cushions and the curtains yellow silk. The six bearers had been chosen for both their strength and their looks, and they matched, all being olive-skinned and dark-haired. No elegant lady would have bearers who did not match.

As I leaned back against my silk cushions, with Pelia waving a peacock feather fan to keep me cool, I tried not to think about last evening's dinner.

"Oh, stop fanning me," I said to Pelia. "Heaven knows, it doesn't make it any cooler. Are we near the dressmaker's yet?" I pulled the curtain of the litter aside and looked out. A thrill of surprise went through me.

There, on the crowded market street, young Caesar came walking along, his fair hair shining in the sunlight. He was flanked by two other well-dressed young men, who I supposed were his friends, and trailed by a knot of servants.

I would ask myself afterward why I did what I did then. Certainly I felt a pull of attraction and a nudge of sympathy. Maybe

Caesar's youth called to me because I was also young. I would not have sought Caesar out, but now, seeing him, I acted on impulse. I ordered my litter bearers to stop and said to Pelia, "That young man—" I pointed. "Run and tell him that the lady Livia Drusilla would like a word with him."

She jumped out of the litter and did my bidding. When Caesar came walking back with her, he looked rather grim, but I did not stop to wonder why that was.

"Last night, at dinner, after you left—" I spoke in a whisper because I did not want the litter bearers to hear. I knew I could secure Pelia's silence, but I did not trust them.

"Last night?" Caesar said. He leaned close to hear, so close his nose was almost through the parted curtain.

"There was talk about you—your future. And Cicero said something." I repeated the words and made the little gesture Cicero had used, pointing upward.

Even as I spoke, I feared that Caesar would look at me as if I were a fool and say, *So what? Praised, honored, elevated? What could be better?*

But he did not. "Elevated?" he said. "You heard the way he spoke. What do you think he meant by that word?"

"I can't be certain if he meant removed from power or . . ."

"From this earth?"

"It could be dangerous for you to trust him."

"There could never be any question of my trusting him. But 'the boy must be praised, honored, and elevated'? Those were his exact words?" Caesar shook his head. "And here I thought he was getting to like me a little. But obviously, he has no liking for me at all." He added in a hard voice, "And what's more, he has no respect."

I noticed only at that moment the change in Caesar's appearance. The evening before, he had looked positively blithe. Now his eyes were bloodshot, and there was tension and pain in his features. "Something else has happened, hasn't it?" I said. "Something bad?"

"My mother died suddenly last night."

"Oh! I'm sorry."

He looked away. "She always worried about me. Too much. I think worry helped kill her." He shifted his focus back to me. "Thank you for what you just told me. Did I say that already? I'm a little distracted. But thank you."

The implications of what I had done pressed in on me. I reached out and gripped his hand. "I don't ask for thanks." I kept my voice down. "But please, promise me no one will ever know I told you what Cicero said."

"I promise." He added, "You can take my word."

"I know I can take your word." Somehow I did.

"I would value your friendship."

There was a world of meaning in how he said the word "friendship." Oh, no romantic meaning, which was how some women might have heard it. I released his hand, as quickly as if it had burnt my fingers. "I won't be your spy."

He nodded, unsurprised.

"The truth is, I can't be your friend." These words stuck in my throat.

His mouth tightened. "I understand. Obviously your loyalties lie elsewhere."

My loyalties. Yes, I had loyalties. But I had betrayed them, betrayed the confidence of Cicero, who was my father's ally. It amounted to a betrayal of my father. I felt disbelief at what I had done just moments before, and I almost blamed Caesar for it, as if he had exerted some iniquitous pull on me. But the fault was mine. I was drawn to him, and should not be. I raised my hands and covered my face, shaken and ashamed.

"Livia Drusilla, what's wrong?"

I lowered my hands. "I regret what I've done. I owe my father every loyalty."

He nodded, and said in a bleak voice, "Of course. Loyalty to your own blood is the foundation of all virtue." Then he smiled faintly. "Don't be too hard on yourself. After all, your motives were good, weren't they? Just pure kindness?"

I did not answer.

"My mother was so kind," he said. "I've been feeling today as if most of the kindness has gone out of the world. For me, anyway. In general, women are much kinder than men. No man living would have brought me a warning about Cicero and asked nothing in return."

"No?" I said.

"Don't you realize that?" He shook his head, as one might over the simplicity of a child. "Livia Drusilla, I've been keeping you here talking, but sooner or later someone may notice, and that could be awkward for you. So in a moment I'll say farewell and walk away. But I want you to know that I never forget a favor or an injury, and I make it a practice to pay both back with interest. Thank you for the kindness you just did me. Maybe you won't end up regretting it after all."

"Cicero thinks you will forgo vengeance for your uncle. But he's a fool, isn't he?"

"Only my friends have the right to ask me that kind of question," Caesar said. His eyes altered, took on an inward look. It was so cold, so removed from me, I felt as if I were gazing at someone I had never met before. He pressed his lips together, as though he was trying to hold back words it was better not to utter. But then his expression softened, and he spoke. "I'll say this—if you can detach your husband and your father from their allegiance to Brutus, they'll probably thank you in the end."

I recoiled. The implicit threat to both my husband and my father was clear. I understood the full magnitude of the sin I had committed. This man who I had tried to help was my family's deadly enemy.

He read my face, I am sure. Accurately, and with no surprise, and yet with a certain sadness. If he could read my expression, I could read his too. It was almost as if he had spoken his thoughts aloud: *So now you truly see me, and you don't like me anymore. I can expect no more kindness from you.*

"I have to go and buy mourning clothes for my mother's funeral," he said. "Farewell, Livia Drusilla." He walked away.

My mother called on me that afternoon. It was not like her usual visits. She often came to see me, usually bringing Secunda with her. She would inspect my house, frequently finding dirt in corners that I had not noticed. "You must keep in mind that even the best slave will do only the minimum that is required," she would tell me. "That is human nature. If you are too lazy to discipline your servants, you will wind up living in squalor." I would nod my head obediently, and Secunda would nod too.

This time my mother had left my sister at home and was uninterested in housekeeping. We sat in the garden. She said to me with no preamble, "Your behavior at dinner last night was unseemly and rude. I am most displeased, and so is your father."

Silent, I gazed at the tree near the garden wall, which was flowering with peach blossoms.

She leaned forward and gave me a hard tap on the knee. "Livia, pay attention. It is possible for a woman to influence public affairs. I'm not saying that one should, but that one can. Everyone knows Cornelia, mother of the Gracchi, did it."

In the Forum stood statues of the Gracchi brothers, great political reformers and champions of the common people who had lived three generations ago. Nearby was a statue of their mother—our only public statue of a female that was not a goddess or an allegorical figure but an actual Roman woman who had once lived.

"A woman can exert influence through her sons, as Cornelia did," Mother said. "Or through her husband. And in no other way. Can it really be you don't know this?"

"In some countries, women are queens and rule kingdoms," I said.

"I am talking about Rome, not barbarian lands. Listen to me. What you should have done, if you decided Cicero—Cicero!—needed your advice was whisper what you thought into Tiberius Nero's ear." Mother averted her gaze for a moment. "At a time when he was likely to be receptive, that is what I mean. And if you were truly clever you would arrange matters so that he arose next morning convinced that it was he who had worked out why Cicero was going down the wrong path. He would have emerged from the house eager to seek Cicero out and show him the flaws in his thinking."

And Cicero would have heard him, I thought. *The old goat would probably not have changed course anyway, but at least he would have had to listen.*

"There are ways for a woman to get what she wants in this world. If you are wise, you will use them."

"I will remember what you said, Mother."

She let out a breath and settled back in her chair. "See that you do."

As long as I could remember, a distance had existed between Mother and me. Yet at that moment I felt she did care about me, in her way. It made me wish to confide in her. I repeated to her the words that Caesar had said, which I had taken as a threat to Father and Tiberius Nero.

She grew somber. "Well, your father should certainly know about this."

⋙⋙

In keeping with their policy of honoring Julius Caesar's memory, most of the Senate joined the procession taking his niece Atia's body to the Field of Mars. My mother, sister, and I walked beside Father and Tiberius Nero. Father spoke to me in a voice so low I could barely hear it above the wails of the hired mourners who led the cortege. "Your mother has repeated to me what young Caesar said to you. I'm not surprised that he has no love for those who killed his own kin. It doesn't surprise me either that he spoke to you with boyish bravado."

"I don't think it was just bravado," I said. "You should have seen the look on his face."

Father gave a snort of amusement. "I'm sure that boy can look very fierce, talking to a girl he wants to impress."

"Father, how can it make sense to give him the right to raise an army?"

"Cicero has spent many hours in young Caesar's company and has come to the conclusion that he is a loyal son of the Republic."

"What if Cicero is a fool?"

"Cicero," Father said with asperity, "is considered the wisest man in Rome. I was appalled by the lack of respect you showed him when he dined with us. But your mother says she discussed that subject with you, and so I don't need to."

"Father—"

"That's all I wish to say. Let's both be quiet now and honor the dead."

At the Field, I stood with my family to the side, at the front edge of the great crowd, as Atia's body, draped in a shroud, was reverently lifted and set on a pile of wood. The air was thick with the smell of incense. Priests chanted, and the hired mourners continued their loud wailing and tore at their clothes. At first I did not see young Caesar because a dozen men wearing wax masks, portraying his mother's illustrious ancestors, blocked my view.

There was a hush. The men in masks moved out of the way, and young Caesar approached his mother's pyre, a flaming torch in his hand.

I could see his face clearly in profile. He looked very pale and grim in his black-dyed toga. Beside him stood a woman, his elder by a few years, with fair hair and pretty features, surely his sister.

What I felt made no sense. I could summon up no wariness when I looked at Caesar. My heart went out to him. I wished that, instead of being in my place with my family, I could go and stand beside him.

He touched the torch to his mother's pyre, which burst into flames. He stepped back and for a few moments stood like a statue, still holding the torch, watching the smoke rise. Then he did something that people might have thought odd, if anyone but me had noticed it. He turned his head and looked toward the place, some yards from him, where senators and their families stood. His gaze moved over the throng, as if he were seeking someone. Our eyes met.

I felt as if through the force of my own emotion I had somehow reached out and touched him, and impelled him to look at me. We held each other's gaze for a long moment.

He broke off the contact, threw the torch into the flames, and stood in the smoky haze watching the pyre burn. He was still there, watching as a filial son should, when my family and I left the Field.

>>>>>>>

Afterward, Caesar Octavianus and Cicero continued their public love affair. Caesar told one and all that Cicero stood in the place of a father to him. Cicero made a series of speeches in which he attacked Mark Antony not only as a public figure but as a man, accusing him of corruption and every conceivable sexual filthiness. On the other hand, he praised Caesar, calling him "this heaven-sent youth." "It is my solemn promise to you," he told the Senate, "that he will always be what he is today—the kind of citizen we have all prayed for."

With Cicero's endorsement, Caesar was named a propraetor of Rome. He continued to expand his army, acting fully within the law, and after the turn of the year, he marched off to help save Decimus Brutus from Mark Antony. The force that went against Antony included Caesar's own soldiers and a larger army, under command of the two newly chosen consuls.

In April, they met Antony in battle. Both consuls were killed. Caesar fought well despite his inexperience. Routed, Antony and his army fled.

Caesar now led the consular army as well as his own force. The Senate sent him a dispatch, ordering him to turn command over to Decimus Brutus. He wrote back courteously explaining why that was impossible—many of the soldiers were veterans of Julius Caesar's army; they could hardly be expected to follow the lead of one of his assassins.

When a delegation from Decimus Brutus arrived in his camp, wishing to negotiate an accommodation and suggesting a meeting between the two commanders, young Caesar explained that this was impossible too. Decimus Brutus had participated in the murder of his great-uncle and adoptive father. "Nature forbids me either to set eyes on or talk to Decimus Brutus. Let him seek his own safety."

In other words, tell Decimus Brutus to run for his life.

Decimus was caught between Caesar's forces and those of Mark Antony. His soldiers began to desert. He and a little band of loyalists tried to escape to Macedonia, where Republican forces had begun to gather under the leadership of Marcus Brutus. They were captured by a tribe of Gallic savages.

The Gauls, fearful of Roman power, sent word to Antony, asking what they should do with their prisoners. Antony said to kill them. So the savages whooped with pleasure and hacked them to death.

>>>>>>>

Caesar had secured the loyalty of eight legions, fifty thousand men. A deputation of four hundred centurions from his forces arrived in Rome. They put two demands before the Senate. For Caesar's soldiers, they required a bonus in gold. For their commander, they demanded the consulship.

Tiberius Nero tried to talk sense to them. The centurions, men of plebeian background raised to positions of authority because of their judgment and courage, heard him out because they respected him as a soldier. For the Senate, they had only contempt. "They said the Senate has done nothing for the common people, ever," Tiberius Nero told me. "They worshipped Julius Caesar and insist that young Caesar is the one great hope for Rome's future. I couldn't change their opinions."

The next day, several centurions addressed the Senate. One of them pulled out his sword. "Make Caesar consul, or we'll get the consulship for him with this," he said.

The Senate ordered the centurions to go back to Caesar and tell him that his demands had been rejected. Soon after, we learned that Caesar Octavianus was marching on Rome.

It was winter. The days were short. Caesar's army approached the city. We had a family dinner, my mother, my father, Tiberius Nero, and me. Secunda was at the table too. Her lower lip trembled. I wondered how much she understood of what was happening. Perhaps only enough to be afraid.

"Cicero urges negotiation," Father said. "But the boy has already said there's nothing to negotiate."

Mother gestured for a slave to serve the second course and fill our wine cups. "Not the ordinary wine," she said. "Bring in the Judean vintage." She gave my husband a tense smile. "Our son-in-law is here, after all."

"Thank you, Alfidia," Tiberius Nero said. "But really, the ordinary stuff is good enough for me."

"Don't be silly."

"Negotiation would be pointless," Tiberius Nero said to my father. "The wonder is Cicero is not ashamed to show his face."

"He was misled by a scoundrel," Father said. The scoundrel he meant was Caesar.

"I hope the chicken is well done enough," Mother said.

The slave came back with the Judean wine and poured some into each of our cups. The second course was served. Even in these circumstances, Mother had ordered the cook to prepare roast tuna in a mint-and-vinegar sauce, as well as baked chicken. There was also a dish of lentils with coriander. But none of us were hungry.

"It's very good chicken, Mother," Secunda said. She looked as if she might cry.

"I don't suppose there is still time for us to leave the city," Mother said to Father. "It's too late for that, I suppose?"

"Much too late," Father said. "All the roads are clogged. Decent people are being set upon by thugs as they try to escape from Rome with their goods. And Caesar's army is rapidly advancing toward the city. It's more dangerous to go than to stay."

"I see," Mother said.

We were quiet for a while, doing our best to down our dinner.

I had known for two months that I was with child, and my husband fervently hoped I would give birth to a son. Every morning I rose to vomit my insides out. A hostile army approached Rome; and the child in my belly made me feel even more vulnerable than I might have otherwise.

"I don't see how it's possible to make a stand," Tiberius Nero said. "With what troops?"

"Are you suggesting capitulation?" Father said. "Has it really come to that?"

"What's the alternative?"

Father ran his hand over his face.

Would the Senate put up a fight when Caesar tried to enter the city? Everyone knew who would win such a fight. And then what—when the battle was over? Would Caesar order the execution of all men allied with the killers of his adoptive father? Might he wreak revenge on their families?

What if it came to the worst?

If it did, then I would go as a supplicant to Caesar, clasp his knees, and hope he remembered that I had once done him a kindness. I would beg for the lives of my father and my mother and my sister—and yes, even my husband. I would plead for my own life and that of my unborn child.

My father had an empty, wounded expression on his face. Perhaps he wished he could go back in time and relive the last year. Despite his keen intellect, he had followed Brutus's lead and then Cicero's, even when they acted foolishly. He was a loyal man who had put too much faith in the judgment of others. I could have wept for him.

I decided that if I survived I would never do what Father had done, never defer to anyone's judgment or refuse to look clear-eyed at the world. I would never be so blind, never.

If I survived.

Chapter 5

"You were quiet at dinner," Tiberius Nero said when we arrived home. "It's unlike you."

"There are no words," I said. "For a Roman to march on Rome, demanding to be consul! What kind of man could do such a thing?"

"Try not to distress yourself," Tiberius Nero said. "Think of the child."

Think of the child.

I imagined afterward, that the baby, having received a hint of what the world was like, thought better of the idea of being born and declined to join the dance of folly. Tiberius Nero and I went to bed, and in the middle of the night I awoke in pain, as if someone were driving a knife into my belly. The miscarriage was an ugly, bloody business, and the midwife could do nothing to make it easier for me. For several days afterward, my husband and my father and mother feared that I would die. As for me, I never realized my danger but lay in a stupor of pain. Then I began to recover.

I had felt little pleasurable excitement anticipating the birth of my child, perhaps because I was sick so often or because of the worries that occupied my mind. Yet I felt the loss keenly, as if a part of me had been ripped away.

As I lay in bed, feverish and ill, I thought of how it would have been to hold my baby in my arms, to guide his steps as he grew. I imagined a son, a small boy running through the garden to me, shouting, "Mother!" and grieved for the child who would never be born.

I was still confined to bed when I learned that Caesar's army had paused, a day's march from Rome. He exchanged no messages with the Senate, made no threats. Silently, he waited.

The Senate capitulated and made Caesar consul.

>>>>>>>>

I sat up in bed, my back resting against a pile of pillows. Tiberius Nero entered the bedchamber, dressed in his senator's toga with its purple trim. He sat down on the bed beside me. For many nights, sleep had eluded him, and his eyes were hollow with exhaustion. But he gave me a reassuring smile.

So, I thought. *We will all go on living.*

I struggled to frame a question that would not be humiliating for my husband to answer. "How did Caesar act?" I asked finally.

"Oh, he was very polite, very reasonable. No boyish arrogance—he could have been a fifty-year-old magistrate, the way he acted. He thanked us all for coming to the Appian Way to greet him and escort him into the city—"

"The whole Senate was there?"

"Yes, certainly. The whole Senate."

My father too? I almost asked. But Tiberius Nero had already said *The whole Senate.*

"Well, we welcomed him warmly, of course. Many men kissed him on the cheek. I didn't. Maybe I should have. Perhaps he'll remember that I didn't and hold it against me. But in any case, he said how moved he was by our wonderful welcome. He sacrificed at the Temple of Jupiter officially as consul. And then we escorted him to the Forum, to show himself to the people. All along the way, there were cheering throngs. He made a speech from the Rostra, quite a smooth speech, about what he intends to do."

A consul's role while in Rome was to preside over the Senate and carry out senatorial decisions. But everyone knew that with an army at his back, Caesar would do more than preside. He would dictate. With the Senate's acquiescence, he would do just as he wished.

"And what does he intend?" I asked in a taut voice.

"First, to set up tribunals to try the killers of his 'father'—"

I clutched Tiberius Nero's arm.

"No, dearest, he doesn't mean the mere accomplices, just the men who actually wielded the knives. They've all left Rome anyway. There'll be one-day tribunals, which will return a directed verdict—'guilty, guilty, guilty.' Brutus and the others will be condemned in absentia."

"Not you and my father?"

"No, certainly not. Didn't I say how reasonable Caesar is? He asked us to allocate public funds for a statue of his great-uncle, to be built in the Forum, but only if we—the Senate, that is—thought it fitting. That statue will be built, believe me, posthaste." Tiberius patted my hand. "The day after tomorrow, Caesar will march off, with his army—he's up to eleven legions now, he happened to mention. He will defend the Republic from Antony, who—Caesar informed us—is a considerable threat to its stability. Gods above, we ate gall and wormwood, but Caesar has no plans to kill anybody, and he acted as if he couldn't wait to leave town."

"Who will govern here in Rome?"

"I'm sure Caesar will have picked men of his own to do that. And Livia, do you know what I found out today? The boy doesn't shave yet. He's very fair, and naturally not very hairy, so he's only now getting much stubble on his chin. And he has new hair on his upper lip, I noticed. But he said he has sworn never to shave until he has avenged his so-called father. It will be a new experience for him—shaving." My husband averted his face. "How the gods must be laughing at us."

⋙⋙

I ask myself now, was what I felt then for Caesar pure loathing? Did some part of me thrill to the audacity of what he had done? If so, I did not acknowledge the feeling. Caesar was a threat to all those I loved, and to everything my father had taught me to believe. I had reverence for the vision of the Republic that Father had shown me. In much of the world there were kings, and people bowed to the rule of one man. We in Rome had had a government based on law, in which the people elected magistrates, and from these magistrates senators were selected. The senators were once men who wished to serve the common good. I knew that the government had become corrupt, that over the last hundred years rich and powerful men had resorted to outright violence to subvert the people's will, that the Senate had become a narrow, despised oligarchy. But, like my father, I had believed the Republic could be purified and once more be what it had been long ago. If Caesar had his way, that would never happen. I tried to consider him in that light, and only that light, not as a man I had felt drawn to but as a problem to be solved.

The next day, while tribunals met to obediently condemn Brutus and the rest, I summoned Caesar Octavianus into my presence. Oh, not the boy himself, but his phantom image. I sat, leaning against pillows in my bed, and imagined him, resplendent in his purple-edged consular toga, perching on the stool near my feet. I visualized him with his shining good looks, and added the new chin stubble and the hint of a moustache my husband had mentioned.

What do you want? I asked him.

He answered, *Supreme power.*

What else?

I want to avenge my father.

Because you loved him so much?

They came at him, fifty against one, men who received only good from him. They stabbed him and stabbed him and stabbed him. Do you think I forget that?

Your great-uncle—

Young Caesar interrupted me. *Kindly do me the courtesy of calling him my father. Julius Caesar was the father I longed for. The father who begat me died before I could well remember him.*

How strange it was. I felt no sympathy for Caesar Octavianus now, or so I believed. Yet there was an odd tie, as if I were able to sense his feelings.

I saw myself in Julius Caesar just as he saw himself in me, the phantom said. *I did love him.*

But it's not all a matter of love with you. That's not the only reason you seek revenge.

No, I have to avenge my father for my own credit. My soldiers will worship me less and hesitate to follow me if I don't do it.

You are giving this matter of the tribunals a high priority. You want to appear to be acting within the law.

The phantom smiled. *Exactly.*

You will convict Brutus and the rest, and then rush off to fight . . . Antony?

Caesar tilted his head and gaped at me. *Now why would I do that?*

You said you would.

He laughed. *But Livia Drusilla, we both know I don't always do what I say.*

⋙⋙

The armies of Caesar and Antony marched toward each other, Caesar coming from Rome, Antony from Gaul. They both stopped at the Lavinius River, and camped on opposite banks. In the middle of the river sat a tiny island, linked to both shores by bridges. Lepidus, a former consul, walked over to the island from Antony's side of the river. This Lepidus had ranked next to Antony among Julius Caesar's supporters. Now he dutifully searched for hidden weapons and lurking assassins. When he found nothing, he waved his cloak, the agreed-upon signal. Caesar and Antony, alone and unarmed, crossed the bridges to the island.

⋙⋙

My father came to see me shortly after word reached Rome that Caesar and Antony had forged an alliance. The two of us sat alone in the library, my favorite room of the house I shared with Tiberius Nero. Autumn sunlight streamed through the window and turned Father's gray hair to gold.

He told me that forces were coming into alignment for a great battle in Greece, with Caesar and Antony on one side and Brutus on the other. "Now, since I am a senator, some men would argue that I could be of more use by remaining in the city, holding myself in readiness to act politically when the time comes," he said. "Tiberius Nero has intimated that he'll stay here. That is an honorable path. But this is a battle in which the destiny of our country will be decided—a battle in which I must personally take part."

Desperately, I begged him to remain in Rome. He would not listen and delayed his departure only long enough to see to the marriage of my sister, Secunda. She was just twelve, and in ordinary times Father would never have given her in marriage so early. But he wanted her safely ensconced in a nonpolitical family, shielded from hardship in case his cause went down to defeat.

I never heard Mother question Father's decision to join Brutus and fight for the Republic. Whether she did so when they were alone, I do not know. But at the family dinner before Father departed from Rome, her face was full of dread, and there was such love and fear in her eyes when she gazed at him that I ached for her. My mother and I shared the same terror—that Brutus would be defeated and we would never see Father again.

Kissing him good-bye, I swallowed unshed tears. It was a dreadful parting.

\>\>\>\>\>\>\>

We heard that Caesar had wed Mark Antony's stepdaughter, Claudia, a distant cousin of mine. The girl was only ten; the consummation must wait for two years, but the marriage created a familial bond between Caesar and Antony.

For a while, events slowed to a creep. I brooded about what the last eight decades had been like in my country. Again and again in Rome, men had died for political causes they considered good, and left behind wives and children scratching for survival.

I didn't so much dread poverty as I did something worse and less distinct. What I feared—though I had no clear idea of what form it might take—was the utter destruction of my family.

⋙⋙

My menses had always been perfectly regular, and I felt certain of my second pregnancy early on. I calculated that I would bear a child in November, and wondered if the great battle my father had spoken of would take place by then. If the Republic went down, and my father and my husband went down with it, what would I do? How would I care for my child?

Tiberius Nero never said anything directly, but he carried himself like a man who suspected he had chosen the wrong side. I had the feeling, though, that he was ashamed to fully admit this even in his own thoughts, to say to himself, *Well, I have been a fool, and now I must turn tail and run for safety.* The sense of shame kept him paralyzed.

One night, after we coupled, I whispered in his ear, "Dearest, now that Julius Caesar is gone, who do you think is the best general alive?"

He laughed. "Is that what you call pillow talk?"

"Who?"

He answered in the voice of one indulging an inquisitive child. "The best general is Mark Antony, beyond any doubt."

"Yet young Caesar's army defeated him the one time they clashed."

"Caesar's army defeated him not because Antony is not a great general, but because most Roman soldiers, even those who follow Antony, refuse to fight Julius Caesar's chosen heir."

"So Antony is the best general, and young Caesar has the loyalty of the soldiers. Do I have that right?"

"Yes."

"And they are allies now?"

"Again, yes," Tiberius Nero said, the lightness no longer in his voice.

"You never raised a hand against Julius Caesar. For years you followed him loyally."

"What are you saying, Livia?"

"Only that it's not as if you had a long-standing enmity against Caesar. And his friends have no knowledge you were aware of the plot to kill him. They have no special cause to hate you. Young Caesar certainly does not. And Mark Antony—I doubt if he bears you any great personal ill will."

"Bears me personal ill will? Why should he? I fought under him in Gaul. He commended me. Apart from that, his brother Lucius is a good friend of mine. Here's something I don't like to boast about—in battle I once saved Lucius's life."

"You did? You never told me that."

I drew out of him the whole story of how he had warded off a sword blow aimed right at Lucius's neck. I suppose it is the kind of thing that often happens in war—one soldier saves another. However, Lucius had thanked him in emotional terms.

I lay with my cheek against Tiberius Nero's shoulder, and touched my belly, where I was sure the new baby lay asleep. *This—this must be my highest loyalty.*

"Why all these questions? What are you trying to suggest?" A wariness had come into Tiberius Nero's tone.

I did not answer. Instead I said, "I think I'm carrying your son."

"Truly?" He kissed me. "This time nothing must go wrong. I'm practically forty years old—very old for a first son. It's not as if the years ahead are endless."

"You aren't old," I said. "And he'll be here before you turn forty—in November, before next winter comes. Our Tiberius will be born by then."

Our son would be named for his father, as custom demanded, but he would be my child, my boy. He must be no orphan, kicked about and scorned, but carefully nurtured and protected as he grew to splendid manhood.

"Would you feel better—more secure—if I came to some agreement with Antony?" Tiberius Nero asked me.

"I think it would be prudent. And Antony needs friends in the Senate, doesn't he? He's not so powerful that he doesn't need friends?"

Is it I who am saying this? I? Father's Livia Drusilla?

My husband let out a long sigh. "Still. To go crawling to Mark Antony."

"But you wouldn't have to go to him, would you? Not directly? If you were to contact Lucius, who is your friend and owes you so much . . . ?"

"Yes, Lucius is a good sort." Tiberius Nero stroked my hair.

"There are ways you could get a message to him? To Lucius?"

"There are ways."

Forgive me, Father. Forgive me. Forgive me. Forgive me.

"If Brutus wins—and yes, yes, O Jupiter Optimus Maximus, let Brutus win!—it won't matter," I said. "It won't even become publicly known, will it?"

"It still sticks in my craw," Tiberius Nero said.

"Of course it does. Because you are good and honorable. But these are awful times. And—look at it this way. Will it add one soldier to Caesar and Antony's army? Will it take one man away from Brutus? Of course not. You won't be offering Antony anything more than . . . future friendship."

"But I hate the thought of it. I wouldn't even consider it except that I don't want you to be fearful of the future, while you're carrying our child."

"My love," I said, "I think you would be wrong to offer Antony your loyalty as a free gift. Why should you? You are Tiberius Nero, a great soldier who saved his brother's life. Make it clear to him you want something in exchange. I know—why not tell him you want the praetorship?"

Tiberius Nero laughed aloud. "Gods above, with Lucius as my advocate, Mark Antony just might go for it."

With this inducement—the possibility of high office—any doubts my husband had were resolved. And so the message was sent, and the bargain sealed.

⋙⋙

Two months later, proscriptions came to Rome. They were carried out by order of Antony, Lepidus, and Caesar, who now formed a triumvirate. It was said that Caesar had agreed to proscriptions reluctantly. But he acquiesced, at the insistence of the other two.

Names were scrawled on whitewashed wooden boards set up in the Forum. If your name was on the list, you could be killed by anyone, and your killer would receive a share of your property, with the rest of it going to the triumvirs to pay their army. Those named were the political opponents and personal enemies of the triumvirs.

Many of those killed were wealthy men who lived on the Palatine Hill, as I did. On the very first day of the proscriptions, I walked out of my door and saw a headless man in a toga sprawled in the street. I stood and stared, amazed at how much blood he'd had inside him, how far across the roadway the puddle stretched. Then I turned and walked back inside. I clasped my hands together to still their shaking, feeling as if I had been transported from Rome to a wasteland prowled by ferocious wolves.

During the proscriptions, about two thousand men were killed. Among the dead was Cicero. His head was cut off, on Antony's order—and also his right hand, the hand that had written speeches against Antony—and they were displayed in the Forum.

The killers came after the sun had set, because they wanted their faces hidden. They searched every hiding place, every back alley. I never felt safe, even though my husband was now counted among Antony's supporters. At night, I lay wakeful, clutching my belly, whispering soothing words to my unborn child.

My father's name, of course, appeared on the white boards. All of Father's property was seized. Mother fled to us when men came to break into the house. She managed to take her jewelry with her but lost everything else. She spoke of how all that had been seized would be returned to her when Brutus and his forces triumphed. But I heard the fear in her voice—fear of losing more than a house and property—and she had the look of a woman who expected to forfeit everything she valued on this earth. Father was constantly in her thoughts, as he was in mine.

>>>>>>>

When all of those condemned who had not fled Rome had been killed, the proscriptions ended. Antony, Lepidus, and Caesar left the city to march to Greece, at the head of an army that had swelled to one hundred and twenty thousand men.

Mother lived with my husband and me, a silent, somber presence. Once, as we sat spinning wool together, I said, just to draw her into conversation, "Oh, Mother, I wish I could know if I'm going to have a boy. November is so far away. It seems such a long time to wait."

"There is a way to know, sooner than that." Mother did not look up from her spindle. "It's supposed to be very sure. But it's troublesome. You must get a newly fertilized chicken's egg, and hold it in your hands to warm it until it hatches. If the chick is a hen, then you are carrying a girl child. But if the chick is a rooster, then the baby will be a boy."

In answer to my eager questions, Mother—who had grown up on her father's farm—told me it took twenty-one days, more or less, for a chick to hatch. My maids could hold the egg when I couldn't, but it must always be warmed by a woman's hands.

"Then you must wait at least another thirty days after the chick is born, and see if red bumps appear on its head," Mother said. "You're not going to ask me what the red bumps mean, are you?"

"It means it's growing a comb and is a rooster."

Without bothering to say if my guess was right, Mother went back to her spinning.

I sent a slave to a farm on the outskirts of Rome to get an egg for me—one the farmer swore was newly fertilized. Every day I held the egg cupped in my hands. While I bathed, dressed, ate, or relieved myself, my maid Pelia or Mother held the egg, and while I slept the female servants took turns sitting up in the atrium and holding it.

To some degree, this hatching of the egg was a thing I did for Mother's sake, to divert her mind from her troubles. It also distracted me a little from fear for my father. I did my best every day to concentrate on cradling the egg in my hands, and on making sure neither I nor my servants were careless with it for a moment. I yearned to bring a boy into the world—a warrior, not a female who would have to wait at home while distant events decided her fate—and I half convinced myself that if only the egg successfully hatched, the chick would be a rooster and I'd have the son I wanted.

"Mistress! Mistress!" A little before dawn, I heard Pelia's cry from the atrium.

I rose from my bed and in my haste ran out of the bedchamber barefoot. An oil lamp burned in the atrium, and Pelia sat in a chair in the center of a pool of light. She held her hands palms up in her lap, and there lay the egg. Leaning over, I could see a crack in it, and a tiny beak breaking through.

This was the first time I ever saw any living creature born. I have visited many temples, but I never felt such a true sense of the sacred as I did then, as I stood for nearly an hour, all the women of the household gathered round, watching as the chick slowly emerged in Pelia's hands.

As a gift after I conceived, Tiberius Nero had bought me two little twin boys, pretty Syrians, named Talos and Antitalos. It was a fashion to keep such children as pets and allow them to walk around naked, and train them to sing and tell jokes. They were fascinated by the chick and helped me care for it—keeping it in a small wooden crate in a corner of the atrium and feeding it worms from the garden. They even gave it a name—Aquila, "Eagle"—certainly a grand name for a chicken.

One morning, when the chick was past a month old and had begun to sprout feathers, Antitalos pointed at its head and said, "Look, Mistress."

I could see tiny red bumps on the chick's head, and my heart soared. I knew I would bear a son.

Tiberius Nero was as overjoyed as I was, though he pretended skeptical reserve and suggested we fatten the chick—now a little rooster—for the cook pot. I gasped, "You want to eat Aquila?"

For a while, I would not part with Aquila at all. Eventually, though, his crowing proved irritating. Tiberius Nero owned several farms outside the city, and we sent the rooster to one of these, with strict instructions it was never to be eaten but used for siring more chickens.

>>>>>>>>

When I was in the seventh month of my pregnancy, a letter came from Father. Mother read it first, while I sat beside her watching her face. I saw her eyes light up, and when she handed the waxed tablet to me, I read the letter eagerly. It was brief. Father told us that a brave army of over a hundred thousand men had gathered around Brutus, and they looked forward to reclaiming Rome. We must keep up our courage, pray to the gods, and await a joyous reunion.

The messenger could not tarry long. Mother and I rushed to compose short letters to Father. I wrote, *Beloved and revered Father, in just a few months I pray you will hold a newborn grandson in your arms, in a free Republic. And we will all be together and never part again.*

Full of hope, I had no trouble drifting off to sleep that night. But then I had a nightmare. I found myself in the middle of a battlefield, surrounded on all sides by men locked in armed struggle. Two caught my eye. They thrust and parried with huge, glinting swords. I could not see their faces, but though I did not know who the men were, I feared for them both. I shouted, "Stop! Stop!" but they did not hear me. As they fought, I could only watch, sick with horror. Finally, one man lunged with his sword, and the other warrior fell to the ground. I cried out, ran and knelt beside him, and stared up at the man who had slain him. It was my father, who looked at me with stony eyes and said in a contemptuous voice, "A wife should weep for her husband." I gazed down at the warrior he had killed. I expected to see Tiberius Nero.

The man's face was like a death mask, frozen, icy cold, but not a corpse's face, nothing as human as that. It was not Tiberius Nero. The dead man was young Caesar. As soon as I saw who it was, I began to shriek and rend my garments.

When I awoke, my cheeks were wet with tears. I lay in the darkness, Tiberius Nero snoring beside me, and understood something that I had not allowed myself to know before: I would mourn Caesar if he died in battle. Even though he was my father's enemy, even after the proscriptions. And there was another searing truth, plain in the dream, that I had not previously faced. When the two armies met, it was almost certain that either my father or Caesar would not survive. There was not enough room in the world for men like Father and Brutus *and* for Antony and Caesar.

I did not know if my nightmare contained any true prophecy. Perhaps a priest of Apollo could have interpreted my dream to me, but I had no desire to confide it to anyone. The self-knowledge it brought me made me feel like a traitor in my heart. I loved my father. But if Caesar died in the coming battle, I would weep.

⋙⋙

It was almost November. Soon my child would be born. Heavy and sluggish, I often lay on my bed fully clothed during daylight hours, and sometimes dozed off. I woke one day from a nap, a couple of hours past noon, jarred out of sleep by shouts coming from outside the house. I could not make out the words. It sounded as if two or three men were arguing in the street.

The shouts continued and grew louder. What did this signify? My mouth went dry with fear. I had to push on the bed with both hands to get myself up since my belly was so huge. I slipped my feet into sandals and went to the atrium.

Mother and Tiberius Nero stood there. Mother had her fist pressed to her teeth, and her expression was all desolation. When she saw me, she spoke in a controlled voice. "Livia, come here and sit." She led me to a couch and sat beside me. Tiberius Nero came and sat on the other side of me.

"If it were possible to keep what has happened from you until your son is born, we would do it," Mother said. "But it's not possible, so you must hear it. You must keep calm, lest you injure the child. Do you understand me, Livia?" Just at the last, a tremor came into her voice. "Will you be calm?"

"I will be calm," I said.

Mother tried to speak again, but instead choked and shut her eyes.

Tiberius Nero gripped my hand. "Word's come—it's not by an official dispatch, you understand, just a man on a horse racing here with the news. But I think he's telling the truth. And the news is being shouted through the streets now. The armies met at Philippi in Greece. Antony and Caesar won the battle. Dearest, remember that I'm Antony's friend, and we're perfectly safe."

I looked at Mother. "Is Father alive?"

She shook her head.

I pressed my face against her shoulder. I wept, and Mother wept too. Inside myself, a voice screamed, *Father! Father! Father!* I had never known such tearing grief. But I did not cry out, and I did not rend my garments. My mother had said I must contain myself, for the sake of my son.

Later, reassured by my self-control, Tiberius Nero told me all he knew about the battle and its outcome. He said that Antony alone had led the forces that opposed Brutus, for illness had come upon Caesar—dropsy—and swollen with fluid, unable to rise from his cot, he had taken no part in the fighting.

After the battle was over, Brutus quoted some poetry about virtue and the caprices of fortune, then got a soldier to hold a sword so he could run upon it.

Tiberius Nero volunteered nothing about Father's death. But I had to know how he had died. I steeled myself and asked, "Did Father survive the battle too?"

"Yes," my husband said gently.

"Did he die by his own hand?" I asked the question in a quiet, composed voice, so that Tiberius Nero would not hold back the truth.

"He fell on his sword," Tiberius Nero said.

No one who fought for the Republic died a more exalted and noble death.

>>>>>>>

On the day when we learned the outcome of the Battle of Philippi, grief settled in my heart that would never leave entirely; I would carry it until the day of my own death. And there was guilt also. When I urged my husband to ally himself with Antony, I betrayed my father. I could argue that I had not changed his fate one iota. But I had done what he never would have: chosen safety over honor.

Mother, Secunda, and I put on the white garb of women's mourning, but we did not have Father's body to tend and could not even expect it would be treated with honor by the victors. That deepened our grief.

When word of Philippi's aftermath trickled back to Rome and came to Tiberius Nero's ears, I insisted on knowing what was happening, however awful it might be. I learned that after the battle, Caesar Octavianus, still so sick he could barely walk, sat in a curule chair of office and, with Antony, judged those who had surrendered. Every one of Julius Caesar's assassins who was taken alive was executed. No matter how they pleaded for mercy, young Caesar always spoke the same words: "You must die." He and Antony looked on as prisoners were thrown on the ground and decapitated.

That Caesar wanted to put all his "father's" assassins to death surprised no one. The savagery of his manner was the shock. One poor man begged Caesar to at least allow him a decent burial. Caesar said, "Take that up with the crows."

The bodies of the dead were burned in piles like the carcasses of foundered cattle.

Young Caesar ordered one of his own bodyguards, a veteran of Julius Caesar's Gallic wars, to cut Brutus's head from the corpse. On his instruction, this soldier galloped to Rome, carrying the head, stopping only to change horses. When he reached the city, the veteran rode his horse into the Forum, straight up to the statue of Julius Caesar that had been erected on young Caesar's order. "See this vengeance, O gods!" he shouted. He threw the head down at the statue's feet.

Now when I remembered the attraction I had felt for Caesar Octavianus, I recoiled. But strangely enough, I still could not help putting myself in his place. I felt in my viscera what Caesar must have felt, when his body failed him just before the great battle to avenge the man he called Father. He saw himself transformed again into the boy he had been, too sickly to hope to play a man's role in the world. I imagined his unbearable humiliation. Perhaps this had helped to fuel the rage he displayed after the battle.

If he meant for men to call him merciless rather than say he was a weakling, he managed that very well. He performed only one clement act. Tiberius Nero came rushing home to bring me the news. Seeing my stricken face—what could I expect but word of another enormity?—he blurted, "No, for once I bring you some comfort. Truly. An unbelievable thing has happened—but my source is irreproachable."

I sat in my sewing room, where, with the heart to do almost nothing, I accomplished little work these days. I slipped my needle into the cloth for a tiny tunic I had been trying to make for my coming child. "What has happened?"

"Caesar gave your father a funeral."

I rose. "What?"

"He gave him a perfectly proper military funeral, with sacrifices and incense, and legions lined up in rows to do him honor. He lit his funeral pyre himself."

"Did he say why he treated my father differently?"

Tiberius Nero shook his head.

Caesar had informed me that I could expect repayment of a debt. When he avenged his "father," he demonstrated to all Rome that he paid back debts with interest. I was sure he gave Father a funeral for my sake. This did not make me think well of him. It was just knowledge I could not escape.

"I heard Caesar has recovered from his illness," Tiberius Nero said. "What a pity, eh?"

"A pity," I echoed.

⋙⋙⋙

I wondered what had become of Marcus Brutus's wife, Portia. She had ardently espoused the Republican cause and encouraged her husband in the course he had taken. The day after we heard news of my father's funeral, word came of her fate. Often when a man is impelled by honor to take his own life, his wife will do the same. And so Portia did, most painfully, jamming a hot coal down her throat. When I heard of this, fear tugged at me. What if my mother should also resolve to die?

What anchored Mother to life was my pregnancy. She was aware, as all women are, that first births are very dangerous. As the moment for my baby's birth approached, Mother did not treat me with any new warmth. But she hovered over me as she never had before, prepared special foods that were supposed to be particularly nourishing for women facing childbirth, and hung an amulet round my neck that she had worn when she gave birth to her children.

I felt the first pangs of labor early in the morning a fortnight after I heard the news of my father's death. What I learned on the birthing chair was this: my body's capacity for pain. The midwife, Mother, and Secunda all stayed in the room with me. They wiped my face with cool water, and they murmured encouraging words. But they could not ease my agony or make the baby come forth. I did not call on Diana or any other god or goddess; they all seemed so far off. I felt I had only my own strength to rely on as I pushed and pushed, gripping the arms of the mahogany chair. I knew if I won the struggle I would live, and my son would live. Otherwise we would both die.

When the day had waned and come again, sunlight slanting in through the bedchamber windows, and still the baby had not been born, I saw grave looks on my mother's and the midwife's faces. As for Secunda, she had already begun to cry.

I was beginning to lose my battle, that was plain. Something in me revolted at this thought. I would not lose. *Would not.* I said to myself that when the sharpest pains came again I would push with all my might, while I still had strength left to make this attempt, push and push and push and hold back nothing, and not cease until the baby was born. Live or die: I would stake everything on one toss of the dice. As soon as the pain came, I did just as I resolved, biting on the strip of leather the wet nurse had given me, refusing to scream. I felt my insides being torn asunder. I did not know I had won my battle until I heard the midwife cry, "A son! And he is perfect!"

What more honored estate can there be for a woman in this world than to be mother to a son? But I was too exhausted to feel triumphant.

Later, I held my son in my arms and counted his fingers, almost suspiciously. Five on each hand. I told myself that proved he was perfect, just as the midwife had said. They say every child looks beautiful to his own mother, but the truth is, he did not seem beautiful to me. His tiny, wrinkled red face reminded me of a peevish little old man. Yet I loved him.

⋙⋙

We hired a woman named Rubria, whose own baby had died, to serve as wet nurse for the child. Right after the birth, of course, the midwife had laid the swaddled baby at Tiberius Nero's feet, and he—exultant—had lifted it in his arms, signifying his decision to rear, rather than expose it. I have never known a wealthy father to cast out of doors a healthy, legitimate child, even a girl.

Nine days after the birth, as custom required, we held a naming ceremony for the baby. The celebration was a small one, since Father was so recently dead. There sat Mother, Secunda, and I in our white mourning clothes, trying to balance grief and happiness. Tiberius Nero hung a child's protective amulet—a bulla—on the baby's cradle. Our guests applauded, which made the baby wake up and wail. I rocked him, but could not soothe him. Finally, Mother lifted him, and little Tiberius Claudius Nero quieted in her arms.

Mother put the baby back in the cradle. "You feel quite well now, don't you, Livia? No signs of fever? No weakness?"

"Mother, I'm fine."

She brushed my hair back from my face. "Always so messy. Ah well, life goes on."

I went to bed rather late that night and also slept late, long after Tiberius Nero and the rest of the household were up. A knock on the bedchamber door roused me. I opened it to find Antiope, the maid who waited on my mother, looking anxious. She said she had repeatedly knocked on the door of Mother's bedchamber and was concerned that Mother did not answer.

I raced to Mother's bedchamber. Before I threw the door open, I suspected what awaited me there. Mother lay across her bed, dressed just as she had been for yesterday's ceremony. Her head rested on a pillow. Her legs were crossed at the ankles. The folds of her stola were carefully arranged. There was a smear of yellow across her lips, and in her hand she clutched the kind of vial used to hold expensive perfume. Her eyes, wide open, gawked at the ceiling.

A waxed tablet with writing on it lay on the stool at the foot of her bed. I snatched it up with desperate eagerness, as if words could somehow make everything right.

> *Livia, I have gone to join your father. The loss of our property has played only a minor part in my decision. Certainly I have no desire to be a burden to you or your husband. But I have chosen this course because it pays the greatest honor to your father and our marriage. I am sure you have enough daughterly reverence that you would not dream of questioning the rightness of my action.*
>
> *Secunda is to get my emerald necklace, which I promised her; you may divide the rest of my jewelry with her as you think just.*
>
> *I forbid you to follow my example, and hope I need not remind you of your responsibilities to your husband and your son.*

I had received the news of my father's death calmly; Mother was there to order me to be calm. She was not here now. I sank down on my knees, howled like an animal, and tore at my clothes.

Tiberius Nero came running. It was a long time before he could get me up on my feet. He made me down a sleeping draught, and I soon fell into a stupor. I think my husband was afraid that if he did not give me the draught I would do myself harm.

Chapter 6

December is the most joyous month of the year, the time of the Saturnalia, of games and feasting, and at the end of the month, new year's presents. Fresh grief at this time walls you off from everyone. With so many people dead in the proscriptions and in battle, the revels that year had a forced quality, but one still heard music in the streets and smelled honey cakes and spiced wine. When I had to go anywhere, I kept the curtains of my litter closed. Young as I was, I did not know that mourning passes, and was as defenseless before grief as the young usually are.

I did not take much pleasure even in my son. I felt terrified if he so much as sneezed. What if I lost him as I had lost my parents?

Soon it was time for me to take up my duties as a wife again. They were less onerous than they had once been. Tiberius Nero's ardor in the bedchamber had lessened. I suspected that he began seeking other women during my pregnancy, and having fallen into this habit, he never stopped. For men of the nobility this was expected, conventional behavior. It still would have upset me, if I had loved him.

I no longer had the illusion that my marriage might help save the Republic. The Republic was quite dead. Antony, Lepidus, and Caesar had carved up the empire between them. Antony was in the east, Lepidus in North Africa, and Caesar remained in Italy.

Tiberius Nero was named a praetor. Lucius Antony stayed in Rome, having been chosen consul. People said that Lucius could almost be taken for his brother's less competent and vital twin; he had the same tall, husky build and fleshy face as Mark Antony. He would frequently dine at my home, and then he and my husband would withdraw to confer for long hours.

One evening at dinner, I heard Lucius say something that terrified me. "That little swine Caesar wants to act like he's the third Gracchi brother. It's too much." Looking intently at my husband, he added, "I've written to my brother that he can absolutely depend on you."

"Of course he can," Tiberius Nero hastened to say.

Caesar was almost never in the city of Rome, and he shared the governing of it with Antony's men. His priority was to hold the loyalty of his soldiers, and so he was settling his veterans on small farms. Since the time of the Gracchi, it had been considered a great injustice for Roman soldiers to return from the wars to nothing. Their commander was expected to see to it that when they mustered out they got small plots of land.

Like the Gracchi, my father had loathed the latifundia, the great estates worked by slaves, which ate up so much Italian land. He said the latifundia owners often drove poor citizens off the land by foul, illegal means. If he approved of nothing else that Caesar did, he would approve of this—that he was going about Italy, breaking up latifundia so he could give his veterans small farms.

"What is Antony depending on you to do about Caesar and the latifundia?" An edge in my voice, I asked the question of my husband that night as we prepared for bed.

"There are legal matters that fall under my jurisdiction," Tiberius Nero said. His duties as praetor were largely those of a judge.

"He wants you to rule in favor of the latifundia's owners? Just to thwart Caesar?"

Tiberius Nero did not reply.

"He does, doesn't he?" I gasped for breath as if all the air had drained out my lungs. "The question of land—it drips blood. It always has." Strife in Italy had first started nearly a century ago over this very matter.

"Now, dear, calm yourself."

The guttering candle on the table beside our bed flickered feebly. I could not see my husband's face. "This is ruination."

"It would be ruination for me not to do what Antony requires," Tiberius Nero said. "I have no choice. Not if I want my head to stay attached to my neck. Do you think I like this business?"

"Caesar and his men won't stand for this," I said.

The carnage, the civil war, would all begin again. This present lull was only a brief holiday from the Roman habit of self-destruction. What made matters worse—what had me sick with despair—was that my husband's allegiance, and therefore mine, had to be with Antony in a battle in which right and justice were with Caesar.

>>>>>>>

I wonder how many women from time immemorial have thought that if only women could rule the world it would be better than it is. Really, has any woman *not,* some time or other, thought that? Of course I thought it too. I believed women were unquestionably less bloodthirsty than men. Then I met Fulvia.

She was Mark Antony's wife. Her husband, whom she was said to love passionately, had assumed control of the eastern empire, gone to Egypt, and fallen into the snares of Cleopatra. One might, as a woman, have sympathized with her if she had had a shred of decent human feeling. She did not.

When Tiberius Nero and I went to have dinner at her home, the mourning period for my father and mother had not yet elapsed, and I wore white. Fulvia looked me up and down and said, "Oh, you poor creature, you just lost your parents, didn't you? What a pity they chose the wrong side."

She was about forty years old, tall and full-busted. Her bright makeup was just this side of grotesque. I did not reply to her remark about my parents but returned her gaze steadily, while wishing her in the hottest corner of Tartarus.

She ushered Tiberius Nero and me into her dining room. Murals depicting Dionysian revels adorned the walls. Her brother-in-law Lucius was already eating dinner, along with a raven-haired girl of ten or eleven.

"That slimy little beast has divorced her," Fulvia informed me, when she saw me gazing at the child.

"Caesar?" I said.

"Who else do you think I mean? To think that the poor child lived with him for months on end," Fulvia said.

"Lived with him?" I stared at her.

"Well, she lived in his house," Fulvia said. "He didn't touch her. He didn't touch you, did he, Claudia?"

The girl shook her head. "He said I was too young."

"The day after the divorce he married a relative of Sextus Pompey," Fulvia told me. Sextus, the son of Julius Caesar's great enemy, Pompey Magnus, was at that time gathering military support and preparing to seize Sicily. "Scribonia. She's skinny and ugly and at least thirty-five years old. He's desperate for Sextus's help against Antony, you see. The coward. It won't do him any good. I'm raising such a force in Italy that it will be simple—like that"—she snapped her fingers—"to obliterate him."

"*You* are raising a military force?"

"Of course," Fulvia said, and looked at me as if I were stupid.

»»»»»»»

Throughout dinner, it was embarrassing to hear Fulvia bark orders at Tiberius Nero and Lucius Antony. She acted as if the Roman government and Antony's army in Italy were in her hands. Neither of the men dared to say no to her. Such was her force of will.

Fulvia never recruited as many troops as she hoped to, but it was not for lack of trying. And for month after month, she put pressure on Tiberius Nero to give legal rulings inimical to Caesar. Then, not content with this, she ordered her soldiers to harass Caesar's veterans. Skirmishes were fought in which men died. Caesar could not control his veterans' resulting fury. They demanded Caesar lead them against Fulvia and cursed him when he seemed to hesitate.

Fortune favored my husband and me. When Caesar and his veterans began their march on Rome, we heard about it early enough not to be trapped in the city.

We knew Tiberius Nero would have to flee. No one doubted that, as the man who had handed down judicial rulings as Fulvia had instructed, he would be torn limb from limb by Caesar's troops when they took Rome.

On a sunny morning, I stood in the courtyard clutching my son in my arms as Tiberius Nero told me that Fulvia, Lucius Antony, and their supporters had decided to withdraw from Rome to Perusia. A small city a hundred miles away, it was highly fortified and could hold out for a long time against an attacking army.

"Livia, you and the baby must come to Perusia with me," Tiberius Nero said. "Caesar hasn't gone in for murdering women and children yet, but there's always a first time—and besides, the gods alone know if his troops will obey him once they enter Rome."

The risk of staying was too great. I held my son more tightly and buried my face in his curling dark hair. We were fortune's playthings and might lose everything. But I promised myself that whatever happened, I would keep my child safe.

Perusia did not seem like a city at all to me but only a walled town, for it was tiny compared to Rome. Guards opened the city gates for us. Our cart drove down narrow streets to Perusia's forum, an unimpressive square ringed by one-story brick buildings. It was filled with soldiers, armed and wearing breastplates and war helms. A runner had been sent from the gate to tell Lucius Antony of our arrival. He came through the press, smiling. "Welcome, my friend," he said to Tiberius Nero. He looked at me. "I hope you and your child are no worse for the trip. I have a house prepared for you."

The house that Lucius had commandeered for us stood not far from the forum. It had belonged to one of the city's leading men, but when we entered and I glanced around the atrium, I was taken aback. There were a few old couches, a couple of plain oak tables, no frescoes on the walls, nothing costly or beautiful.

Tiberius Nero looked around somberly.

I felt I must keep up his spirits as well as my own. "This is better than I expected," I said. "We can be very comfortable here."

A rough-faced former legionary named Buteo, once Tiberius Nero's armor bearer, had accompanied us to Perusia as a servant. Rubria had come too, to help care for little Tiberius. While Buteo carried our things in from the cart, Rubria and I explored the house and found a little room where she could nurse the baby. She seemed perfectly accepting of the situation in which she found herself. She sat down on a stool and bared her breast, her plain, broad face placid as she placed her nipple in my son's mouth. I went back to the atrium, where Tiberius Nero stood with Buteo.

"I want to start putting our things away and making us comfortable," I said. "You'll help me, won't you, Buteo? Will you carry that chest into the room on the left side of the atrium?" I pointed. Buteo grimaced but picked up the chest.

Later, when we were alone, Tiberius Nero touched my cheek. "Little dove, do you truly understand what is going on here? Do you realize what will happen if Mark Antony doesn't get here in time with an army?"

"Yes," I said. I put my arms around him and rested my cheek against his shoulder. Shared misery seemed to deepen the bond between us, and I felt true affection for him at that moment. "We're together. You, me, and our boy. That's the most important thing."

"You're brave," my husband said.

"I'm not," I said. "I'm frightened. But if my father were here, he would say that this is a moment when it is necessary to be brave." *Now,* I thought. *In this miserable city, waiting to be besieged. Now. This is a time when the gods are at work to forge our souls.*

⋙⋙

We settled down and lived as best we could. I had been trained in all housewifely arts by my mother, on the theory that it was necessary to know how a task should be performed in order to supervise the work of others. No one could get house servants in Perusia. Well, Fulvia could and did. But virtually all of the town's womenfolk—except for those at the bathhouse that doubled as a house of prostitution—had fled to surrounding farms or other towns. So I scrubbed our clothes and cooked the meals myself. Buteo helped with the heaviest work, though always with a scowl. Rubria pitched in generously.

The country people, who came to the city gates to sell us food, brought news of Rome. Caesar and his veterans had marched into the city. There was some looting by soldiers, but in the end Caesar had restored order.

"Next he will want to assert control over all of Italy," Tiberius Nero said grimly.

We had been in Perusia barely a month when Caesar's army arrived and camped outside the town. Fulvia mounted the public speakers' platform in the Perusian forum. Over her woman's garb, she had strapped on a sword. In a voice as carrying and confident as any man's, she addressed the troops and told them they need not fear. Her husband was on the way; his army would soon arrive to defend us. She pointed at her two little sons, who stood at the foot of the speakers' platform. Mark Antony would not abandon his wife and children.

Even in the insane times in which we were living, women did not don swords and deliver speeches. This was more than outlandish—it was as if the moon had fallen to Earth. But I admit that much as I disliked Fulvia, I felt a little shiver of admiration for her audacity. Though some snickered at first, in the end the soldiers all cheered her—after all, she had promised them help.

Fulvia on the speakers' platform with her sword—a repellent image, surely. And yet it pulled at my mind: a woman wielding unvarnished political power.

>>>>>>>

Caesar encircled Perusia. His army commenced to dig a ditch all around the town and to build a rampart. They would starve us to begin with, and then, when we were weakened, climb over the town walls.

Our soldiers fired slings full of pebble-sized lead balls and stones as big as a man's fist over the walls at the enemy, and received the same in return. Soldiers etched insulting messages into the lead pieces. References to intimate parts of Fulvia's body adorned most of those that came flying in our direction. "I seek Caesar's ass" was one of the milder messages on the balls our side fired. Very amusing, except that those lead balls, like the stones, shattered soldiers' skulls.

How strange it felt to be in a town besieged by a young man with whom I had chatted at my father's dinner table, a young man to whom I'd felt attraction. I wanted to plead with him, *Why must we have this conflict? Can't you call off the siege and go away?*

Though greatly outnumbered, Lucius Antony and my husband again and again led out soldiers to attack Caesar's troops. They could not defeat Caesar's army but hoped to slow down the construction of the rampart, which would completely seal off the town. Our hope was that Mark Antony, summoned by Lucius and Fulvia, had left Egypt and was sailing toward us with the bulk of his army. After all, we were fighting not just to hold Perusia but for dominance in Italy. We prayed that Mark Antony would reach us before the rampart was finished and we began to starve.

Every time Tiberius Nero left me to attack Caesar's forces, my heart constricted. What if he were killed, what if I were left alone in this besieged town with only my baby and two servants? But I knew my role was to see him off with a calm and confident face. I always did.

Once, Tiberius Nero brought home a wounded soldier, a boy who had distinguished himself with gallantry in a raid. With Buteo's help, he managed to carry him back into the city from the place outside where he had fallen. The young soldier had a deep wound in his back that slowly seeped blood. He could not live. But because he was no more than sixteen or seventeen and had been so brave, Tiberius Nero did not want him to die in the grisly hospital barracks. So he put him in our bed, without saying a word to me. And I, equally silent, brought water and washed the boy's face, which was streaked with the blood and mud of battle.

The young soldier lay on his side, very still. He had dark, wavy hair and smooth olive skin. I noticed his eyelashes. What a strange thing to notice, but they were unusually long and thick. I was sure girls had sighed over him.

Once, he said a word, "Water." So I held a cup to his lips. He tried to drink, but it was beyond him. I dipped my fingers in the cup and moistened his lips. Then I sat and held his hand.

He opened his eyes wide and seemed to truly see me for the first time. He looked surprised to find a woman beside him. Then he smiled. I wondered if he mistook me for some girl he fancied. Or perhaps he had a sister. I hoped he took me for whatever woman he preferred that I be. He shut his eyes again and seemed to sleep.

Look what the fools have done to you. Caesar and Antony and Fulvia—all those fools.

I held on to the boy's hand, even though I knew he was no longer aware of my presence but was far away, and going on a farther journey still.

Why don't the gods intervene and stop this slaughter? I would do it if I were them. If I had power, that is what I would use it for. I do not care if Caesar rules or Antony does. We must have peace.

The young soldier died before morning, died because Rome could not govern herself. His passing reawakened memories of the loss of my father and mother, and took me to a place beyond tears.

>>>>>>>>

Once, Tiberius Nero came home from a raid flushed with rage. His manner was so grim that at first I thought it best not to question him. After I helped him to take his armor off, and bound up a small flesh wound on his right forearm, he said, "Oh, Livia, we almost got him."

"Got whom?" I said.

"Him. That piece of manure, Caesar."

I stared. "You mean, you were that close? You actually saw him? What happened?"

"They were holding some ceremony—he stood at a little makeshift altar with a knife in his hand, about to sacrifice a sheep. And we came at them, suddenly, in force. I threw a javelin, and it almost hit him. I swear to you, my aim was true. But he saw it coming and he ducked, and it went over his shoulder. And then all his men came surging around him, and—well, he escaped. Maybe this all would be over if I had just managed to kill him."

But it was not over, nowhere near the end.

Water we had in ample supply, because there were many wells in the town. There was no way the enemy could make us die of thirst. But very soon we ran out of eggs and fish. The small amount of produce that one saw in the market—roots, mostly—looked half rotten and gnawed by vermin. Silos stored a limited supply of grain. We made it into porridge or had it milled into flour and baked a gritty and tasteless bread. We did not precisely starve.

I was often hungry but had no right to complain. We, Tiberius Nero's family, received more generous grain rations than the ordinary soldiers did. What was most important to me was that Rubria, our wet nurse, had enough to eat, and that little Tiberius did not go hungry.

My son had turned one year old. He was big for his age and confidently walking. It was good that he was still nursing, but he required other food too, and more than just grain.

I ventured out of our house only to go to the marketplace. Tiberius Nero insisted that Buteo accompany me, for he did not want me alone on the streets of a town that was almost womanless and packed with thousands of soldiers. Except for Fulvia, Rubria, and me, there were almost no women in Perusia who were not prostitutes. So with Buteo's grudging company, I searched the market for food. I was quite willing to stick several gold coins into a butcher's hand in exchange for some decent-looking meat. But it became hard to find meat that did not seem tainted. All the horses and mules in the town not immediately needed for military purposes were slaughtered and eaten early on. Then people killed the dogs and ate them.

Once I stood at a butcher's stall, looking at small cubes of flesh. "What is that?" I asked.

"Chicken," the butcher said. He wore a frayed gray tunic that was spotted with blood. Though he made a point of looking me in the eye, I knew he was lying.

"What is it?" I asked again.

He laughed. It struck me that he looked extraordinarily well fed, and that there was something brutal about his features. "Rat," he said.

My stomach turned, though I knew people were trapping rats and eating them. Then another thought came into my mind. Perhaps an old slave of his had begun to seem useless, a burden to feed, and perhaps . . . Or was this just a sick fancy, the product of my hunger?

I did no more shopping that day, and all but ran home. But the next day I was back in the marketplace, searching again for meat.

One becomes numb to many things when one is continually hungry. But I was never too numb to feel afraid. My greatest fear was that privation would cause my little boy to sicken, that he would die as a result of this siege. Or that when the enemy came over the walls, an arrow or spear would find his little heart.

I remember once clutching him to me, near despair. "Oh, my son, what is going to happen to you?"

A soft voice said, "Don't worry, Mistress. We will keep him safe." Rubria had appeared beside me.

"Will we?" I said.

"Oh, yes. We are both strong, and we will keep him safe together."

Rubria rarely spoke unless she was spoken to. She had told me only a little about her life. I knew she had lost both her husband and her son in a tenement fire in Rome, and she had turned to selling the one thing she had—her milk—to survive. Though she was quiet and inexpressive, she was a person I could rely on.

As winter wore on, we all grew hungrier. And still Mark Antony did not come.

⋙⋙

It was spring and the fifth month of the siege. Tiberius Nero told me that Fulvia and her sons had left Perusia. "She used an old passageway that goes under the city wall," he said. "Almost no one knows about it."

We stood in our bedchamber. I knew we had been utterly abandoned, that Mark Antony would never come now, that Perusia would fall. "Let's leave too," I said.

"I can't. I'm not a deserter."

The resolute set of his jaw infuriated me. "My son is not going to be here suffering as the food runs out," I said. "When Caesar and his army come climbing over the walls to sack and burn this town, my son won't be here, do you understand me?"

Tiberius Nero touched my shoulder. "I'll do all I can to get you and the boy away from here safely. But as for me—no."

Tears came to my eyes. I had been his wife for more than three years. Still, my soul was not knit to his soul, as my mother's had been to my father's. And yet I could not leave Tiberius Nero to die for Perusia.

"If you were fighting for Rome, I would never ask you to walk away," I said. "But this is not for Rome. Tiberius, I cannot bear—I truly cannot bear to see you die for such a ridiculous cause, for no cause at all. I don't want my son to be without a father. I won't leave without you."

Tiberius Nero shook his head. "You'll leave with the boy. I'll arrange it."

"No." I looked deep into his eyes for a long moment. "You have to find a way to save us all," I said.

In the end he went to Lucius Antony, and Lucius gave him permission to leave, on one condition. After he escaped, he must try to raise an army to relieve Perusia, by offering freedom to any slaves who would fight against Caesar. It was an absurd idea. But if Tiberius Nero had told me that in order to get Lucius's permission to go—without which he would not leave Perusia—he must agree to try to construct a great machine to carry Lucius up to the heavenly vault, I would have said, *Certainly, agree.*

We made preparations for our escape. Rubria and Buteo would accompany us. We would take my jewelry and what money we had, nothing else. Tiberius Nero told me that after we emerged from the underground tunnel, we would have to walk about five miles down a path that took us close to Caesar's camp, near where his lookouts were. To keep the baby from crying and giving us away, he would obtain a sleeping draught for him from one of the army physicians.

⋙⋙⋙

The tunnel that led under the city wall of Perusia stretched for nearly a mile and was so narrow that the four of us had to walk single file. Moisture clung to the walls, and the air had a dank smell. Buteo, who knew the way, walked first, holding a torch. He wore breastplate, helm, and a sword. Slung over his back, tied on so his hands could be free, was a heavy sack that contained some of our valuables. I walked next. I had put on first one tunica then another till I ended up with four, one over the other. I also wore a cloak. A pouch that contained my jewelry dangled from my waist. I carried my baby in my arms. Fearful of harming him, I had given little Tiberius only half the draught the physician recommended. But he had quickly dozed off.

My breathing began to labor. I seemed not to be able to get enough air in my lungs. I told myself this was only a silly imagining. There was enough air in the tunnel. I touched my son's chest. He breathed normally.

On and on we walked. Something slithered over my foot. I bit my lip. There was no point in screaming.

We knew the tunnel ended in a place deep in the woods. Our ultimate destination was the city of Neapolis, many miles away, where Tiberius Nero had a good friend who was a supporter of Mark Antony. We hoped the friend would not be afraid to give us shelter.

We would be fugitives. Caesar now ruled all of the Italian mainland. I told myself I must not think of the uncertainties ahead. It was hard enough to live through these moments, to keep on walking, to try to get enough air, laden down as I was with jewelry and with my baby.

Finally, Buteo muttered, "Here."

I saw stone steps. They seemed to be leading up not into any aperture in the tunnel but into a pile of tree branches. But then Buteo pushed the branches aside, and we saw light. He extinguished his torch. I followed him up the steps. Rubria and Tiberius Nero came after us. I stood blinking, half-blinded by the sun. Tiberius Nero and Buteo piled the branches back over the hole in the ground that led to the tunnel. If Caesar's troops found that hole and used the tunnel to attack the city, defending Perusia would be impossible.

When my eyes grew accustomed to the light, I saw that we were in a forest, trees on all sides of us. The air smelled of rotting leaves. Ahead was a dirt trail. Buteo pressed his finger to his lips. He did not have to tell me we must be absolutely silent. Caesar's soldiers patrolled these woods.

Buteo—who had reconnoitered the area—led the way down a narrow dirt trail, the rest of us following in single file. Then suddenly he paused and raised a hand.

I heard voices. Two men—not close enough for me to make out what they were saying.

I glanced back at my husband. Tiberius Nero had his hand on his sword hilt.

In a flash, I imagined a scene of horror. A fight, Caesar's soldiers shouting, many more soldiers coming to their aid. My husband and Buteo killed. Rubria, me, and the baby defenseless. What would the enemy do to us?

The voices faded. We walked forward again. We had gone perhaps a hundred yards when the baby woke and started crying. I pressed my hand over his mouth. But then I was terrified. Could he breathe?

"Hush, hush, my little lamb, my little dumpling, my son, my son," I whispered. I took my hand away. He howled.

In an instant, Buteo snatched my son away from me. His hands were underneath the baby's armpits, as he held him up high in the air. I knew he meant to dash him against a tree trunk or the hard ground to kill him. I reached up to grab the baby from him, to fight for the life of my child.

Little Tiberius stopped crying.

I seized the baby and backed away from Buteo. Looking down at little Tiberius, all I could see were his eyes, great staring eyes in his small, pale face. My mouth was dry with fear. But he was safe in my arms.

Later, Tiberius Nero would try to convince me that nothing dreadful had happened. Seeing I was unable to quiet the child, Buteo did his best to distract the baby by swinging him up in his arms, he said. Luckily it worked.

But I knew what Buteo's intentions had been. And I believe little Tiberius knew too. For the rest of our journey on foot, I held him tightly wrapped in my arms, and he never made another sound.

⋙⋙

We made it to a farmhouse at the edge of the forest, where horses could be obtained. It was necessary for us all to ride astride down paths where a wagon could not pass, and so I mounted a horse for the first time in my life. My heart thudded. I was up so high. I kept thinking how far I was from the ground, and that I would fall. And yet I was young and this was adventure: to ride a great powerful beast, with my tunica hiked up above my knees, cold air filling my lungs. Rubria rode beside me. I don't think she found any pleasure in the experience. But there were moments when I truly felt like Hippolita riding out to battle.

Eventually we were able to exchange our mounts for a horse and cart. For four days we traveled by little-used roads, and ultimately we reached the city of Neapolis, where Tiberius Nero's friend gave us shelter.

Rubria stayed with us, but I insisted that my husband dismiss Buteo. I could not stand to look at the man and would not tolerate him around my son.

The next days run together in my mind. I waited in the friend's house while every morning my husband went off to try to raise a slave army. I knew he would fail, and feared he might get himself killed trying to carry out Lucius's mandate. But I thanked Diana that at least my baby and I were no longer in Perusia.

And then, we heard that the city had fallen. The memory of what happened there is one to make all Romans weep. The defenders were slaughtered in their thousands, the city itself sacked and burned to the ground. When men tried to surrender, Caesar by and large refused to show them mercy. He spared Lucius Antony, though—not wishing to provoke all-out war with Mark Antony.

There was now no reason for Tiberius Nero to continue his fruitless efforts to rouse the slaves.

Shortly after Perusia's fall, we learned that Caesar's soldiers were on their way to take charge of Neapolis. Tiberius Nero and I fled with our child. Rubria, who deeply loved little Tiberius, begged to be allowed to come.

Tiberius Nero brought our horse and cart to a stop when we were miles away from Neapolis, in a forest glade. His cheek was twitching with nerves. I told him we had to decide on a destination, but without a word he jumped off the wagon seat and went walking off to disappear among the trees.

Rubria stared at me. I saw the question in her eyes, the same one I had asked: Where were we going?

We waited for a time for Tiberius Nero to come back. When he did not return, I put the baby in Rubria's arms and went into the woods to search for my husband. I found him leaning against a tree, one hand pressed to his eyes. "Tiberius?" I said softly.

He straightened and looked at me. I was relieved to see that at least he was not weeping. But he seemed absolutely spent. "It may be I've come to the end of my road," he said. "Maybe rather than running away and being hunted down like a wild beast, I ought to think of dying like a soldier of Rome."

Perhaps he was just succumbing to momentary despair. He had walked off to be alone and collect himself, and I had come after him and found him at his lowest ebb. But with the deaths of my father and mother still so fresh in my memory, I did not take his words as a mere expression of wretchedness.

"Do it then," I said. "But don't expect me to honor your memory or to teach your son to honor it. I assure you, we will remember you as a coward. And be very certain, we will not die with you. My son and I will survive."

He stared at me in disbelief.

"Coward." I spat the word at him.

"How dare you call me that?"

"Are you angry, Tiberius? Good. Perhaps you're a man after all."

He struck me across the mouth with the back of his hand. I went reeling from the blow and tasted blood in my mouth.

He had never hit me before. I had not expected that. And yet I had wanted to rouse his anger, and even this rage seemed better than talk of suicide.

His hands were knotted into fists. I could tell he was fighting to keep himself from hitting me again. I wiped blood from my lips. "The time may come to die with honor," I said. "But it has not come yet."

"Do you understand my position? I must flee, but I don't even know where to flee to. Anywhere in Italy, Caesar's men will hunt me down like a rat."

"Mark Antony—"

"If I wanted to go to him, where would I go? I don't even know where he is. In Egypt still? Egypt is far away."

I thought for a few moments. Then I said, "Sicily is closer than Egypt." Sicily was governed by Sextus Pompey, who had lately forged an alliance with Caesar. But the bond between the Claudians and Sextus's family was ancient; there had been friendships and marriages going back many generations. "From what I hear, Sextus Pompey is a man who honors old ties."

Tiberius saw where I was leading him. "I doubt Sextus would kill me or turn me over to Caesar. Whether he would offer me any real help is another question."

"He would shelter us, at least for a time, and he would not kill you," I said.

My husband gazed at me with compunction. "Look at your lip. Why in the world did you insult me that way?"

To rouse you, I thought. *Because my son needs the protection of a father.* I would have taken many more blows if it would have helped us survive. "I was overwrought. Forgive me," I said. "Shall we go to Sicily?"

He knotted his brow for a few moments. Then he let out a deep sigh and said, "Yes."

⋙⋙

It was not easy to get us aboard a ship bound for Sicily without being caught by Caesar's forces. But Tiberius Nero managed it with the efficiency one would expect of a former praetor of Rome. We arrived on the island and stayed in an inn so primitive it had dirt floors and a thatched roof. Sextus Pompey had no eagerness to see us, but after a month finally sent for us.

At the age of thirteen, Sextus had seen his father killed before his eyes. His family estate had been seized by his father's enemies. Now in his mid-twenties, he had lived a brigand's life for years. Yet with fellow Roman aristocrats, he behaved with honor.

"I would truly like to help you," he said, seeming to speak more to me than to Tiberius Nero. "But allied as I am with Caesar, that's rather awkward." He told us, though, that he was willing to help us get to Mark Antony, who was now in Greece. Since this was the best offer Sextus was likely to make, Tiberius Nero accepted it.

Sextus had the sea, as well as Sicily, for his domain. Men called him the favorite of the god Neptune. He had made himself feared, but to me he looked sorrowful and lost. Maybe I looked lost to him too. On parting, he gave me a bleak, oddly tender smile, and bent and kissed my cheek.

>>>>>>>

My mother had said that Mark Antony had little eyes like a pig. Meeting him, I saw the aptness of her description. But despite that, his fleshy, florid face, dominated by a jutting chin, was handsome. He gave off a musky smell—sweat and wine and some strong masculine essence. Sprawled on a dining couch, wearing not a toga but a Greek chiton made of red silk, sipping from a gold wine cup decorated with rubies, he eyed my breasts. When a serving girl came to refill his wine cup, he fondled her buttocks.

"How are you enjoying Athens, Drusilla?" he asked me.

I felt a burst of irritation, which I was careful to hide. Antony had kept Tiberius Nero and me waiting here in Athens for an audience with him—that was what this dinner was, an audience—for an incredible four months. And from the moment I met him, he insisted on calling me not "Livia" or "Livia Drusilla" but "Drusilla." It was a completely pointless affront. No one ever called a woman by just her second name.

"Athens is just as beautiful as I expected it to be," I said.

"Yes, we've been seeing the sights and having a pleasant time." Tiberius Nero managed to sound as if he had not spent the last months consumed with anguish, in dread about his future. I never knew before that he was such a good actor.

"Any city would seem a fine place after Perusia," Antony said, looking at me. "You were there during most of the siege, weren't you?"

I nodded.

"You look as if you've recovered from the privations you suffered. My poor Fulvia never did."

I had heard his wife had died of a fever not long after she and her children joined him in Greece. "I am so sorry—" I began.

"I know she meant well. But what a debacle that whole business was. How foolish, to stir up all that conflict with Caesar over the latifundia." Antony shook his head. "It's a shame no one informed me of what was happening in Italy." His gaze shifted to Tiberius Nero. "I've often asked myself why you didn't restrain Fulvia and Lucius. A prudent fellow like you, a praetor—how could you have gone along with that lunacy?"

"To be honest, I never doubted for a moment that they were taking orders from you," Tiberius Nero said.

"Taking orders from me?" Antony roared. "Are you insane?"

My stomach jumped. "My husband is only saying that this was the impression we got from Fulvia and Lucius," I stammered.

Antony gave a contemptuous snort.

I did not believe he had not known about Fulvia and Lucius's actions. Even if they had wanted to keep him in the dark, surely

Caesar would have sent him messages of protest. No, Antony had let them try their luck against Caesar, and then left them both—and even his two small sons!—undefended in a city under siege.

What had kept him from relieving us in Perusia? I wondered. Prudence? The tentacles of his mistress, Cleopatra, the Egyptian queen, tying him to her side? Some other, unfathomable thing—perhaps pure sloth?

"Well, past is past." Antony took a stuffed mushroom from his plate, studied it as if it might tell him something, then popped it into his mouth, chewed, and swallowed. "What are your plans now, Nero?"

"That rather depends on you," my husband said. "Naturally, I hoped—"

Antony interrupted him. "I'll be frank. My house here is going to be crawling with Caesar's representatives soon. His sister's husband must be seventy years old, and his health has taken a bad turn. She's twenty-five and supposed to be a peach, and—well, now I'm a widower. So I may agree to marry her, if the old stick dies. It would be a good way to smooth things over. There'll be a big wedding—maybe the little snake will agree to come here for that. Do you follow what I'm saying?"

Tiberius Nero nodded. "You are going to forge a new alliance with Caesar."

"Exactly. And do you know whose face I don't want Caesar and his friends seeing? Yours. What will they associate you with? Perusia and all that stupid business with the latifundia. I don't want them noticing you in my entourage."

"I see," Tiberius Nero said.

Antony lay back on his dining couch and looked meditatively at the ceiling, which was decorated with paintings of pink cherubs. "Now, matters could change. You were a bad praetor, but you're a good military man. I'm not throwing you to the dogs. Look, the Claudians have lots of ties to Sparta, don't they? Aren't there hordes of people there your grandfather or some relative or other once helped?"

"True. I have guest-friends in Sparta," Tiberius Nero said in a wintry voice.

"Well, that's good." Antony turned over on his side and flashed a boyish smile. "Sparta's under my jurisdiction. Isn't that convenient? As long as you're there, you don't have to be scared of Caesar. What I suggest is that you go to Sparta and tell your friends that you've come to call in some old debts." He looked at me. "Drusilla, you're going to love Sparta."

We were quiet for a while, absorbing the fact that our immediate future lay in, of all places, Sparta. Then Tiberius Nero said, "About my property . . ."

"Your what?" Antony said.

"I understand that Caesar has seized all of my property in Italy."

"Well, that's a pity," Antony said. "But you can't expect me to do anything about that."

I swallowed my anger and my sense of betrayal, and my husband did the same. We were powerless. What rankled most was that we had served Antony loyally and had suffered for his cause. That meant nothing to him.

Looking back now over the years, I remember how it felt to be helpless. I hated it. And whatever my failings, I can say I have never cast adrift someone who was loyal to me. I would never even treat a slave so.

After dinner ended, a high-ranking officer of Antony's named Pomponius took Tiberius Nero and me aside. He had served with Tiberius Nero in Gaul. He advised us to go to Sparta and lead a quiet life, and not expect any aid from Antony, ever. "If information comes my way that can help you, I will write to you," he said. "You can depend on my friendship."

⋙⋙

So we went to Sparta. Tiberius Claudius Nero and the daughter of Marcus Livius Drusus Claudianus received a warm welcome. The Claudians had been associated with this city for generations, protecting Spartan interests in the Senate of Rome. A man named Cadmus made a house available to us without charging any rent. It was a good house, with a roof of red tile and a fig tree in the garden. Other Spartans gave us food and clothing.

The Spartans' charity could not go on forever. I foresaw a time when I would have to sell my jewelry so that my family could eat. Nevertheless, when I put my son in his little bed at night and saw that he was healthy and safe, life did not seem too terrible.

Little Tiberius was two years old now and talking volubly. Sometimes he seemed overly serious for a child so young, and I wondered if what we had suffered through in his short life had somehow marked him. But then I would watch him happily playing and feel relieved.

For some time, Tiberius Nero and I had felt so harried, we rarely coupled. We had become friends, though, true comrades in adversity; and one night in Sparta my husband did desire me, and that night I opened to him in pleasure, as I never had before. Still, I did not love him. And yet, in that little house in Sparta, for the first time I found a measure of delight in his arms. I think it was on that night—or other nights like it, soon afterward—that I again conceived a child.

⋙⋙

We heard from travelers passing through Sparta that Caesar's sister Octavia had been widowed and that Antony had married her. Not long after we learned about the marriage, Tiberius Nero received a letter from Pomponius, saying there had been a realignment of the borders between Antony's territory and Caesar's. Antony could have warned Tiberius Nero of this, but he hadn't chosen to. "Caesar gets Sparta," my husband told me. "His soldiers are on their way here now."

We fled, with our son, and with the ever faithful Rubria, and with the new baby in my womb. Cadmus told us about a dwelling in the woods he used when he went hunting. It was only a two-room shack, situated in a small clearing.

When I looked at the shack in the woods for the first time, I remembered my home in Rome and wanted to burst out in hysterical laughter. To come down in the world was one thing—but to come down as far as this? Who had ever heard of such a descent?

A stern voice in my mind reminded me that even now things could be worse. After all, we were alive.

We deposited our possessions in the shack. It was what you would expect a hunter's hut to be, furnished with a few cots. I asked Cadmus, who had led us through the woods to our new home, "Are there wolves in this area? Any beasts we need to fear?"

"So close to the city? I don't think so." Cadmus had white whiskers and shining dark eyes. His face was scored with wrinkles, especially when he smiled.

"Those caves we passed. There are no bears in them?"

"No bears," he said.

"Well, then all is well," I said.

"Is there a source of water nearby?" Tiberius Nero asked.

"There was a stream near here," Cadmus said. "But we've had so little rain lately it might have dried up."

We walked to the stream—or rather, to the place where the stream had once been. It no longer existed. Tiberius Nero cursed.

"There's a lake a couple of miles away," Cadmus said. "Anyway, you don't plan to stay here long, do you?" Friendship was friendship, but he would have been a fool if he had not been thinking of whether his association with Tiberius Nero could endanger him.

"No, we won't be here long," Tiberius Nero said.

We walked back to the hut, where Cadmus took leave of us. Tiberius Nero went into the back room of the shack. I followed after him. He sat on a cot, his head in his hands.

"I think we should go far, far away, forget Rome, and start a new life," I said.

"What I don't understand," he said, "is Antony failing to warn me that Caesar's soldiers were coming. Antony knew I was in Sparta. He was the one who suggested I go there. What would it have taken for him to send me a message? If Pomponius weren't my friend, I would be dead."

"Forget Antony."

Tiberius Nero nodded. "Antony has abandoned me. Caesar has seized my property and wants to kill me. Sextus Pompey—well, we've seen how little we can expect from Sextus's goodwill. The three of them have divided up the world, and there is no place for me in it."

"Not the whole world," I said.

"Very nearly."

I could not dispute what he said. In most of the world—in all the world that mattered to us—there was no place for him, and therefore none for me and my son and the child to come.

Tiberius Nero rubbed the side of his face. "Where should we go? Go running back to Sicily, so Sextus can ship us somewhere else? Go and clasp Antony's knees? I almost think the best thing would be to march into Sparta, present myself to Caesar's men, and say, 'Here I am.' I am a Roman citizen, after all; they would not crucify me. I think death at their hands would be quick and relatively merciful."

"That last thing you must not do," I said. "There is always a way to survive."

"No," Tiberius Nero said. "You are showing how young you are when you say that. Believe me, there is not always a way to survive."

"There is for us," I said. "Look, we have shelter, we have food. We have freedom of movement. Who knows? Perhaps Caesar's soldiers will leave and it will even be possible for us to go back and live in Sparta." Returning to that little house in Sparta would have given me the greatest joy.

We settled into the hut. Days passed. We got water from the lake every morning for ourselves and our horses, and every day Tiberius Nero went to the edge of the forest to meet Cadmus. He brought us both food and information. Yes, he said, Caesar's soldiers were in Sparta and seemed likely to stay. Where exactly were the new boundaries of Caesar's domain? Where would we be safe? Cadmus said he would try to find out for us.

As time went by, Tiberius Nero's meetings with Cadmus began to worry me. The man had been nothing but kind to us, but I imagined betrayal. What if his association with Tiberius Nero seemed a liability now, and he sold him to Caesar's soldiers? I brooded about this. And yet Cadmus was our one link to the outside world. We could not sever ties with him.

It was early in the month of Julius. The heat was intense, and the land was dry, parched. Vegetation crunched under my feet as I walked. I noticed how yellow the grass was, how leaves hung limply from the parched trees. One morning, Tiberius Nero went off as usual to meet Cadmus. Rubria took little Tiberius to pick berries. She carried a large sack of rough cloth, the only container that was handy, to hold the berries. I meanwhile, in my third month of pregnancy, felt familiar nausea. I went behind the hut to the ditch that served us as a latrine. The sun was hot, and the stench was overpowering. My head swam. I vomited again and again.

Often I felt the need to maintain a façade of strength for the sake of my husband and child, but now, all alone, I cried. I wanted my father and mother, and I wanted the life I had once had.

Eventually, I wiped my eyes and returned to the front of the shack. Our two horses, which were hitched to a post there, started to snort and rear for some reason. Maybe Cadmus had been wrong, and wolves *did* stalk these woods? I looked around, but I could see no threat. I was afraid to approach the horses when they seemed so wild. While I looked on, they broke free of the post and went racing off in the direction in which Rubria and my son had gone.

Another disaster. Would we ever get those horses back? The idea that our already miserable existence had become worse almost made me burst into tears again. Then I smelled smoke.

I looked in the direction from which the odor came and saw a glint of red, up in the trees. I whirled and headed down the path Rubria and little Tiberius had taken. Remembering stories I had heard of how quickly forest fires could move, I began to run.

In the distance, down the path, I saw Rubria hand in hand with little Tiberius. I cried, "Rubria!" She spun around. I saw horror in her face and knew she saw the fire. "Take the baby! Run, run!" I screamed. It was unnecessary. She had scooped up my little boy and was already running.

I sprinted after her, the smoke already thick around me. "Diana, save me!" I cried. I ran so fast my heart felt as if it would burst, gulped for air, and breathed in smoke. Smoke burned my eyes. The fire was so fast, much faster than I was. I could feel heat on my back and knew I was about to be burned alive.

"Here, here!" Rubria shrieked. I could not see her. I ran in the direction of her voice. Then I did see her, through a haze of smoke. She stood in the entrance of one of the hillside caves in which I had feared there might be bears. I dived for the cave entrance and fell in the dirt screaming.

"Roll in the dirt, roll in the dirt!" Rubria cried. "You're on fire!"

I rubbed my body on the ground and threw dirt on myself. Rubria beat at my hair and my tunica with the sack she had brought for berries, beating out the flames. As she did it, I heard her crying out—surely with pain. Was she burning herself? I felt no pain, just unimaginable terror. Rubria stopped beating out the fire, and I crawled deeper into the cave.

"Your hair was on fire, your hair and your clothing," Rubria said, sobbing. "Oh, my hands, my hands . . ."

She had burned her hands putting out the fire. I threw my arms around her neck and began to cry. We clung together. Then I heard my son crying and reached for him. I could hardly make out his face in the smoky darkness. His little body trembled.

We went as deep into the cave as we could go. The entrance filled with smoke. Outside, the fire raged. I remembered my unborn child, and clutched at my belly. *Are you all right, little one? Are you all right?* Rubria, little Tiberius, and I stayed huddled together, coughing and choking. The smoke burned our eyes and our throats. "It hurts, Mama," my son sobbed.

I held him close and told him he was my brave boy and he must breathe, keep breathing what air there was. I was in terror for him. What if he succumbed to the smoke, passed out, and smothered? "Breathe," I whispered. For what seemed like hours, the three of us sputtered and coughed and did our best to inhale air.

Finally, the air cleared, and we ventured out of the cave. We saw no fire, just what the burning had left behind, scorched land, trees reduced to charcoal. I looked at Rubria, who was in tears because her hands were so painful. They were deep red, the skin peeling. "I owe you my life," I said.

She whispered so that my son could not hear her, "Mistress, you were truly on fire."

"I'm not burnt," I said.

"Look at your tunica."

I followed her eyes and gazed down at the tunica's hem. It was burnt black.

"And your hair," she said. "Your hair is singed."

I shook my head in disbelief.

"The gods must love you," Rubria said.

Little Tiberius clung to my hand, his eyes wide as he gazed at the desolation around us. Ashes covered the ground under our feet. The three of us walked back toward where the shack had stood, not knowing where else to go. It was gone, of course, and everything inside gone with it. "You have to go back into Sparta to get salve for those hands," I said to Rubria.

"I think we should both stay here until the master gets back," Rubria said.

"Your hands—"

"I've been burnt before."

I looked at her in surprise and remembered that her husband and child had perished in a fire. "When you lost your family?"

"Oh, no, another time, when I was a girl. The tenement I lived in burned to the ground. Many people died that time too." She gave me a smile laced with pain. "I know these burns are not very serious. I will recover."

My life had been hardship only lately, but she was used to nothing else.

We walked back to the cave—it was shelter, at least—and sank down on the ground.

Rubria's face mirrored my own exhaustion. I lay with my head cushioned in the crook of my arm. My son cuddled next to me, his head on my breast, and Rubria sprawled beside us. "From life in a mansion on the Palatine Hill to living in a cave," I said to her. "And you think the gods love me?"

"They didn't let you burn," Rubria said.

⋙⋙

We did not live in the cave long, as it happened. Tiberius Nero followed our trail, and just before sunset, he found us. He pressed his hand to his mouth, staring at me wide-eyed. "I was afraid you were all dead," he finally stammered. "But Livia, what's happened to you?"

"I'm fine," I said. "Just my hair and my tunica got burnt. But Rubria got hurt, saving me. We must take her to a physician."

Tiberius Nero nodded. "We can all go back to Sparta right now," he said. I thought he had taken leave of his senses, but he added, "I'm no longer a hunted man."

He brought remarkable news. Cadmus had given him a letter from Pomponius. It explained the provisions of a three-way treaty concluded by Caesar, Antony, and Sextus Pompey—provisions of earthshaking importance to us. Caesar had agreed that a certain number of supporters of both Antony and Sextus, who had fled Rome, would be allowed back to their homes. They would receive one-quarter of their confiscated property back. Antony and Sextus had each submitted lists of supporters to Caesar. One of the names on the lists was that of Tiberius Nero.

It was not Antony who had put Tiberius Nero's name on his list. Sextus Pompey had done it, purely as an act of kindness.

"I will have my Senate seat again," Tiberius Nero said, "and while one-quarter of my property will not allow us to live in luxury, it will allow us to live."

My mind spun with questions. Could we trust Caesar to honor this agreement? Might unanticipated danger await us back in Rome? But I voiced none of my trepidation. What choice did we have but to return home and reclaim what we could of what was ours? And I wanted to be back in the city that I associated with childhood happiness. In particular I longed to see my sister. I had been able to write her one letter from Sparta, and she had written back, telling me all was well with her. But it had been nearly two years since we had set eyes on each other.

As soon as we could arrange passage, my family returned to Rome, to live under the rule of Caesar Octavianus. I prayed that Diana would keep us safe.

Secunda was no longer the young girl I remembered, but more womanly and solemn. "I thought I would never see you again," she told me. "Even after I received your letter, I thought of you as lost—almost as lost as Mother and Father. It seems like a dream to have you back again."

"It seems a dream to me that you're grown up and a mother," I said. She had just given birth to a daughter. Her husband was a wealthy merchant, and life outside the perilous circle of Roman politics seemed to suit her.

Tiberius Nero and I were able to reclaim our home and get most of our house slaves back from their new owners; this included the ones I most cared for, Pelia and the twins, Talos and Antitalos. The familiarity of our surroundings—even the familiar faces of our servants—comforted us, but we knew that comfort could only be temporary. Tiberius Nero's fortune was so greatly reduced that we would have been fools to try to sustain such a lavish way of life. Soon, we knew, we would have to sell the house and buy a smaller one, and even resort to selling some of the slaves—always a miserable business when it comes to house servants one has known well. Tiberius Nero put off making hard decisions for the time being, and I did not blame him.

The one servant I would never, ever consider parting with was Rubria. Her hands healed—though scars remained—and she continued to live with us and take care of little Tiberius, whom she loved as her own child. We would sit in the garden together sometimes, watching my son at play, quiet but both remembering, I think, the dangers that little boy had gone through. Rubria oversaw his meals and his bath, but usually I was the one to put him to bed in the evenings, and in the mornings I would wake him with a kiss. My husband, too, doted on our little son.

All in all, Tiberius Nero and I had to be thankful for our present circumstances. I suppose we would have been unreservedly happy, if only our situation had been secure. But we felt it was not. The reason: Caesar Octavianus.

The Senate, like every other instrument of government in the city of Rome, was firmly under Caesar's thumb. Though Tiberius Nero regained his Senate seat, he was aware of holding it at Caesar's sufferance. Caesar often attended Senate sessions. He spoke courteous enough words when he and Tiberius Nero met. And yet Tiberius Nero said he noticed something disturbing about Caesar's gaze.

"Maybe you're imagining it," I said.

"No, I'm not. I think he recognized me when I threw that spear at him outside Perusia. I was close enough that he certainly could have seen me clearly. I'm convinced every time he meets me, he remembers ducking my spear. That is not exactly the sort of memory that makes for warm feelings between two men."

It did not ease Tiberius Nero's mind that the first important matter brought before the Senate after his return to Rome was the execution of a fellow senator, Salvidianus. This man, who had commanded an army in Gaul, had tried to go over to Antony, taking Caesar's Gallic legions with him. When Caesar and Antony reinstituted their alliance, Antony revealed Salvidianus's disloyalty to Caesar. He was recalled to Rome on a pretext, and the Senate unanimously voted to accede to Caesar's wishes and put him to death.

We had an additional cause for apprehension. The treaty between Caesar and Mark Antony, cemented by Antony's marriage to Caesar's sister, held up well. But the peace between Sextus Pompey and Caesar broke down almost as soon as it was sealed. One heard varying stories about whether Sextus was mainly to blame, or Caesar. Their forces had clashed at sea, and now Sextus's navy was raiding the Italian coast and even preventing the arrival of needed grain shipments to Rome. Tiberius Nero, of course, had been claimed by Sextus as a supporter.

When one feels uncertain and on edge, it is natural to try to think of a course of action to bolster one's position. Tiberius Nero came home from the Senate one day and said, "Livia, here is what I must do—invite Caesar to dinner."

This idea struck me as bizarre. My face must have shown it.

"No, listen to me. I have to reach some kind of personal accommodation with him. All the leading senators are inviting Caesar and his wife out socially. I'm a former praetor—and a former enemy. If I don't invite Caesar when everyone of my rank is doing it, that in itself is a pointed gesture. It's a declaration of enmity, don't you see?"

I shook my head, feeling almost dazed. The idea of the two of us, after all that had passed, inviting Caesar to our home for a friendly dinner seemed grotesque. Then I thought: *How will it feel to see him again?*

"There's no need to upset yourself about it," Tiberius Nero said. "First of all, once I invite him, he won't come that soon. He is very busy; he is always putting off invitations. It may be months before we actually have to entertain him, but the important thing is that I will have tendered the invitation. Then I will invite other couples, senators and their wives, negligible sorts he can't object to. We'll have a regular dinner party when he comes, so you won't have to talk to him that much. From what I understand, he is always the last guest to arrive, and the first one to leave. Half the time he doesn't even bring his wife—she's pregnant right now and prefers to stay home. So he will come for a couple of hours, eat dinner, and leave—and Livia, he likes very plain food. It's not as if we even have to serve him an elaborate meal."

I remembered a beautiful boy smiling at me at the chariot races. I saw him looking at me after he lit his mother's funeral pyre. Then I thought of what had taken place since, the proscriptions, the deaths of my parents, the siege of Perusia. "Surely you realize feeding him a fancy dinner is not what I'm objecting to. After all that has happened, how can we have that man in our home?"

"We can do it because we must," Tiberius Nero said. "Dear, all I want is a peaceful life now. I don't want to have to go wandering all over the earth with my wife and child—soon two children. I've gone through enough—we have both gone through enough."

I noticed how tired he seemed. He was not quite forty-three years old now, but the deep lines in his forehead and the gray streaks in his hair made him look older. As for me, in three months my second child would be born. The thought of our having to flee again was unbearable.

"We can spend a couple of hours entertaining Caesar, if it helps secure our future," Tiberius Nero said.

What would happen when Caesar and I came face-to-face? Would I hate him? Or feel something else? Surely not attraction. No.

Perhaps I did not wish to know what I would feel when I saw him, and that was the true reason why I balked at the idea of inviting him to dinner.

"Livia, this is necessary."

I straightened my spine. "All right. Invite him."

The next day, Tiberius Nero came home nonplussed. "Well, I invited him, and he said yes. And—here's the surprising part—he didn't put me off."

"You mean he's coming soon? When did you invite him for?"

"Three evenings from now. He said he was delighted by the invitation and was definitely coming."

Caesar did not arrive late. I heard the slave admitting him when I was in the dining room with the first two guests who had arrived, a senator, Rullus, and his wife, Nepia. Tiberius Nero gave me a meaningful glance. We excused ourselves and went to the atrium. Twelve lictors stood there, Caesar's official escort, bearing the rods and axes that signified high office. There were also four bodyguards armed with swords. In front of this crowd of men, Caesar waited to be greeted. He wore the purple-trimmed toga of a proconsul and had a closely clipped golden beard.

A beard has unpleasant associations for most Romans. Men stop shaving when they are in mourning, after all. And I have always connected beards with uncivilized peoples. So I recoiled a little at the sight of Caesar's beard. Despite that, and despite all that had transpired since I had last set eyes on Caesar, I felt a pull looking at him. Oh, I felt it, immediately and intensely. Even with that repulsive beard, he was as beautiful to me as any statue I had ever seen of the god Apollo.

"Caesar," my husband said, "how wonderful it is to welcome you to my home."

"I hope I'm not inconveniently early," Caesar said. "I have something of a name for always being the last guest to arrive. I'm trying to reform."

"You're right on time," Tiberius Nero said. "Two other guests are already at the table."

"Oh? Good." Caesar smiled at me. "Livia Drusilla, it's been a long time. You were practically a little girl when I saw you last."

"No I wasn't," I said. I suppose I wished to contradict him in order to discomfort him a bit. I was remembering what I had felt when I first met him. My feelings had not been those of a child.

Tiberius Nero turned his head to look at me.

"You were a new bride," Caesar said.

"Yes," I said.

"I've heard you have a son."

I nodded and smoothed my stola down over my pregnant belly.

"I'm afraid my wife is unable to attend this evening," Caesar said, addressing both Tiberius Nero and me. "She sends her apologies."

"What a pity she couldn't come," Tiberius Nero said. "Shall we go into the dining room?"

Inside, Rullus and Nepia greeted Caesar with great enthusiasm. Tiberius Nero gave him the place of honor on his right.

Our other guests, another senator and his wife, Fannius and Valeria, soon arrived. They all but ignored Tiberius Nero and me, their hosts. "It's a privilege to be able to spend some time with you this way, informally," Fannius said to Caesar.

"I can't tell you how we have been looking forward to this dinner," Valeria said, clutching Caesar's hand.

Caesar's lips twitched, and he gave me a look. It was the briefest of looks really, and yet strangely intimate. *Aren't some people silly?*

I glanced away and motioned to a slave to serve the first course. "I hope everyone likes goat cheese," I said.

Everyone agreed they liked goat cheese.

"I've heard you eat only the simplest food," Nepia said to Caesar. "Is that true?"

He nodded, munching his cheese.

"And is it true you drink only two cups of wine, mixed half and half with water, per day?"

He nodded again. I imagined her sharing this fascinating information with all her friends: Caesar eats only simple food, and he severely limits his wine. I remembered Caesar's health problems and felt certain some high-priced physician had advised his austere regimen.

The conversation turned to the chariot races. Caesar said he liked the Reds this season. Everyone agreed the Reds were a good team.

"Even five years ago, you preferred the Reds," I said.

Caesar's eyes lit up. "Oh, you remember that?"

"The first time we met, you said the Reds would win, and they did." I drank some wine.

Tiberius Nero said, "That was at Julius Caesar's funeral games, wasn't it?" I could tell he was speaking only because he was the host and thought he ought to contribute something to the conversation.

"Yes, his funeral games," Caesar said. His eyes seemed to go a little cold.

Everyone else at the table froze.

Caesar glanced down at his plate, picked up a piece of cheese, and nibbled it. He looked up and seemed surprised by the silence. "This cheese is delicious," he offered. He looked at me—it seemed in appeal. *Say something.*

"Does anyone want more cheese?" I asked. "If not, I think it's time for the second course."

We began the second course—baked mullet fillets with no sauce at all, since we had been told by people who had previously entertained Caesar that he liked plain, unseasoned fish. I tried to avoid gazing at him. My eyes kept straying in his direction, without my volition. I looked at him—I looked at him more closely than I usually looked at anyone. I noticed the tilt of his head as he talked, and how his fair hair tumbled over his forehead. The fine gold hairs on the backs of his forearms. His hands—the long, tapered fingers.

Nepia started talking about the Temple of Minerva near the Forum. It had lately been renovated, much of the brick replaced by marble. "It's one of the most beautiful temples in the city now," Nepia said.

"You think so?" Caesar sounded gratified. Repairing the temple was one of the public works projects he had recently undertaken; I was certain Nepia had known that before she spoke.

"It's perfect," she said. "I go inside and feel so reverent. And Minerva is my favorite deity."

"Really?" Caesar grinned at her. "I would have guessed Venus."

She giggled.

Caesar looked at me. "Who is your favorite deity, Livia Drusilla?"

"Diana," I said.

Rullus, Nepia's husband, gave a mock shiver. "The goddess of chastity."

"Why do you choose Diana?" Caesar asked me.

"She is the protector of the Roman people."

Everyone began to say who his or her favorite deity was. Tiberius Nero said, "Mars."

"Given your military record, that is the perfect choice," Caesar said.

Tiberius Nero smiled at the compliment.

"Mars isn't your choice?" Valeria said to Caesar.

He shook his head. "Who do you guess it would be?" His eyes were on me.

"Apollo," I said.

Caesar laughed, delighted as a child. "You're absolutely right. How did you know that?"

Because you are beautiful, just as he is. I shrugged and noticed I had begun to feel uncomfortably warm. *No more wine.* I motioned for a slave to pour some water to dilute the wine already in my cup.

"Why do you pick Apollo?" Nepia asked him.

"He is the god of knowledge and of light." Then, eyes back on me, Caesar said, "Do you remember how Apollo and Diana are linked?"

"They're surely not lovers?" Rullus said.

"Not exactly," Caesar said, still looking at me.

"They are twins," I said.

Caesar nodded.

I raised my chin. "Diana was the elder of the two, the firstborn."

"Absolutely true," Caesar said, "but there's more to the story. Diana emerged from the womb and then became her mother's midwife. She helped Apollo to be born."

"Imagine a baby acting as a midwife," Fannius said. "These old stories are so strange. But you go out in the countryside, or even into the city slums, and you'll find people who believe them. Amazing how credulous the common people are."

"There's another kind of truth, besides what is literal," Caesar said. His eyes met mine. "Don't you think so?"

"There is also poetic truth," I said. "The stories about the gods are true, in the same sense great poems are." I glanced away. "My father always used to say so."

"And the stories about the gods are beautiful, like the most magnificent poetry," Caesar said.

When I looked back at him, I saw that he was leaning forward and his eyes had not strayed from my face. I could feel color coming into my cheeks. Caesar saw; I was sure he did, because of the way he smiled at me. And yet, no one else at the table seemed to notice. We were having a staid conversation about religion and poetry.

I imagined the two of us alone. I imagined him making love to me.

He no longer smiled. His lips were parted, and his gaze had an intensity it had not held before. I felt he had read my mind.

"Do you enjoy poetry, Caesar?" Valeria asked him.

"Yes, very much." Caesar settled back on the couch. "There was a time when I thought I would be a poet and write tragic plays."

Nepia laughed. "Oh, no. A tragic poet? You?"

He smiled at her. "It was a serious ambition. I even had one play all plotted out. Not, mind you, that I ever wrote a single line of it."

"What was the subject?" Valeria asked.

"Ajax."

"Oh, in the *Iliad,*" Valeria said. "The Greek warrior."

"Why him?" Tiberius Nero asked. "Is he interesting? I thought he always came in second to Achilles."

"That's true, he did," Caesar said. "But I thought Achilles as a subject was overworked. And Ajax—" He looked at me. "Can you guess what I like best about Ajax?"

"His prayer," I said.

Caesar nodded.

"What prayer is that?" Tiberius Nero asked.

"On the battlefield of Troy, Ajax was the one who prayed for light," I said.

"That's it," Caesar said. "Can you visualize it? The battlefield is full of fog and darkness, and Ajax lifts his arms up to Zeus and prays. You remember the prayer, don't you, Livia Drusilla?"

If someone had asked me that at another time, I am not sure I would have remembered it, though when I was a child my tutor had insisted I commit vast segments of the *Iliad* to memory. But just then, the words came into my mind, effortlessly. I raised my arms as a priestess would and declaimed in Greek,

> *"Lord of earth and air!*
> *O King! O Father! Hear my humble prayer!*
> *Dispel this cloud, the light of heaven restore;*
> *Give me to see and Ajax asks no more;*
> *If Greece must perish we thy will obey,*
> *But let us perish in the face of day."*

I lowered my arms. For several moments, there was silence. Caesar lay motionless, a look of longing on his face. Then he began to clap his hands.

Everyone joined in the applause, and cried, "Bravo!" I gave a little bow.

When the applause had died down, Caesar said, "Ajax uttered those words, and the darkness lifted. There was light, and Greece did not perish. Greece prevailed."

"Yes, it's quite beautiful," Valeria said.

"I see—it's symbolic, of course," Tiberius Nero said, smiling. "It's not just literal sunlight the poet is talking about, but enlightenment.

The light comes, and Greece prevails." I knew he was thinking that the dinner was turning out well; certainly it was less unpleasant and strained than he had feared. And Caesar seemed to be having a good time, which was the main thing.

"You're exactly right," Caesar said, eyes shining.

Gods above, I thought, looking at Caesar, *I believe I know why, even now, that prayer means so much to you. You think Rome is Greece, and you are the light bringer. You actually think that, don't you?*

"If I'd written the play, that prayer would have been the centerpiece," Caesar said. "And I wanted to actually shroud the stage in fog and darkness. Ajax would speak his prayer for light, and then all of a sudden sunlight would flood the stage. I'm sure a really good theater director could figure out a way to do that."

"It would be wonderful," Nepia said.

But let us perish in the face of day.

At that moment, I thought of my father and mother. As soon as I did, the sight of Caesar, happy and at ease at my table, seemed more than I could bear. The desire I felt for him revolted me.

"But what would you do about the end of the story?" I asked.

"The end?" Caesar said.

"When Ajax runs amok and kills the Greek leaders who have slighted him?"

"I'd just show him covered with blood," Caesar said. "And he doesn't actually kill anyone."

"That's right," I said. "He only kills sheep, doesn't he? He *thinks* they're the Greek leaders, because he's insane. So your play would be about a man who prays for light, but ends up raving and covered with blood?"

"It would be a tragedy, remember," Caesar said.

"You can't have a tragedy without blood and insanity," Fannius said.

"It sounds as if it could be very good," Valeria said. She looked at Caesar. "You should go ahead and write it."

"I don't have the time," Caesar said. "And the truth is I probably don't have the talent either."

My eyes met Caesar's. "I think you could write a very good tragedy." I spoke gravely, even gently.

Caesar shrugged, expressionless. "Maybe I'll write it one of these days. As I said, right now I haven't the time."

Fannius laughed. "Yes, I could see how you might be too busy."

The atmosphere at the table had changed. Tiberius Nero, with a trace of anxiety in his voice, led Rullus and Fannius into a discussion of recent boxing matches they had seen. Valeria and Nepia listened, looking bored. I lay toying with my food. Caesar lay toying with his food too, every once in a while contributing a succinct assessment of one boxer or another.

When I glanced up from my plate, I found him gazing in my direction. He looked like someone who was wounded but prepared to forgive the wound. For a while, I tried avoiding his eyes. Then, because I did not want to be a coward, I met his gaze. He gave me a small, rueful smile.

Suddenly, Nepia said in a high, bright voice, "Caesar, are you planning on keeping your beard? I hope you're not about to shave it off."

"I haven't given it much thought."

"You should keep it," Valeria said. "I think all Roman men should start wearing beards again, as they did in olden times."

"Yes, beards are very manly," Nepia said. "A man with a beard really looks like a man."

"You could set a new fashion," Valeria said.

"If you keep your beard, every man in Rome will eventually grow one," Nepia said. "Oh, please say you won't shave off your beard."

Caesar looked at me. "Livia Drusilla, don't you have an opinion?"

I heard a slight barb in his voice, as if he were daring me to say something disagreeable. "Since you've asked me, I feel obliged to be honest," I said. "My opinion is that you should shave it off. I think it makes you look like a savage."

Beside me, I heard Tiberius Nero sharply inhale.

Caesar rubbed his chin. "Really? Is it as bad as that?"

I nodded.

He smiled, a little stiffly. "My sister said exactly the same thing, the last time I saw her."

There was a silence. Valeria hastened to fill it. "Oh, well, if your *sister* doesn't think you should have a beard—"

It felt unbearably hot and close in the dining room. "Excuse me," I murmured. I got up, exited, and walked through the atrium, past Caesar's lictors and guards, out to the garden.

»»»»»»»

I can't stand any more. It all crowded in on me. Caesar's presence, having to treat him as an honored guest. Memories of my father and mother, stab after stab of grief. The knowledge that I ought to wish to destroy Caesar, that I should feel a rage at him as pure as flame. And the realization that there was no purity in me. I was sinking in the muck. Because I could not look at him without desiring him.

A pregnant woman, full of lust for her husband's guest. An undignified spectacle in any circumstances. In the present circumstances, utterly repellent.

What am I?

The sun had begun to set, casting long shadows across the garden. It was late summer; the marigolds were in full bloom, and the air was perfumed. I told myself I should go back inside. Go and act like a good hostess and a proper wife. But I could not make myself do it, not immediately. A woman, visibly with child, can leave her guests at the dinner table, even for an extended period, and people will imagine reasonable excuses. No one will think too badly of her. That was what I told myself as I lingered in the garden. I would take a little time, calm myself, then return to my guests.

Finally, I let out a long breath and reminded myself that after all, the evening was almost over, and I must see it through. I steeled myself to go back inside. Then, a shadow moved at the edge of my field of vision, and I turned, expecting to see Tiberius Nero, coming to fetch me back to the dining room. But the man standing at the perimeter of the garden was Caesar Octavianus.

He came closer. "Why are you hiding out here?"

"I'm not hiding," I said. "I just wanted to breathe some cooler air."

"If you find it so unpleasant to be around me, you shouldn't have invited me."

He spoke as if I were some unreasonable child who had fled from him. I felt a rush of deep anger. I wanted to shatter his complacency so much that I did not guard my tongue. "I didn't invite you—my husband did. Everyone in the Senate has to invite you, because you might take it personally if they don't. And then they don't feel too safe. You must know that."

"When somebody invites me to dinner, I don't generally analyze the reasons."

"You just assume you're loved wherever you go."

"No, I'm not that much of an idiot." He frowned. "When I was a boy, there was an elephant they used to bring out every time there was a fair. And the elephant had one trick. You could go up to it and put a coin in its trunk, and the elephant would put the coin in its master's purse. What I remember is how everyone approached that elephant. Like this." He mimed going forward on tiptoe, tentatively holding out a shaking hand with an imaginary coin. "Everyone was scared to death of being trampled. Most people approach me now like I'm that elephant."

"And that surprises you?"

"Not in the least," he said. "I'm only saying, if I avoided socializing with people who were afraid of me, I would have a remarkably narrow social circle."

Yes, you would, I thought. But what struck me was that I was not afraid of him. Perhaps I should be, but I wasn't. Of all the feelings he drew from me, fear was absent. And all things considered, that was strange.

He glanced up at the sky. "It's very clear out."

"Yes," I said. "It's very clear." The sky was violet, and there were no clouds. A few stars had emerged.

"You know, I'd like to have an ordinary conversation with you, just ordinary as if I was a human being and not some mammoth beast. But that's not going to work so well, is it?"

"Probably not."

"Let's try anyway. Say something ordinary."

I would humor him for a moment, I thought, and then extricate myself and go inside. "I was a little surprised your wife didn't come with you this evening," I said. "But I've heard she's about to have a child."

"Yes, she is, but the reason she didn't come is that the marriage has never been more than a political arrangement, and we don't like each other. It's more convenient for her to stay with me until the baby comes, however, so we're both being patient about the divorce. The moment that baby is born—that day—I'm divorcing her."

I stared at him.

"It's by mutual agreement," he said. "Really. We'll probably be much better friends when we don't have to live in the same house."

I noticed fireflies in the bushes, near the garden's south wall. Their lights flickered.

We were silent. It was palpable—this thing between us that did not fit with recent history or with the fact that we were relative strangers. And I knew he felt it too, and that was why he had come out into the garden after me.

"For us to be out here together is not at all appropriate," I said.

I was six months pregnant. My husband was in the dining room not thirty feet away. It was the kind of situation you would not find even in the most vulgar kind of farce. But I didn't move to go back inside.

"I'm sorry that there has been so much . . . disruption in your life. The disorders we have been through should not touch the lives of women. The fact that we men can't resolve our differences in some decent way shouldn't create havoc in the . . . domestic sphere."

"Wouldn't it be pretty if that were so," I said.

He seemed to be deep in thought, his expression troubled. Then he asked, "Do you blame me for your father's death?"

"I blame you, among others. For his death and for the death of my mother."

"I had nothing against your father. Still less your mother. I'm not by nature a violent or a brutish man."

I thought of the merciless actions I knew he had committed. I said nothing.

"So you regard me as an enemy?"

"I regard myself as being at your mercy," I said. "I'm a woman with a little child and another on the way, and a husband who lives by your sufferance. I must swallow the drink the gods have put in my mouth. You have nothing to fear from me and mine. Isn't that obvious?"

"Yes," he said. "Of course it is. And you have nothing to fear from me. The difficulty, as I see it, is that you think you're supposed to hate me. And you don't." He paused, studying my face. "You don't, do you?"

"I thought I did."

"But you don't." There was a trace of triumph in his voice.

I do not hate you. Of all the emotions I could feel, fear and hatred are the ones that make sense. And those are the ones I feel no trace of.

"What do you feel?" he asked.

I shook my head.

"If I were to go to kiss you, you wouldn't back away, would you? You wouldn't do that."

I took a sharp breath. My heart hammered. A part of me wanted to feel his lips on mine. A part of me wanted to run. "Don't," I said.

"Well, you're right, this isn't the place or the time. But strangely enough, I still feel like doing it."

I made myself say, "There is no place and no time. There can never be a place or a time."

"Livia, if I had had the opportunity after Philippi, I swear to you I would have let your father live. I would have done it for your sake."

I said nothing.

He must have thought he saw disbelief in my face, because he said, "If you think I'm lying, then consider this: Do you know how many of Brutus's supporters I conducted a funeral service for? Exactly one. I did it for you."

"I've believed all along that you did it in return for what I told you about Cicero," I said.

But it was one thing to honor a dead enemy, something else to leave him alive and dangerous. Would Caesar truly have done that? There was no way of knowing. "If you want thanks for granting my father a funeral, then thank you."

"What kind of man would want thanks for that?"

A monster, I thought. *A monster would want thanks.*

"It wasn't in return for what you told me about Cicero," he said. "It was because of what I feel for you. What I felt from the first time I met you."

The question was on the tip of my tongue: *What do you feel for me?* I would not ask it. Instead I said, "Let's go back inside."

"If you want to."

I walked back into the house, and Caesar followed me. Returning to the dining room, I registered the guests' attempts to keep from staring at the two of us. Nepia's look was knowing and, I thought, jealous. On Tiberius Nero's face I saw amazement and dismay.

I tried to say something, but no words came. Caesar rescued me. As if nothing unusual had happened, he asked if anyone had seen the statues of a sculptor named Massilus. "I think his work is overrated, personally. But perhaps I'm missing something. Rullus, you know more than I do about art. What do you think?"

Rullus began criticizing Massilus's work. "Most of his statues look unfinished. You feel that with a little more effort, he might produce something truly beautiful. But it hasn't happened yet."

I motioned to a slave to serve dessert. An array of dates, plums, peaches, and grapes was placed on the table.

The dinner party continued for a while longer and ended pleasantly. Caesar thanked Tiberius Nero and me for our hospitality in the friendliest possible way before he left.

When we were alone, Tiberius Nero turned on me, his voice shaking with anger. "What were you doing?"

"What do you mean?"

"You came very near to insulting Caesar. And then what—were the two of you off somewhere talking?"

"Yes, we were talking. Tiberius, forgive me. I was upset, thinking about all that's happened, all we've been through. And he—Caesar was very understanding."

"Understanding," Tiberius Nero repeated. "Well, how did you leave it with him?"

"Leave it?" I stared at him.

"You seemed to part on good terms. I'm asking if you really did. Or did you make that man our enemy?"

"He's not our enemy. I swear he's not. Yes—we parted on good terms."

"Then that's all right, I suppose," Tiberius Nero said.

»»»»»»»

"Are you sleeping with Caesar Octavianus?" my sister, Secunda, asked me, three days later. She had come to visit me, and we were in my sitting room, just chatting, or so I had thought.

"Am I what?"

She averted her eyes. "Sleeping with him."

"Why are you asking me such a question?"

"I've heard talk."

"From whom?"

"From the women at the market." Secunda reached across the space between us and pressed my hand. "Livia, please—you can admit it to me."

I had been away from the city so long I had forgotten how gossip attached to the great in Rome, and how quickly it spread.

I had not considered the obvious: that everything Caesar did was liable to be discussed and twisted and picked apart by everyone, and that any hint of impropriety relating to him would be seized upon with lip-smacking relish. "What exactly are people saying?"

"That as soon as you came back to Rome, you seduced him. Oh, I'm sure that's not true, I'm sure he seduced you—or forced you, even. Livia, did he force you?"

I shook my head. I did not elaborate. I was too stunned.

"People are saying that because of you he has told his wife he wishes to divorce her. And that the baby you are carrying is his child. And—I've heard that he's shaving off his beard just to please you."

"And you, my sister, believe this?"

"I didn't say I believed it," Secunda said. But then she pressed her lips tightly together in a reproving frown. She looked at that moment very much like our mother.

I ran my hands over the bulge in my abdomen. "Oh, yes, certainly, it's his child. Have you forgotten that I'm six months along, and six months ago I was in Greece and Caesar was in Italy?"

"I know it's not his baby," Secunda said.

"How clever of you to deduce that," I said coldly.

"I was just speaking out of sisterly concern," Secunda said. "And—well, he *is* all of a sudden planning to hold a great festival, to celebrate when he shaves off his beard."

In our strata of society, young men sacrificed at the Temple of Jupiter after they shaved for the first time, and their families celebrated the occasion. Caesar had pledged at age nineteen not to shave until his adoptive father was avenged. Before that, he had never celebrated his first shave. Now he had announced publicly that he would shave off his beard on his upcoming twenty-fourth birthday. Rather than just holding a private party, he had decided to invite all of Rome to the festivities—to hire street musicians and distribute food and drink throughout the city. It was an intelligent thing for a young politician to do, a way to curry favor with the people.

"What does Caesar shaving off his beard have to do with me?"

"People say that you told him at a dinner party that you hated his beard, so he is shaving it off to please you," Secunda said. "Are you telling me that's not true?"

My behavior with Caesar when he dined at my home had given rise to gossip. I knew the other guests had been talking. "I just gave him my opinion when he asked for it. For heaven's sake, that doesn't mean I'm having a love affair with him."

My sister peered at my face, then nodded. "I'm glad," she said. "Of all the men you could have a love affair with—not that you should have one with anybody, of course—he would be by far the worst choice. Why, he's a tyrant, isn't he, as bad as his great-uncle? Oh, Livia, what would Father and Mother say?"

It was not uncommon for married women to have love affairs, but I had always been chaste. Some men tolerated unfaithful wives; some divorced them for adultery. I believed if I strayed, Tiberius Nero would be extremely upset and angry. I wondered if any of the talk Secunda referred to had come to my husband's ears. After she left, I had the impulse to broach the subject with him, but in the end I could not bring myself to. Ever since the dinner party that Caesar had attended, he had been cool to me. I had thought that he blamed me for not being pleasant enough to Caesar. Now I asked myself if he suspected me of being altogether too pleasant to him.

But the next day Tiberius Nero came home from the Senate smiling. "Caesar has invited us to celebrate the shaving of his beard!" he announced.

"He has invited the whole city," I said.

"He asked us to the private party he is giving at his home. Livia, we are part of a very select group!"

I felt sad, seeing how happy my husband was. It seemed a bit pathetic. I remembered how brave he had been at Perusia. Truly, he had always shown exemplary valor in war. But he had no more taste for playing the bloody game of Roman politics. All he wanted was to live quietly in Rome, enjoy what was left of his possessions, and feel safe. The invitation delighted him because he considered it a sign of Caesar's goodwill. I don't think there was anything he desired more at this point than to be regarded with benevolent eyes by Caesar Octavianus.

I dressed with care for Caesar's celebration. But if anyone had dared ask if I wished to make myself beautiful for him, I would have said no. After all, I felt obliged to dress well; I was a senator's wife, and this was the social event of the year. I wore a pale green stola, green being becoming to me with my red hair. I disliked the look of women weighted down with gold and jewels, and I wore only an emerald necklace and plain gold earrings, no bracelets or brooches. The locks of my hair that had been singed in the woods outside of Sparta had, of course, long since been cut away. My hair was still shorter than usual, but Pelia, who had developed into a skilled *ornatrix,* arranged it becomingly in soft curls around my face. She applied rouge to my lips and touched my eyelids with kohl.

Pelia held up a silver mirror, and I studied myself for a moment. Fortunately, pregnancy did not cause my face to become puffy, as it did with some women. I had prominent cheekbones, my complexion was clear, and my cheeks had a natural blush. I was nineteen years old, and except for my swollen figure, I was as beautiful as I would ever be at any time in my life.

As I rode down the Palatine Hill to Caesar's house, Tiberius Nero, who felt like stretching his legs, walked beside my litter. We heard singing and laughter on every street we passed. The air was full of the odors of spiced wine and sweet cakes. The celebration Caesar had sponsored already engulfed the whole city.

It struck me as odd that someone as rich as Caesar did not live on the Palatine Hill but in the commercial district near the Forum. Was he trying to pose as a man of the people? His house stood at the end of a lane of shops selling signet rings. A throng of Caesar's supporters had gathered outside. Half of them were drunk, but their mood was amiable. My bearers had no difficulty getting through the crowd and carrying me right up to Caesar's threshold.

Tiberius Nero helped me from the litter, and we approached the solid oak door. As soon as we knocked, the door was opened by an extremely well-dressed slave. We stepped inside, and Caesar and his wife, Scribonia, came forward to welcome us. Caesar was clean-shaven. Scribonia looked old enough to be his mother and was heavily pregnant.

Tiberius Nero congratulated Caesar on his first shave and on his birthday.

"I'm so glad to meet you, my dear," Scribonia said to me. She seemed to be looking over my shoulder, as if someone more interesting had come in behind me. But there was no one there.

I assured her that I was glad to meet her too. As the four of us exchanged pleasantries, I was struck by how young Caesar looked without his beard. A certain boyishness softened his features. I gazed at his smooth skin, blue eyes, and golden hair and could almost imagine people saying, *What a pretty young man.* But I doubted they ever said it—not if they noticed the tense energy that animated his whole being and the way he seemed to be probing your defenses even when he smiled.

Other guests were arriving, and we were shown to a dining couch inside. The atrium was crowded with couches on which guests already reclined—distinguished men in purple-trimmed togas, with their bejeweled wives. From what I could see of it, the house was nothing special, no larger than most senators' dwellings. But the harpist, who played during the first course of the meal, was first rate. The food and wine were abundant and very good—Caesar had not imposed his health regimen on his guests. We ate thrushes on asparagus, roast peacock, mussels and eels in a delicate onion sauce, and ham boiled in honey. Caesar, I noticed, did not recline and enjoy his meal but kept circulating among his many guests, talking to them and making them feel important, as a public man should.

Shortly after the second course was served, Tiberius Nero caught sight of an old friend, an officer he had served with in Gaul, across the room. "I haven't seen Vitellus for ten years," he said. "Excuse me, Livia. I must greet him."

As soon as he walked away, Caesar—so quickly that I almost gave a start—came and sat down on the couch on which I was reclining.

The dining couch was narrow. If I had moved my leg a few inches, we would have been touching. "What do you think?" he asked, rubbing his chin.

"I approve," I said.

He leaned closer and whispered in my ear, "I did it for you, you know."

"No you didn't," I said.

He laughed. "I didn't?"

We were both now talking in low voices not meant to be overheard by the other guests. "Why would you shave off your beard for me?"

"That's a good question. What do you think the answer is?"

I did not say a word.

"Tell me to do something else," Caesar said. "I'll do it. What else would you like me to do?"

"Don't be silly."

"All right, I won't be silly. The truth is I was probably going to shave off my beard eventually, but I wasn't in any hurry. I didn't want to look like a savage to you. Is it really an improvement?"

"Yes."

"I'm glad you think so." He looked into my eyes. "Now what?"

"There is no 'now what.' I'm a married woman, and you're a married man."

"I'll soon be divorced. I told you that already."

"I'm a married woman."

"Shall I tell you how it has been for you? You were fourteen, fifteen years old, and your father said, 'Marry this man.' So of course you did, and ever since then you've been trying to feel more for your husband than what—tolerance? Friendship? Maybe you are friends. You don't want to injure him; he's the father of your son. That's admirable. But are you planning to pass the rest of your life without ever experiencing passion?"

This conversation was taking place in the middle of a party attended by the most prominent members of the city's elite, with people reclining across the table from me and surrounding me on all sides. My husband stood in my line of vision, across the room sharing a toast with his friend from the Gallic war.

"I'm pregnant," I said.

"You won't be forever."

"I don't indulge in adulterous affairs."

"Of course not," Caesar said.

My eyes darted around the crowded atrium. Everywhere I saw people on couches, laughing and talking. My mouth felt dry. I took a sip of wine. I put down the wine cup, and smoothed back a lock of my hair.

"Your hair is fine," Caesar said.

"Everyone is watching us."

"No one is paying attention."

"Yes they are." I felt as if my body, every inch of skin, were stripped bare.

"No one hears us," Caesar said. "I'm having a perfectly proper conversation with one of my honored guests. There's not a thing in the world wrong with that."

"There will be gossip," I said. "There is gossip already."

How could I feel what I did for him? It would have been easy to tell myself I simply experienced physical desire for a handsome man. That would make it almost impersonal, as if I looked at Caesar as I might have gazed at a statue by Phidias, approved the symmetry of his features, and decided that yes, he was beautiful. But when I was in his presence, I felt an emotion deeper than lust. That was what was most awful—that I felt inexplicable tenderness for a man who had helped to kill my father.

Caesar went on talking in a voice barely above a whisper. "I've been married twice, but I feel as if I've never been married at all. It's because my marriages have been nothing more than political arrangements, which could be ended whenever the wind shifted. The way most of the Roman nobility marries these days—the countless divorces—has never seemed natural or right to me. Because out in Velitrae, where I grew up, people marry for life."

"Maybe when your baby is born," I said, "you ought to stay with its mother, and not divorce her after all, since you have such proper views about marriage."

He recoiled a little, as if he had been lightly slapped. "No, I can't stay with her. You see, I don't like her."

You liked her enough to beget a child on her. I imagine that if I said that, he would look puzzled. He would say, *What does that have to do with liking her?*

He went on talking. "And I'm in love with another woman. I think I've been in love with her for—what is it?—close to five years."

My heart pounded. For one moment, I melted, and he saw me melt. All I felt for him was surely in my expression. But then I became fearful and said, "You must take me for a fool."

"No," he said. "I don't."

"You've been in love with me for five years, and you married twice in the interim—and you just discovered this great love you've been nurturing in your heart for me?"

"You make it sound absurd. But I've been focused on survival—and still, I always remembered you. It's only lately that I've been able to breathe, let alone give any thought to personal happiness or love."

"I suppose you expect me to believe any nonsense you tell me," I said.

"Evidently a love affair with me has no attraction for you," he said.

"That's right. It has none." For that was not what I wanted—something quick and tawdry. To be used and discarded. I wanted more than that.

His eyes went cold. "You could at least have said that a little more kindly."

It struck me then that I was talking to the absolute ruler of Rome. I thought, *What have I just done?*

What words could I speak, to make it right? To ensure that I had at least not done some terrible injury to myself, to my family? *Yes, I will have a love affair with you. As soon as my husband's child is born, I will run straight to your arms.*

What I said was ridiculous. "I didn't mean to hurt your feelings."

"Oh, thank you for that," he said. "I profess love for you, and you mock me and then you say, 'I never meant to hurt your feelings.'" He shook his head and looked so comical suddenly, so disappointed and amazed, that the trepidation I felt disappeared. "Livia, are you telling me you don't feel anything for me? Was I so wrong to think . . . ?"

Of course his approach had not come uninvited. I had desired him from the first moment I saw him, nearly five years ago. And he had known it from the first. He had to have known it. And when he had come to my house for dinner I had not been able to take my eyes off him.

My face flamed. I wanted to run away and hide.

"What do you feel for me?" he asked.

"All your guests are looking at us." The truth is I was beyond focusing on other people's faces. I could not tell if we were being watched.

"If you care nothing for me, say you care nothing, and I'll leave you alone. But you must spell things out for me, just as if I were some provincial boy from Velitrae. Because that's actually who I am in these matters, and I have to know."

"I will spell this out for you: I remember who my father was and who my mother was. And you should remember it too. I can't help what I feel. But I'm not to be had cheaply." My gaze traveled around the room. I could see more clearly now. On the opposite couch, two women stared in my direction. I whispered, "And by sitting here, talking to me in this way, you are making me an object of gossip and disgrace."

He stiffened. "I'm sorry I've given you offense," he said. Then he got up and walked away.

I stared after him. Of all emotions, what I felt was this—longing. Because he was gone.

I became aware of Tiberius Nero sitting down beside me. "In the name of all that's sacred," he said in a low hiss, "what is going on between the two of you?"

"Nothing," I said. "Nothing at all." My voice sounded far off, remote. I felt almost disembodied, as if my husband's presence had no reality for me.

"He looked put out or insulted when he walked away."

"Yes, perhaps he felt put out or insulted."

"If he suggested something improper—"

"No, he didn't. He didn't suggest anything."

"Then what—? Was he flirting with you? Couldn't you just be pleasant to him?"

"No, I really couldn't," I said.

Tiberius Nero said, "I think you've lost your mind."

⋙⋙⋙

I knew what I had done. I had not done it with forethought. Still, I had done it.

Caesar had said, *If you care nothing for me, say it, and I'll leave you alone.* But I had not said that, had I? No, for all my indignation, I had not. I had told him that I was not to be had cheaply. Those words—it seemed to me my usual self had not chosen them. Yet they had not come to my lips accidentally. They had been honed by a part of me with which I was barely acquainted.

I imagined Caesar examining my words, holding them up in the sunlight, so to speak, slowly taking in their meaning. And then deciding how he would respond.

Four days later, Caesar's wife gave birth to a daughter, and that day the new parents divorced. People said Caesar had ended his marriage for love of another woman, and they knew the other woman's name, Livia Drusilla. Meanwhile, we hadn't even kissed. But I had become a public figure, of a certain kind. My sister came to me almost weeping because she had seen a picture, supposed to be me, drawn on a fence—a grotesque charcoal sketch of a lewd, naked woman with a pregnant stomach. And scrawled beneath the drawing was a dirty joke about Caesar's whore. "What is happening?" she demanded. "What are you doing?" When I told her there was nothing—nothing!—between Caesar and me, I knew she didn't believe me.

It was impossible that Tiberius Nero, by this point, did not know about the talk. But he did not confront me. I think he was in a state of stunned disbelief. He was out most of the day or else behind the closed door of his study. We hardly spoke to each other.

Then, early one morning, a message came from Caesar, not for me but for my husband. Would Tiberius Nero please call upon him that day? There was a matter they needed to discuss.

Tiberius Nero sent the messenger back to Caesar. "Say I will visit him within the hour." He looked at me when the man had gone. "Livia, do you know what this is about?"

I did not say, *How would I know?* I just shook my head.

You would have had to have been acquainted very well with Tiberius Nero to notice the tight set of his mouth and recognize it as a sign of fear. My husband had a grievance against Caesar, not the other way around. Caesar was rumored to have seduced his wife. Just a few generations before, it would have been considered an outrage for a public figure to have carnal relations with a married woman. Divorces were rare and viewed as an affront to the gods. Roman women were expected to be chaste, and did not even recline at dinner parties but sat upright like well-behaved children. It was not even considered proper for us to drink wine. A man could kill an adulterer—however prominent that adulterer happened to be—and everyone would applaud him for it. Under the Republic, it would have been Caesar who had cause to be afraid of my husband. But the Republic was dead.

Tiberius Nero went and donned his toga. I watched him leave, and then I walked out to the garden. It was late September. I could smell autumn in the air. Sometime after the new year, I would bear my husband's child.

What would happen between these two men? I could imagine, like scenes in a play, two benign possibilities. In one—which I did not for a moment believe was even possible—Caesar had perfectly valid and mundane senatorial business to discuss with Tiberius Nero; it turned out this summons had nothing to do with me at all. In another, more likely scene, he acknowledged the unfortunate talk about us, assured Tiberius Nero it was groundless, offered him some office or honor as a sop, and sent him on his way.

Other possibilities, I refused to allow myself to envision.

As I sat on a garden bench, waiting for Tiberius Nero to return from seeing Caesar, the baby inside me began to kick frantically. I caressed my belly and murmured reassuring words to my unborn child.

I asked myself what I wanted. What I should want was obvious. For my husband to come home to me, for our life together to continue unchanged. To remain a faithful wife to the man to whom my noble father had given me.

What did I actually want? Two contradictory things. I wanted to be a worthy child of my parents, not to be defiled by passion for a man who had helped destroy them, to keep my wholeness and integrity. And I wanted Caesar's arms around me, his lips on my lips, to be pressed to him, body to body, soul to soul, in excruciating and unending bliss.

Chapter 8

When Tiberius Nero came home from his encounter with Caesar, he walked silently past me into his study and sagged into a chair. He called for a slave to bring him wine, though he rarely drank it so early in the day.

I sat down on the study couch. The slave came with the wine. "Leave us—and close the door," Tiberius Nero told him. He drank a cup of wine in silence. When he finally spoke, his voice had a stilted and pedantic tone. "Livia, Caesar feels that by reason of your Claudian bloodline and your father's rank among the defenders of the Republic, marriage to you would bring him unique political advantages. It would help conciliate certain portions of the nobility, you see. Therefore, he has asked me to play the part of a patriot and, for the peace of Rome, free you so that you can marry him."

I absorbed it. Caesar wanted me to be his wife. I looked down for a moment. I did not want Tiberius Nero to see my joy. "He asked you to divorce me?"

"For Rome's sake."

"And what did you say?"

Tiberius Nero shut his eyes.

"What did you say?" I asked again. I waited, unable to breathe.

He licked his lips. "I told him I would not stand in your way."

A woman's heart is not a simple thing. I had never been in love with my husband. But when I realized Tiberius Nero would not fight for me I felt as if I had been slapped across the face. I wanted him to give me up to Caesar, oh, I wanted it. And yet in this moment it stung me that he would agree to do it.

I suppose what he read in my expression was contempt. He flushed. "Understand, I don't believe Caesar has taken it into his head to marry you without encouragement from you. I'm not as big a fool as you may think. I won't destroy myself for a woman who's given her heart and her body to another man."

"I haven't given him my body."

As soon as the words were out, I realized what I had revealed. I doubt I had fully admitted the truth to myself until that moment. I covered my face with my hands and began to weep.

Tiberius Nero cursed softly.

After a time, I stopped crying. I went to my bedchamber and called Pelia to bring me a basin of water and my mirror. I washed my face, and Pelia combed my hair. Then I ordered my litter fetched.

When I was walking through the entranceway, about to leave, Tiberius Nero came after me and caught me by the arm. "I hope you'll admit that I have been no bad husband to you. If you suffered hardship, it wasn't through any fault of mine, but because of the times we're living in. If anything, I've been only too willing to accommodate myself to your wishes."

"What you say is true."

Why was he saying it, though? I realized that he feared my enmity, and this shook me to the core. I could have wept again over the awfulness of the situation. I carried my husband's child but was betraying him. And instead of living in the virtuous Republic of my father's dreams, we were ruled by a young man with an army at his back. A senator even feared saying no to this young man when he asked for his wife. To give it all one final twist—it was this young man I could not help loving. None of it was as it should be.

I had no right to blame Tiberius Nero for anything, I thought. What a net he had been caught in. "Why, Tiberius, you are the father of my son and the child I will soon bear. I will always be your friend."

He dropped my arm and took a step away from me.

I went outside, where my litter was waiting. I told the bearers to carry me to the house of Caesar Octavianus.

>>>>>>>

His slave led me in through the entranceway, and Caesar met me in the atrium. We stood still at first, just looking at each other.

He thought that by asking my husband to divorce me so that we could be married, he was doing what I wanted him to do. But we had not discussed this explicitly. I believe he considered it possible that I had come to tell him that he had misunderstood, that marriage to him was not my desire. So there was a moment in which I saw doubt and vulnerability in his expression. This moment was inexpressibly sweet to me. But it passed. He said in a businesslike tone, "I'm glad you're here, Livia Drusilla. There are matters we must discuss." He led me into a small room furnished with worn-looking couches.

My litter, of course, lay outside his door. Someone would recognize it; the gossip mills would be at work. People would imagine what was happening inside between the two of us. They no doubt conjured up scenes of passion. Meanwhile, we sat down on couches facing each other, as if we had met to negotiate some business contract.

"What you told Tiberius Nero makes little sense," I said. "I don't think marriage to me is a good political move for you."

"No?" he said, his expression impassive.

"No. If I were unmarried, it might be. Some people might be reassured by your choosing to marry someone of my background. However, the idea that you will heal whatever breach exists between you and the nobility, by demanding the wife of one of the nobility's more prominent members, is on the face of it absurd."

"You think so?"

"I am sure of it," I said.

Caesar shrugged. "It's hard to ask a man to give you his wife, without in the process paying him such a mortal insult that he'll gladly sacrifice his life to stick a knife in you. I think my meeting with Tiberius Nero was a great success because at this moment you are here with me, and he and I are both alive. It was better to spout nonsense about politics to him than to say the truth."

"By the truth, do you mean that you're in love with me?"

He said in a constricted voice, "I already told you I want you."

He did not say the word "love." But why shouldn't he be guarded? I had replied with mockery when he spoke of love before.

"I'm afraid that this marriage will bring you ill fame," I said.

"Everything I have done for the past five years has been so well calculated. Don't I have the right to just once . . . ?" He paused as if unable to find the right words.

". . . act foolishly?"

"Livia Drusilla, I've considered all the possible consequences of marrying you. I find them acceptable. I'd like you to tell me if you wish to be my wife."

This was the moment of choice I had never had before. I would decide my destiny. I could say "No." I knew that if I did, he would not force me to marry him. Or I could say "Yes."

People would whisper that I'd angled for what marriage to Caesar would give me—power and riches. I would not have sold myself for either. I saw Caesar sitting there, his features tense, his eyes on mine, waiting. What I wanted was not power, not riches, but him.

I said, "I wish to be your wife."

He smiled. "Then all is well."

"No," I said. "All is not well. Don't you see? You were my father's enemy. And I'm married. I have two children—one not even born—whom I will lose if I divorce. I feel—terrified."

"Sometimes you reach a place where the earth seems to open in a great fissure," Caesar said. "Retreat is impossible. So what you must do is leap."

"Leap," I repeated.

"Livia, it can't be all perfect and right the way you want it. You have to choose between two imperfections, because that's all there is. Either you stay Tiberius Nero's wife, or you divorce him and marry me. We can't change your parents' fate. As for your children—a father must have custody, but do you think Tiberius Nero will try to prevent my wife from seeing her children? I doubt if he'd even want to. I promise you, you'll see them every day if that's your desire."

"Do you know what I wish?" I found that for the second time that day I was crying. "I wish it were five years ago. And I had never married, and a boy from Velitrae came to my father and asked to marry me. And since he was such a fine young man, with such a good head on his shoulders, my father liked him the moment he set eyes on him. And there was no such thing as civil strife in Rome, and so we married and prepared to lead very uneventful lives. Why couldn't it have happened that way?"

Caesar came over to the couch I was sitting on and put his arms around me.

I imagined the last five years had never happened. All who had died in these years, beginning with Julius Caesar, still lived, and Caesar Octavianus was that boy from Velitrae, an innocent boy with no blood on his hands.

I raised my face. I wanted to be kissed by that boy. And he kissed me.

To be kissed by the person you have longed for so deeply is joy beyond measure.

He held me close. My arms were around him. I felt the soft wool of his tunic, and I was conscious of his body underneath, its clean male scent. Our lips met again and again in burning kisses.

When I finally drew away from him, I was trembling. The air felt warm. He stroked my cheek, and his merest touch filled me with longing.

Only the most virtuous and pure, they say, go to the Elysian Fields after death. In that far-off place, existence is unending bliss. I am sure my father and mother are there. I doubt if I deserve to join them. But I experienced Elysium on earth, in the presence of Caesar Octavianus. To sit in a room with him, alone as we had never before been alone. To rest my head against his shoulder and feel his warmth. To hear his voice. To look at him. That was bliss beyond bliss to me.

"Caesar—how can I go on calling you Caesar? It sounds so formal—so—" It was a name I associated with years of enmity.

He hesitated and then said in a low voice, "My family has always called me Tavius."

"Tavius," I said. The boy from Velitrae was called Tavius.

At that moment, Caesar Octavianus became Tavius for me.

We were strange people, Tavius and I, as anyone who had watched us during those first hours we spent alone together would have realized. If his oddity and mine did not take precisely the same form, still the edges of one seemed to fit those of the other, like two sides of a split piece of pottery. Maybe in some way we had both sensed this, and this was part of what had drawn us together. Every time his hand so much as brushed mine, I felt desire. But it was not the moment, with me pregnant, for us to consummate our love. So what we could do was talk. We did not exchange sweet nothings or fantasies of our future life together. We talked about Rome. A conversation began that day that would continue for a very, very long time.

I remember him saying in an almost harsh tone, though we still sat pressed together on the couch, "Livia, do you think things have happened the way they have because I'm ambitious? Oh, I am, but it's also the situation. Things have gotten so rotten that someone had to come along and not flinch from doing what was necessary to put them right. Had to. Sometimes I can feel history blowing right on the back of my neck, pushing me along."

"You feel history blowing on the back of your neck?"

"I was using a metaphor. Look, do you think we can go through another ninety years like the last ninety? Even another ten years? How much more can any country stand? I sometimes wonder why Italy hasn't broken off from the mainland of Europe and sunk into the sea."

He went into an account of the last ninety years. Assassinations of the good and pure. Senators, holding office for life, who would do nothing to address Rome's ills but would kill to protect their own wealth and position. Times of relative peace ending in violence. Civil war and again civil war. His account was detailed and complete and brilliant. I was sure he had gone through it before, probably many times, maybe to persuade others of his viewpoint, or maybe to persuade himself. It was self-justifying; I knew that, even as I sat there listening, loving him, and, if such a thing were possible, falling even more deeply in love with him because I perceived the luminous nature of his mind. The Republic had been governed by a corrupt oligarchy. Rome needed to be led by a single strong and enlightened leader. He was that leader.

"Do you know what troubles me most?" Tavius asked. A shadow passed over his face. "That after all this is over, people will say Caesar Octavianus destroyed the Republic. Destroyed a thing that has been in its death throes for much, much longer than most people live. That was actually struck dead the first time a senator murdered his political opponents and was lauded for it."

"We took the wrong turn in the road," I said, which was a great understatement.

"Again and again," he said. "And if there is a way to go back, I don't know it. But I know a way forward."

I thought about the ideal my father had died for: a just and harmonious Republic in which the nobility acted for the benefit of the people and the people admired their leaders and followed them loyally. There had been a time, surely, when a Republic of this kind had actually existed, but that had been long before my birth. I no longer dreamed that the Republic could be restored. My hopes for my country were much narrower. I wanted us to live in peace.

"You are saying we were unworthy of the Republic," I said to Tavius. "And so the Republic is dead, maybe forever, or at least for a very long time. And we are left with one alternative, preferable to complete destruction. You."

"That is a grim way to put it," he said, "but yes, it's what I believe."

"My father believed in the Republic, with all his heart," I said. "And yet—the thing he believed in, what had it become but a government run by and for a tiny clique? Run ineptly by them. Those who tried to help the people were slaughtered. And so the Republic, as it was constituted, deserved to die. But you—you must offer the people something real, to make them loyal to you. Your rule must be based on more than fear."

"Of course," he said.

I thought he assented too quickly. I studied his face.

He caught the look I gave him. "Livia, don't assume I'm completely self-serving or that I don't love my country. Those are wrong assumptions to make." Ardor entered his voice. "Understand, I come to Rome as a builder, not a destroyer."

If you gaze into a cup of wine mixed with water, it is hard to tell how much of each liquid is present. It is much easier to say that the cup contains both water and wine. I knew Tavius was driven to seek preeminence, but I was ready to believe he also wished to serve a greater purpose.

He and I had been born in a terrible time. We sought a path out of darkness. My prayer is that when the gods judge us they remember this.

I surrendered my father's dream, fully aware of the moral gravity of what I did. "The civil strife must end," I said.

"I will end it," Tavius said.

And I will help you do it, I thought.

\>>>>>>>

I spent most of that day with him. At noon we were served an extremely simple meal of bread and cheese. "Moderation in all things, that's my motto," Tavius said.

He had made himself ruler of half the Roman empire before his twenty-fourth birthday, and he told me his motto was "Moderation in all things."

We ate out in the garden. It was small, as was to be expected in a crowded, commercial district. "Why do you live in this part of the city?" I asked him.

"It has never mattered much to me where I lived."

"We will, of course, move to the Palatine Hill."

He smiled, amused. "Of course." We ate in silence for a while, then Tavius said, "I want to marry you immediately."

I nodded. "As soon as my child is born."

"No, right away. I've consulted the College of Priests."

"You've consulted them—already?"

"Yes. The last thing I want to do is offend the gods. It turns out we can't have a religious rite while you're pregnant. The College has advised me that we can go through two separate marriage ceremonies—one immediately, the ordinary ceremony the common people use, and then after the birth, the religious rite proper to patricians."

"Two marriage ceremonies?" I said.

"I'm told that as long as Tiberius Nero and I agree he is the father of your child, an ordinary wedding won't compromise the baby's legitimacy as a religious rite would. We can hold a religious ceremony after your baby is born."

"But Tavius, there will be a scandal over our marriage in any case, and all this rush will only add to the talk. For me to marry you when I am carrying another man's child will reflect badly on both of us. Why not just have one proper wedding after I deliver my baby?"

"Because I don't want it that way," he said, and for the first time I heard steel in his voice.

I felt an inward jolt. Where was the man who had so sweetly agreed to our moving to the Palatine?

He sensed my dismay. "There are all kinds of strange twists on this path I'm on," he said. "I might have to go and put down an invasion by Sextus Pompey at any time. Suppose we must part for months, without a marriage to bind us. What then?"

We could lose each other, I thought.

"If you prefer it, I won't touch you until after you have your child. Believe me, I know how to wait. But I want you here, in this house with me for these months, as my wife."

We had lived through the same cataclysms, even if we had been on opposing sides. We both had a sense of how quickly unforeseen calamities could overtake us. I understood his sense of urgency.

"Livia, don't you *want* to be with me?"

"More than anything on this earth."

⋙⋙

Just before I left him to go home as I must, Tavius said, "Would you like to see the baby?" A few times during the hours I had spent with him, I had heard an infant crying somewhere in the house. With my mind elsewhere, I barely noticed the sound; it might have been a servant's child. Now I realized the baby he referred to was his new daughter. I wondered if Tavius's former wife, Scribonia, often visited her child, and how much of a presence she would be in our lives.

I said that of course I wanted to see his daughter. I realized I would soon become this little girl's stepmother. So we went into the nursery, where a maidservant sat rocking the cradle. Smiling, Tavius lifted the infant.

I am not the sort of woman whose heart thrills with tenderness whenever she sees a baby. What moved me, became a picture I always would carry in memory, was the vision of Tavius, the happy and loving new father.

"Julia," he crooned to the child. He looked up at me. "Isn't she pretty?"

To me, she was only a tiny red mite, no different from any other child. She was not mine. But I promised her silently that I would be no evil stepmother to her. It struck me that by the nature of things I would spend more time in the future with Tavius's daughter than I did with my own children. Certainly I would visit little Tiberius and my baby after it was born. But I would miss those small, important moments—when my son wept and needed soothing, when the baby spoke its first words or took its first steps. I would not be there with my little ones but living in another house. This thought hurt me and made me question the course I was taking. How could I leave my children?

Tavius gave the infant to her nurse, and we walked to the entranceway. He put his arms around me. "I can't stand to let you go," he said.

"But I must go," I told him.

"I know. And it will only be for a little while. But it's hard."

My pregnant state felt like a physical barrier between us. But we kissed, and when I drew away, I whispered, "Beloved." I had never spoken that word before, to anyone.

I rode back home in my litter, the curtains drawn, my mind pulled this way and that. And yet my thoughts came back to Tavius, always to Tavius. I dreaded that the huge scandal attached to our marriage might threaten his rule.

Many Romans would have said Caesar Octavianus needed as much protection as a scorpion did. But mixed in with my passion for him there was, from the first, fear for him, and a desire to keep him safe.

He had said he had the right to act foolishly just this once, that is, to act on the basis of desire and human emotion. But his rule was still new and fragile. He could be doomed by even one foolish action. I did not want my marriage to him to cause more bloodshed, least of all for it to bring him harm.

Men might look at his taking me from Tiberius Nero as one more exchange of partners among the sophisticated Roman elite, an ordinary divorce and remarriage. Or they might believe they saw an act of infamy, a tyrant wrenching a wife away from her lawful husband.

Tiberius Nero might smolder in the Senate House. I could imagine a group of malcontents gathering around him, and finally striking Tavius down. I could just as easily see Tavius recognizing the threat and putting Tiberius Nero and others to death. I wanted neither of these eventualities. I was not like Fulvia, ready to exacerbate our rifts. My marriage must somehow become a part of Rome's healing. I came to the conclusion that how the wedding was conducted mattered; and Tiberius Nero's attitude mattered greatly.

As soon as I entered the house, I went looking for my husband. I found him in his study, staring grimly into space. Awkwardly, because of my pregnancy, I sank to my knees before him. "Forgive me," I said.

Surprise flickered across Tiberius Nero's face, but he said nothing.

"I will marry him. Forgive me," I said.

Still, he did not speak.

"Do you know what I have been asking myself?" Though I remained on my knees, my voice sounded ordinary to my own ears. I was speaking, as a friend, to a man I had known well for a quarter of my life. "I've been wondering who will give me away, at the wedding. There must be a man to stand up with me. But my father is dead. And my male cousins are scattered to the wind. So who will do it?"

Seeing me kneeling softened Tiberius Nero somewhat, I think. He said in a reasonable enough tone, "All you have to do is let Caesar know the difficulty, and he'll snap his fingers and some senator will leap at the chance to do you this service. This is really a very small problem. Why you are talking to me about it I can't imagine."

"I'm sure you're right. I just—I want my father. And if it can't be him—well, I think to myself that I should ask one of his friends. And then I go down the list in my mind, and I find that they're all dead. Who will give me away, in place of my father? Marcus Brutus? Decimus Brutus? Cicero?"

"Livia—"

I allowed myself to cry. My grief was real, and the tears were genuine, and yet I knew weeping would serve me. "Forgive me. I realize that I deserve no kindness from you. But what occurs to me is this: that you were my father's friend and also his cousin."

"You can't mean . . ."

If he had become enraged, I would have fallen silent, risen, and withdrawn. But he just seemed amazed.

"You are the leader of the Claudians now, the senior member of our lineage. It is up to you to act for our family. I ask you to act—for the sake of the peace of Rome. It would be a noble deed. And it would win you Caesar's undying gratitude."

Tiberius Nero said nothing.

I added in a low voice, "It would bind you to Caesar as an in-law."

I wanted Tiberius Nero to see that although he was losing a wife, he still stood to gain in the transaction. Nothing served so well to solidify political alliances than for one man to give another man a female relative to be his wife. The fact that Tiberius Nero was my husband made our situation peculiar. But he was also my kinsman; and only a few days before, he had desperately wanted Tavius's favor.

"You truly want me to give you away?"

"It would mean everything to me."

In the tone of a prince granting a favor to a milkmaid, he said, "I suppose I could do it."

When I suggested that he hold the wedding banquet for Tavius and me here in his home, he muttered assent. With a grave face and downcast eyes, I rose and withdrew from his presence.

That night, as I did for the few more nights I remained Tiberius Nero's wife, I slept in a little spare room. I fell asleep quickly, but I had a bad dream.

I stood on a high pinnacle. Below me lay a ravine. I saw with horror that it was filled with corpses, twisted and gray. They lay in a sea of blood.

Across the ravine, also on a pinnacle, stood Tavius. He extended his hand to me and commanded, "Leap!"

My heart pounded but I obeyed him. I flew like an eagle over the ravine, over the corpses. Tavius grabbed me in his arms. I clung to him with all my might, certain that if we let go of each other we would fall. I would not let him go. We stood there, pressed together, swaying, for an unimaginably long time. I felt wave after wave of terror, because I knew how likely it was that we would eventually fall and land on the pile of corpses, shattered and broken.

I woke in darkness. I did not have to ask myself what the dream meant.

\>>>>>>>

Early the next day, I received a note from Tavius, scrawled on a tablet in his own hand, carried by a messenger: *Dearest love, come and visit me at midday, for I cannot go a day without seeing you. And we have most urgent matters to discuss, specifically our wedding.* I noticed his handwriting, which I had never seen before. I could sense how quickly he wrote, how the stylus ripped through the wax. His writing was so different from Tiberius Nero's schoolmasterish hand.

A memory came to my mind, of the time I had ridden a horse. All that power, between my thighs, under my control. Then I realized where my thoughts were leading me, and I almost blushed.

Of course I wanted to control Tavius—to an extent. And to our mutual benefit, and the benefit of Rome. Any woman who says she does not want to guide the actions of the man she loves is, in my opinion, lying.

I took a leisurely bath with scented oils, and then Pelia helped me dress and arranged my hair. I thought that I would bring her with me when I married, and also take the gardener, with whom she cohabited, and their little child, to keep her happy. In addition, I would keep the twins Talos and Antitalos, of whom I was fond. They could all count toward the repayment of my dowry. Its full amount must be returned; of that I was determined. Forfeiture of half the woman's dowry was the penalty for adultery. For me to ask in private for Tiberius Nero's forgiveness was one thing; to be publicly besmirched by the loss of any part of my dowry was another. Given Tiberius Nero's reduced circumstances, returning all he owed me would create problems for him. But I had a plan to deal with that.

These mostly pleasant thoughts occupied my mind while Pelia rouged my lips and applied kohl to my eyelids. Then I thought of Rubria. I regretted that I could not take her with me when Tavius and I married. I would always be a friend to her, but she had to stay in Tiberius Nero's household, to look after my son.

When I remembered, again, that little Tiberius must stay with his father, the room seemed to go dark, or rather, I was drawn into a dark place within myself. I saw in the mirror Pelia held up to me a ruthless, selfish woman about to abandon the child she had already borne and the infant she would bear. I imagined what my father and mother would be thinking of me, if they could know, in Elysium, that I intended to leave my husband and marry, of all men, Caesar.

"Why, the kohl isn't too much, is it, Mistress?" Pelia said to me. "You said you liked the way I did it last time, and this is just the same."

She was responding to the expression of dismay she saw on my face.

"The kohl is not too much," I said. "It is exactly as I wish it." I stood up, threw my shoulders back, and summoned my litter bearers to carry me to Tavius's house.

⋙⋙⋙

Tavius had lived a very strange and perilous life for the past few years. Despite his steadfast courage, this had taken a toll on his nerves. That was how I understood the fact that he greeted me not with pleasure so much as relief, as if he were not sure I would come at his summons. Enfolding me in his arms, he said, "I keep thinking this great happiness is not for me, that it's going to be snatched away."

Caesar—the man so many had reason to fear, the one who had ordered executions—that was someone else. I wanted to believe that. Tavius gave me every reason to believe it. Of course, I knew the other part of him existed. Love did not make me a simpleton. But that part seemed to have no relevance to our life together.

"I have news to tell you," I said, when we reclined in his dining room, over another of his exceedingly plain meals.

"What?" he asked tautly.

We must marry as soon as possible, for his sake. In the meantime, for love of me, he will be a tortured soul. This thought made me smile.

"Good news," I said. I told him that Tiberius had agreed to give me away and to host our wedding.

"You got him to agree to do *that?*" Tavius said. He saw immediately how Tiberius Nero publicly blessing our marriage would be to everyone's benefit.

While he was still rejoicing, I said, "I don't want our marriage to cause any resentment of you in any quarter. Tavius, may I ask you this? Please treat Tiberius Nero with the greatest respect and kindness."

Tavius laughed. "Why not? He'll be my new, most treasured friend."

I looked down at my food. "Then you'll see to it that his property, which you seized, is returned to him?" I raised my eyes to find Tavius staring at me, not precisely with dismay but certainly with surprise. "It will sweeten him even further," I said. "And it's good for men to know that those who accommodate you don't go unrewarded." I smiled. "Beloved, I have an interest in this too. I want my dowry back. Also, what Tiberius Nero owns will eventually belong to my children."

Tavius tilted his head and assumed an inward look. This pose of his would soon become very familiar to me. I knew at once that it meant that he was thinking, of course, but I had only a dim sense as yet of what it meant for Tavius to think about a problem. In time I would come to understand that he did not ponder just what was on the surface but plotted out all the strategic implications of any move he made, as if life were some incredibly complex board game.

Presented with a question such as whether he ought to return Tiberius Nero's property, he considered not only the effect on Tiberius Nero and on me, but how other men, allies or adversaries, would interpret such a gesture, whether they would be soothed or irritated by it, where the money would come from, how it otherwise might be spent, and other repercussions of which I never would have conceived.

Everything was weighed and balanced in a few moments. He smiled and said, "Done."

We were reclining together on one couch, and I kissed him. He stroked my hair and ran his fingertips down my throat and, lightly, over my breasts. I wished my baby were already born. Because I was vain enough to want my body perfect, not big with child, the first time we made love, and yet I desired him so. Lying there with him, I was sorely tempted to go beyond kisses and caresses, and I think so was he. But then I thought, no, it was better to wait until I was not another man's wife and carrying another man's child. I did not want our first time together besmirched by any hint of what was wrong, ungainly, or absurd, but to be an act of beauty. Perhaps he felt the same. Before long, we drew apart.

We discussed our wedding and whom we wished to invite. The religious rites, such as the sharing of the consecrated cake, would not take place, but we would observe most of the usual customs. Tavius said, however, that he saw no reason for me to walk from the wedding banquet to his house. "It's no requirement. I'm sure you'll be more comfortable riding in a litter."

"Dearest," I said, "I'm touched that you want to protect me. Thank you. But I think it is important that people see me walk to your home, and do it serenely, on our wedding day. Because I want to leave no doubt in anyone's mind that I'm no Lucretia."

Tavius's eyes widened at this. But he understood my meaning.

Roman men are complex beings. Some might think—I have at times thought it myself—that their wives and their daughters, and women in general, matter not a pin to them. They certainly have been known to act as if that were so. But there is a whole other aspect of their minds and hearts. After all, the birth of the Republic—the overthrow of the monarchy under which Rome was founded—can be attributed to good men's indignation over the rape of a woman. One of the sons of Rome's tyrannical king ravished Lucretia, a pure young wife. She told her husband and her father of this, before she committed suicide. The uprising that followed overthrew the monarchy for all time.

If I had wanted to destroy Tavius, and had been willing to lay down my life to do it, the means were in my hands. All I would have to do was stab myself to death on his doorstep. The men of Rome would avenge me.

But in fact I wanted to preserve his life and his power. I could best do that by walking through the streets to him, pregnant though I was, and showing the world that I consented to our marriage.

Though I was caught up in the joy of love, the political implications of our marriage kept dogging my thoughts. Let Rome laugh at all three of us, Tavius, Tiberius Nero, and me. Let them crack jokes because Tavius and I did not have the self-control to wait for marriage until after the birth of my child, guffaw about this cool and calculating young man making a fool of himself over a woman. Let them assume Tiberius Nero was so venal that for political advantage he would cheerfully give away his wife. I could even bear being called an adulteress, much as I hated that. But no one must talk about a tyrant dragging an unwilling wife away from her husband. Of that, I would make sure.

>>>>>>>

When I left Tavius that day, I did not go directly home but paid a visit to my sister. We went into the garden of her house and sat on a marble bench. Secunda pursed her lips and waited for me to speak.

"In a few days," I informed her, "Tiberius Nero and I will divorce, and Caesar and I will marry."

"Livia!" She wailed my name. "How can you do such a thing?"

I lifted my chin. "Caesar and I have fallen in love."

Concern for me, dismay, and outrage warred in her expression. Outrage won. "Well, I certainly will not attend the wedding."

"Did I invite you? I don't recall it."

"Not invite your own sister to your wedding?"

"I admit I intended to, but if you will not come, you will not come. What you must do is this: Tell your husband that he is about to be linked by marriage to Caesar Octavianus, and you've decided to deliver this deadly insult, and have refused, on behalf of you both, to go to the wedding. I'm sure he'll be overjoyed at how well you're managing his affairs."

As I walked out of the garden, and out of my sister's house, I heard her calling after me. I ignored her, and, getting into my litter, ordered the bearers to take me home. Then I cried.

It was not because I did not expect Secunda to attend my wedding. I knew my sister. She was not, fundamentally, a fool. There would be an apology. She would beg to be allowed to come to the wedding, and I would let her come.

I cried because I saw in what she had said a reflection of what my parents' reaction would have been, if they had lived. What if, by some miracle, my father had survived, and I had gone to him and told him I intended to marry Caesar? He would have considered me a traitor to the Republic. Whatever anguish it caused him, he would have turned his back on me forever.

Father, Father, I called to him in my heart. But there was no answer. There would never be an answer.

I wept all the way home. And then, before I exited the litter and put my foot down once more on the hard ground, I promised myself I would never cry again for this cause. I would not attend anymore to my guilt, or my regrets about the past. I would turn my face away from all that and look toward the future. That was what was required of me as Tavius's wife.

⋙⋙⋙

The day before my wedding, I went to the Temple of Diana on the Aventine Hill. This particular temple, ancient, fortress-like, and associated with the cause of the common people, breathed an awful history. Eighty years before, in front of the temple, senators led by a vicious consul had slaughtered Romans who espoused democratic political reform.

I entered the temple's bronze doors, which bore scratches and dents, marks of the arrows and spears cast long ago. I promised myself that I would get Tavius to refurbish this place and make it beautiful. With me I brought a white lamb, which I gave to a priestess. She cut its throat, and as its blood fell on the floor's ancient, broken tiles, I raised my eyes to the statue of Diana. I silently spoke to her of the boy who had died in Perusia holding my hand.

Here, near the place where many of Rome's best men had died, slain by their own countrymen, I begged her to end the killing. I asked that no more Romans die in useless civil strife, and I prayed that the marriage of the daughter of Marcus Brutus's noblest supporter to Julius Caesar's adopted son would help to bring Rome peace. Stretching forth my arms, my heart full of fervor, I also prayed that she extend her benevolent protection to Tavius.

Chapter 9

Rome may have seen stranger weddings than mine to Gaius Julius Caesar Octavianus, but people would be hard put to think of one. The role that Tiberius Nero played became a part of our legend—that is, Tavius's and mine. Some interpreted his giving me away as a deed of patriotic self-sacrifice, some as something much less lofty. But Romans will never forget it.

Early in the morning, long before the wedding guests arrived, Tiberius Nero and I went through the formalities of a mutually consensual divorce. The seven required witnesses arrived at our house, sent by Tavius, who had taken many of the arrangements for the day into his hands. Tiberius Nero and I met them in the atrium, where slaves were dragging in couches for the wedding banquet. I stole a glance at my soon-to-be former husband. How does a man appear when he is about to be incorporated into another man's legend? Not too happy. But at least he did not look enraged.

Before the seven witnesses, he spoke the traditional words to me. "Take what belongs to you and go."

"I consent," I said.

Our marriage was over. Acting as my kinsman and guardian, he glanced at the marriage contract that Tavius had sent him. The main provision transferred my dowry to Tavius's control. Tiberius Nero pressed his signet ring into the wax seal on the document. "Thank you," I said. I slipped off my gold betrothal ring and handed it to him. He looked down at it in his palm, closed his fingers around it, gave a little chuckle, and walked out of the room.

An important bond had been severed, and I felt an ache, remembering times of affection and shared joy. I had come to Tiberius Nero a girl and grown into a woman as his wife. I had not wanted him as my husband, but we had come to rely on each other. I told myself I would be a friend to him just as I had promised to be, and there was comfort in that thought.

I went to the nursery, where Rubria was dressing my son. As soon as I saw him, I felt the start of tears. But I had promised myself not to weep anymore about what was already unalterable, and I did not want to act in front of little Tiberius as if some tragedy were befalling us. I blinked away my tears and managed to smile at him.

"I will want to see him tomorrow," I said to Rubria. "I'll send the litter, and you'll bring him to me."

"Of course," she said.

"And you will care for him just as you always do." My son was gazing up at me with puzzled eyes. He was two months short of his third birthday. How could he understand what was happening? I fell silent.

"Of course," Rubria said again.

I remembered that she had lost her husband and her own child in a tenement fire—a common circumstance in Rome's slums, one she could certainly not prevent—and I wondered what she thought of me. In her plain, patient face, I could find no clue.

I kissed little Tiberius on the forehead. Then I left him with Rubria and went to prepare for my marriage ceremony.

⋙⋙

I have had to pause for a while in my writing. My mind was so full of memories of my son as a small boy. And then I recalled I have yet to reply to a letter he recently sent me.

The waxed tablet stamped with his seal is here on my writing table. He urges me to rest more and to leave my business affairs entirely in the hands of trustworthy servants; he would be glad to suggest able men I could rely on. My holdings are extensive. I have brickyards, a copper mine, granaries. It is too much for me, at my age, he says, to involve myself in overseeing these many ventures. Moreover, I should not go out among the poor, as I still do, and personally distribute largesse. As he has done before, he hints that this activity is hardly suitable even for a woman in the prime of life.

My son's tone is almost one of entreaty. I will write him back a polite reply, thanking him for his filial concern. But as always, I will refuse to be bound by his efforts to restrict my actions.

My son Tiberius can be harsh and overbearing in his dealings with others. With me, he at least softens his voice. He takes care to be courteous. But he looks at me—at any woman—with a narrow vision. He is most at home in a military camp, among men.

There were proscriptions in Rome when I was carrying him. While he was a baby, his father and I fled from place to place with him, often in great fear. Then came my divorce and marriage to Tavius. Did those past events affect who he is today? I wonder. Sometimes I think he lost some of his ability to trust—in particular, to put faith in any woman—because I abandoned my marriage to his father.

I remember the confusion in my son's eyes when I took leave of him on that long-ago wedding day, and even now I could weep.

⋙⋙⋙

The wedding's ridiculous aspects were dwarfed for me by joy—Tavius's as well as my own. He was marrying a woman big with another man's child who would not be ready for months to be a true wife to him. But he came through Tiberius Nero's entranceway smiling with happy anticipation. Then he saw me in my wedding finery—the long white tunica, the sheer crimson veil—and his lips parted as if he were gazing at a miracle. In the head wreath of red and yellow flowers he wore for the occasion, he looked young and pure, like a boy who had never seen a bride before.

He embraced Tiberius Nero like a brother. The strain that might have been expected got swallowed up in Tavius's happiness and goodwill. The moment when the two men exchanged copies of the marriage contract, even the moment when Tiberius Nero placed my hand in Tavius's, passed quickly and in a civilized way.

We—Tavius and I—stood with our hands linked. I looked through my sheer red silk veil into his eyes and spoke the words of consent. When I said, "Where thou art Gaius, I am Gaia" to Caesar Octavianus, I meant it. With him, I would stand or fall. I was a young woman in love, but I also felt like a general who chooses the ground for his battle, knowing, whether he has chosen rightly or not, there can be no retreat, that he will either win or die.

Tavius placed a gold ring on my finger, the same finger from which, only hours ago, I had removed Tiberius Nero's ring. At that moment, I felt no doubts, but rather a sense that what had come to pass was right and inevitable, because Tavius and I were twin souls, and the love between us was vast.

Shouts of "*Feliciter!*" filled the air.

I lifted my wedding veil. We reclined together, receiving congratulations from numerous guests. Tiberius Nero lay on a couch in the place of honor to our right, as the bride's nearest relation normally would. I watched out of the corner of my eye as people approached him. They were respectful, but they groped for words, since it did not seem right to congratulate him.

I thought, *Well, this is my wedding. I must act as if I am enjoying it. But I will be so much happier once this day is over.*

I spoke polite words to guests and listened as Tavius responded to their congratulations. He was never at a loss for what to say; in that, he seemed like any seasoned politician. But he did not rattle on and bore people, as public men are prone to do. I asked myself: *If you heard his voice, and did not know him, who would you imagine him to be?*

Oh, a well-bred young man, but not a native of the city of Rome; he speaks just a bit too softly and courteously for someone born here. You might think, "I hope Rome is not too rough a place for him."

My sister and her husband came forward to greet us. She wore a pretty light green stola and her finest jewelry. Her husband beamed. Secunda looked at Tavius as if he were a lion and I were reclining there with him on a leash. Poor thing, she had no talent for masking her thoughts. She said, "May the gods bring luck to your marriage," and tried to smile. Then she darted an amazed look at Tiberius Nero, who was making short work of the first course of the wedding feast while talking with other guests.

Tavius was convivial with her husband and gentle with her. But Secunda looked relieved when she could go back to her dining couch.

Tavius's sister could not attend the wedding, since she was far away with Mark Antony, her new husband. But I met two men at the wedding banquet who were as close to Tavius as brothers, Marcus Agrippa and Gaius Maecenas.

Agrippa approached us first. He said, "*Feliciter,*" and Tavius introduced him to me.

He was tall, muscular, and ruddy-faced, good-looking in a rugged way. I knew he'd had operational command of Tavius's forces during the siege of Perusia. I pushed thoughts of Perusia away and said, "I'm happy to meet you."

"And I to finally meet you."

Tavius had talked to him about me, obviously.

I caught the wariness in Agrippa's eyes. I did not hold it against him. His future, his whole life, was bound up with serving Tavius. He had never had to take Tavius's first two wives into account. It would be different with me, and he knew it.

People gossiped about Agrippa's low birth. His father owned a rich estate near Velitrae, where he, like Tavius, had grown up, but his grandparents had been freed slaves. I was a daughter of the Claudians. I think he feared my scorn. We exchanged pleasantries, sizing each other up.

Soon afterward, I met Maecenas. Physically he was Agrippa's opposite—short, dark, and plump. I had heard he had royal Etruscan blood.

"*Feliciter,* my dear," he said to me. His voice was extremely pleasant, almost musical, but a bit high for a man. He gave me a charming smile. "I won't keep you now, but I'm looking forward to getting to know you. I'm determined that we'll be the best of friends."

"I hope so," I said.

"Oh, we will be," he assured me.

He has made a decision, I thought. *He will befriend Tavius's new bride, to reinforce his position in Tavius's innermost circle.*

I smiled back at him. We understood each other.

In the past years, as he jockeyed for power, Tavius had had only two advisors who mattered, not wise graybeards but these friends his own age. The two had certainly served him well, judging by the results. I would therefore never do anything to injure their relationship with my husband. On the contrary, I would make it my business to win their gratitude and loyalty.

Most of the Roman nobility looked down on both of them, of course. Agrippa could never be forgiven his forebears. And Maecenas—well, his royal descent would pass muster even with patricians. But the impression he gave, not only of softness but effeminacy, brought him mockery. These two had been Tavius's closest friends at school. Who was he when he first met them but the sick one, the boy who could not endure exercise or military training? It struck me that in that school for the sons of the provincial elite of Velitrae, he, Agrippa, and Maecenas all likely had been, for different reasons, outsiders.

The three had already demonstrated, not just to their old schoolmates but to the world, how foolish it was to discount them. I saw myself as the fourth member of that golden circle. But not ranked number four, no. I would be the one closest to Tavius, his mate in every sense. I'd be content with nothing less. And the world would learn it was wrong to discount me too.

⋙⋙⋙

People remember a certain incident that occurred at the wedding banquet. Talos and Antitalos, wearing jeweled sandals for the occasion though otherwise naked, had been brought in to entertain. They sang a funny little song, and afterward went about from table to table, babbling amusing nonsense. Then Antitalos, the wittier of the two, came up to the couch on which Tavius and I reclined. His black eyes rounded with mock incredulity. "Mistress—Mistress—"

"Yes?" I said, and waited for the joke.

His face turned into a mask of comical dismay. "Oh, Mistress," he said in a loud voice, "what in the world are you doing over here . . . when your husband is over there?" He pointed at Tiberius Nero.

For a moment, it could have gone either way. We all could have been greatly embarrassed. But Antitalos, though only nine years old, was a comic genius in the bud, and had a gift for gauging such things. This jest touched on the tension beneath the wedding's festive mood, and exposed to the light and air what had previously been unmentionable, the peculiar circumstance obvious to all. Everyone exploded with laughter. In particular, Tiberius Nero and Tavius both laughed until they were red-faced and looked ready to choke.

I, too, dissolved in helpless laughter.

Now I remember Antitalos's years on stage, the acclaim he won. He acted in comedies after I set him and his brother free, and eventually he had his own theater. There are three sets of twins among his grandchildren. In my mind, I picture him as he is today, a dignified old man with a glint of humor in his eyes, and then I again see that little naked child.

As I stroked Antitalos's silky black hair, his young face glowed. I wondered if he knew what a risk he had taken, and how completely he had conquered us all.

The cook had outdone himself with the main course—tender cuts of beef in a delicious sauce flavored with cumin, dates, and honey. Tavius did not taste it. Throughout the wedding banquet, he adhered to his usual simple diet and drank only a single cup of wine mixed with water.

As I nibbled on a fig pastry, part of the dessert, which he also eschewed, he whispered, "It'll be over soon, and we can go home."

I smiled at him.

"Don't walk there," he said.

I shook my head.

"Are we going to have our first argument, as man and wife, over this?"

"Very likely," I said.

"People may shout . . . ugly things."

I felt a tightening around my heart. But then I thought of myself running through the forest outside Sparta with my hair and clothes on fire, and I laughed. "I assure you, I've been through worse."

He frowned and said nothing.

"Please, let me do it," I said. "It is for our benefit that I show myself. And even if some people scorn me, it doesn't disturb me, because I know I will conduct myself in such a way that they won't scorn me in the end."

A little later, we stood outside, hand in hand together as the wedding torch was lit. A great crowd of Tavius's supporters had gathered. I felt their eyes on me. They shouted good wishes; they were our friends. Tavius squeezed my hand and then let go of it, and disappeared into the crowd. Two little boys, Tavius's cousins, took my hands. With a boy of twelve or thirteen carrying the wedding torch before me, I started my walk to the home of my new husband.

I wore my veil raised back over my hair. I wanted people to see my face and know that I was happy.

Tiberius Nero's house stood only a third of the way up the Palatine Hill. The walk down the slope, into the Forum, and from there to Tavius's house would be no strain for me, even in my pregnant condition. People sang bawdy songs just as they had when I married Tiberius Nero. But the crowds that came out to watch this wedding procession greatly outnumbered those on that occasion.

Look your fill, I thought.

The people of Rome. My eyes fixed upon individuals. A harsh-faced woman in a tattered tunica, who held the hand of a sweet-faced little girl. A long-nosed fellow in a workman's rough tunic. A somber man in a toga, whom I recognized as an old acquaintance of my father's. Dozens and dozens of others. They stared at me, and I looked back at them.

The sun had set by the time I reached the foot of the Palatine Hill. Someone deep in the crowd shouted, "Whore!" I pretended I did not hear this, and went on walking.

The faces I saw in the torchlight looked at me without hostility, even with goodwill. These were my people, the people of Rome, and in marrying Tavius I intended also to marry myself to their service. Did they sense this? Did they see something about me to like? Or did they just fear Caesar? Whatever the reason, I heard no more hostile shouts.

Finally, I reached the unprepossessing house in the commercial district. Two young men lifted me over the threshold. Inside the entranceway, I found Tavius waiting for me, smiling with relief. *My husband.* I felt as if I had no heart room for all the joy and love I felt. His eyes glowed like blue jewels. We looked at each other, dazzled by the dream that had come to pass. Then he concluded the wedding rites by giving me a cup of water and a burning twig—sharing water and fire, elements that sustained life—and leading me into the depths of the house, where I lit the hearth fire.

A few days after our wedding, we sat, two lovebirds on a couch, my head on Tavius's shoulder. On his lap lay a waxed tablet. In his hand he held a stylus. Anyone looking at us might have imagined he was writing me a poem. But no. "Show me the world as you see it," I had asked him. So he was drawing me a map.

"This is us, Italy. This is Spain, which is also mine. Besides that, I have most of Gaul, where Agrippa is heading right now. His task is to secure the border." Tavius drew lines on the western edge of Gaul. "That's the savages trying to invade our territory."

"Should I worry about them?" I asked.

"No. Agrippa will defeat them. But I'll have to keep an eye on that border forever. Now here's North Africa." He drew a circle, beneath the Italian boot. "Held by Lepidus, who is not my friend. And here to the east, we come to Antony."

"I don't like Antony," I said.

"Personally, I can't stand him. But we're allies. I married my sister to him."

"Does your sister like him?"

"Yes, strangely enough she does. But she's so sweet-natured she likes almost everyone. Anyway, for now at least, I don't worry much about Antony."

"Good," I said and nibbled Tavius's ear.

"Are you sure you want to wait until the baby is born to consummate our marriage?"

I found it hard to keep from touching him, hard to exercise restraint. But the fact that I was carrying my first husband's child remained a barrier, in my own mind at least. "I'm sure," I said.

"Now we come to Sextus Pompey," he said briskly and drew Sicily off the Italian coast.

"I rather like Sextus. He was very kind to me." Snuggling with Tavius, I felt so comfortable, I spoke without thinking. I recognized my mammoth blunder even before a look of displeasure crossed his face.

Tavius drew one slash mark after another, coming from Sicily into Italy. "He raids my coast. He covets everything I have. When we made peace, he broke the terms that same month."

Maybe Sextus would have said Tavius had broken the terms. Julius Caesar and Sextus's father had been enemies and rivals, and the enmity had inexorably carried over into the next generation. "It's all-out war between the two of you?"

Tavius nodded. "There's a lull now, but yes. It will be war to the finish."

Since the day of our wedding, I had felt as if no grief could touch me in my happiness. Now I saw how foolish that sense of invulnerability was. I quailed at the thought of more civil war. "That's a pity," I said.

Tavius gave me a sharp look. "You truly have a soft spot for Sextus, don't you?"

"Not if he's your enemy."

A brooding expression settled on Tavius's face. "Most of the nobility in Rome has a soft spot for him. He was born one of you. I wasn't. So they prefer him." Tavius's mother had been patrician, but his natural father sprang from humbler, rustic roots.

I touched his cheek. "Why should anybody prefer Sextus to you? Or anyone on earth to you? I can't imagine why anyone would." I brushed my lips against his. "We will have to open people's eyes."

"We," he said. He spoke the word as if he were not sure he liked the sound of it.

"We," I said.

There are people who say that from the moment Tavius and I married, I grasped for power. None of them ask, power for what? I wanted Rome's citizens to be content. I knew that all but the most savage form of government depends on the people's sanction. And the most savage kind does not last long. I dreaded another Ides of March.

With my marriage, I had made a commitment not only to Tavius as a man but as a ruler. I saw his intelligence and strength. Of course I loved him; it would not have been strange if that had affected my view of what his leadership could offer Rome. But many others—military officers, common soldiers, and hard-eyed politicians—shared my assessment of his qualities. And if some followed him only for gain, not a few looked to him to save our country. Like me, they were patriots. Rome cried out for wise government and stability. That was what I hoped Tavius would bring us.

My parents had numbered among those defeated and destroyed. It was natural for me to feel for the plight of the vanquished. I imagined myself making Tavius's rule gentler than it had been.

"I want people to talk about how great and good you are, not because they're afraid not to but because they mean it from their hearts," I told him.

"And you'd bring about that delightful state of affairs . . . how?"

You will have to become great and good.

"Good works," I said. "As much as we—or the treasury—can afford. And we should entertain all the people who matter. I want them to see a likable young couple, so devoted to each other. We must be models of old-fashioned virtue. I'll make all your clothes at home. Well, oversee the maids making them. But a woman spinning wool has a special meaning. It's associated with all the old virtues in people's minds. Everyone should know that I do spin wool."

Tavius looked as if he might laugh.

"You don't believe that symbols can be potent in politics?"

"I believe they can be. But I wonder how much time you plan to spend spinning wool and making my clothes."

"Not much," I said.

He grinned. "We shall be virtuous and austere. I'm all for it."

Of course he was humoring me. I charmed him, I amused him, he desired me. Did that mean I could take him down a road he never would have stepped on otherwise? I did not know. But I had a vision of what we could be together. "I'm in no rush to move to the Palatine Hill," I said, "because this house is ideal in a sense. It's so humble. Even when we move, I don't want a very grand house, just the kind any senator might have. No one should look at any aspect of our lives, and say, 'That's how a king and his queen would live.' It's so important that we shape how people see us."

"What's important is how the army sees me. And I have vigilantly attended to that."

"You think popular opinion doesn't matter?"

"I didn't say that." Tavius almost snapped out the words.

Perhaps he had heard criticisms in what I intended as helpful suggestions. It struck me—not for the first time, but forcefully—that I must make a regular study of this complicated being who was my husband. I had not yet completely gained his confidence.

He carried crushing burdens, and felt himself alone with them. I perceived and spoke to his loneliness. "Do you know why I care so much about these matters?" I asked. "Because I love you. Everyone else has interests of their own, which are separate from yours. How can they not? If Agrippa or Maecenas did not have their own ambitions, you would be the first to say they were pathetic creatures. But I—I just love you."

I reached up to stroke his hair. Just perceptibly, he narrowed his eyes. An image came into my mind of a boy I had once seen taming a half-wild puppy. Soft words and gentle pats had done the trick; before long the puppy ate right out of his hand. Here was my poor love, who had lived through such great dangers. He needed kind handling.

"Do you understand how much I adore you?" I said. "How close to you I want to be—how very close? You can tell me anything, and no matter what, I'll always be on your side. I'll always think first of you."

He said in a constricted voice, "But just a little while ago you were saying you 'rather like' Sextus Pompey." His eyes stared into mine. "Is that true? Do you like him?"

I thought of that sad young man, Sextus, who had gone out of his way to do Tiberius Nero and me an enormous, unexpected favor. From the bottom of my heart, I wished him well. "I barely know Sextus Pompey."

"He is my enemy. Do you like him?"

I faced a test. I could not have Tavius doubting my loyalty. "He did me a kindness. I would prefer he were your friend. But if he makes war on you, then he is my enemy." I sensed these words were not enough. Part of me recoiled, but I said, "If he makes war on you—if he would harm you—then I want him dead."

Tavius watched me carefully. "Well, then you should be happy soon. Because he'll meet the shade of his beloved father, and I'll have Sicily. Will you be happy?"

"As long as you're safe and glorious, I will always be happy."

Tavius must have heard the ring of truth in my voice, because he smiled. "I probably haven't paid as much attention lately as I should to popular opinion, or to cultivating the nobility," he said. "It's stupid to be neglectful, but with war in Gaul and with that viper's son Sextus—well, you can only attend to so much at a time. I'm only one person."

"You used to be only one person," I said.

His expression turned slightly skeptical, but he did not contradict me.

>>>>>>>

I set myself the task of winning Tavius's unlimited trust. Was it hard? Not really. Occasionally I had to choose my words carefully and even shade the truth, in order to convince him of my all-embracing commitment to him. But it is not so difficult to convince a man of what he wants to believe. After all, he was in love with me. He wanted to trust me. And I suppose he sensed my fundamental sincerity. I did adore him.

If ever a man needed a wife ready to be a true partner, Tavius did. He governed a vast territory and was fielding two armies, one in Gaul, the other readying to do battle with Sextus Pompey. Soon after we married, he showed me into a great room he had set aside in the house just for the three freedmen who screened petitions and letters that arrived for him. In the midst of stacks of waxed tablets and parchment scrolls, the secretaries scrambled to keep up with a constant inundation.

"Somewhere here there's important information I absolutely need," Tavius said. "But it's hard for anyone else to sort out what I should know about. So I read a lot of letters and petitions myself. I could spend all day every day just reading my mail."

Tavius hungered for real achievement, not empty honors. He wanted to bring effective government to Rome and the provinces under his rule. Often, he would work all day, and then after dinner with me go back into his study and work some more. His conscientious drudgery would have amused Mark Antony and other public men who lacked his diligence.

If there was an administrative snarl in some wretched backwater he governed, people appealed to him, and he tried to unravel it. When a road leading into Rome fell into disrepair, someone would come whining to Tavius, and he would see that it was fixed. Every time the grain deliveries for the bread distribution to the city's poor arrived late, that became his personal problem. He labored to set up efficient governmental structures that would not require his constant attention. Meanwhile, day to day, he juggled a thousand details, trying to bring order out of chaos. This was his reward for winning a desperate struggle for power—exhausting labor and a constant flood of supplications.

The three freedmen overseeing his correspondence had been picked for their acumen and efficiency. But naturally, they enjoyed only so much of Tavius's trust and could exercise only so much authority.

"You can't do everything, dearest," I said to him one day as we sat on the couch in his study. "You need a helper you can truly rely on, who understands your goals and can exercise discretion."

"I can't figure out what color your eyes are," Tavius said. He took my chin in his hand and tilted my face so he could see it better.

"I have ordinary brown eyes."

"There are flecks of gold in them right now. But in certain light, I can't see those flecks at all. Sometimes, I swear, your eyes are absolutely black." He kissed me on the mouth, then on the throat.

A shivery sensation ran through my body. I wanted him so. "Soon, my beloved. Soon," I murmured.

He drew away, his face tense with need. "O god Apollo," he muttered under his breath.

I was still a not-quite-attainable object to him, the wife he had married but not yet slept with—literally; as usual in noble households when a wife is many months pregnant, we had separate bedchambers. This left Tavius in the grip of passionate, obsessive desire. At times, I would be reading and would raise my eyes from the book to find him sitting there, quietly watching me. Sometimes, wakeful in the middle of the night, he came into my bedchamber with a candle, to sit and watch me sleep. He looked at me the way a man might at some incredibly precious object he had just bought for a great price. It was as if he did not fully believe I belonged to him.

And I? When I gazed at him, sometimes I forgot to breathe. I imagined all the delights ahead and ached with longing. And I visualized a marriage far different from the one I had known, both passionate love and an affinity of mind.

I pressed my hand against his cheek, ran my fingers across his lips. "Tavius . . ."

"What?"

"I want to supervise your mail," I said. "I'll be very good at it. If you tell your freedmen to report to me, I promise you won't regret it."

"Do you know how much work you're asking for? Why do you want to work that hard?"

"I just do. I'm peculiar."

Of course I wanted to help him and ease the load he had to bear. But I also sensed the influence it would give me if I took charge of Tavius's correspondence. To decide which information came to his attention and which did not, to be ready to urge action or no action on a host of matters, to draft his replies to letters from important men all over the empire . . . that would surely give me a kind of power. I could foresee, also, that as time went on, it would seem more and more natural that I handle many matters on my own.

"I love you," I said. "Let me help you."

"That's what you want?"

"More than anything."

He tilted his head, thinking. Even in the first rapture of love, Caesar Octavianus did not act impulsively when it came to matters that touched on his political survival. I did not press him for a decision. Delicacy, gentleness—those were my tools. I waited.

Then one day he brought me into the study and showed me the pile of scrolls on his wide, oak writing table. "How can I read all those petitions and do anything else?"

I clucked my tongue. "If you only had the right person to sort through all that . . ."

"All right, we'll try it," he said.

Before my child was born, before I was in the full sense Tavius's wife, I had an unofficial role of authority in his government. I reached for it with both hands, and once I had it, I felt like an eagle chick that for the first time had a chance to fly. That is to say, I took to it.

I might read through a long, rambling missive from the chief magistrate of a little provincial town, and also letters from his groaning subjects. *This is why the magistrate wants to raise taxes, and this is why it might be the wrong time for it,* I would tell Tavius. He would decide what he wanted to do about taxes, and I would draft a reply to the magistrate for him. Our working together was not separate from our personal bond, the heart of our marriage. Rather, it was like our two minds making love. We meshed so well—and this melding came about so quickly—it startled and delighted both of us.

One evening when we dined alone, we had a discussion that greatly moved me. "Sometimes I feel certain the gods favor me," he said. "Not because they love me, you understand, but because they love Rome, and I'm what Rome happens to require. When both the consuls died right after I became propraetor, it looked so convenient some people thought I must have secretly murdered them. But I didn't. They just died and cleared the path for me." Tavius shook his head, remembering. "It seemed uncanny."

"Fortune favors the brave," I said.

"Suppose the gods decided what I needed now was to marry an extraordinarily intelligent wife? I think they're fully capable of arranging that, don't you?" He spoke earnestly, not as if he meant to flatter me but almost as if he were talking to himself.

If he had written me a dozen poems rhapsodizing about my eyes, my hair, and my dulcet voice, it would have meant far less to me. It is a joy to be appreciated for the thing you want to be appreciated for. To be appreciated as a woman, and also to be appreciated as a creature with a mind—what more could I have wanted?

>>>>>>>

I had flown high and had great reason to be happy, but there is no such thing as perfect contentment on this earth. Whenever Tavius left for a session of the Senate I remembered the fate of the man he called his father, and I feared knives. Apart from that, my life had its complement of mundane difficulties.

No marriage ends with absolute finality when a child of that marriage is loved by both parents. Scribonia regularly came to visit her little Julia. She would fuss over the baby and imply that much was lacking in the child's care. Tavius had a way of being nowhere to be found when she arrived. I would be left to placate her. Meanwhile, my son was being reared in his father's household. I saw little Tiberius as frequently as I wished, just as Tavius had promised. Tiberius Nero also remained a presence in my life. My heart was not rent by guilt when I saw my former husband; there was too much steel in my character for that. But I felt a sense of obligation. He knew it. He had a way of finding little chores for me, small domestic problems he expected me to solve. Luckily Rubria was extremely competent, and willing to help me, for I essentially had charge of two households. All in all, my life was extraordinarily busy.

I gave birth in mid-January. My second son arrived with much less travail than his brother had. Afterward, I lay in my bedchamber, the swaddled infant in my arms. The baby looked so beautiful to me, so perfect. He even smelled sweet. He had wailed just after his birth, but now slept peacefully. I wanted to hold him forever.

Tavius came and sat on the edge of the bed. "Do you know what I wish?" I asked.

"The same thing that I'm wishing."

If only that baby had been Tavius's son.

"He'll always be special to me," Tavius said, "because he was born to you, here in my house." He peered at the baby, a tender half-smile on his face. "Livia Drusilla's son. Little Drusus."

"His father intends to name him Decimus Claudius Nero," I said.

"Why shouldn't he have two names? And two fathers? I can testify that more than one father can be a great advantage to a man."

I smiled. But my son had to be acknowledged by Tiberius Nero. His place in the world depended on my former husband's prompt assertion of paternity. "The baby must be wrapped up warmly and carried to Tiberius Nero's house," I said to Tavius. "Will you give the orders, please?"

Tavius nodded. "You should rest now." He grinned. "The sooner you recover from the birth, the sooner we can set about making sons of our own." Clearly he did not understand what it would cost me, to send my newborn baby away. I felt as if I were tearing out a piece of my heart.

Jokes circulated about how Tavius and I had managed to produce a child so soon after our marriage:

Fortunate are the parents for whom
The child is only three months in the womb.

But little Drusus—the nickname stuck—was acknowledged by his father on the day he was born, and well-informed people did not doubt his legitimacy. This included, of course, Tiberius Nero. He rejoiced, as well he should have, at the birth of a second fine son.

I engaged a wet nurse for Drusus, just as I had for little Tiberius. My former husband was only too happy for me to supervise the care of both my sons. I told myself I was doing what any woman of my rank would do—overseeing servants who looked after my children. I tried to believe it did not make a great difference that we lived in separate households. But of course it did. If they woke up sick or afraid in the night, Rubria and a staff of servants would tend to them. Their father was there too. But not their mother. Never their mother.

There were times when I imagined my sons crying for me, in their father's house. I ached to hold them. And sometimes when we were together I thought I saw an accusation in little Tiberius's eyes. *Why did you leave me?*

>>>>>>>

Tavius and I had a second marriage ceremony just three days after my second son's birth. The timing was my choice. Tavius said, "Why rush? It's not as if we can consummate the marriage yet, so why put yourself through a wedding ceremony before you're fully up to it?"

"We are a traditional patrician couple," I informed him. "We would not dream of living together one day more than necessary before we have our marriage sanctified."

I spared Tiberius Nero the duty of giving me away a second time, but I put on a bride's scarlet veil again. The priest of Jupiter sacrificed a pig, examined its entrails, and said that heaven smiled. Tavius and I ate the consecrated cake. Then after we shared dinner with a handful of guests, we kissed, and I went back to my own bedchamber and fell asleep.

On the ninth day after Drusus's birth, Tavius and I attended the naming ceremony Tiberius Nero held for him. I expected Tavius and Tiberius Nero to be cautiously polite with each other, but they seemed at ease. At one point, Tavius said something—I was not close enough to hear his words—and Tiberius Nero's face lit up with a smile.

"What did you do, offer to make him consul?" I asked Tavius later.

He shook his head.

"What then?" I asked.

He touched the tip of my nose. "Must you know everything? I promised him that I would always do whatever I could to further his sons' future careers."

My first thought was *Their future careers? One is a newborn baby, and the other is a three-year-old.* But I could see from Tavius's face that he meant it as a solemn pledge, and I sensed that this promise could someday matter greatly to my boys. So I threw my arms around his neck and told him how kind he was. He smiled and shrugged. He loved nothing better than being congratulated on his benevolence.

»»»»»»

By then I had learned some of Tavius's foibles and flaws. I knew how he could all at once become guarded and curt, even with me, and then quickly turn cheerful and affectionate again. He always ate sparingly, never drank much—but he loved to gamble. He would bet on anything—a footrace, a boxing match, what the weather would be like. When he took time to relax, his favorite recreation was shooting dice with Maecenas or with members of his bodyguard. The intense look in his eyes when he watched the dice fall amazed me. So did his exhilaration when he won even a tiny bet, and his brief but real chagrin when fortune did not favor him. But he won more money than he lost, so I had little to complain of.

From the beginning of our marriage, I had avoided entering his bedchamber, fearing he might take it as an invitation I was not yet ready to make good on. But one night, a fortnight after Drusus's birth, he smiled and said, "You can come inside, you know. Oh, just for a moment, to wish me sweet dreams. I won't bite you." So we walked into his bedchamber, his arm around my shoulder, my arm around his waist. The room contained a plain, low sleeping couch, a cedarwood cabinet, and a small oil lamp, lit and hanging from a hook.

He pulled me close. His breath felt warm on my neck. I closed my eyes, lost in the sensation of his body against mine. I could have sobbed with my need for him. He drew me toward the bed.

"Tavius," I said, "it's too soon. Tavius . . . not yet."

He let go of me and gave a rueful laugh.

"Soon," I said.

I went back to my own chaste bedchamber, blew out the oil lamp, lay down, and pictured him on his bed, gnashing his teeth. I tossed and turned. Five years had passed since the first time I looked at him and wanted him. Now I needed to wait only a little longer to have my desires fulfilled. But as I lay in the dark, the waiting seemed cruel. Every particle of my being anticipated his touch. I imagined ecstasy, the moment when we would be one flesh.

Physically I had not yet recovered from Drusus's birth. But since my wedding, I had been living in an idyll of love. Though I had not yet slept with my husband, exquisite expectancy colored all my days. Oh, sometimes I felt a twinge of apprehension. What if when we finally made love, reality fell short of my imaginings? Or worse, of Tavius's? There were even dark moments when I thought: *What if he should compare me to others and find me wanting?*

I tried not to notice the women—the women I saw looking at him with hungry eyes every place we went. He had great power, wealth, and beauty. They gazed at him as they did at champion gladiators or famous charioteers. When they smiled at him, he would smile back. I told myself, *If all they do is look, why should I mind? I am his wife. He loves me, not them.*

One evening in February, we held a small, informal dinner party to which we invited a few of Tavius's closest supporters. At one point, I sat on Maecenas's dinner couch while he kept me entertained with anecdotes about young poets and artists he knew. "You see, I've staked out my territory," he said. "I'll meet these people, cultivate them, and introduce the best of them to Caesar. He will help them, and they will add luster to his name. That's the greatest contribution I can make to the rebirth of Rome."

The gravity with which Maecenas said this surprised me. He was rarely grave about anything. When anyone asked if he wanted an official role in the government, he looked as if it had been suggested he be put on the rack. But Tavius valued his political advice, and when difficult diplomacy needed to be conducted, it was Maecenas he turned to. He said Maecenas had a wonderful gift for charming people even as he eviscerated them.

I became aware that Maecenas's wife, Terentilla, had gone to sit on the couch on which Tavius was reclining. They did not touch each other, but I was struck by the familiar ease with which she sat there. Maecenas noticed my glance. "They're old friends," he whispered.

Everyone knew that Maecenas's marriage to Terentilla provided companionship and not much else, that both had male lovers who came and went. I drank some wine, my eyes never straying from my husband and his "old friend."

"I'm not sophisticated," I said in a low voice.

"It's good you're not," Maecenas said. "Caesar prefers you that way."

"Is he . . . sophisticated?"

"He is and he isn't. He's like a schoolboy in love when it comes to you."

I watched Tavius and Terentilla. They were just talking. But I felt tension in the pit of my stomach.

"The town we grew up in wasn't a sophisticated place," Maecenas said. "There's a part of him that's remarkably straightlaced. But what did you hope? That he'd lived like a eunuch?"

I shook my head. My eyes were still on Tavius and Terentilla. She had bright yellow hair—dyed, I was sure—arranged around her face in ringlets. As I watched, she smiled into Tavius's eyes.

"Terentilla seems to know him very well," I said.

Maecenas leaned close and whispered in my ear, "It's over between them. I swear to you, it's been over for a while."

"That's good," I said, still watching them. "And all the others—the others I see eating him up with their eyes?"

"Is it permitted for me to offer you some advice?" Maecenas asked, his voice kind.

I shrugged, gritting my teeth.

"There are few women in Rome Caesar can't have. You're bound to see them throwing themselves at him. You must learn to look away, because it will take on exactly as much significance as you give it. Think of it this way: *It's beneath your notice.*"

I nodded.

Then I got up and walked to Tavius's dining couch. I looked at Terentilla. Not angrily. I just gazed at her and waited. Her eyes widened. As if she had suddenly remembered an urgent errand, she rose. She went to recline on Maecenas's couch, and I took her place beside my husband.

"I have been having the most wonderful conversation with Maecenas," I told Tavius. "I agree with him completely about patronizing artists and poets. You'll do it, won't you, dearest?"

"Yes, you should," said Metella, another of the women present. "Everyone should know the best artists are in Rome, not in Athens or some other remote village. You can make the arts flower, Caesar."

"I intend to." He smiled. "Insofar as I can afford it, anyway."

"Thank you, my love," I said, and kissed him on the lips.

>>>>>>>

He was patient in letting me decide the moment when I would become his wife in body as well as in heart and soul. And I loved him the more because I could see that this patience cost him something.

One night, I took him by the hand and led him into my bedchamber. The question in his eyes made me smile.

I had prepared the room with scented candles. The air was full of a sweet, subtle musk and smells of cedar and roses. Red silk pillows and a coverlet of red silk, decorated with gold thread, lay on the bed.

"I love you," I said. "I will love you all my life."

He gazed at me for a long time, his head tilted to the side in that way he had. His pupils were dilated, and his blue eyes looked almost black in the candlelight. He bent to kiss me, and my arms went about his neck. I caressed his shoulders and tangled my hand in his hair. He held me close and whispered my name.

All that night, we were lost in each other.

Chapter 11

I knew that in the spring, Tavius would leave for war. He planned an all-out attack on Sextus Pompey, an invasion of Sicily. Only a short time together was vouchsafed us. We spent a great deal of time in bed—in bed but not sleeping. We would talk and make love, make love again and talk some more. I loved him so, I could not get enough of his body. I only had to look at him to want him. He would kiss me on my breasts, my thighs, and I would feel fire where his lips touched. I had never known such delicious sensations before, never knew what ecstasy was possible.

Now across the years I remember the sound of his young voice, whispering or filled with laughter, and his scent, and the warm feel of him. No one had ever touched me with as much tenderness as he did. I was so new to such joy. Often it seemed as if the words "Where thou art Gaius, I am Gaia" were literally true, that there was no division at all between the two of us.

But of course we were separate beings. I would go for a time believing Tavius and I shared the same view of the world. Then would come a moment of surprise and dismay. We did *not* look at everything with the same eyes.

"Do you think I should let the Senate name a month of the year after me?" Tavius asked me once, as we lay together and he stroked my thigh.

It was nearly noon. The shutters of the bedchamber were half opened, and I could see his face clearly. His lips turned up at the corners in a faint smile.

"Who suggested such a thing?"

"A friend of mine. Numerius." He named a senator who was a particular sycophant.

"That man is no friend of yours," I said.

Tavius stopped petting me. "Actually he is."

"He is an idiot. You don't need idiotic friends."

"Oh, no?"

"No."

Tavius went back to fondling me, and I touched him in a place that made him gasp and for a while we stopped talking.

Later I murmured, "The month of Octavianus, is that what Numerius had in mind?"

"I suppose so. My father"—he meant Julius Caesar—"had the month of Julius named after him."

I almost blurted out, *And that's one reason your "father" is dead.* But even when we lay in a warm embrace, I did not speak carelessly to Tavius about political matters. On the contrary, I plotted out important conversations with him. I sensed we were about to have an important conversation now. In fact, we were treading close to dangerous ground.

"Livia, I won't have a month named after me," Tavius said. "I never considered it. I was just curious to hear your reaction."

"I am your wife who loves you, and therefore my reaction is absolute horror," I said.

He frowned. "Because you love me so much."

"Because I adore you."

"You think a little thing like having a month named in my honor would get me knifed?"

My mind groped for a gentle way to say what I needed to. Tavius treated the memory of Julius Caesar as sacred. I feared that for this reason he had not been able to extract the right lessons from his "father's" assassination.

"You're getting that veiled look of yours," Tavius said, leaning over me.

"What look is that?"

"The one that says 'How can I break the truth to this poor fool?' I can read you as well as you can read me, my love. Tiberius Nero never could, I know, but I certainly can, and don't forget it. Say what you have to say to me, before I get annoyed."

I reached up and ran my hand through his hair. How pleasant it was to touch that golden hair of his, to curl a smooth lock around my finger. "Have you ever analyzed what mistakes your father made that contributed to his assassination?"

"Certainly. He forgave people who had betrayed him, who then turned on him again. He showed too much clemency. Excessive clemency, you may have noticed, is not a vice of mine."

"He had another, worse failing," I said. "I see it beckoning to you every time a false friend lavishes you with flattery."

"What failing are you referring to?"

I pressed my face against his shoulder.

"What?" he said again.

"Do I have to say it?"

"I think you're talking about hubris."

"Your father was not satisfied with power—he had to have the trappings to go with it. He named a month after himself. He was dictator, but he made it clear he wanted to be king. Knowing that Romans hate kings. All his mercy won him no goodwill, because he rubbed senators' faces in the fact of their subjection. He didn't let them pretend he was their equal."

Tavius moved away from me and lay back on the pillow, gazing at the ceiling. I could not tell if he was angry or just pondering what I had said.

I could not restrain myself at that moment. I leaned over him, and said, "A man who suggests you name a month after yourself is inviting you to die! The sycophants are your enemies, Tavius. They will lull you into thinking you can do whatever you want and still be safe. And you can't!"

"Why are you getting upset?" Tavius asked in a mild voice.

"Because I'm afraid for you. And I'm terrified you won't hear what I'm saying."

He pulled me on top of him and locked his arms around me. "Do you know what you and I are, Livia? We're the kind of people—well, if there were a great shipwreck, say, and only two people were left alive, washed up on shore, the two would be us. We would somehow find a way to not get swallowed by the sea."

If the sea is fierce enough, it swallows everyone, I thought. *And in the end, a great sea swallows us all.*

But this much is true: We would neither of us be easy to drown.

I kissed him again and again. His lips, his neck, his eyes. "I'm going to make old bones," Tavius whispered in my ear. "And then, when I'm a decrepit old stick, do you know what I'll do?"

"You'll make them name a month after you."

I could feel him silently shaking with laughter. I laughed too, thinking, *O Diana, please let it happen that way. Let us have all those years together.*

>>>>>>>

After my son Drusus's birth, I began giving dinner parties to which I invited mainly senators and their wives. The evening that Mucia came stands out in my memory. My mother had liked and admired her, and as a child I had regarded her with awe. With her perfectly coiffed white hair and dark, knowing eyes, she looked just the way I imagined Cornelia, the mother of the Gracchi, must have. Mucia and her husband, a senator named Atratinus, had survived the past five years by remaining aloof from partisan battles. They were people of integrity and had a large and devoted circle of friends.

When Mucia arrived, she embraced me and whispered, "I see so much of your mother in you." I had to blink away tears.

She and her husband politely greeted Tavius, who stood beside me. I noticed the tensing of small muscles around Mucia's mouth and eyes as she looked at him. Later, as we dined on the first course, I felt her unobtrusive scrutiny and could almost read her mind: *Here is Alfidia and Claudianus's daughter, poor child, married to this savage, Caesar. Gods above, what the world has come to.*

My role as hostess was to put people at ease and get them talking. But this evening, I made it my business to draw out not my guests but Tavius. What did he think of this poet, that architect? At first he looked puzzled to be put through his paces this way, but soon he became absorbed in talking about art. Surely, I thought, no one who listened to him could take him for other than what he was—a charming, brilliant man. *See,* I was telling Mucia. *He is not at all what you thought. He is civilized. Really. He has elevated tastes.*

And he is quite tame. I took a grape from my plate and put it in his mouth. He chewed and swallowed. I fed him several more grapes, which, listening to guests' talk, he hardly noticed.

I caught Mucia's glance and spoke to her without words. *He loves and trusts me. You may have heard that my influence with him is substantial and growing. Believe me, that is true.*

Some would say it hardly mattered what women thought of Tavius, that even senators' wives, like Mucia, had no power to shape events. But what if Portia, Brutus's beloved wife, rather than encouraging his plan to assassinate Julius Caesar, had told him he would pointlessly destroy himself and others? I think Portia might have changed history.

The dinner ended; nothing important seemed to have happened. But as Mucia took her leave, she said, "Livia, dear, I'm having a luncheon soon with a few ladies. It would delight me to have you come. Four days from now. Is that too soon?"

I told her I was perfectly free, and when she and the other guests left, I threw my arms exultantly around Tavius's neck. "You're so happy to receive a lunch invitation from that woman?" he said.

"That invitation matters. It will be to our benefit," I told him.

We walked into the atrium. A yawning slave was extinguishing the lamps—all but the small one on the altar by the entranceway; that one would be kept blazing all night. Tavius drew me into his arms. I remembered a night from my childhood—peeking out from my bedchamber, watching my parents arrive home from a social engagement. They were in a gay mood and, not knowing they were observed, embraced and kissed.

"And now you're sad." Tavius had said he could read me, and he could.

"Mucia was my mother's friend," I said. "She wants to be kind to me for my mother's sake. Seeing her brought back the past."

"You have to forget the past."

"I try to," I said. "And most of the time, I succeed, don't I?"

"Come to bed," Tavius said. "I know how to make your sadness go away."

⋙⋙

For Mucia's luncheon, I wore a new stola of fine yellow linen, expensive but austere, trimmed only with thin scarlet edging. Pelia draped it so that it fell in perfect, graceful folds. I put on gold earrings, a ruby necklace, and a gold rose-shaped brooch I had from my mother. My hair was arranged in tight curls around my face, pulled back over my ears, and pinned up. If any hairstyle could make a political statement, this one did. Because it was so simple, people associated it with the old-fashioned Republican virtues. I had taken to wearing it whenever I appeared at Tavius's side in public, and for all other important occasions.

I sensed that Mucia's luncheon qualified as important. As it happened, I was right. All the other guests were wives of high-ranking senators. None of their husbands could be considered Tavius's firm friend; in fact, if I had wanted to recruit a cabal to overthrow my husband, I probably would have approached those very men. So, I had my work to do.

The scent of expensive perfume hung in the air. Emeralds and pearls glittered on throats and wrists. Delicate hands lifted pastries filled with spiced meats. Rouged lips sipped wine from silver cups. There was the tinkling sound of feminine laughter. At first the conversation was just what you would expect at a gathering of patrician matrons. We discussed the merits and demerits of several dressmakers, at length. Meanwhile, my every word and gesture was being analyzed by a half dozen shrewd and wary minds.

I was the wife of Rome's ruler. Most of the women spoke to me with more than a hint of deference. In return, I was gracious, even cordial. They appreciated that and relaxed a bit. They knew I had been born noble. I was a Claudian; I was one of them. It would be impossible to overestimate how much that mattered. I could feel a softening under the careful courtesy. Why not accept me, why not make friends? Still, one of the women, Caecilia, was cool, if not hostile. I sensed she thought it would be wise to be pleasant to me, but could not manage it. When we spoke of children, she said, "It must be so hard for you, to have such young children and not have them living with you."

"It is hard not to have them under my roof," I said, "but my former husband is very kind, and he allows me to direct their care."

"How fortunate," she said.

Mucia gave Caecilia a barely discernible reproving glance and changed the subject. A flutter of small talk rose. Then, Papiria, the youngest woman present, said, "Has anyone seen a good play lately? I would love to see a good play."

I leaned toward her. "Do you know what play I would like to see, which is almost never presented? It's Greek. Surely you have heard of it. *Lysistrata.*"

Papiria smiled. "Isn't that the one in which all the wives refuse to make love until their husbands bring a terrible war to an end?"

I nodded.

"It's a comedy, of course," Caecilia said.

"Yes," I said, "it's a comedy. And it deals with the Peloponnesian War between Athens and Sparta, which went on for only twenty-five years."

"Only?" Hirtia, another of the women, said.

"Greeks killed Greeks for twenty-five years," I said. "By Roman standards, what is that? We've been at it much longer."

Papiria laughed. "A pity Rome has no women like Lysistrata."

"Yes," I said. "A pity."

"What are you suggesting?" Caecilia asked. "That we all refuse to couple with our husbands until Italy is at peace?"

"Oh, no," I said. "Nothing as crude as that." I shrugged. "I don't think it would work. After all, the man now breaking the peace is Sextus Pompey, and he's outside our influence. But I believe women should give serious thought to peace and what is likely to bring peace—what and who." I nibbled a pastry.

"By 'who' you mean Caesar Octavianus," Caecilia said, almost accusingly.

I smiled into her eyes and said, "Yes, actually I do." I looked at Mucia. "The pastries are delicious. If your cook would give mine the recipe, I would be so grateful."

I had planted a seed, and that was all that I had intended. In the months and even years ahead, I planned to assiduously water and tend it.

When the lunch ended, several of the women came up to me and, looking abashed, drew sheets of folded parchment from the folds of their stolas. One wished a certain piece of confiscated property to be returned to her family; another had a husband who sought an official appointment; a third had another favor she wanted from Tavius.

Then Caecilia approached me. "My brother," she said, her face burning. "He is in exile. It's destroying him, not being able to come home." She held out a document warily, as if she expected me to refuse to accept it.

But of course I took it. "I will do my best for you," I said.

She looked at me with doubt in her eyes.

"Truly," I said.

I went home to Tavius with these petitions, and after dinner, we curled up on a couch in his study in the mellow lamplight and scrutinized them together. I did not need to tell him why I wished for the petitions to be granted. He knew. He hoped I would help to sway the nobility to his side, and these women with whom I had lunched were the cream of the nobility. The favors requested were hardly earthshaking, and he quickly granted three of them, partly, I suppose, to please me but also because doing so was in his interest.

Then he said, "Caecilia's brother . . ."

"Is he a threat?"

Tavius shook his head. "He's an obnoxious little toad who was disloyal to my father. I have absolutely no desire to pardon him."

Could I get him to do it, just to please me? What would be the best way of going about that? As I pondered these questions, I studied his face and noticed blue half-moons under his eyes. "You look tired. You need a holiday."

He grimaced.

"We ought to get away from Rome for a few days, now while things are quiet," I said. "We could do that, couldn't we?"

"Maybe. I have a villa halfway between here and Neapolis. I almost never go there, but it's beautiful. Would you like to go?"

"Yes, very much."

He smiled faintly. "I expected you to say, 'Certainly, let's go, but first pardon Caecilius.'"

Poor man. Everyone was always importuning him to do this or that. Each morning a crowd of favor-seekers stood waiting before our door, and they dogged his steps when he went out. Imagine what it would be like, to have a wife who acted like she was only another in that horde of supplicants. "Forget Caecilius," I said.

There were chariot races the next afternoon at the Circus Maximus. Tavius and I sat in the large private box that was now reserved for us, and we were the focus of all eyes. He won two big bets, which delighted him. But though he enjoyed himself, by the time he finished giving out prizes to the winning charioteers, night was falling and he was too tired to keep from yawning. "Let's go to the country soon," I said.

Torches lit our way home. We rode through the streets in a great litter, borne by eight bearers. We opened the curtains to wave at people who came out to cheer.

Later, at home, we lay entwined in each other's arms. "So . . . you want me to pardon Caecilius," Tavius said.

"Note that you are bringing it up again, and I am not."

"But you want me to pardon the little snake."

"I want you to be magnificent, I want you to be merciful," I said.

"But you see, dear love, I'm not merciful. What I am is rancorous and vengeful."

"You're a being of light."

The being of light kissed me. The next day he pardoned Caecilius, and we left for the country.

⋙⋙

Sometimes he did things he might otherwise not have done, for no other reason but to make me happy. Perhaps he wanted to live up to my dream of him. The question of whether pardoning Caecilius was wise policy or not was not settled for him, even after he did it. He chewed on the greater implications of this act.

"It's a puzzle," he said to me, as we traveled in a closed carriage together, surrounded on all sides by his mounted bodyguard. "I ask myself how much one should strive to be feared, or alternately, to be loved. There's no sure answer."

"Oh, better to be loved," I said, and took his hand.

He smiled. "In some relations, undoubtedly. But in public life?"

"You've made yourself sufficiently feared," I said. "Now it is vital that the nobility see you as moderate and the opposite of bloodthirsty. All men must understand you are a safe harbor for Rome after the bloodshed of the past. Then they will support you."

"That's how you see it?" he said, pondering.

"I believe too much fear can lead to hatred and desperate acts," I said. "And many people can be conciliated by kindness."

"I think you trust too much in what kindness can do," he said. "But I'm willing to give this more consideration."

For the rest of the trip, we spoke of lighter matters.

Tavius's villa had been left to him in Julius Caesar's will. Once there, we walked through stately rooms and vast gardens, and saw works of art everywhere we looked. Early in our stay, we lay on our bellies on smooth marble slabs after a dip in the pleasantly warm swimming pool, being pummeled by specially trained slave masseurs. I turned my head to look at Tavius and said, "You own this, and you almost never come here?"

"I've been busy," he said, the corners of his mouth twitching at the understatement.

"But I have the feeling money and what money can buy means nothing to you," I said.

"No. Money can buy armies. It's a great help to a political career."

Despite the opulent surroundings, we mainly engaged in simple pastimes. It was not yet spring, but the weather was warm. We felt so free, outside alone without hovering bodyguards. There were fields and orchards where we could just walk and walk. And one day Tavius with his own hands hitched a pony to a little open carriage—painted red with a red leather harness—and took me for a carriage ride, through orchards he owned.

During that carriage ride, an eagle swooped overhead. It seemed to be flying right along on the same path we took. Tavius kept glancing up at it. The eagle flew lower. "Look," Tavius said, "it has something in its talons."

It did—something white in color. A bird, I thought. Was it a dove? No, a bigger bird than that.

"Maybe this is a mother eagle, who has been out hunting and is going home to feed her young," I said. I thought of little Tiberius and Drusus, with their father back in Rome. I had never before been away from my children for even a few days. Pleasant as this holiday was, I missed them.

Even as I spoke, the bird the eagle had been carrying somehow broke free—or else the eagle dropped it. Wings fluttering, it plummeted toward the ground, the eagle diving after it. The eagle swerved away, just before the bird landed in my lap.

I gazed down at a small white hen. On its sides, I saw traces of blood from the eagle's talons. But the hen was alive and looked up at me with bright, black eyes. In its beak, it clutched a stem with some leaves on it.

Tavius gazed at me, openmouthed.

I stroked the hen's feathers. "Poor thing. Do you think it will live?"

Tavius gave the hen a closer look, but not to judge its injuries. "That stem is from a laurel bush."

"Are you sure?" I asked.

"Yes." He said the word flatly. He had gone a little pale. Laurels. Associated not only with victory but with his patron deity, the god Apollo.

We both knew that something uncanny had happened. Oh, perhaps eagles do sometimes drop their prey, and people just happen to be underneath and catch birds out of the sky. But how to account for the laurel twig?

"We must keep that hen," Tavius said, "see that it recovers from its wounds, and never harm it. The steward who runs the farm here must take the greatest care. As for the laurel, we should give it to the gardener and tell him to treat it as a cutting, and see if he can grow a new tree from it. I'm sure that's what a priest would tell me to do."

I nodded. Then, because Tavius looked so grave, I said, "It's an omen of victory, isn't it? It has to be!"

"It's an omen of victory. For you."

"But dearest, 'Where thou art Gaius, I am Gaia.' It's for both of us, surely."

"A *hen* with a laurel twig, dropped in *your* lap? No, that doesn't sound like an omen for *me,* Livia."

I stared at him in dismay.

"Don't misunderstand," he said. "I'm pleased. This is a very fortunate omen."

He did not sound pleased, however. We rode back to the villa, neither of us saying a word, me clutching the hen all the way. I think we both felt somewhat chastened. I remembered the days I had spent holding an egg in my hands, wanting so much to hatch a rooster chick, harbinger of a son. Now the gods had deposited a hen in my lap, in her beak the laurel of victory. Could there be a rebuke in that?

Later, Tavius seemed happier about the omen. "I'll publicize it, of course," he told me over dinner. "And all the sophisticates will be sure I made it up. But the simple folk will believe and be awed. This can only add to our stature." He had already sent a messenger racing to Rome, to consult the College of Augurs as to the omen's exact meaning.

The augurs sent our messenger back to us with great speed, bearing a letter that Tavius read at once. "They said I'm to take good care of that hen, and plant the twig, just as I thought," Tavius told me. "You see, I was right."

"And the meaning of the omen?"

He read aloud from the letter. "'The eagle is Rome's symbol and is also a sacred bird belonging to Father Jupiter. The hen is female. The laurel means victory. Therefore, we understand that Jupiter grants victory or great benefit to Rome, through a female.'" Tavius looked at me. "Specifically, through you." He gave me a slightly grudging smile, then glanced down at the letter again. "Nothing in here about me, except, oh yes, the gods obviously approve of my marriage, since the hen fell into your lap while I was riding with you."

I remembered how as a girl I had wanted to perform mighty deeds for my country, and how out of reach that had seemed because I was female. Now the gods seemed to be saying that as Tavius's wife I could indeed accomplish great things for Rome. It was wonderful to think that this could be so.

I was especially affectionate to Tavius in bed that night. We were happy together, and omens and augurs' verdicts were banished from our minds.

The days we had to be together, free of responsibilities, passed quickly. "Before we go back to Rome," Tavius said one morning, "I want to take a side trip. There is an important supporter who has been begging me to visit him. Vedius Pollio. Have you ever heard of him?"

I had not.

"Well, he's eccentric," Tavius said. "But he is extremely rich and was loyal to my father."

We set out the next morning for Vedius's villa in a carriage, accompanied by Tavius's bodyguards. Our time of bucolic peace was over. As if to emphasize the point, the weather had turned bitter cold. It was a three-hour journey, so I pulled my cloak tight around me. Tavius, also warmly dressed, began to wheeze a bit. I looked at him with concern.

"Sometimes cold weather has this effect on me," he said indifferently.

"Maybe we should visit Vedius another time," I said.

"Certainly not."

"Tavius—"

"*I am not sick,*" he said.

So we continued on.

Vedius's villa resembled a small city more than a house. As I stepped down from the carriage, at the front gate, I stared wide-eyed, amazed by the villa's sheer size. Vedius came out to greet us. "Caesar!" he cried, and threw his arms around Tavius. "And your beautiful wife!" He did not hug me but contented himself with grabbing my hand and wringing it.

Despite the cordial greeting, on first sight I did not like the man. I did not like his thick lips or his bulging eyes, or how his graying hair ringed his forehead in pomaded curls swept forward to hide the fact that he was going bald. I did not like his wife, Opimia, with her wide, brittle smile, or their eagerness to show off the house—or rather the palace—they lived in. They took us on a tour, through room after room filled with exquisite Greek statues by famous masters. We also passed wall murals of incredible vulgarity, showing gods and goddesses in sexual congress. Gold and silver glittered everywhere.

They led us out on a balcony that overlooked a pond. The pond, a perfect oval, was gray beneath the cloudy sky. The banks were paved with black marble. The air had a dank, unpleasant smell. "The pond's not natural," Vedius informed us. "Did you think it was? No, no. I created it. It took months to dig."

Tavius and I both admired the pond, as Vedius expected us to.

"And what do you think I have it stocked with? What do you think?" Vedius looked at me.

"Fish?" I suggested.

"No, no. Eels! And not just any eels. Lampreys! Their tongues have teeth on them. They can clamp their tongue on a man and drain him of blood. Imagine being attacked by a hundred of them, two hundred! Anybody who falls in that pond dies a very unpleasant death, believe me!"

Tavius had said the man was eccentric. I did not ask why he would want to have a pond filled with lampreys beside his house. I was mainly interested in getting off that balcony. But Tavius leaned over the balcony railing and gazed into the pond, trying to see the lampreys lurking in its depths. "Do you feed them?"

"Of course, Caesar," Vedius said. "Whenever one of my slaves does something to annoy me, I throw him to the lampreys!"

It was Vedius's notion of a joke. Tavius chuckled.

The tour continued. We saw more artwork, more furniture with gold trim. Compared to this, Tavius's villa—which I had thought luxurious—seemed like a simple country house. I did not feel envy, though, just a strong desire to leave.

Tavius acted like the soul of amiability during the whole tour. No doubt he reminded himself that the friendship of a man as spectacularly rich as Vedius could come in handy. The house was warm—golden braziers in every room. At least he had stopped wheezing.

Finally, Vedius led us into his dining room. He introduced us to two other guests, a young couple, his nephew and the nephew's wife. Slaves scurried about, serving us from huge platters of food. We lay on carved ivory couches with green silk cushions and drank sweet wine from costly crystal goblets that sparkled bright as diamonds. I admired the goblets, I must admit. I had rarely seen any so fine.

"That's quite a mural," Tavius said, gazing at the wall.

It depicted a centaur ravishing a nymph.

"Stunningly lifelike, isn't it?" said Vedius's nephew.

Slaves brought in the second course, along with wine of a different vintage. The crystal goblets we were using were being exchanged for new ones, equally beautiful. Suddenly we heard a crash. I turned my head to look. One of the slaves had dropped a crystal cup. A lanky young man with a lantern jaw, he stood stock-still, gazing down at the shards at his feet. His face looked corpse-like, tinged with green.

"You idiot!" Vedius shouted, getting up from his dining couch. He rushed toward the slave. I was sure he was going to pummel him.

Well, one does see these scenes sometimes even in the homes of well-bred people, I thought. A server spills some wine, and his mistress slaps him. Or a cook spoils the dinner, and his master insists on flogging him before the dinner guests. I personally found such scenes repulsive, but one cannot tell other people how to treat their own slaves.

But Vedius did not lay a finger on the man who had broken the goblet. Instead he yelled, "Krito, do you know what this means? I'll tell you, you clumsy fool! It means you're going to the lampreys!"

My stomach clenched, but I thought, *Of course it's an empty threat. Who would condemn a man to be eaten alive for breaking a cup?* I looked at Tavius. He gave me a slight smile and shook his head. He thought as I did, that we were watching a cruel piece of theater, nothing more.

I glanced at the slave. His eyes darted around wildly. He took his master at his word.

Vedius clapped his hands and shouted, "Lecto! Brumio! Phaedo!" Three other slaves—brawny fellows—rushed into the dining room. "To the lampreys," Vedius said.

The slaves started toward Krito. He backed away, looking around for an avenue of escape. Then he threw himself down on his knees before the couch on which Tavius and I reclined, grasped the edge of Tavius's toga, and cried, "Lord, save me! Help me, please!"

Tavius smiled. It was a rather stiff and embarrassed smile. "Krito, your master doesn't intend to throw you to the lampreys." He looked at Vedius and, still smiling but with something hard in his voice, said, "I'm sure Krito has learned his lesson and won't ever break another of your cups. In any case, we've had enough of this, don't you think?"

"You're right about this much, Caesar," Vedius said. "He'll never break another of my cups."

Tavius went rigid. The smile died on his face. "You're not serious."

"But I am," Vedius said.

"For heaven's sake, Vedius," Tavius said, "this is absurd. Even if you have no human feeling—it's a stupid waste of a valuable slave."

"It's worth it to me," Vedius said.

"Over a *cup*?" Tavius stared at him. "Don't you think it's out of proportion? To have a man eaten alive over a cup?"

I imagined being Krito, kneeling there on the floor, listening to this conversation.

"He's my slave, and I can do what I want with him," Vedius said.

"No one is suggesting otherwise," Tavius said.

Krito groaned.

"Vedius," Tavius said, "I'd appreciate it if you would change your mind. You see, the man appealed to me for help, and I feel a kind of obligation." He managed to sound as if he were asking a reasonable person for an ordinary favor.

"I'm sorry I can't oblige you, Caesar," Vedius said.

No one should ever interfere between master and slave. So I had always been taught. But my heart constricted when Vedius gestured to the men he had summoned to drag Krito away. I looked at Tavius. He compressed his lips, and his face went flinty. *And so we will watch, and allow this awful thing to happen,* I thought. My mind groped for words to move Vedius. But what words could affect this madman?

Tavius's voice rang out. "Aulus!"

The head of his bodyguard came racing in from the atrium, followed by five soldiers.

"Get every piece of crystal in this house and bring it in here," Tavius said. "Every piece, you understand?"

Aulus stared at him for one moment, then spun on his heel and went off with his men to do Tavius's bidding. Everyone else in the dining room had frozen: Krito kneeling on the floor, the slaves who had been about to haul him away, Vedius, the other guests. All eyes were on Tavius.

Tavius stood and picked up the goblet he had been drinking from, looked at it for a moment as if to assess its worth, and then, half-filled with wine as it was, threw it to the floor. It crashed and shattered.

"Caesar!" Vedius wailed as if a child of his had just been slaughtered.

Tavius ignored him. He looked at me and wordlessly extended his hand for my goblet. He was white with rage, his eyes like blue points of fire. I gave him my cup. He flung it to the floor. Then he went in turn to each of the other people at the table. He held out his hand. No one spoke. Each person handed him a crystal goblet. *Crash! Crash! Crash!*

Tavius went to Vedius's place at the table, picked up his goblet, and threw it down. Broken crystal and spilled wine lay all around us. The bodyguards by this time were lugging in a fortune's worth of fine crystal. Tavius motioned for them to put it on a side table, but it was already piled high with plates and platters. Tavius removed all these objects with a sweep of his arm. They crashed to the floor. The bodyguards piled the crystal on the table. There were goblets, vases, more than one fine decanter.

Tavius gazed at the crystal pieces for a moment. Then he said, "Break them."

The bodyguards broke all the crystal pieces by hurling them to the floor.

Vedius stood motionless, like a rabbit watching a hawk descend. Krito, who still crouched on the floor, was surrounded by shards of crystal and looked like Pandora must have when she opened the chest and accidentally loosed all the world's demons. Even the bodyguards, who now stood straight at attention, appeared scared. As for me, I didn't move or say anything. I had no idea what Tavius would do next.

He took a deep breath and gazed down at Krito, pointed at him, and said, "You are set free." The slave gave a delighted, incredulous cry and clasped Tavius's knees in gratitude.

Tavius stared across the table at Vedius. At that moment, I felt true terror. The force in that stare—the deadly force of it—made me quail though I was not the recipient. Vedius trembled. I think he expected Tavius to order him thrown to the lampreys. I half expected that myself. But Tavius said, "You will fill in your pond. You understand me?"

"Yes, Caesar."

"I don't expect to ever hear again of you doing something like this."

Vedius grabbed Tavius's hand and kissed it.

Tavius wiped at his hand with a napkin as if someone had smeared mud on it. He spoke a few words to one of his bodyguards, making official provision for freeing Krito. Then he looked at me and said, "Come," and went striding out of Vedius's house so quickly that I nearly had to run to keep up with him.

When we were in our carriage again, riding back to the villa, Tavius said, "He was actually going to have a human being eaten alive for breaking a cup. Gods above, I know what scum men are, and how filthy the world is, but I would not have believed it."

His sense of right and wrong had been truly violated, and the anger he had shown was righteous anger. *Pity anyone who provokes that anger in him,* I thought.

This side of him, which was so just, appealed to me. I had seen only hints of it before. He kept it buried within himself. *Imagine who he might have been,* I thought, *if he had been born a hundred years ago, when the world was less filthy. Imagine what a champion of right and justice he would have been.*

When we had gotten a mile or two away from Vedius's estate, Tavius began to wheeze, as he had earlier. The wheezing got worse as the trip continued, until he could only take quick, shallow breaths.

"What is it?" I asked fearfully.

"Nothing," he gasped.

"You need a physician," I said.

He looked at me with anger. "Didn't you hear me? I said it's nothing."

>>>>>>>

Soon after, when I was back in Rome while Tavius was away overseeing the final preparations for the invasion of Sicily, I invited Maecenas over for a private discussion. We chatted, and I told him about how Tavius had broken all the crystal in Vedius's villa. Maecenas chortled. "Every last piece? How fitting! I'm going to see that this story is widely told. It will add to his legend."

"Yes. But right now I'm less concerned about his legend than I am with him." I got down to the purpose of our meeting. "What can you tell me about my husband's health?"

"Surely the person to ask about that is Caesar," Maecenas said.

"Don't say that to me, please. He takes it as an insult if you imply he is not well. But he's not. Why can't he breathe properly when it's cold?"

Maecenas gave a deep sigh. "Livia, dearest Livia, queen of Roman womanhood, flower of all the world, for whom I would ford rivers and climb mountains, fight lions, walk through flame . . . don't you see that you're putting me in an uncomfortable position?"

I did see it. On the one hand, Maecenas wanted my friendship. He rather relished the role of wise guide to Tavius's bride. But he kept Tavius's secrets and was wary of betraying him.

"Almost every morning when Tavius is in Rome, he goes to the Field of Mars for military exercises," I said. "I think he hates it, but he goes. Often he comes home limping, and if I ask him what happened, he always has a different story. He pulled a muscle while riding, or he tripped while fencing. But I've noticed that it's always his right leg that gets hurt, never the left one. Then, he will eat only a few foods—a very few, when I think about it. It's peculiar the way he eats, how he scrapes sauce off his meat, like it was poison."

"So he likes a plain diet," Maecenas said.

I was filled with frustration and fear. Something was the matter with Tavius—gravely the matter—and nobody would tell me what it was. "Liar, liar, liar," I said. "How can you look at me and lie?"

Maecenas rubbed the side of his face.

"Tell me the truth. For heaven's sake, I'm his wife. Why must he keep things from me?"

"Think of how he is situated. He needs to project strength and invincibility."

"He needs to project invincibility—with me?"

"Do you expect instant and total trust? He already lets you read his mail. Have a little patience."

"Have a little patience? I would like to know if he is fatally ill."

Maecenas shook his head. "He's not. When we were younger I used to stand vigil at his sickbeds and go home and weep. But he would always come bounding up again. I finally realized he is one of those people who is never truly well, but still will probably outlive me."

"What's wrong with him?"

"This and that." We were in a small sitting room, and I had ordered fruits, nuts, and wine served on a side table. Maecenas ate a fig, frowning, then sighed and said, "He has a weakness in his right side, so sometimes he limps. If it's too cold or too hot he has trouble breathing. I don't know why. It's strange. He can't take smoke or dust or— Once a bee stung him, and he swelled up and almost died. There's a lot of food he can't eat, because if he does he gets violently sick."

"Violently sick?"

"Livia, please try not to get so distressed," Maecenas said. "The difficulties with his health come and go, but they will never be allowed to impede him. And they will certainly never kill him."

"How do you know they won't?"

"I know his strength of will. He'll do what he has been put on earth to do."

"How in the world can he go off and lead an army when he's so . . . sickly?"

Maecenas looked around as if he feared someone were listening to us. "Please, don't ever let anyone hear you call him that—least of all him." He added, "Do you know what is going to happen to me if you let him know I discussed this with you?"

"What?"

Maecenas ran his finger across his throat.

"Truly?"

He grinned. "No. But he'll be furious. So use some discretion, will you?"

I kept Maecenas's confidence. And when Tavius returned to dispose of business at home before leaving for war, I did not say, *You can't possibly go, because you are not a well man.* The girl I had been at fourteen would have said it. The woman knew he would go whatever I said.

»»»»»»»

"Dearest," I murmured one night in bed, "I have something important to ask you."

Tavius paused from nibbling my neck. "What do you want?"

I want you home and safe. I want an end to the civil wars. "When you're away, someone who truly cares ought to be overseeing your finances. I think it should be me."

He chuckled. "You like to be in charge, don't you? Do you know who you remind me of?" He whispered the answer in my ear: "Me."

Only a few days before, I had wished to sell a little farm that was part of my dowry. Of course I had to ask Tavius's permission to do it. As my husband, he was my financial guardian, and I needed him to stamp with his seal every business contract I made. He readily acceded to my request, and yet I felt angry, as if it humbled me to ask him. Here I was helping him to govern Rome, but because of the laws that applied to women, I could not freely dispose of a bit of my own inheritance. I certainly did not want some male factotum controlling all our money while Tavius was gone.

"I'll hold your seal for you while you're away?"

"Oh, let me consider that a little," Tavius said. But his tone told me he would agree.

He did give me his seal without my having to ask again. But the thing I wanted more—peace—*that* I could not get so simply.

A few days later, I stood in the atrium, clutching Tavius in my arms. Fear of loss had turned me into a coward.

The knowledge of Tavius's infirmities tore at me. Military life was so difficult. What if hardship made him fall seriously ill? I wished I could go to war in his place. At least I didn't have his host of physical ailments.

The woman who had coolly asked to hold the purse strings while her husband was away—that woman had vanished. I felt as if something had broken inside me. I remembered my last parting with my father, and pressed my face against Tavius's shoulder. The metal of his breastplate was hard against my cheek. Civil war had robbed me of my parents, and now it would rob me of my love. I wept.

Tavius had never anticipated this sort of parting. "Livia, please, don't act this way."

"I love you too much," I said.

"For heaven's sake, I'm coming back."

How do you know?

"Wipe your eyes, will you?"

"Forgive me. You'll come home in triumph, and I'll laugh at what a fool I was."

He kissed me, and I let him go.

»»»»»»»

I looked after our affairs in Rome. Lonely months passed. I waited for news of success in Sicily, and felt dread—dread that was not completely misplaced. One day a message came from Tavius:

> *My love, the invasion did not succeed. We will have to try again. I am coming home. Please, however disappointed you may be by this news, keep a cheerful countenance when you are among others. Let them know I am still in charge.*

He was alive, he was coming home. That was what mattered most to me. But when his fleet had met that of Sextus Pompey at sea, he lost. In every battle he had fought before, his had been the winning side. Being ever victorious was part of what had kept him in power. I feared that, seeing him weakened, all those who submitted to his rule only out of fear would be emboldened. His political enemies might soon be on him like a pack of mad dogs.

Chapter 12

I stood on the edge of our little garden. Tiberius Nero had gone away on holiday and left our sons in my charge. Rubria had also come to stay with me. Drusus was in his cradle, sweetly dreaming, my perfect baby who hardly ever cried, but would wake to reach for me with his tiny hands, cooing. Beside Drusus, in another cradle, Julia lay asleep. Rubria sat watching over the two of them.

Meanwhile, little Tiberius played at battle, jabbing his small wooden sword into the rosebushes. "That's right," I said. "Fight hard. You will be the victor."

He darted a quick glance at me. He had my eyes exactly—wide set and unusually large. He went back to fighting his imaginary enemy. Tiberius Nero had shown him how to hold a sword, and, at only four years old, he knew to keep his sword arm close to his body except when he made a thrust. I felt a rush of pride, gazing at him.

I sat down beside Rubria. "I've had a letter from my husband. The invasion did not take place. It's all to be done again."

She looked at me questioningly.

"It's a setback, that is all," I said.

Rubria, this plebeian woman so different from me, had become my confidante. She studied my face for a moment, then relaxed. *Good,* I thought. *If Rubria doesn't know that deep down I'm quailing, no one else will.*

Trepidation filled my mind. After a defeat, would Tavius keep the loyalty of the people of Rome? Sextus, son of a famous father, had his own appeal. And people like a victor.

How could I help my husband?

"If you wanted to endear yourself to the common people of Rome, what would you do?" I asked Rubria.

As she stared silently across the garden, I could not tell if she was thinking or if she had somehow not heard my question. At last she said heavily, "I would do something about the fires in the tenements." I knew she was remembering the deaths of her husband and child.

The wooden three- and four-story tenements in the poorer parts of Rome easily burst into flame. Private fire brigades would put the fires out—but only if the owners could pay. A tenement owner might stand desperately dickering while a fire raged. Meanwhile the flames would engulf nearby buildings.

I hurt, thinking of Rubria's loss. I knew she did not want me to allude to it, so I said, as if the matter had nothing to do with her, "I've heard some cities have public fire brigades always on alert. But in Rome we have never had them."

I found myself imagining how it must feel to be trapped inside a burning tenement. I myself had almost died by fire, and my mental pictures were all too vivid. I shuddered and resolved that Rome would have public fire brigades.

>>>>>>>

In the next days, as I awaited Tavius's return to Rome, details trickled back about the defeat. There had been a battle at sea. Sextus—who liked to call himself Neptune's son—had arrayed his forces skillfully. The admiral in charge of Tavius's forces had been outmatched. More than half of his galleys had been sunk. Tavius himself had come close to drowning and was lucky to survive. Many men died.

I did what I knew Tavius wished me to. I attended the theater and the chariot races. I dined with senators and their wives almost every evening. I kept a cheerful countenance.

"How is Caesar? Have you heard from him?" a senator might ask. "How do matters stand now with the war?"

I would sigh and shake my head. "Caesar, oh, he's fine, but not happy." Who would believe me if I said he was happy? "He wrote me that he will have to launch the invasion all over again. He is very irritated about it, as you can imagine. He hates delay." Then I would put my hand on the senator's arm and ask him what he thought about establishing public fire brigades in Rome. How would one go about doing it? And would it be horribly costly?

Maybe after we parted the senator thought, *Well, I suppose the Sicilian disaster is not irreparable. Caesar's wife is cheerful. In fact, all she wants to talk about is public fire brigades.*

That at least was my hope.

>>>>>>>

A month after I first had news of the Sicilian defeat, I heard a clatter in the atrium and found Tavius there with a group of high-ranking military officers. I wanted to throw myself into his arms. As I approached, feelings surfaced on his face; I saw that he had longed for me. Then his expression changed. He was controlled, a commander surrounded by his men.

"Dearest, welcome home," I said, smiling. I greeted the soldiers as graciously as if they were guests at a dinner party.

Tavius wheezed with each breath. I could not keep myself from giving him an anxious look.

"I caught a little head cold," he said.

"Mucia was just telling me about a medicinal drink made with herbs, very good for head colds," I said. "I'll go and brew you some."

I left him with his officers, went to the kitchen, and gave the cook instructions to mix up a heated drink. Then I went into the corridor leading to the atrium and listened to snatches of conversation. I learned that we were in no immediate danger from Sextus, but Tavius was determined to launch another invasion soon. I heard no enthusiasm from his officers until he said, "Agrippa will lead it." Then the relief in their voices was palpable.

Agrippa had just won an enormous victory in Gaul. This was good, of course. Our position would have been horrible if we had been losing two wars. But the contrast between Tavius's failure and his friend's glorious success was stark.

Still, listening to Tavius's voice, I heard only confidence. Even I could not tell how much of that was for show. But he could not keep from coughing.

When the officers had left, Tavius did not come looking for me, as I had expected he would. I found him in his study, examining the correspondence that I had put aside for him to read.

"You're going to sit there and read letters—now?"

He raised his eyes from the documents. I saw a flicker of emotion in his face, but it passed before I could even decipher it. "What would you like me to do?" he asked in a cool voice. "Sit here and weep?"

"I'd like you to tell me what our situation is."

"We lost. So we will mount another invasion, which will succeed."

The cook arrived, with a cup full of Mucia's remedy. I held it to Tavius's lips, and he took a sip. "At least it doesn't taste as awful as it smells," he said.

"Drink it all," I said.

He made a face but took the cup and sipped from it.

I stroked his hair. "I missed you."

He nodded. His features were grim. I felt that inside himself he was reliving the defeat.

"I want to organize public fire brigades for Rome," I said, trying to distract him. "I have plans, figures."

"It's a bad time for a large outlay of public money."

"They'll cost less than you probably imagine."

"How much, exactly?"

It said something about us, I suppose, that we could put thoughts of the Sicilian defeat aside and sit there and discuss public fire brigades.

Later that afternoon, Tavius summoned Maecenas. "I want you to go to Mark Antony in Athens," he told him. "You and my sister must persuade him it's in his interest to help me destroy Sextus."

As I sat by, listening, something in me flinched at those words: *Destroy Sextus*. Sextus had shown me only kindness. But he and my husband were locked in a life-and-death struggle. I had to harden my heart.

"What Antony will want," Maecenas said, "is a promise of assistance from you when he invades Parthia." Antony at that time was planning to become another Alexander the Great by conquering the Parthian empire.

Tavius nodded.

"Meanwhile, you'll bring Agrippa home?" Maecenas asked.

"Of course." Tavius looked away. "It's a great victory he won in Gaul. By rights, he deserves a triumph."

Maecenas frowned.

To publicly celebrate Agrippa's victory—to emphasize it after Tavius himself had suffered a staggering defeat—would be like announcing to Rome which of the two was a great general. But every military commander dreamed of riding through the streets of Rome in a triumphator's chariot. To deny Agrippa a triumph would be to risk alienating the one friend we most needed now.

"You do intend to grant Agrippa the triumph he deserves?" I said to Tavius.

He looked at me for a long moment. Finally he nodded.

"Will you help me write Agrippa a letter?" he asked me, after Maecenas had gone. "I don't know if I can manage the right congratulatory tone."

The letter to Agrippa was dispatched to Gaul that day, and the reply came back with lightning speed. I sat with Tavius in his study when he received and read it. He swallowed and looked shaken.

"What in the world did he say?" I cried. For I imagined disaster: Agrippa inflated with pride, refusing to come home and help us, instead setting himself up against Tavius.

"He said he will come home at once, and we will defeat Sextus. And he is full of boundless gratitude and will never forget that at such a moment I offered him a triumph. I can see, just by these few words he's written, how much that mattered to him. But he absolutely refuses to have a triumph now."

"Why?"

"'It would not be appropriate at this time.'" Tavius read the words from the letter, then shook his head in wonder. "That's all he says."

>>>>>>>

Maecenas wrote from Greece that Antony wanted to speak to Tavius personally about allying with him in the war against Sextus. Tavius agreed to meet him in the city of Tarentum. He wanted me to come. It would in a sense be a family gathering since Tavius's sister—whom I had never met—would be there. There was no question, though, of bringing the children on what would be an uncomfortable overland journey through swampy terrain. Julia's mother would happily take charge of her, while my boys did not live with me in any case. It would be less than a month's absence. Still I hesitated to leave them—to leave all three of them, because I oversaw Julia's care as if she were my own child. But in the end I gave precedence to Tavius's needs and kissed my little ones good-bye.

Tavius and I traveled five days by carriage. After an uneventful journey, we arrived in Tarentum. It was a beautiful, small city—full of gleaming marble buildings and exquisite public statuary—located in Southern Italy but founded by Greeks. Antony owned a villa here. He greeted Tavius with a boisterous shout and hugged him, then embraced me too. Octavia was more quiet in her greeting, but I saw tender love in her face when she looked at Tavius.

Tavius had once told me that his sister liked nearly everybody. Well, she did not like me. I knew it from the first. When she smiled and greeted me, her eyes—Tavius's blue eyes—were empty of warmth. "I'm so pleased to finally have a chance to get to know you," she said to me, in the strained tone of an inexpert liar.

At twenty-seven she was milky-skinned and girlish looking. She had a quality one hopes to see in Vestal Virgins but usually does not—not quite of this earth. Pregnant with her first child by Antony, she was mother to a boy and two girls by her first husband, an aged senator she had married at fifteen. If I guessed rightly, there had been no awakening to passion in her first marriage, and Antony had not awakened her either. She must have known Cleopatra had borne Antony twins and that people still spoke of their scandalous love affair. I don't think it occurred to her she ought to try to compete on that particular playing field, the one on which Cleopatra won every prize. But she was aware of her responsibility to the Roman world to help keep peace and amity between her husband and her brother. I knew from her letters to Tavius, which he often shared with me, that she did everything she could to make each see the other in the best possible light.

Given Antony's power, many would have regarded him as a supremely desirable husband. But with the perquisites of rank came—Antony. I doubted he was remotely the mate Octavia would have picked based on personal affinity. Tavius spoke of her almost reverently, sometimes with a hint of guilt. He knew the burden he had placed on her, and he appreciated the fact that she never reproached him even implicitly by seeming unhappy.

How could Octavia and I have liked each other? When she looked at me she saw a woman who had forsaken husband and children—abandoned duty, when duty was Octavia's life—for a love match. I saw in her the epitome of a womanly ideal I could have realized only by smothering myself.

Inside the villa, our husbands tried to settle the fate of the world. Meanwhile, Octavia and I sat for hours on end amid roses and irises in a fragrant garden, enduring each other's company and making endless conversation about our children and domestic matters. I have rarely found it so hard to talk to anybody. Both of us were chary at first about bringing up politics. I could not even discuss clothing or hairstyles with Octavia, because she showed no interest in either. Eventually, I discovered that she read a great deal—far more than I had time for anymore. So we talked about poetry, especially about the new poets Maecenas discovered and acted as patron to. Then she said, "Did you know Tavius once wanted to be a poet?"

"And write tragic plays. Yes, I know."

"He used to write beautiful poems when he was a boy. My mother saved them, but I couldn't find them after she died. That's such a pity. I wanted them to keep. He doesn't write poems anymore, does he?"

"When would he have time?"

"It's as if he has killed part of himself."

I stared at her.

"I mean by abandoning his poetry." She bit her lip and avoided my eyes.

I finally broached the subject uppermost in my mind. "Do you think Antony will help him with the war?"

"Oh, yes. He'll join in declaring Sextus an outlaw, and he'll give Tavius some ships, and then when he goes off to Parthia, he'll expect Tavius to lend him some legions. To fight yet another war." She let out a long breath. "It could at least build goodwill between them, but it won't, because of the way Antony is doing it. He had to make Tavius come, to personally ask for his help."

"You couldn't persuade him to do it differently?" I asked.

"No. I tried. I know Tavius is sensitive. It kills him to beg for anything. It kills him to be made to feel weak or small. But Antony doesn't see that. He only sees that *he* should have been Julius Caesar's heir. He expected to be, you know. He told me about it, one night when he had a bit too much wine. The way he fought for that man—how he was discounted—" She stopped. "I pity everyone. That's a weakness of mine." Her expression changed. It was like a door closing. "You don't have that weakness, do you?"

I tossed my head, and said, "No." Then I added, "Maybe I did once, but I outgrew it."

It was the wrong thing to say to her. She looked insulted—as if I had called her a child. In truth, I had misspoken and expressed what I truly felt. In some ways, she did strike me as childlike.

We spent two more days in each other's company, and never said another word to each other that mattered.

⋙⋙

Antony and Tavius sealed a pact, taking sacred oaths to support each other in peace and war for a term of five years. Afterward, Antony hosted an extravagant farewell dinner meant to foster personal ties. All I remember of it is Antony needling Tavius. As he drank cup after cup of wine, the needling got worse. "Drusilla," Antony said to me—he still refused to call me by my proper name—"I had to respect your father. At Philippi he put up a fight. Believe me, he was no coward. I saw him in the thick of it. But I looked around in the midst of battle—and who did I *not* see?" He laughed. "'Where is he?' I asked. 'Where is Julius Caesar's chosen heir? In his tent? How, by Jupiter's cock, can he still be in his tent?'" He looked at Tavius and shook his head, grinning. "Just your miserable luck, right? To take sick on that day."

"Miserable luck," Tavius echoed, and he smiled. But his eyes—his eyes. They looked just the way they had at Vedius's villa. Cold blue fire. I felt fear. Fear for whom? I suppose for Antony. Incredibly, for Antony. The thought came to me—ridiculous on the face of it—*Tavius will kill him.*

Octavia started talking about nothing at all. "Have you noticed how cool the weather has been? It will be hot soon enough. Then we'll want it cool again, won't we?"

"This little man will be born, once it gets warm," Antony said, and placed a hand on her belly. As they lay together on the dining couch, they looked like an affectionate couple, though one of them—Antony, of course—was red-faced with drink.

Next day came the final parting. We stood in the road outside Antony's villa, Tavius and I ready to climb into a carriage to begin our journey back to Rome. Antony towered over Tavius by half a head. His shoulder muscles bulged under his tunic. He had a neck like a bull. As he and Tavius stood next to each other, I saw how unequal the two were physically. Antony's bulk seemed to symbolize the greater strength of his military—the reason why all through the conference Tavius had grimly taken what Antony dished out.

Antony had officially allied himself with Tavius against Sextus, and given him 120 war galleys. Yet the two parted worse friends than they had been before. Still, here stood Octavia, carrying Antony's child, Tavius's nephew or niece. She was the unbreakable link that held our world together.

Tavius took her in his arms. He and his sister did not seem able to let go of each other.

Antony gave Octavia a clumsy pat on the shoulder. "Look, honey-girl, you don't need to be parted from your brother for too long a time. Soon I'll go to war. Why should you wait for me in Greece all alone? You can go to Rome then, for a good long visit. I still have a house there; you'll be comfortable. Take your children and my sons with you—the whole tribe. I don't want Antyllus and Jullus to forget they're Romans. Do you like the idea?"

I had never seen Antony be kind to anyone before. It surprised me that he had it in him to be kind.

Octavia let go of Tavius and threw her arms around Antony. "You are so good to me. Oh, yes, I like the idea. And can I really take the boys? I just wish you could come to Rome with me too when I visit."

I truly think Tavius felt warmed by this exchange. I saw his face soften. Octavia embraced him again and said, "I'll see you soon then."

"I'm grateful," Tavius said, looking at Antony. He kissed his sister. "To have you back in Rome, even for a while—"

And then, Antony, being Antony, had to ruin things. "All right, boy," he said. *Boy*. He gave a great, roaring laugh. "In the meantime, just make sure you don't sink my boats like you did your own."

Those were the final words Antony said to Tavius in parting. They were the last words either would ever say to the other, face-to-face.

»»»»»»»

Maybe some malicious spirit heard those words, *Don't sink my boats.* Maybe Neptune himself did, when he was in a wrathful mood.

Tavius and Agrippa prepared a two-pronged attack on Sicily. They each headed a huge fleet. By some magic diplomacy, Maecenas induced Lepidus to come from North Africa to assist them; he succeeded in landing twelve legions of his own on Sicily's shore. Then an enormous storm struck. The fleet under Agrippa's command managed to ride it out. Tavius ordered his own ships into a bay on Italy's coast that should have been well-protected. As if directed by some evil intelligence, the storm headed for that bay. It was impossible for the ships to escape by going out to sea; they were pinned.

On the day I heard the news, all Rome heard it too. Another fleet had been lost. Tavius, half drowned, made it to shore and shouted into the wind, "I will win this war even if Neptune doesn't want me to!" Then he stood for a long time looking into the bay, which was filled with the bodies of his dead soldiers.

I could not go out this time and smile and pretend nothing dreadful had happened. On many Roman streets one could hear the sounds of mothers wailing for their dead sons. The loss of life dwarfed the first defeat, and now it was disaster piled on disaster. This was a horror, and everyone knew it. I could not even say, as I could have the first time ships were lost, that this resulted from Tavius receiving bad advice. In turning into the bay he had followed his own instincts.

Some street poet, aware of Tavius's fondness for gambling, made up a ditty for the occasion. I never saw the wit in it but knew it was repeated everywhere.

He took a beating twice at sea,
And threw two fleets away.
And now to achieve one victory,
He tosses dice all day.

Tavius came home, pale and exhausted, and muttered barely a word of greeting to me. He went into his study. I sat beside him while he stared at the wall. I asked him nothing. I feared he would shut me out entirely, tell me to go away. I could imagine him doing this out of shame. Two fleets, gods above, he had lost two fleets. Who, in all of Roman history, in such a little space of time, had ever lost two fleets?

Why did he have to turn into the bay? And why had he ever chosen to wage aggressive war on Sextus? Might there not have been an accommodation?

I did not feel honey sweet sitting there beside my husband. No, when I thought of the decisions he had made that had brought us to this pass, I could have slapped him. I imagined him sinking, and me going down with him. To say he had been weakened did not begin to tell it.

It was too late to sue for peace with Sextus. Tavius had to somehow garner a victory after this debacle. Only victory could justify the losses his forces had suffered. I knew enough of recent history to foresee the pattern events might take otherwise. Another defeat, and the army would begin to abandon him. I was certain if he were deposed from power, he would not survive it. He would be hunted down and either murdered by his enemies or given no honorable alternative but to take his own life. And I would leave my children to their father's care and do what Portia had done, what my mother had done. I, who had called Tiberius Nero a coward when he spoke of suicide.

I sat there filled with fear. Then Tavius gave a deep, hollow cough. Strangely, the sound of that cough was all I needed to remember how desperately I loved him. I studied his face. He looked as I had never seen him look before—empty, inconsolable. His pain was mine. He could have lost a hundred fleets and I would have loved him.

No, I thought, *we will not die. Neither of us will die. Whatever happens, we will both live. Somehow. I will not allow him to be destroyed. I will not.*

I said, "This is only a testing time. It befalls heroes on the path to their destiny. The gods want to see what you are made of."

When he spoke his voice seemed to come from a great distance. "Do you truly believe that?"

"I'm sure of it. Watch. The war is about to turn in your favor. Lepidus has landed in Sicily, hasn't he? And Agrippa's fleet wasn't touched by the storm. You will be victorious. You've only to keep faith." I thought of the hen that had dropped from the sky with a laurel twig in its mouth. Surely the gods had promised us victory.

"Only a few days ago I heard from the steward at that wonderful villa of yours. Do you know, the laurel cutting has taken root? And the hen hatched a brood of chicks. Remember, I wondered if she would even live?"

"But that omen was for you, not me."

I shook my head. "My fate is not separate from yours. I want no separate fate. I do not want it, and I will not allow it."

People commonly assumed that I had left Tiberius Nero for Caesar Octavianus out of opportunistic motives. Maybe Tavius himself believed I adored him in good part for his shining success. If so, he began at this moment to see that my love for him was different from what he had imagined it was—fathoms deeper.

I had sensed up until then that he would not want me to touch him. He seemed walled off. Now the barrier between us dissolved. In a perfectly natural and easy way I took his hand. "You will win," I said. "Don't you see? Nothing else is possible."

He said in a low voice, "You can't imagine what that storm was like. The screaming men, the sinking ships. The water. There was so much water—coming from the sky, from the sea. I don't know how anyone survived."

"Remember you told me once we would both be hard to drown? That's the truth," I said. "And you didn't drown, did you?"

"No. It's Sextus—the one who calls himself the son of Neptune—who's going to drown." There was something forced and tentative about Tavius's voice. But still, he sounded more alive.

My role in our unhappy circumstance was to be that hen with the victory laurel in her beak, fluttering down from the sky. "Of course the war will continue?"

"What else? Unless I take Sicily before winter sets in, it's over for us."

>>>>>>>

There was a gladiatorial exhibition a few days later in the amphitheater at Rome. We went because we nearly always attended these events, and did not want it to look as if we were hiding.

Tavius and I had our own private box at the amphitheater, which saved me from sitting with the other women in the back where I could see nothing. I enjoyed the bouts, but I preferred it when no one died. So did Tavius. And particularly at this moment in our lives, with our own existence so precarious, neither of us wanted to look at killing.

The first match was exciting. The defeated gladiator fought reasonably well, and at the end, with a sword to his throat, raised his hand to appeal for mercy. Tavius made the downward gesture with his thumb that indicated the sword was to be lowered. So both fighters survived.

The second fight was tedious, repetitive thrust and parry, on and on. People went to buy refreshments; they nibbled their lunches. I could smell sausages and cheap wine. My mind wandered miles away. Then a shout rose in the amphitheater and brought my attention back to the sands beneath us. The contest was over. The wounded fighter dropped his sword and sank to his knees—injured, but probably not mortally. He raised his hand toward Tavius in the box.

Half the arena crowd shouted for death and half for life. A senator named Corvus was sitting with us. "Death this time, I think," he murmured to Tavius. "Really, the fight was dreadful." Maybe Tavius was feeling squeamish, and that was why he lowered his thumb again. A mutter rose from those in the crowd who had wanted death.

Next, a gladiator with a dagger and shield and another with a trident and net walked out onto the sand. The muttering turned to shouts of "Neptune, Neptune!" I felt a chill up the length of my spine. Of course, Neptune is often depicted holding a trident. But everyone knew Neptune was the patron deity of Sextus Pompey.

Buoyed by the cheering, the trident man caught his opponent in his net and skewered him like a sardine. Those who wanted death got it. The victor pulled his weapon away, with the fallen gladiator's guts on it. Blood stained the sand. The victor waved his trident, guts flying in the air. A roar rose from the amphitheater. Tavius and I dutifully clapped. And then a good part of the crowd began to chant, "Neptune, Neptune, Neptune!" The chanting had a menacing sound, like distant thunder. It was not a tribute to the victorious gladiator.

Romans liked victors. They didn't like commanders who lost fleets. If the people of Rome had been offered a free choice between Sextus and Tavius at that moment, they would have taken Neptune's son.

The chanting grew louder. Anger and scorn darkened the faces turned toward us. I sat still and looked straight ahead. Any other action could be read as weakness. My heart raced. I half expected people to rush us in our box. In that event, would Tavius's bodyguards, who were standing by, be enough to protect us? Or would we be torn limb from limb?

Corvus spoke in a low voice, addressing Tavius. "My advice is to send some soldiers over there—see on the right where they're doing the most yelling? You have to shut them up."

I was terrified that Tavius would do what this fool suggested, and that would be just the thing to provoke a riot. Before I could say a word, Tavius managed a laugh. "My friend, I wouldn't dream of it. They're free Romans. Who am I to tell them not to chant for Neptune?"

Two new gladiators walked out on the sand, distracting the crowd. When they began to fight, the chanting stopped.

"Can we go?" I whispered to Tavius.

"No, dear," he said. "Not quite yet." He smiled at me. Anybody looking at him would have thought we were talking about the most pleasant subject imaginable. "If we run like prey, some of them may follow like a wolf pack," he whispered. "We are going to sit here and watch this contest. Then, if everything is peaceful, we will leave—very slowly."

"Of course, you're right," I said.

"Keep smiling, my love."

I watched the next contest without seeing it. The defeated gladiator must have fought well, because when he lay on his back raising his hand for mercy, almost all the crowd wanted him spared. Tavius acceded, and while the amphitheater roared its approval and the two gladiators went staggering off the sand, he and I rose. My mouth was dry. We exited the box with slow, deliberate steps, bodyguards on all sides of us, both of us smiling until we were out of there.

>>>>>>>

As we rode back home in our litter, my terror subsided, replaced by anger. A part of me was screaming at Tavius, *I keep telling you, you don't pay enough attention to your popularity with the people. Look what comes of it. "Neptune, Neptune, Neptune!" What have you done for Rome? Repaired a few temples. Why aren't there more public improvements for citizens to point at and admire? If you had followed my counsel, at least set up fire brigades, the people would love you, and maybe they'd stand by you now. Maybe they wouldn't be chanting for that miserable pirate Sextus!*

I bit my tongue. It was not the time for us to have an argument. And the Roman people had at times abandoned even the leaders who had done the most for them, when their stars fell. Nothing but victory could offset a double defeat. Yet it seemed to me Tavius had done little to win the people's love, and it was worth having. In a crucial moment it might serve as some protection.

The next day, in soft and gentle tones I told Tavius more or less what I thought. He looked at me blankly and said, "Worry about fire brigades now? I am fighting a war."

You are losing a war. I took a breath. "I want the people to love you, as I love you."

"Sometimes you're wearying to be with," Tavius said. "All my resources—*all* my resources—are going into cobbling together another fleet for Sicily."

We were in Tavius's study. He picked up a tablet from the stack of correspondence that lay on his writing table and began reading it. To my annoyance, he would do that sometimes, start reading while I stood there. It was his way of telling me I was dismissed.

I ruffled his hair, as I might have with one of my sons. When he looked up, I smiled at him and caressed his neck, then ran my hand under his tunic and stroked his shoulder. He put down the tablet he was reading. I could feel his hand wandering under my stola, caressing my knee, moving up my thigh. A shiver went through me.

Shortly after this, I finally got my public fire brigades, or I should say, Rome got them. And not long afterward, Tavius addressed the Senate about a vast new program of public works he had in mind, designed to benefit Rome's citizenry—though it was as yet only in the planning stage, to be carried out once Sicily was taken. This was in line with my thinking and pleased me greatly.

⋙⋙

Soon he took leave of me again. On a doleful morning, I stood just inside our entranceway, again about to see Tavius go off to fight Sextus, feeling in the depths of my heart that another defeat would doom us both. I was determined not to let my courage waver. *Come home victorious,* I intended to say with confidence, just as the wives of Roman generals had said it from time immemorial.

But I said something else. "Beloved, if it is possible for you to show mercy in this fight, please show it. Even to Sextus—if you can spare his life, I beg you to do it."

Given the situation, the last thing Tavius expected was to be asked to show mercy to Sextus. At first he looked disconcerted and amazed. Then his eyes lit up. "Well, I see you truly have faith in my victory."

"I do," I said. "And I believe the gods love mercy. They will favor you if you are merciful."

A small, lopsided smile played around his mouth. "You truly believe that?"

"Yes."

Tavius looked at me the way loving husbands look at wives when they talk foolishness. He embraced and kissed me, and once again, he left.

⋙⋙

I saved the letters Tavius wrote me when he was away. Frequently they were no more than scrawls on waxed tablets. The writing eventually faded into the wax. But sometimes he would write me a longer letter, on papyrus. He was not writing for history, only for me; the letters employed bits of cipher and private code, and they were frank—even more candid, sometimes, than he might have been if we were face-to-face. When I read his letters I imagined him in some miserable army tent, after a day of maintaining a posture of might and infallibility. He longed to drop the mask, and he could do that with me.

My love, I trust this finds you well and also the children. By the time you read this, you will have heard the final outcome of the Sicilian campaign. But knowing you, you want the entire story. You would certainly worm it all out of me if I were there beside you, as I wish I were.

I've often wanted you here so I could make love to you. But how much time can even the most ardent lover spend in conjugal embrace? And how many hours when I'm home do we spend talking? Here I'm surrounded by friends and supporters, but it still feels as if I have no one to talk to. Right now more than anything I wish you were here just so I could talk to you.

I imagine you saying, "The war, Tavius. I want to hear about the war." All right, but don't expect a heroic tale.

We had an excellent plan, and everything did begin well. I gave the command of most of my warships to Agrippa so he could keep Sextus busy and distracted. I filled other vessels with troops, planning to land them in Sicily and join Lepidus's forces there. Agrippa engaged the enemy at sea and won a victory. However, Sextus's forces withdrew in good order, and when I started to cross from Scolacium in Italy to Sicily, they were ready to pounce.

We fought two engagements. My ill luck at sea is one constant in a world in flux. Many of my galleys were captured; others were burned. My own ship sank. I climbed into a small, barely seaworthy craft and, with this boat taking in water and Sextus's forces giving chase, managed to make it back to the shore of Italy.

I had only my armor bearer, Gnaeus, with me, and distant shouts told me I was being hunted by many men. I had resolved at all costs not to be taken alive and while we were still at sea had induced Gnaeus to swear a sacred oath to kill me if I were at the point of being captured. I suspected my fate was now at hand. Gnaeus and

I darted along the beach, crouching in the forlorn hope of not being seen. Incredibly, a couple of friendly peasants came sprinting onto the beach out of nowhere and offered me help. They said they knew who I was and were admirers of my father. I had my doubts, but all I could do was trust them.

They led me to their little fishing boat. Gnaeus and I scrambled aboard, and they took us to a point on shore where some of my own troops were gathered. So there I was, amazed to be among friends and even more amazed to be alive. I was able to launch a ship and finally got across to Sicily. Agrippa's and Lepidus's forces had been victorious. By the time I arrived, they were in possession of most of the island.

Livia, my love, I confide in you as I would in my own soul. Let me briefly tell the rest. Sextus, with only the north tip of Sicily in his hands, decided to stake everything on a great sea battle. I was arming, about to go out and lead my forces, when . . . I don't know what happened. I found myself sprawled on my cot. Gnaeus stood over me, wringing his hands, and informed me that I had passed out.

My strength had all drained away, at a most crucial moment. Every time I tried to rise, I got dizzy and collapsed. I finally just lay there in a daze. Even the memory of this is absolutely awful.

Agrippa came running into the tent, wondering where I was. He has always been a kind friend, and when he saw my condition, he said, "You probably have a fever, so don't strain yourself. All you have to do is give me your command to commence hostilities."

I told him he had my command.

People will tell all kinds of stories about why I didn't take part in the final battle for Sicily. If you can think of something better to say than that I got sick, I would be grateful.

Agrippa sailed off to confront Sextus without me. Fortune favored him in a remarkable way. Early on, one—only one—of Sextus's many ships got rammed and surrendered. Some of our men raised a paean of victory, and it spread to our other ships and finally to our troops watching from the shore. This song—that was all it was—shook the confidence of Sextus's whole navy, and a rout began. One of Sextus's two admirals fell on his sword; the other surrendered.

The commander of Sextus's ground troops promptly surrendered too. Agrippa granted quarter to the common soldiers, which I'm sure will please you. He informed the officers that they would have to apply to me for pardon. I had their heads chopped off. No, dearest, I didn't. I emerged from my stupor long enough to wave a benevolent hand and pardon all of them. Now aren't you happy?

What, you wonder, happened to Neptune's son? He packed his close friends on a small boat, and according to our best intelligence, he is going east. I think he will fall into Antony's hands, and that will be it for him. I'm sorry if that makes you sad.

When I recovered from my fever, or whatever it was—the camp physicians scratched their heads—I leaped off my cot assuming I owned Sicily. I quickly discovered, however, that Lepidus had no intention of honoring his agreement to cede Sicily to me. We prepared for yet another battle. I sent out some spies, though, and got welcome reports about the mood of Lepidus's army. Suffice to say, his troops did not love him.

There are times when you have to throw the dice. I suspected they would desert him for me, if I made the right gesture. So I recruited some volunteers from my cavalry and rode to Lepidus's camp. We left the horses at the fringe of the encampment and with a half dozen companions I went walking through the lines, smiling amiably. I was recognized, and soldiers saluted me.

Unfortunately, someone told Lepidus what was happening. He sent a squad of loyal officers to repel this invasion of his camp. My men and I went running out of Lepidus's camp. I could hear the ring of mocking laughter behind me, but no one gave chase. Back in my own camp, I sat in my tent on my cot with my head in my hands. I thought a battle would have to be fought. Then Agrippa came in smiling and said, "They're all deserting and coming over to us."

A while later, Lepidus surrendered. When he entered my tent and began to fall down to clasp my knees, I grabbed him and told him that was unnecessary. I gave him some wine because he looked about to faint. "I have Sicily now, and expect you to cede North Africa too," I told him. He gave me his pledge to retire from public life, and I shipped him home to his villa on the Italian coast.

My darling Livia, I imagine you reading this and thinking, "What a malleable husband I have. I ask him to be merciful, and all of a sudden he is sparing a viper like Lepidus." But you know the truth is more complicated than that, don't you?

Do the gods really favor the merciful? My reading of history does not uphold that point of view, though it's an appealing belief that reflects well on you. I don't have your gentle spirit. But I feel as you feel—as all Rome feels, by now—that all this mutual slaughter has got to end. I'm sick of it. We're all sick of it.

My niece's birth delighted me mainly because it made Octavia happy. But politically speaking, it's good Antony and I have become linked by blood, through little Antonia. Remember that map I once drew you? Sextus was on it, and so was Lepidus, and coming in from the west, marauding Gauls. It's a simpler map now. Antony and I are the only ones left.

Tavius took a month settling affairs in Sicily, and then he came home. I could not let him out of my arms. He said the tale of the Sicilian war was not heroic. To me it was. Tavius had won a war necessary to our survival. In addition, he had spared every life it was possible to spare. The people of Rome, especially the nobility, would now see him in a wholly different light—that of a restrained and judicious ruler. To prevent the spilling of more Roman blood, he had gone bare-handed into the camp of an opposing army. What act, in all our history, surpassed that in courage?

The Senate fell over itself voting him honors. They even commissioned a gold-plated public statue of him.

His fainting spell in Sicily worried me, though he told me there had been no recurrence. One day his trusted physician, Fustinius, happened to visit our home to attend a sick servant while Tavius was out. I seized the chance to invite him into my study and question him about Tavius's health. In particular, I demanded to know why he had passed out in Sicily.

The physician equivocated and rubbed his chin but finally said, "Well, Caesar was born with a sensitive constitution. Rich foods, any uncleanness—what you or I might easily tolerate has an adverse effect. Exposure to heat and cold worsens his condition. And of course worry, apprehension, and mental burdens . . ." He made a vague gesture with his hands.

I stared at him. Was he saying Tavius had fainted in Sicily because of mental burdens? "You know who my husband is. You do realize he bears enormous mental burdens every day of his life?"

"Yes. It's not what I would recommend."

I could not change the circumstances of Tavius's life. At this time, my interest in brewing curative potions increased, for what else could I do but try to minister to him as best I could? Malicious people would later read a sinister meaning into my study of medicinal plants. But I intended only to help my husband.

On a glorious day in late autumn, he stood on the Rostra, the stone speakers' platform from which our foremost leaders addressed the citizenry. People filled the Forum to overflowing. Cheering throngs stretched out on all sides of him, a sea of adulation, waiting to hear him report the victorious outcome of the Sicilian war. There was no place for a wife at such a gathering. But I had a runner stationed on the fringe of the square, to come back at once and tell me how he was received. No one chanted "Neptune, Neptune!" "Caesar!" was the name the multitude shouted. And "Imperator!"—a title reserved for our greatest military commanders. When the crowd quieted, Tavius spoke the words that made all Rome delirious with joy. He said, "The civil wars are over."

He believed these words when he spoke them. His thoughts were filled with plans for governing a land at peace.

Chapter 13

We finally moved to the Palatine Hill. Our new house was just what I wanted it to be—not larger than an ordinary senator's, nothing to excite malignant envy, but beautiful, with glorious murals on the walls, a huge study for Tavius to work in, and another study, almost as large, for me. On each side of our front door, Tavius ordered a laurel tree planted, symbols of victory. We grew them from cuttings of a tree that had sprouted from the stem the hen had held in her beak when she fell from the eagle's claws. Privately we gave the trees silly names, Pompo and Tatilla, and pretended they were a married couple. Out of war's shadow, we were in the mood for such nonsense.

Tavius generously rewarded those who had served him well. The peasants who had rescued him when he was hunted by Sextus's forces did handsomely. Maecenas gained a large estate in Sicily. But no one deserved more of Tavius's bounty than Agrippa, and no one received more. Extensive Sicilian holdings made him an extremely wealthy man.

I was present when Tavius told Agrippa he was to oversee a vast renovation of Rome's aqueducts, sewers, and public buildings. Agrippa just nodded.

"You will be city aedile," Tavius said. "That's the proper title, given what your new responsibilities will be."

Agrippa nodded again. Titles did not matter to him. He began to ask questions of the most practical kind. How many buildings would be rebuilt? How extensive a sewer renovation did Tavius have in mind? He and Tavius were soon engrossed in a long, technical discussion.

Then Tavius said, "There will be a great new temple for all the gods, a Pantheon. You should put your name on it. We'll have 'Marcus Agrippa built this' carved in stone where everyone can see it. How will that be?"

"That will be fine." Agrippa smiled. Then he went back to talking about drainage ducts.

"He will do everything I asked him to do," Tavius said to me later. "And watch—he'll do it all superbly."

I said I did not doubt it. Agrippa excelled in every practical art except, happily, political maneuvering. He was as faithful as a good hound. The thing was to keep him that way.

A few days later Tavius and I sat together in our large and lush new garden. "Do you know what Agrippa needs?" I said. "A wife."

Tavius gave me a quizzical look.

"I know just the right one. She is rich, attractive, and well-born. And"—my eyes roamed across the garden, to where a slave was trimming the hedges so no branches stuck out—"she is personally loyal to me." The last thing I wanted was to see Agrippa marry some fool who would try to sway his allegiance.

"Who is this paragon?"

"Caecilia."

"The one whose brother I pardoned?"

I nodded. Her husband had recently died and left her a young widow. Though frosty at our first meeting, she had become one of my dearest friends. And she was wise. She had seen men in her family destroyed by misplaced ambition; she would never urge any foolish course on her husband. Also, she had the discernment to look past Agrippa's lowly pedigree to his true worth. "A highborn wife will give Agrippa the luster he needs," I said.

Before long, they married. Both thought they had made a good bargain and were grateful to Tavius and me, just as I had hoped.

There are periods when life is so pleasant one can almost imagine the world is sun-dappled and safe. At this moment, everything I touched seemed golden. My new house was a short stroll from Tiberius Nero's residence, so I lived close to my sons. Tiberius Nero had not remarried; people whispered that a slave girl he bought himself could pass for a twin of me at fifteen. When I glimpsed her I did not see the resemblance, except that she had red hair. Be that as it may, Tiberius Nero treated me as a friend, and he was a reliable supporter to Tavius in the Senate. It pleased him that other senators deferred to him because of his ties to power.

No one ever lost by giving Tavius or me their loyalty, not the highest, not the lowest. I began a practice of setting free, after a time, each of the women who attended me personally; Pelia, who rose to a position of authority in my household, was the first of these. Rubria, of course, was freeborn. It frustrated me that she, to whom I owed a huge debt, wanted little I could give her. I rewarded her well in a material way for the care she gave my sons. She thanked me, but I noted her basic indifference. Then one day she said to me, quite shyly, "Do you know who Marcus Ortho is?"

We sat in the courtyard of Tiberius Nero's house. My sons, whom I had come to see, were wrestling on the ground like lion cubs. I would have put a stop to it if I had feared little Drusus would get hurt. But Tiberius, who was big for his five years and could be rough with boys his own age, always took care not to injure his brother.

"Marcus Ortho?" I looked at Rubria questioningly. "The name seems familiar, but I can't quite place it."

"He is a member of Caesar's bodyguard," she told me. Then she blushed.

At last I had found the reward she desired.

Because Rubria was alone in the world and my dependent, I investigated Ortho. He was temperate, honest, and, I learned, even had a good head for figures. So I took charge of the practical arrangements for the marriage. Ortho left the army, and I set him up in a jewel-importing business, which thrived. He allowed Rubria to continue to oversee the care of my sons. It was a happy arrangement for all concerned.

Around this time Tavius's health improved. Perhaps this was due to the curative potions I brewed him, or maybe respite from war and turmoil helped Tavius more than any drink could do. He coughed and wheezed less; he took more time to relax, and joyously welcomed his sister, Octavia, when she arrived in Rome. She had been dispatched by Mark Antony as he prepared to leave for Parthia, and she moved into his huge mansion on the Palatine. Along with her came her own children and Antony's two boys.

Octavia still did not like me, but one day as we sat together at the chariot races she smiled with unexpected warmth. "I'm so happy," she said. She glanced at Tavius, who stood out of earshot, talking to a senator. "But I feel embarrassed about telling *him* the news. Isn't that silly? He'll surely want to know, and be glad for me. Still, I'm not used to discussing such matters with my brother. Maybe you'll tell him for me?"

"Tell him what?"

"Oh, didn't I say?" She laughed. "I'm expecting another baby."

It annoyed me that she was too delicate to tell this to Tavius herself; and for some time I had been fretting because I had yet to conceive a child by my beloved. We had been married for two years, but I had been pregnant on our wedding day, and Tavius had been gone for months at a time. Still, the lack of a child worried me. So when Tavius came back to where we sat, I told him coolly, "Your sister is with child again."

Octavia looked appalled; no doubt she wanted more fuss and ceremony in the way I conveyed the news. But Tavius smiled and kissed her.

This pregnancy, even I had to admit, was an excellent omen. When it became generally known that Octavia would again bear Antony a child, everyone thought their marital felicity almost guaranteed civil harmony. Rome wanted no more war between countrymen, and so Rome rejoiced.

One cloud had appeared in the azure sky of my happiness. Month after month, I had my hope to become pregnant dashed. No one thinks a man's seed is to blame in such a case. And Tavius's brief, chilly marriage to Scribonia had resulted in Julia's birth. So surely the fault was mine. I ached to have Tavius's child, longed to hold that small, warm bundle in my arms. I resolved not to speak of this to him. And yet one night, in bed, the words slipped out, bald as my announcement of Octavia's pregnancy.

"Tavius, I want a baby."

"It's just a matter of time."

"I hope so." I snuggled up against him and said lightly, "Otherwise you'll have to divorce me."

"What are you talking about?"

"An empire needs an heir," I said. "You need a son."

"Livia, how old am I?"

"You are twenty-six years old."

"How old are you?"

"Twenty-one," I said.

"I would say we have a little time left to get an heir," he said. "Will you explain this to me: Why do women conjure up difficulties where none exist?"

"Because women are wise, and they see the future coming down the road long before men see it."

"Oh. I thought it was because they delight in misery." He pulled me closer. "But if you feel we should try harder to get an heir, I'm all for redoubling our efforts."

So we laughed and made love, and put the subject aside.

⋙⋙

A day is a day whether you are a washerwoman or a baker or the ruler of Rome. You can't increase the number of hours. People laughed when they heard Tavius used two barbers, that he would have one man shave one side of his face while another did the other side. They had no notion what the press of time was like for him. He had so much to accomplish.

We had so much to accomplish. Increasingly, I handled correspondence from provincial governors on my own. I often met with senators on Tavius's behest. He could not do everything, be everywhere, himself. And he knew he could rely on me.

I did not see much of my sister. I helped her, of course; her husband became even wealthier than he had been before. But Secunda moved in a different circle than I did. Political life frightened her. When I broached the idea of elevating her husband to the Senate she looked at me with such horror that I dropped the subject and never raised it again.

She often did not even tell acquaintances that I was her sister. I tried not to take that personally. In a way, the inconspicuous role she had chosen was useful to me. I had recruited a group of confidants who told me what people were saying about Tavius and me. Not informers: Neither Tavius nor I wished to punish people for their opinions. But I never forgot the crowd in the amphitheater chanting "Neptune! Neptune!" I kept an eye on the public mood. Secunda, who chatted with women in the market and dined with merchants and tradesmen, became a source of information for me.

"Do people talk much about the fire brigades?" I asked one day. We sat in my garden. I had my boys visiting that afternoon. Tiberius, Drusus, Julia, and Secunda's little girl, Decimia, were all at play around us—or rather, Drusus and the girls played. Tiberius had a stack of child-sized javelins and had set up a target near the rosebushes, fifteen feet away. As serious as an adult, he practiced his javelin throw.

"Oh, yes, everyone praises them," Secunda said. "But . . ."

"But what?"

"Well, I've heard some people say they're like your private army."

"My army? Not Caesar's, mine?"

Secunda smiled faintly. She took a certain pleasure in bringing me bad news. "Why, practically every time a building catches on fire, you're there with the fire brigades, aren't you?"

I did often go to watch the brigades fight fires in the tenements. I would bring gifts of money, clothes, and food to people who lost their homes. Women and children, especially, would crowd around me, as eager for a kind word as for the coins or material goods I could give them. Tavius could not go out to fires himself, because he could not take the smoke. But I wanted people to feel that he cared about them.

"I have a special sympathy for anyone who has to flee from fire, because I was in that situation myself," I said.

Secunda pursed her lips. "I've heard you even give speeches to the fire brigades."

"I just say a few words sometimes to encourage them." A recent memory came to mind: standing on a pile of rubble, surrounded by burly men with soot-stained faces who cheered as I praised them for extinguishing a raging fire. Gods above, was I turning into Fulvia? "Secunda, what do people say about me? Not about Caesar, but about me?"

"Oh, some say you're good and generous . . ."

"And others disagree?"

She shrugged. I could tell she was enjoying my discomfort.

"Secunda, tell me what they say!"

She leaned forward so her face was only inches from mine. "If you must know, they say you're cold and power-hungry, and you give commands and Caesar obeys. That before he goes to talk to you, he writes down questions and then he writes down your answers. That your marriage is no true marriage but like an alliance between two men."

I kept my expression impassive, not wanting to show I was hurt. Tavius did write notes before and after some of our discussions, as he did with his other advisors. It was for the sake of clarity and order, and to make good use of his time and mine. But he certainly did not obey my commands—though truthfully he did little politically without asking me what I thought. It dismayed me that people should think ill of me for this, though knowing Rome I might have expected it.

Was I cold? Maybe at times I appeared so. For if I sometimes granted people's requests, at other times I had to turn them down; and I cultivated a contained, authoritative manner.

"When I first married Tavius, do you know what I was afraid of? That people would remember the circumstances under which we wed and make up salacious stories about me, which would besmirch my husband. So I have been careful about how I dress, and I never so much as glance at an attractive man in public." My voice trembled. "And so people say I'm made of ice, my marriage is not even a marriage, and I only love power."

A look of sympathy crossed Secunda's face, just for a moment. "For heaven's sake, don't get upset. What does it matter what people say or think? They have to bow to you anyway."

"I do a great deal for the people's welfare," I said. "Is it peculiar that I'd like some appreciation?"

"Appreciation from the Roman people? Don't you remember Father saying that the people never appreciate their benefactors?"

I looked away and watched as Tiberius hurled a javelin and hit the target dead center. "Very good, darling," I called. "You have wonderful aim." He did not even glance in my direction, just shrugged and picked up another javelin. What a grim little man he was.

"Do you ever remember Father and Mother?" Secunda asked me.

"Of course I do. What a strange question."

"You never mention them."

"I mourn for them always, in my heart."

"Do you?"

"Of course. How can you ask?"

"I just wonder sometimes."

I could taste unshed tears in the back of my throat. It was as if a trapdoor under my feet had opened up. It had taken so little to open it. All Secunda had had to do was say, *Do you remember Father and Mother?*

Can they see me now? I wondered. *And if they do, what do they see? A daughter who betrayed them, a power-hungry woman made of ice?*

Drusus came and climbed into my lap. "Are you sad, Mama?" he asked, looking at me with his beautiful dark eyes.

Would my parents recoil at the sight of me now? Maybe they would only be amazed by the shape my life had taken and wonder how they had come to have such an unlikely creature for a daughter. I gazed at my two sons, and I could not account for either one of them—not Tiberius, who silently gravitated to the tools of war; not Drusus, who was so gentle.

I tossed my head, said, "Mama's not the least bit sad," and kissed my little boy.

⋙⋙

On his flight to the east, Sextus Pompey had taken enough gold with him to raise three legions. He offered the services of this army to the Parthian king against whom Antony was about to embark on war. One of Antony's generals marched against Sextus, captured and executed him, on Antony's orders. He deserved a better fate, and I pitied him. But I was relieved he no longer constituted even a remote threat.

Sextus left one child, a small daughter in the care of relatives in Rome. I resolved that, from a distance, I would watch over this little girl, and insofar as I could, smooth her path in life. I did this for the same reason that I aided the people of Sparta who had once helped Tiberius Nero and me. Under Tavius, Rome treated Sparta with special benevolence. It was a matter of repaying my old debts.

Here I was a young woman who just a few years before had cowered in a cave, but I never thought that Rome's dealings with Sparta might be none of my business. The moment when I almost wept in my sister's presence—that was rare. For I loved what I was doing, loved who I had become. I did not pause often to look behind at where I had been. The role I played in Tavius's government felt completely natural to me. It was the limitations imposed upon me as a woman that seemed unnatural. When I met senators, I felt myself their equal in mind and heart. I even thought I would have made a far better senator than some of them—but of course that was a laughable notion. Even in the private sphere, I felt myself hemmed in. The little inconvenience of not being able to independently administer my own dower property continued to irk me. Why must my husband be my guardian?

Of course I had far more important concerns. I worried that Antony, if he conquered Parthia, would be much more powerful than Tavius. He might seek to diminish Tavius's role in the government of the empire. I also feared a growing menace on Italy's northern border, a savage people called the Illyrians who raided our towns. The thought of another war brewing—even war against barbarian tribes, not other Romans—put my teeth on edge.

From time to time, I worried also about keeping my husband's adoration. One evening at the theater I noticed Tavius looking at a pretty young woman. She turned toward him, and they exchanged smiles. I had the feeling they were not strangers. And Tavius was always noticeably friendly with Maecenas's wife, Terentilla. Then too, sometimes at dinner parties, he and a certain senator's wife would talk in voices no one else could hear.

When we returned from the theater or the dinner, I would turn over in my mind what I should do. I imagined a conversation. *Why were you talking to her?* I would ask Tavius. Or, *Why did you smile the way you did?* He would stare at me. *What do you mean, why did I smile?* I would lose dignity, just by raising the subject. For no wife could ensure her husband's fidelity, even if he were a peasant. How, if he governed Rome?

Probably I could have numbered on one hand all the high-ranking Roman men who coupled only with their wives. Could

Tavius be counted in that number? Truthfully, I did not know. I did remarkably well at banishing that question from my mind. I sensed if I went down the other path, if I demanded assurances, I could only do my marriage harm, and so I held my peace.

Tavius came home to me each night, that was certain. We hardly ever even dined apart. He made love to me as passionately as ever. And he did not reproach me for my slowness in conceiving a child.

I watched Octavia's body swell with Antony's baby, while my courses continued, regular and unfailing. I asked the gods why she was fruitful when I was not. When Octavia gave birth to another daughter, she showed some disappointment, for she had wanted to give Antony a son. Still, here was another child, pretty and thriving, to bind her and her husband together; and Antony had male heirs already. Did I only imagine that a wistful look crossed Tavius's face when he saw Antony's two sons?

Octavia and I were so different—not only because at this time fortune favored her in the matter of children. At heart she had as little taste for politics as my own sister did, but she could not follow Secunda's example and keep her distance. She was Tavius's sister and Antony's wife. Now that she was in Rome, she appeared with Tavius and me on public occasions. People would always shout her name. Her role in securing the peace won Roman hearts.

While people watched, we formed a happy threesome. In private moments, strains surfaced. I recall a dinner—just Tavius, Octavia, and me at my villa at Prima Porta. "My villa"—Tavius smiled when I used those words. "It's so kind of you to let me visit your villa," he would joke.

I had decided we needed a country home near the city and had discovered this place. The location was perfect—a few miles from Rome, conveniently close but still far enough away to offer us some privacy as well as relief from the city noise and smells. I carried through the negotiation with the owner and paid for the villa with funds from my dowry. I hired and supervised contractors to improve the building and grounds. So naturally I felt the villa was mine.

"I was very annoyed today," I said, my mind on renovations. "The painter—the one who is doing the murals for the summer dining room—is a genius, so there's no question of replacing him. But he said he wanted approval from my husband before he would seal the contract."

"What effrontery," Tavius said, the corners of his mouth twitching.

We were in the winter dining room, already fully furnished. It was in the warmest part of the house. I had kept in mind Tavius's sensitivity to temperature while setting out a new arrangement for the rooms, for my chief concerns in renovating the villa were his ease and pleasure. Here, out of the public eye, we could allow ourselves the luxury we avoided in Rome. Though Tavius never sought out luxury, he liked it well enough if you offered it to him. Now he sprawled comfortably on a couch outfitted with soft cushions of red silk.

I knew he would love the summer dining room when it was finished. The artist had an uncanny ability to paint flowers, trees, and birds so they all looked real and alive, especially the birds. He would give us a dining room that looked like a fantastic garden aviary. Unfortunately, he was not only brilliantly talented but boorish.

"Yes, I would call it effrontery," I said.

"Take my seal and seal the contract, and tell the painter I looked at it," Tavius said.

"I will do that," I said, "but I find it rather sickening. If I were going to pay him with your money, it would be another matter, but it's my money that's involved."

Tavius clucked his tongue.

I felt a prickle of anger run down my spine. "Do you know what I want you to do for me?" I said. "Pass a law releasing me from any man's financial guardianship. After all, Vestal Virgins are free of guardianship. If they can be, why can't I?" The virgins who tended the sacred fire in the temple of the goddess Vesta had many special privileges.

Tavius munched a bit of cheese.

If a voice in my mind whispered that I was verging toward hubris, the very hubris I had once warned Tavius about, I ignored it. For I had been slighted, and it seemed so unfair that I—I, who helped to administer an empire—could not put my own seal on a simple contract. Oh, looking back now I see I was full of myself at that moment, full of myself as the young can often be. Even my sister's words to me about how I was regarded had gone right out of my head. "I am serious," I said. "I would like you to pass a law. In return for all I do for you, and for Rome. All the load of work I carry. That's what I want. Is it so much to ask?"

Tavius drank some wine.

"You aren't in earnest?" Octavia said. "You're not asking my brother to pass a law for your exclusive benefit?"

"Forgive me, I was leaving you out, wasn't I?" I looked at Tavius. "It would be better if you included your sister in the law. After all, we are both wives of Rome's rulers and equal in rank."

"I would never want a law passed to set me above other women," Octavia said.

I tossed my head and did not reply. Her selfless virtue irritated me. I felt myself judged by her and had a perverse desire to live up to her bad opinion. Truly, Octavia had a talent for bringing out the worst in me.

"This is an academic discussion, because I am not passing any such law." Tavius leaned over the space in between our couches and kissed me. "I can't do it because it would make me look ridiculous. Just keep using my seal."

Our eyes met and held.

"Can you imagine what men would think if I passed a special law for my wife?" he demanded. "So she can buy and sell property without my permission?" A sarcastic edge in his voice, he added, "Forgive me, dear, I don't plan to make myself a laughingstock."

I said nothing. We went on staring at each other for a few more moments. Then I glanced away.

Octavia looked gratified to see me thwarted. "We need to discuss the legions for Antony," she said to Tavius. My foolishness had been dismissed, and now we would turn to important matters—her husband and what he wanted. "In his last letter to me, he asked when he could expect more troops."

"I sent him a thousand men."

"But you promised him twenty thousand," Octavia said.

"The situation has changed," Tavius said.

"But Tavius, dear, one must always keep a promise." Octavia spoke in the gentle, reproving tone she used to chide her children.

I laughed.

My sister-in-law turned toward me. "What do you find amusing?"

"We're not in your daughters' nursery. We're talking about legions here," I said. I thought of Perusia, Antony's double-dealing. A Roman city destroyed by Romans—because of the conflict Antony provoked and yet would not own up to. I remembered fleeing in terror from that city, carrying my baby son. Octavia had always been safe, everyone's cosseted darling, but had she closed her eyes, stopped up her ears? Where had she been these last years, if she thought nursery rules applied to Roman politics?

I feared that Tavius might actually accede to her wishes and act to his detriment just to please her. He all but worshipped his sister.

She looked at Tavius, her face tight. "You gave your word."

"I'll keep my word. Antony will have his twenty thousand soldiers. Eventually."

"But he is waging war against Parthia now."

"He sends constant reports of his victories to the Senate," Tavius said. "What does he need my soldiers for? He has enormous resources in the east. And the trouble in the north keeps getting worse. I'll soon be at war myself against the Illyrians."

"You expect me to write him that you said no?" Octavia looked as if she might weep. "If you don't honor your pledge, Antony will think you are hostile to him."

"I can't spare any legions now," Tavius said. He spoke in a strained voice.

"I think the Illyrians are only an excuse for refusing to keep your word," Octavia said. "And if you and Antony are not friends, where does that leave me and my little girls? Are we to be torn between the two of you? Antony is still my husband. I am his wife. That has not changed."

Tavius compressed his lips.

When Antony had dispatched Octavia and the children to Rome, it had seemed like a kindness. Tavius had thanked him for it—and been made to feel a fool. For it now appeared Antony had only wished to clear the way for his mistress. Before launching his invasion of Parthia, Antony had thrown himself back into the arms of Cleopatra. They made no attempt to hide the fact that they had resumed their love affair, and by the time he left for war she, who had previously borne him two children, had conceived again. Just days ago, we had heard of the birth of their new son, to whom Cleopatra gave the royal name Ptolemy.

Antony might have taken any number of mistresses, and Tavius would have shrugged so long as he did it quietly. In Velitrae, where Tavius's soul had been formed, wives were faithful and men sought their pleasures where they would. But seemliness mattered. No respectable man flaunted his concubines. He might look after his illegitimate children, but there would be no public noise about them; that would be an insult to his wife. This was decency, in Tavius's view. Contrast that to Cleopatra bearing her third child by Antony in sight of the whole world, a few months after Tavius's sister gave him a daughter.

In a shaking voice, Octavia said, "So you are saying you'll deliberately break your word. You won't give him those legions?" She turned toward me. "I blame you for this."

I gazed at her in amazement. "Me?"

"You are so selfish." Her mouth twisted with contempt. "'My villa!' 'My money!' I know the kind of advice you give my brother."

"Good advice. That's why he keeps taking it," I said. She was attacking me—for what? Not taking her childish view of the world? Distrusting Antony, a man who had amply earned my distrust?

Tavius broke in. "Octavia—"

Looking at him, she said in a hoarse voice, "Did it never trouble you, how easily she shed her husband and her children? Didn't that tell you what she was?"

Tavius said, "You need to remember you're talking about my wife."

"And I'm your sister. And when I beg you to keep your word to my husband—"

"I can't do it," Tavius said.

Octavia turned from him and gazed at me again. "You've alienated him from me."

"What a silly child you are," I said.

Her chin began to quiver. Her eyes were on Tavius. Maybe she wanted him to reproach me for calling her a silly child. When he did not, she began to weep, then rose and fled from the dining room. Tavius looked after her, pained.

"You're doing the right thing," I said to him. "You're about to go to war yourself. Antony will have all the power and wealth of Parthia soon, and he could never be trusted to be loyal even to his blood kin. Only a fool would send him more legions."

Tavius nodded, drawing in a deep breath. After a moment, he said, "He is not going to have all the power and wealth of Parthia."

"No?" I said.

"I've gotten reports his Parthian campaign has been one disaster after another. His dispatches to the Senate have been full of lies."

"Truly?" In the circumstances, that was good news. I rose and went to sit on Tavius's couch. "You're sure?"

He nodded. Then he said, "Of all the things I've had to do for Rome, marrying my sister to Antony is the one that turns my stomach."

I stroked his cheek. "I know. But you did it for the sake of peace. And she seems fond enough of him, doesn't she?" I might have alluded to the fact that Octavia's first loyalty was to Antony these days, not to Tavius, but I restrained myself.

"She is fond enough of him," Tavius agreed in a grim voice.

"Beloved, must you lead the army against the Illyrians yourself? Can't Agrippa do it without you?"

"You know the answer to that," Tavius said.

"You must be seen bravely leading your forces into battle," I said.

He pulled me down beside him, and kissed me, gently and almost tentatively. In a moment he was covering my throat with passionate kisses.

I caressed the back of his neck. It felt fragile, vulnerable. He would go to war again soon. That was a painful thought.

He cursed softly.

"What is it?" I said.

"I wish—"

"What?"

He shook his head. He had gone away from me. Maybe he was brooding over the situation with Octavia and Antony, or he was thinking of the coming war. I touched his hair. *Come back, come back.*

I looked into his remote eyes, and a question nudged me: *Does he love me as much as he once did?* Perhaps I wanted a proof of love, or a proof that I counted. What infants we can be, sometimes, wishing to be special.

"Tavius . . . I want charge of my own property. I can't explain to you why it matters, but it matters terribly. I know it's not easy, but don't you think we could find a way—?"

"It's impossible. I said no. What are you, a child who has to be taught the meaning of the word *no*?"

It was like crashing into a wall. I heard anger in his voice and dropped my eyes. "Forget I spoke," I said. When I looked up again, he was staring at me, his expression cold.

I knew I had been a fool, harrying him when he was already upset. I kissed him and sensed for a moment that he wished to push me away, but finally he yielded to my kiss and all was well again.

>>>>>>>

Oh, I did not give up the idea of independently handling my own property. I just had to think of how to do it without making

Tavius look ridiculous in the public eye. It took the better part of a month, but a scheme finally popped into my head—a series of actions that would not only accomplish my goal but serve purposes close to Tavius's heart. His own standing and that of his beloved sister would be enhanced. The popularity Antony still had with the Roman people would be undermined. Also, a heroine whose memory I revered—Cornelia, mother of the Gracchi—would receive an added measure of glory.

I had learned that sometimes it was better to talk over matters with Tavius in bed. "Octavia plays such an important role in maintaining Rome's peace," I whispered into his ear as we lay together in sweet darkness. "She is so well loved. Everyone would praise you if you gave her a special honor. That new portico near the Forum that you and Agrippa are building—I think you should call it the Portico of Octavia. It would be a touching gesture. When the portico is finished, you might make a speech saying she is just what a Roman woman should be—a selfless and virtuous wife and mother. People would be moved."

"My love," Tavius said, "we both know you have no fondness for my sister. So why are you saying this?"

"I respect how much she cares about peace between you and Antony. She deserves to be honored for that. The statue of Cornelia—the one that you are going to have restored—"

"The one you've been after me to have restored," Tavius said.

"I hate to see it looking shabby. If you had it repaired and put it in Octavia's portico, it would join the two together in a vision of ideal Roman womanhood."

"Yes? Go on."

"And then, after you make the speech at the opening of the portico, you could pass a law conferring the rights and protections of a Vestal Virgin upon Octavia. No one would mind. After all, everyone makes way for her, and she gets the best seats in the theater as it is. So people would say, *What's the difference?* But it would exalt her in everyone's eyes."

As soon as I had said the words "Vestal Virgin" I had felt Tavius shift on the bed. But I had gone on talking in the same easy tone. Now I could feel his breath, warm on my cheek. "You are relentless," he said.

"If I am, then I'm like you, aren't I?"

He said nothing.

I said, "Beloved, I'm only relentless about a very few things, the ones that matter."

He was leaning over me, silent. He ran his fingertip over each feature of my face, my nose, my lips, my chin, as if in the absence of light he needed to remind himself of what I looked like—as if he was trying to comprehend who and what I was. He said, "I wonder sometimes why I put up with you." The strange thing was that he said this lovingly.

I smiled into the darkness. "Why *do you* put up with me?"

"Well, you *are* beautiful. But you also have such an interesting mind."

I felt a thrill of pleasure. Nothing delighted me more than when he praised my mind. "It's a good plan, isn't it?"

"The more I build up my sister as Cornelia reborn," Tavius said, "the more people will despise Antony for mistreating her by flaunting his relationship with his Egyptian whore."

"Yes. Here you are, her loyal, devoted brother, and there he is, having children with a foreign queen."

"A foreign queen," Tavius repeated, and all his dislike for Antony was there in his voice. In a different tone, light, knowing, he asked, "What do you get out of this?"

"What do you think?"

"You're her equal in rank. No one will much notice while I speechify about my sister that the law will give you the rights of a Vestal Virgin too."

Including freedom from financial guardianship. "That would only be fair," I said. "And I want that. But Tavius—the people will love you for honoring your sister. For honoring Cornelia, who lives in their hearts and their memory. And that's what I desire most." Popularity with Rome's citizens was one of the pillars of his rule, a guarantee of his security. I saw it as absolutely necessary that he be loved—certainly loved more than Antony.

Not long after this, Tavius made a well-received speech in which he praised his sister as if she were the goddess of peace. The implicit question—how could any decent man prefer an alien like Cleopatra to this pearl of Roman womanhood?—did not even have to be stated. No one quibbled when Octavia got the sacrosanct status of a Vestal or seemed to care that I received it too.

Tavius took my suggestions and went further with them than I would have thought of doing. The chance to make Antony look bad was honey to him. Julius Caesar, while in the grip of passion for Cleopatra, had placed a statue of her in the Temple of Venus. Decked out in Egyptian finery, with her beaked nose, and her full, sensuous lips curved in a hint of a smile, she looked like what she was—an exotic foreigner. Tavius disliked the statue intensely, but did not remove it. However, on either side of the statue of Cornelia that he moved to Octavia's portico, he put up two more statues—one of his sister and one of me. Because Cornelia's statue showed her seated, we sat too. We held our backs rigidly straight and our chins high, just as she did. Octavia and I both found posing for the sculptor wearying, but the result was worth it. We were depicted in extremely modest Roman dress, shawls covering most of our hair, our expressions like Cornelia's, grave and noble.

The sculptures were flattering, but what mattered was the political message. We were Cornelia's spiritual daughters, as no Egyptian queen could ever be. *This is what a good Roman woman looks like*—that was the message.

⋙⋙

How strange it felt to be portrayed in a public statue. Little boys in Rome dream of being important enough that a statue will be raised to them. No girl has such dreams. The first time I looked at my statue it made me feel odd, as if it were only a figment of my mind, or as if it were not made of marble but of vapor and might dissolve at any moment. But I got used to people telling me it was a wonderful likeness, so true to life. And I was touched that Tavius had set up a statue in my honor.

I found that the right to handle my own finances gave me new confidence. The properties I would acquire in the future would be truly mine. No man could tell me what I could or could not do with them. My knack for business fully flowered only after I was freed from guardianship.

I remembered with distaste the self-righteousness in my sister-in-law's voice when she said, *I would never want a law passed to set me above other women*. In fact, the statues and the public reverence Tavius accorded Octavia and me enhanced the respect paid to women generally. Some years later, in order to increase the number of little citizens born, Rome offered freedom from financial guardianship to all mothers of four or more children. I doubt that would have been done if I hadn't led the way. I can say before the gods that the privileges granted to me certainly never did other women any harm.

Of course I knew that however much liberty I grasped at, however high I flew, everything rested on my bond with one man.

Chapter 14

I must not become too lost in my memories. Some of the younger members of my family have come to my villa to visit me during the Saturnalia. I feel almost startled to see them, as if their presence is an intrusion. The people from the past seem more real than these youthful men and women who murmur solicitous words in my ear, always speaking in the respectful tones one uses to an ancient. I notice how my young relatives resemble the people I am writing about, though the bloodlines are so convoluted and intertwined, it is sometimes an effort to remember who is related to whom.

My grandson Claudius arrived here yesterday. He is of course Mark Antony's grandson too, as well as Octavia's. My love naturally goes out to all my grandchildren and great-grandchildren, but Claudius has never been a favorite of mine.

I do not dislike him for his crippled leg or his twitching or his stammering, whatever some people may think. He cannot help all that, poor boy. But his loud, raucous laugh grates on me.

I see Antony in him, especially when he drinks. And he drinks a great deal.

He rarely visits me without a special reason. "G-Grandmother," he said to me this morning. "I h-have a g-great favor to ask of you."

I cocked my head, waiting.

"There are b-books. In your l-library."

It turned out he meant certain books in the Etruscan language, which hardly anybody knows anymore. But Claudius has taught himself this language and plans to write a multi-volume history of the Etruscans. He desperately wanted those books of mine, which it seems concern certain obscure Etruscan kings. I let him have them. Why not? Army service has been impossible for him, and he has stayed clear of politics. He barely gets around, dragging his leg as he does. Writing about the long-dead past is a harmless activity for him.

"Oh, thank you, G-Grandmother," he said, when I told him he could have the volumes to keep. He looked overjoyed. "If I can ever do something for you, you can r-rely on me."

Historian that he aspires to be, I wonder what he would think of this account of the past I am writing.

⋙⋙⋙⋙

Another parting came. I ought to have been used to it. But I never was. "Please," I said to Tavius, before he left to make war on the Illyrians, "don't take any extraordinary physical risks this time."

Tavius smiled, but I saw a clouded look in his eyes. "Many people would find it amusing that you say that to me."

I gazed at him questioningly.

"Philippi. The final battle for Sicily. There are people who say I specialize in not taking physical risks. You do know, don't you, what my enemies whisper about me?"

They whispered that he had been absent from those battles because he was a coward. "You walked into Lepidus's camp barehanded. You are the bravest man I know." I saw a tiny smudge on his bronze breastplate and rubbed it with my finger until it disappeared.

"Sweet Livia," he said. "I wish I could see myself through your eyes. It would be pleasant, I think, but I wonder if I would even recognize myself." He tipped up my chin so he could kiss me.

I wound my arms around his neck and kissed him hungrily, as though for the last time. He drew away a little, as if my passionate kisses perturbed him. But then he put his arms around me, and stood holding me as gently as one would a child.

"Tell me," I said, "why is Maecenas going with you? And that gaggle of poets?"

"They wanted a change from their usual dull lives."

"That sounds likely." I knew that the war would have two aims. To pacify the Illyrian savages, and to fortify what Maecenas persisted in calling Tavius's "legend." "Oh, Tavius, I want you to be careful."

Tavius nuzzled my cheek. "Usually I can talk to you the way I would another man. And then you turn all womanish on me. It's always a surprise."

"What are you planning?"

"Well . . . it would be a novelty if when we go into battle, I actually make an appearance."

He laughed as he took leave of me. As if war were a lark.

⋙⋙

"Why do men love warfare so much?" I asked this question of Tiberius Nero not long after Tavius left for Illyria.

"It allows us to test our mettle," he said.

He had come to pay me a visit at my villa at Prima Porta. He thought he might buy a villa in the vicinity, and wanted to see how I had laid out the grounds. As we went strolling through the gardens, he remarked on the beauty of the marble fountains and the variety of flowers. It is always enjoyable to impress an old friend.

"That is quite lovely," he said, nodding at a statue of Diana, wielding her bow. "You still give her worship above all other deities?"

"I've always believed she was the one who saved me from the forest fire," I said.

"Oh, yes, the forest fire." He shook his head, remembering. "That almost seems like another lifetime."

It was on the tip of my tongue to ask him: *Are you happy? And do you forgive me for leaving you?* But there were things we did not say to each other.

We needed to discuss our son. "Little Tiberius—well, speaking of loving warfare, all he wants to do is practice with weapons."

Tiberius Nero grinned. "He's a natural soldier, isn't he?"

I gritted my teeth. "Yes. But the other day he hit one of my house slaves with his javelin."

"No one has perfect aim."

"He has excellent aim for a boy his age. And I have a feeling he did it on purpose."

"He didn't kill the fellow, did he?"

"No, but he wounded him. And he didn't seem sorry, even after I smacked him."

"Well, if I see him aiming at any of my slaves, I'll give him a whipping." Tiberius Nero smiled. "You have to admit he certainly has the makings of a soldier."

"I want him to be more than just a soldier," I said. "He needs softening and refinement. Next November, he will be seven years old. Will you let me engage a tutor for him? It has to be the right sort of person—someone who can open his eyes to philosophy, art, and poetry."

"Go ahead. But I don't think you'll soften him up much." Tiberius Nero's eyes glowed. "That's *my* boy."

>>>>>>>

My beloved Livia, I would chortle except it hurts so much. Everything hurts. But I am happy. We besieged the Illyrian capital, Metulum, raised wooden gangways, and readied our assault. I stood on a temporary tower, supervising from above as a general ought. But did I stay up there? No. At the critical moment of the assault, overcome by fierce martial spirit, I rushed down from the tower and grabbed a shield from one of my soldiers, who held back, hesitating. I yelled, "Follow me!" and climbed up the gangway.

Did we plan it, you ask? Of course we did. Ten members of my bodyguard flanked me. Still, I personally led the assault. And what supreme commander has ever led an assault on a besieged town? Practically no one. Well, Alexander the Great did it, but he was Alexander.

You'll say: "Tavius, the risk!" My love, it was a risk worth taking. And for once I didn't have some ridiculous ailment putting me out of commission.

Up the gangway I went. My troops were inspired by my heroism—too inspired. An enormous body of men rushed the gangway, which promptly collapsed. I was just about crushed, but I emerged from the rubble in time to see our army win a great victory. Metulum is ours. The whole province is ours.

My cracked ribs are mending well, the doctors say, and Maecenas has his band of poets composing odes to my valor. My sweet love, it was necessary for me to lead that charge. For my credit with other men, for my own pride.

My cup is full to overflowing. I have won, and do you know who has lost? Antony. His Parthian campaign has come to an inglorious end. He overreached. It was a debacle. I genuinely pity his poor soldiers and wrote him a polite letter offering to send him supplies for them—food, clothes, blankets, and whatever else can aid them in their sad condition. He wrote me back saying I could keep my supplies. He will try to conquer Armenia now. If I were just a shade less of a patriot, I'd root for the Armenians.

You, love, have consoled me when fortune frowned. Now please enjoy my good fortune. Celebrate. Don't shudder and say I was reckless. Be happy I threw the dice and won. So what if I'm a little bit battered? At this moment, the only thing on earth I lack is you in my arms.

>>>>>>>

Battered? The word did not begin to tell it. He nearly died at Metulum, flattened and mangled under a weight of men and wood and metal.

At the head of his victorious army, he came home to me. He limped. He coughed. He looked exhausted. It was a hot autumn, and the day after he returned he was fit for nothing but to lay naked on the bed we shared, fresh red scars marking his torso, his arms, and his legs.

I kissed each of his scars. "Everyone is talking about your heroism," I said. This was only a slight exaggeration. He had certainly impressed the people of Rome. "But please never do anything like this again."

Tavius chuckled. The chuckle turned into a cough.

"Let's hope there will be no more wars for a while," I said. "Surely we are due for some years of peace. But if there are more wars, let someone else fight them for you."

"Oh, but Livia, I've gotten a taste for being a military hero. Maybe I'll go and conquer Britannia next."

Tavius meant this only for banter. But I thought of all he had suffered and might yet suffer to fulfill his destiny. At eighteen, he had determined on a course, and he would see it through. Danger and pain would never impede him. At that moment, looking at his scars, I wanted to weep for him. But I did not. He would not have liked it. I said only, "I would rather you let someone else conquer Britannia."

>>>>>>>

The limp had always gone away before. Not after the Illyrian campaign. Though usually only barely noticeable, it was permanent, like the scars. He soon stopped coughing, though, and was out of bed and driving himself as hard as he ever had.

Rubria became pregnant at this time. I was happy for her, of course; no one deserved my good wishes more than she did. But it was getting so I felt a clutch in my heart every time I heard of a pregnancy or a birth. Tavius and I had been married for four years, and there was no sign of a child.

I prayed at temples. I wore sacred amulets to bed. I drank foul-tasting concoctions prepared by Rome's finest physicians. On the Lupercalia, I stood in the street as other barren wives did.

The festival—which honored the she-wolf who had suckled Romulus and Remus—always brought fresh hope to women who wished in vain to bear a child. Priests sacrificed two male goats and a dog. They smeared the forehead of two young men with blood from the sacrificed animals and dressed them in the skins of the dead goats. These youths ran around the perimeter of the Palatine Hill, striking all the women they met on the hand with a leather thong. A lash from one of their whips was intended to ensure fertility.

As I had seen other women do, I held out my hand as the sacred runner approached. He was a husky young man who grinned like a satyr and looked like one, clad as he was in a loincloth and cape made of goatskin strips. He struck my hand hard with his thong as he ran past. The blow stung and left a welt. But I did not become pregnant.

Now that there was no war, Tavius lavished all his energy on building. Rome got a new aqueduct and new sewers, newly paved roads, and shining marble temples and public buildings. Agrippa had day-to-day authority over all these projects, but when it came to the planning, my opinion also carried weight. It was a great joy to know we were remaking Rome. All this building provided badly needed work for poor citizens; and Tavius's popularity with the common people had never soared so high. Politically speaking, he ought to have been content. But the situation with Mark Antony bothered him like a sore tooth.

He said to me one day, "I think Octavia should go back to Antony before he leaves for war in Armenia."

"Why?" I said.

"Either she is his wife or she isn't," he said.

And if she wasn't? What good could come of making that clear to the whole world? Maintaining the status quo might be best for all of us. "Why not just leave matters alone?"

Tavius gave me an annoyed look. "I'll leave it up to her," he said.

"I don't think—"

"I'll leave it up to her," he repeated.

A few days later, the three of us—Tavius, Octavia, and I—sat in the sunlit courtyard of Antony's house in Rome. "Let me bring him the nineteen thousand soldiers you owe him," Octavia said.

"Two thousand," Tavius said. "And seventy warships, and provisions for his army."

"Why not nineteen thousand soldiers? Why not keep your promise?"

"Because I need my soldiers." Tavius tapped on the side of the stone bench on which he was sitting.

"He'll think you don't trust him," she said.

"Well, he'll be right."

"You think he's going to send me away, don't you? You think he wants to divorce me?"

"Look at the facts. He is openly cohabiting with another woman." Tavius spoke coldly. It was not that he lacked sympathy for his sister, but in the present circumstances her continued loyalty to Antony often filled him with an anger he could barely contain.

"I feel sometimes that I don't know you anymore," Octavia said. She turned an accusing gaze on me. "Livia, whose idea was it to have me join my husband in Alexandria?"

"You said you wanted to go," Tavius said.

"Yes. I've been away from him too long. I ought to have insisted on going before this. But you suggest I go to him now. Why?"

"It's only normal, isn't it, for a wife to be with her husband?"

"I think you assume that my presence in Alexandria will embarrass him. And if he rejects me, that will put him in the wrong with all Rome, because you've built me up into a painted clay statue of virtue." She looked at me. "I know whose idea it was to inflate me in the public mind. I never asked for that treatment, but no one consulted me. Of course not. Why consult me?"

I said nothing.

"This plan to suddenly dispatch me to Antony is so sly. It was you who came up with it, wasn't it, Livia?"

"No."

She tilted her head. "Truly? It was Tavius's idea? Well, sometimes it's hard to tell the two of you apart. Even the way you speak—you sound so alike sometimes it makes my skin crawl."

Somewhere in the house a baby wailed. Octavia's little daughter, Antony's child.

"Enough of this," Tavius said, biting off the words.

When Octavia spoke again, her voice shook. "If it ever comes to war between you and Antony, no one can predict who will be the victor. But I will be the most miserable woman alive either way. Don't you see that?"

Tavius's expression was flinty. "I have no more time for this. I have work to do." Without another word, he rose and walked out of the house.

For a long moment, Octavia looked after him, her expression desolate. Finally she turned to me. "Why didn't you leave with him?"

"I didn't suggest sending you to Antony," I said. "And I don't want him to refuse to welcome you. That's the last thing I want."

"It's what Tavius wants," she said.

I shifted my shoulders. "I don't know if that's true."

"Why, I thought you knew every thought in my brother's head," she said, acid in her voice.

I suddenly felt deeply weary and rubbed my eyes. "He hates this in-between state. He wants matters resolved, one way or the other."

She examined my face, distaste but also curiosity in her own expression. "And what do you want?"

"I'm afraid of a breach with Antony. I hate war, and I fear it."

"You believe if Antony rejects me there will be war?"

"That's what I feel in my bones—it will come sooner or later, if your marriage ends. Another civil war." I looked into Octavia's eyes. "When I imagine Romans killing each other again, my soul cries out. I remember the deaths of my father and mother, and Perusia, that agony and destruction. I can't bear the thought of such things happening again. And you're right—no one can say who would win."

She let out a long sigh. "So we are allies, in this. How strange."

I reached across the space that divided us and grabbed her hand. "Don't go to Antony. Leave matters as they are. Wait until he sends for you."

Octavia gently withdrew her hand from mine, stood, and turned away. We were both silent. The only sound came from the garish fountain at the courtyard's center. Rose-scented, gold-colored water gushed out of the mouths of three golden cherubs. Everywhere you glanced in Antony's house you saw this sort of opulence. Octavia, with her simplicity in dress and manner, always seemed out of place here.

I wondered if she wanted me to leave, but after a few moments she spoke. "Whatever Tavius's reasons are for sending me to Antony, I have my own purpose for agreeing to go." She turned toward me again. "Antony and I—well, we have lain in each other's arms. If I were there, I could talk to him. I know I could never make him give up Cleopatra. But—oh, let her be his mistress, so long as I'm his wife! I could get him to understand how much rests on our marriage. If I stay away, I doubt he'll ever send for me. But if I'm there, at least there is a chance that he won't scorn me."

In that moment, I truly looked at her, as perhaps I had not for a long while. She had delicate features, a graceful form. She was not without beauty. Maybe, sated with Cleopatra, Antony would turn to her. Maybe he would even prefer Octavia, once he saw her again.

"I will not take the children with me, though," she said. "Much as I'd like to. The boys miss Antony so much, and he has never even seen the baby. But it's best they stay in Rome for now. I will send for them, if all is well. Livia, can you understand why I won't take them with me?"

I nodded, realizing how little confidence she had that Antony would welcome her as his wife. If he divorced her there in his domain, and the children were present, he could take them from her. If they remained in Rome, I could imagine Tavius saying: *Certainly, Antony has his rights as a father. Let him come and enforce them.*

She feared not only the loss of her daughters but of Antony's two sons by Fulvia. She had grown greatly attached to those boys.

"I have never in my life done anything brave," she said. "All those virtues Tavius has publicly praised me for—do you notice he left out courage? What does a woman need courage for, he probably thinks." She gave a dry laugh. "It will take courage for me to go to my husband—to see if he is still my husband. I imagine the look in his eyes when we meet. I imagine him comparing me to *her*. Well, be that as it may, I am hoping—I am so hoping—I'll be able to have the children come later, and we will all have a wonderful reunion."

I was moved by Octavia's confiding in me as she did. And I thought there was at least some chance her hope would be realized. Antony was unpredictable, but he had seemed genuinely fond of her. Their marriage might be salvaged, the family ties restored. "May the gods make it so," I said.

>>>>>>>

The two thousand soldiers Tavius chose to give Antony were among the cream of the legions. He had them outfitted with magnificent new armor and weaponry. The seventy warships he dispatched, he packed with clothing and foodstuffs, including live cattle, for the provisioning of Antony's army. He also sent sumptuous personal gifts for Antony and his leading officers. Nothing was meanly done. Tavius certainly did not intend his sister to return to Antony with empty hands. Octavia, seeing Tavius lay out generous sums, embraced him gratefully, and they parted on warm terms.

I hoped Antony would accept what had been sent as a token of friendly feeling and restore Octavia to her rightful place as his wife. No doubt he would expect more military support in time, and likely Tavius would be unable to refuse it. Such an outcome, conducive to future harmony, certainly seemed possible.

I was with Tavius when he received a letter from his sister, telling him how she, and all her bounty, had been received. We sat in his study, discussing a small governmental matter. When the travel-stained messenger entered, I could read disaster just in how he carried himself.

He said to Tavius, "Sir, my mistress is returning to Rome by easy stages, for she is rather tired. But she sent me on with this." He handed over a sealed tablet.

My heart pounded. Tavius ripped the letter's seal away, read it, and turned white. He dismissed the messenger in a voice of barely controlled fury.

I did not dare ask him what news the letter held. His whole body shook with rage. Those who would later say—as many did—that he was capable of dealing coldly with the matter of his sister's marriage, using it as an excuse for doing what he wished to do anyway, ought to have seen him at that moment.

He could not bring himself to speak but just handed me the letter. As I read it, I saw in every line Octavia's effort to make what had occurred seem less awful than it was, and to soothe her brother.

I arrived in Athens and wrote to Antony in Alexandria, asking if he wished me to continue on and join him there, or to stay in our house in

Athens and wait for him to come and join me. I told him of course about all the gifts you had generously sent and asked where he wished them delivered. He wrote me back that I should send the gifts to Alexandria, but I should return to his house in Rome.

Tavius, dear, I know this will upset you. But the wording of his letter was not harsh, but entirely courteous, and he did say I was to return to his house. I am still, of course, his wife. One of his soldiers whispered to me that Cleopatra said she would commit suicide if he received me, as he, at first, had every intention of doing. I think his passion for her is a kind of sickness, which will run its course, if I just wait it out. That is what I intend to do.

Naturally I will comply with my husband's wishes. I am sending the gifts on, and I will soon be back in Rome. My sweet Tavius, please do not make more of this rather absurd matter than it is.

I raised my eyes from the tablet, a sinking feeling in my guts.

"He would not even see her." Tavius spoke as if he were trying to make himself believe it. "He just told her to send on the gifts."

I did not think Antony was brain-sick with passion for Cleopatra. The two of them had come together before, had twin children, and then parted for over three years when Antony found it convenient. If he was now swept away by love, it was a late development in their long acquaintance. The queen of Egypt was the richest and most powerful woman in the world. She had personally funded Antony's Parthian debacle. However love and lust figured in the mix, Antony's actions surely reflected political calculation too. He would not receive his wife if it caused him problems with Cleopatra.

And yet he would not divorce Octavia either. He would keep her in his house in Rome, bound to him, dangling. How could he expect Tavius to acquiesce to this treatment of his sister?

Still, I thought, *there must not be civil war again.*

I knew it was not the moment to tell Tavius to put away his rage. I must tread carefully. "Beloved, I share your anger," I said. "All I ask is that you not act precipitously. You are not a creature to be unmanned by passion, as Antony is."

He said in a smothered voice, "Am I not?"

"The only god he worships is Dionysus, but you are the son of Apollo. Reason, knowledge, and light guide your actions."

"If he spat in my face before the whole world, it would be less of an insult than what he's done. This affront to Octavia—no one can expect me to simply bear it."

I could find no words to say that were not likely to exacerbate his anger. Antony's treatment of Octavia was cruel by any standard. Beyond that, it was dishonoring to her family. Tavius could see it only as an expression of Antony's contempt for him as a man—contempt that had always been there, underlying their relations with each other. That all the world must know of it made it doubly shaming.

Tavius let out a long, shuddering breath. "I won't do anything foolish."

Perhaps Octavia preferred a slow journey home because, as her messenger said, she felt weary. Perhaps she needed time to prepare herself to speak of what had happened. She would have had to have been made of steel not to take Antony's rejection as a personal humiliation.

She finally arrived in Rome, and when she had rested, we—she, Tavius, and I—met in the garden of Antony's house on the Palatine. The beautiful summer weather, the exquisitely landscaped garden, the sweet wine, the figs and nuts Octavia had served to us—these would have well suited a pleasant family occasion. But of course, we were all, in our different ways, profoundly upset. Tavius was livid at Antony's actions, Octavia looked deeply sad, and I was filled with dread of what would happen next.

"You will not remain in that man's house another day," Tavius told his sister. I knew he preferred that Octavia not bear the onus of initiating a divorce from Antony. But pride required that she at least take a step toward this severance. "I just bought two houses near mine. I intended to use them for governmental purposes, but you can have your choice of them. While the house is being furnished, you'll come and stay with us."

"I know you mean that kindly," Octavia said, "but I intend to stay here."

"You will not stay here," Tavius said. "I forbid it. You're not going to stay in this house and pretend you're that man's wife."

"But I am his wife," Octavia said.

"It's true he hasn't had the decency to send you a letter of divorce." Tavius's cheek muscle quivered. "But you must know your marriage is over."

I said softly, "Tavius, there are children to think of. You haven't mentioned the children."

Tavius nodded. "Yes, of course. Octavia, you will take Antonia and Antonilla with you. Livia and I will welcome them." He spoke in a flat, stony way only, I think, because he was fighting to control himself. Whatever he had expected when he sent his sister to Antony, he had been unprepared for the outcome. Unfortunately, he had so far not spoken one gentle word to Octavia, who certainly could have used his kindness and comfort. But he did say, though in the same stony voice, "Don't fear separation from your children. I doubt if Antony even remembers they're alive, but if he does, he'll have to walk over my corpse to get them. Those girls are my flesh and blood, and I'll always look after them, just as I'll always look after you."

Octavia acknowledged his words with a bleak half-smile. "That's good of you. But I have other responsibilities that I must think of. To begin with, my stepsons. They are only twelve and eight years old. How can I abandon them?"

Antony's sons by Fulvia? Tavius looked amazed that his sister should give them a thought at this juncture. But with hardly a pause, he said, "All right, I'll take them into my home too, and you can look after them until their father makes provision for them." He could not restrain himself from adding, "If he ever bothers to. He seems not to recollect he has any children but Cleopatra's spawn."

At the mention of Cleopatra, Octavia stiffened and looked away. She said in a low voice, "You're kind to say you will accept the boys. But I have other responsibilities, just as important to me as the children's welfare. I married Antony, for good or ill. I owe him something even now. At least I can wait and see if he comes to his senses. And I owe Rome something." Her eyes returned to Tavius. "You exalted me, beyond my merits. I have become a sort of symbol of peace, and people look to me to guarantee the peace between you and my husband. I can do that only as Antony's wife."

Tavius just stared at her, his eyes burning.

She reached over and touched his hand. "If you are set on war for motives that have nothing to do with me, there is little I can do. But you and Antony are the most powerful men in the world. How would it be if Rome is brought to civil war because one of you is besotted with a woman, and the other is carried away by protectiveness and resentment on a woman's behalf—on my behalf? It would be both tragic and laughable."

"I have not been speaking of war," Tavius said between his teeth.

"But I sense you're thinking of it. If there is to be war, please—don't make any insult to me the pretext. I beg you. I couldn't stand that."

The three of us were silent. Then Tavius said in a taut voice, "I have no intention as of now of breaking the peace. But you're to leave this house. I will not have you stay here."

"Tavius, dearest, I can't leave his house. The only right course for me is to continue on the path I'm on, to walk the very last mile to salvage my marriage."

"For the love of heaven," Tavius said, caught between exasperation and pain for her, "do as I say."

She smiled slightly and tried to speak in a light voice. "I'm afraid that you will have to call your soldiers and have me dragged out of here. Because I won't leave of my own will."

I understood at that moment Octavia's true nobility. In face of the public shame Antony had inflicted on her, she eschewed anger but sought to act in the best interests of Rome and all of us. She was single-handedly making her stand, trying to avert war. It was how I would have wished to have acted in her place, but I did not know if I would have been capable of it.

Tavius did not say another word but rose and left the house.

So she stayed, tending Antony's property, looking after Antony's sons as if they were her own, and being a gracious hostess to any of his friends who visited the city. This earned her general admiration in Rome. But the fact that she continued, though at a distance, to be a loyal, serviceable wife to Antony was a stone in Tavius's heart.

⋙⋙

The peace held, a rancorous peace punctuated by angry letters from Antony to Tavius, and from Tavius to Antony, a raking up of old and present grievances. As this continued for month after month, it seemed possible we would go on this way forever. But the treaty of alliance between Tavius and Antony had a set term—which had less than two years left to it.

Despite the animosity, it was a very good time for Rome. Tavius wanted to solidify his rule. If it did come to war with Antony, he would need the people's love. So the huge building program under Agrippa's management proceeded at a rapid pace, and even expanded. One saw workmen and construction sites in every part of Rome. My good works expanded also.

Just as Tavius did, I set aside regular morning hours in which to receive ordinary people. By this time, I had acquired wealth in the form of commercial farms, granaries, and olive presses. I was not profligate with my money, but I was generous. If a decent, indigent girl found herself hard-pressed, she would, if she were wise, come to me. I would find her a way to survive other than selling her body. Often I made her a gift of a dowry, enough for her to attract some upstanding fellow to marry her. In return, I expected loyalty—and usually I got it, not only from the girl herself but from her immediate circle. I had many clients of my own, people bound to me by ties of mutual loyalty, who ranged from recipients of my charity to senators' wives; in fact, I could even include some senators in that group. The small, daily exchanges of favors to create and nurture political bonds were as much a part of my life as they were of Tavius's.

Every day Tavius depended on me to shoulder a share of the burden of work he carried. He often said he was lucky in the wife he had chosen. But I felt my failure every time I saw a baby—and at this time, it seemed as if every woman I was close to was giving birth. First, my sister had her second daughter. Then Caecilia, now happily wed to Agrippa, had a daughter too. Shortly after that,

Rubria, who still looked after my boys like a kindly aunt, brought her little Marcus into the world.

Tavius and I made an appearance at the naming ceremony that her husband, Ortho, held for his son. Ortho greeted us, flushed with pride. A few years before, he never would have dreamed of having Caesar as his guest, but now the house he welcomed us to was large and grand, and his baby son lay in an ornate cradle, trimmed with carved ivory flowers.

Little Marcus was not red and wrinkled, as many nine-day-old children are, but already handsome. When I peered at him in his cradle, I swear he smiled as if he knew me. I, not one to gush over infants, felt a fluttering in my heart and a rush of longing.

I tore my eyes away from the child and noticed a statue of Minerva in a wall niche across the atrium: a costly statue, delicately painted. It pleased me that Ortho and Rubria could afford such artwork. The celebration, itself, pleased me—the happy guests, the smell of sweet cakes in the air, the wine poured into silver goblets.

Rubria, still recovering from childbirth and looking a bit pale, sat beside the cradle greeting her guests. When I sat down beside her, she gave me a searching, almost stricken look.

"Why, dear, what is it?" I said. "Surely you are happy?"

"It just feels like a dream to me."

I laughed and patted her hand. "It's no dream."

She looked across the room at her husband. "He has become so wealthy, so quickly. Oh, with your help, and we are grateful for it. But it's like watching a shooting star. And a shooting star rises—and then it falls."

Her words chilled me, the more so because Rubria had never before spoken in such a fashion. I said, "After women give birth, they can have strange moods. But that passes."

"I think sometimes that I'm still alone and poor. I'm not a merchant's wife with a house and a son. I have fallen asleep and dreamed this, but I will wake and realize—"

"Stop it," I said, but gently because I was so fond of her. "You mustn't give in to such fancies."

"Is it just a fancy?"

"Of course it is." I knocked on the gilded arm of her chair. "This is solid. And look around you. Here is your house, your husband, your son. And here am I, your loving friend. I assure you, I'm not some dream phantasm."

"Lady Livia, do you think of the forest fire and the cave? Does it never seem dreamlike to you, to have risen so high, after all that? Oh, I am not comparing myself to you. But don't you, yourself, sometimes wonder if you're dreaming?"

"No," I said, "I don't think such thoughts. For one thing, I'm much too busy." The truth was that when such ideas entered my mind, I did my best to push them away.

"And you don't fear that you might fall?"

"I will never allow myself to fall," I said.

Soon Tavius came to whisper in my ear that we had other engagements that day. So we left, borne off in the large and comfortable litter we used when we traveled about the city together. People stood in the street to cheer, and we kept the litter curtains open so they could see us.

"Do you feel it?" I asked Tavius in a low voice. "Do you feel how the people adore you?"

He smiled and lifted his hand to wave at the crowd.

"And I adore you," I whispered. "Do you know how much?"

I think he sensed some need for reassurance in me. He turned his head and gave me a questioning look, but then the shouts of the crowd distracted him, and he looked away.

At that moment—strangely—I had the impulse to pray. Inwardly, I supplicated myself before Diana. I begged her, as I always did in my prayers, to protect Tavius. I begged for continued peace. And I asked for one thing more, a vital thing. I asked that I be allowed to bear Tavius a son.

Sometimes you are going down a particular road, and the journey seems so long that you can almost imagine it will never end. Then you reach a landmark, and that is enough to make you understand that indeed you are covering distance, and reaching your destination is only a matter of time. But what if you don't want to reach the destination at all? What if you wish to pretend to yourself that you are not traveling? A change in terrain can be so unwelcome.

I wanted to believe that Antony and Octavia could live married though apart forever, and that Tavius and Antony could continue to growl at each other but never come to blows. They were not, after all, living in adjoining towns but in distant lands within a vast empire. Maybe Tavius and Antony could just go on, tolerating each other's existence.

Then one day Tavius entered the room in which I was inspecting some weaving done by my maids. "Come into my study," he said. It was unusual for him to fetch me this way, and his eyes were as fierce as they had been at Vedius's house when he smashed all the precious crystal.

We closed the study door behind us. I sat on the couch. "What has happened?"

Tavius did not sit. I felt almost afraid of him, as he loomed above me. His hands were clenched into fists, and he looked as if he wanted to find someone to strike. "I've gotten a report on Antony's doings. He annexed Armenia."

"We expected that, didn't we?" I blurted.

"Livia, will you be quiet and listen? He returned to Alexandria, to Cleopatra. And he went through some kind of marriage ceremony with her."

Oh, no, oh, no, oh, no.

"And he made a speech to the people of Alexandria," Tavius went on relentlessly. "And in the speech he said this—that Cleopatra had been the legitimate wife of Julius Caesar. That her son Caesarion is Julius Caesar's only true heir."

"Antony has always been a fool," I said in a rush. "He does and says stupid things without realizing the implications. He did this, likely, only to please Cleopatra. Knowing him, he might have been drunk."

Tavius said in a furious voice, "He has dishonored my sister, his wife. He has publicly said I am not the heir of Julius Caesar. And you make excuses for him?"

A voice in my mind spoke. It was like a child's voice. *I'm afraid. Please. There must not be war.* I drew in a breath. "Beloved, you mistake me. I don't excuse him. I am pointing out that he is a fool. If he were a rational, sober man and acted this way, I would take it as a declaration of uncompromising enmity against you. But he is Antony."

Tavius nodded, becoming calmer. "Yes. He's a fool." He sat beside me. "My informant sent me this." He opened his hand. In his palm lay a large silver coin. I took it and examined it. On one side of it was a portrait of Antony in profile, on the other the profile of Cleopatra. I knew that in the kingdoms of the east, this was how kings and queens symbolized their rule.

There were inscriptions in Greek on both sides of the coin. Above Antony's portrait: "Antony after the conquest of Armenia." Above Cleopatra's: "Cleopatra, queen of kings and mother of kings."

"He wishes to establish a monarchy independent of and even hostile to Rome," Tavius said. "He wishes to dismember the empire that generations shed blood to win, so he can become an eastern potentate, with her by his side."

Was that truly his aim? How could we know? "He is erratic. Sometimes he acts with no serious aim at all. He may intend only to gratify her."

"And what does she intend?" Tavius said.

"She?" I said. I had often wondered about Cleopatra's motives. But Tavius had previously spoken of her as if she had no existence apart from Antony.

He gave a mirthless chuckle. "Do you discount her because she is a woman? I don't. Haven't you ever given thought to who and what she is?"

"She is a queen," I said, "and I do not discount her."

"I met her when my father was consorting with her," Tavius said. "She never struck me as beautiful, but she has, when she wishes to exert it, enormous charm. She speaks six languages fluently—oh, she is learned. Learned and also savage. The royal line from which she springs is known for treachery and murder."

I nodded; I knew this. But Tavius went on speaking as if reciting the ugly details gave him a perverse pleasure.

"When Cleopatra was small, her older sister rose in rebellion against her father. He executed his own daughter. After her father died, to secure the throne, Cleopatra murdered both her brothers. This included the one who was also her husband. The royal family of Egypt practices incest—though the boy did not live long enough to consummate the marriage. Cleopatra's younger sister, Arsinoe, showed herself no friend of Rome, but because she was just a young girl, my father spared her life. Do you know what happened to Arsinoe, a few years ago?"

Of course I knew. Cleopatra had insisted that Antony order Arsinoe put to death. He had her dragged out of a temple sanctuary and executed.

Cleopatra had used every gift of guile and feminine allure to maintain her rule of Egypt. She had slaughtered members of her own family to keep her power. But what would she have said if forced to explain herself? No doubt she would have spoken of the struggle with disloyal kin and the need to hold her kingdom against Rome. She might have maintained that her choices were dictated by necessity.

It would be wrong to say I felt a shred of kinship with Cleopatra. But I remembered that Tavius and I had gone down twisted paths we never would have trodden if we had been born in a well-ordered Republic. Who could say what I would have done in Cleopatra's situation? It might be that she and I had more in common than I could comfortably admit. I wondered, did she love Antony as I loved Tavius?

Was she simply laying claim to a husband now? Or was it an empire Cleopatra was claiming?

"I don't know how any man, even Antony, could prefer that woman to my sister, who is kind and good, and I swear to you, more beautiful," Tavius said. "But he's become her creature. They had a great public ceremony, at which he awarded his older son by her the whole Parthian empire he has yet to conquer. Their daughter, he gave Crete and Cyrenaica, and the younger boy got Syria and Asia Minor. Caesarion he dubbed 'king of kings' just as his mother is 'queen of kings.'"

From a Roman point of view, these were bizarre doings. But several kings reigned in the territories Antony governed, subordinate to Rome and to Antony himself. If he wanted to make his children vassal rulers, some would argue that was within his authority and need not injure Rome. I said this to Tavius, and he did not contradict me. Still, I felt he did not hear me.

"Antony has obviously lost his reason," I said. "And who can predict what a madman will do? Just because of that, you should not take any precipitate action. You need to know his and Cleopatra's true aim. And if there is to be war—" I nearly choked on the word. "If there is to be war, all of Rome must be on your side. They look upon you, with good reason, as the man who has brought them peace. They love you for that. You must keep their love, now more than ever. They must be made to understand that war, if it comes, is Antony's fault, not yours. Then they will support you. And then you will win."

"Those are exactly my own thoughts," Tavius said.

So we would wait.

Chapter 15

The next day, Tavius, Octavia, and I had another of our three-sided talks. Speaking as gently as I had ever heard him, Tavius apologized to his sister for ever asking her to marry Antony, and acknowledged that she had done it for his sake. "I never should have tied you to that man. I made a foolish mistake, at great cost to you. It's time to undo my error. You must divorce him." As he had before, he said she should come and stay with us, that he and I would do everything we could to ensure her comfort and happiness.

"I will not initiate a divorce. I will not leave Antony's house," Octavia said.

Tavius's entire manner changed. "Antony has married another woman," he said angrily. "What do you plan to do, live in a polygamous arrangement as if you were some barbarian slut?"

"Whatever he has done, he has not married her. He could not do that, not lawfully. He is married to me."

Tavius fell into a paroxysm of coughing. He coughed more, lately; I took it as a sign of his unquiet mind. I felt his anguish and wanted to help him but was at a loss. I feared what would happen if Octavia divorced Antony. I imagined a war that Tavius might lose, a war that might take him from me forever.

When Tavius could speak again, he addressed his sister in a low voice. "Do you realize that the man you call your husband announced that Julius Caesar had one heir, and it wasn't me? It's as if he drew a dagger and aimed it at my heart. He spat on both of us. Don't you have any pride?"

"I don't want anyone to die for my pride." She reached out and stroked his hand. "Least of all you."

He suffered her touch for a moment, then jerked his hand away and got to his feet. We were in the garden of Antony's house. Tavius looked around him as if even the flowers and the trees were his enemies. "Stay here then," he said to Octavia. "If I loved and honored you less, I would have you carried out of here. But go ahead, stay. I see that you've gone insane. I can only hope you will recover." His gaze shifted to me. "If I did to you what Antony has done to her, you would want to dine on my kidneys, and you know it. But you sit there and say not a word. I think you want my sister to tolerate this disgraceful treatment. Why?"

I felt his anger like a blow. Once we were so united we were like twin souls. Now it was as if walls had sprung up between us. "I only want peace," I said in a shaking voice.

"Peace," he repeated, as if the word disgusted him. He swung around and strode out of the house.

Octavia and I sat silently for a while. I struggled to keep from weeping. "I heard something about this so-called marriage of Antony's," she said finally. "Oh yes, I have my own sources. It was a strange half-Greek, half-Egyptian ritual. He dressed as Dionysus and she as some Egyptian goddess or other. They played at being god and goddess, as they and their guests feasted and drank. It was nothing like a Roman wedding."

"It was a public event," I said.

"It was foolishness. Antony is like a boy in some ways. Children can be cruel, but it's unthinking cruelty. So we have to forgive them."

Do we? I almost said. Antony had gone beyond all possibility of forgiveness, as far as Tavius was concerned. And to my mind he deserved whatever disaster came of this. But we did not. Rome did not. I imagined mothers mourning their sons because of Antony's folly. Romans killing Romans again as we were all dragged into a civil war. A war that might destroy Tavius.

»»»»»»»

There was coolness now between Tavius and me. He had wanted me to help persuade Octavia to leave Antony's house, and I had not done it. I daily felt his silent displeasure. And then, to further darken the skies, a fever swept through Rome. It had happened before; it would happen again. Physicians could do little. At night, one heard wagons rolling through the streets, collecting bodies. Tavius conducted a great sacrifice on behalf of Rome at the Temple of Jupiter to mitigate heavenly wrath, but this had no effect. Tiberius Nero went away to the country with our two boys, for there were few deaths in the countryside. Octavia left the city as well, taking her children and Antony's sons, and little Julia too. Tavius and I were too busy with affairs to leave Rome.

I worried about Tavius's precarious health. But he did not come down with the fever. Meanwhile, several senators I knew died, and so did two of my slaves. Then word came that Marcus Ortho had fallen ill. "I should go to Rubria," I told Tavius.

"Send her husband the best physician we know," Tavius said. "But I won't have you going there to expose yourself to contagion."

"There is contagion here in our own house, among the slaves," I said.

"No," he said. "The ones who were sick have either died or gotten well. You're not to go to Rubria's house."

So I stayed away and only sent physicians. Then I heard that Ortho had died and Rubria herself had fallen sick.

"I might have been burned alive if not for her," I told Tavius. "I have to be with her now."

We were in his study. Tablets and papyrus scrolls covered his writing table. I always kept them in order, but it was still daunting to look at the piles of documents and think of all the matters that demanded his attention. Gaul, North Africa, Sicily—a thousand voices clamored for Caesar's notice. He had taken on this burden gladly, but that did not mean it did not wear on him. Beyond that, there was this sickness in Rome, and always, casting a cloud over everything, the threat of Mark Antony and Cleopatra. His face tight with strain, Tavius said, "Is it impossible for you to obey me for once, instead of adding to my worries? Can't you just obey me as a wife is supposed to obey her husband?"

"Forgive me, I can't. Not in this."

I summoned my litter and started out for Rubria's house. I could not do otherwise. The fear of losing Rubria clawed at me, and somehow I felt that if only I were with her, I would be able to save her from death as she had once saved me.

Her house, so festive mere months before, now seemed like an ornately decorated tomb. Entering, I immediately heard weeping. Slaves weeping for their master or for fellow servants who had also died? Or for their mistress who might soon set out on the same journey? Fustinius, the physician I had dispatched here, came into the atrium to greet me, grim-faced. He said, "She is dying. It can't be helped. There's no good you can do here. I advise you to leave."

"Is she awake?"

"At times."

"Then I will see her," I said.

She lay looking pale as a wax image, covered with a blanket of clean white wool. I would not have known that she still lived except I could see the blanket move slightly with the rise and fall of her chest. Her eyes were closed. She did not stir when I entered and took a chair near her bed. I thought: *She will not awake. I should leave now, for safety's sake.* But then I noticed her burn-scarred hands, resting above the blanket, and whispered, "Rubria, I am here." She surprised me by opening her eyes. "Don't be afraid," I said. "You will get better."

She stared blankly at me, as if I were a stranger.

"Do you know who I am?"

She nodded her head.

"Then you know I can't do without you. You must not leave me."

"The gods say differently." She barely breathed the words.

"You deserve a long and good life, and to watch your son grow up. I say you will get well. Do you understand me?"

She whispered, "Do you think you can control life and death?"

I felt myself rebuked and pressed my lips together.

"I was happy . . . for a little while." She spoke with effort, to console me.

"Were you?"

She did not answer. She seemed to sleep. Then she opened her eyes and said, "My son. Who . . . ?" A look of terror came over her face. "He has no one."

"I will care for him," I said.

The fear did not leave her face. I wondered if she had even heard me.

I said in a louder voice, "Rubria, may Diana witness my oath, I will raise him as if he were my own child."

She looked doubtfully at me.

"He will be my son," I said. "I swear it."

Gradually her face became peaceful. I waited, to see if she would speak again. But she never did. I could not tell the moment of her passing, it was so gentle.

After I closed her eyes and put coins on her eyes to pay the ferryman, I ordered Rubria's servants to bring little Marcus to me. I carried him out to my litter and held him cradled against my breast all the way home.

"I just hope he doesn't infect us all," Tavius said when I told him Rubria had died and I had brought her child with me.

"Oh, thank you for those kind words," I said, tears of grief in my eyes.

"Let me see him."

We walked into a side room, where the baby lay in a cradle. Tavius looked down at the child.

"You see? He is healthy," I said.

Tavius's expression was bleak. Perhaps at that instant he imagined, as I did, how it would have been for the two of us to stand like this over the cradle of our own son.

"I gave my word to his mother I would raise him as my own," I said.

"As your own?" He stared at me. "Without asking me, you swore that?"

At that moment terror filled me—terror of the chasm opening between us. I felt such a deep dread that we could lose each other that I think I must have pleaded with him with my eyes. "Beloved, how could I not go to Rubria? And how can I not care for her child now? You and I—we pay our debts. You would do the same thing in my place."

"You're that sure of what I would do?"

"Oh, yes. I know you."

Tavius stood frowning, and I felt a chill around my heart. But finally he said, "Well, his mother was a loyal woman, and his father always kept faith. I suppose we can make something of him."

I kissed his cheek.

He did not offer to legally adopt little Marcus; making the child one of his heirs would have been a great matter. But he tolerated the child's presence in our home, and soon began to take the same kindly, if rather distant, interest in him he did in my other two children. There were fewer silences between us. And so my deepest fear passed, and I did my best to forget about it.

⋙⋙

There were no more deaths from fever among people I knew, and few new deaths in the city. Rubria's passing was a great blow to my sons, and to Tiberius in particular. He wept long and hard when he heard the news. Then he never spoke her name again.

The months passed, and Antony and Tavius continued their angry correspondence. Tavius urged Antony to return to his lawful marriage and start acting like a Roman official, not a Greco-Egyptian potentate. Antony said his personal affairs were his own business. Tavius strengthened his army, as was only prudent. In Rome, he continued his feverish building. The common people looked at all the scaffolds, all the busy workmen, all the glittering marble, and they applauded him. They applauded me too. But no one had a stronger claim on their affection than Octavia did. She was seen as tolerating a painful marriage for the sake of Rome.

"The people love her," I told Tavius one day. "And they love you too, for keeping the peace."

He grimaced. "The simple hearts of the Roman people."

"Everyone speaks about Octavia's greatness of soul."

He sat on the couch in his study, looking over some petitions from the provinces. He threw the document in his hands on the side table. "Why do you keep praising her?"

"Because I feel for her. She said to me the other day that you hardly speak to her lately. That you don't even like to look at her."

His face flushed. "Gods above!" he shouted. "Are you too obtuse to understand? For her to let Antony treat her as he does turns my stomach. She's my sister. This situation is a dishonor to *me*. Don't you even see that?"

I did not bite my tongue or try to soothe his wounded spirit, for the tension we lived under had frayed my nerves just as it had his. I shouted back at him, "Can't you think of her? Or think of the men who will die if there's war between you or Antony? Can't you ever think of someone besides yourself?"

Then we both fell silent and stared at each other.

He said in an icy voice, "It's good to know my honor means nothing to you."

I was shaken. "Your honor lies in preserving the peace. In serving Rome."

"Yes, in serving Rome," he said.

We said no more. Afterward I walked on tiptoe with him. I feared that if he flung harsh words at me, I would fling them back, and then where would we be? I could not for the life of me find the right phrases, the loving touch that would have served me. Then a most remarkable thing occurred.

At first, I thought I had miscounted the days. I recalculated. No, I had made no error. Well, perhaps I had some small bodily indisposition. When a half-month had gone by and I still had seen no stain on my undergarments, I began to believe my greatest hope would be realized. Still, I said nothing to Tavius, for fear of disappointing him. I noticed an aching in my breasts and remembered that as an early sign when my sons were conceived. Even so, I feared that I could be wrong.

I made a decision to wait ten more days, just to be sure, before I told Tavius the news. But he knew me too well. On the second day, as we prepared for bed, he took my face in both his hands and studied me. "I see that little secret smile of yours. What are you keeping from me?"

"What do you think it is?"

"You invested in more vineries, didn't you? Without telling me? Didn't I say it's a time to be especially cautious with our money?"

I smiled up at him. "I haven't bought any vineries."

"Then what?"

"I'm carrying your child."

As time had gone by, Tavius had tried to act as if our childlessness did not matter. I had never believed this pretense. Now, seeing how his face lit up, I sensed how desperately he had wanted us to have a child.

He kissed me until I was breathless. "Our son will rule the whole empire," he said. "All of it. I swear to you."

I felt a cold prickle on the back of my neck and almost said, *What about Antony?* But he had spoken in wild exuberance. It seemed foolish to make an issue of his words.

"Can we still—?" Tavius murmured.

"Of course," I said.

I had to keep whispering words of reassurance: "Beloved, the baby won't mind." We came together so gently that night. Out of our happiness grew a fresh flowering of love. The soft, unhurried caresses, the murmured endearments, the all-encompassing tenderness reminded me of how it had been when we first married.

⋙⋙

Perhaps it was the greatest joy I ever experienced in my life. To lie in my husband's arms and know his child nestled within me, to picture a little boy with his blue eyes. To know I had not failed him after all. It had taken so long. We both felt as if we had been blessed with a miracle.

I made thank-offerings at all the temples. In particular, I thanked Diana. I asked only one thing more of her—that I bear a male child.

Yet, even at this time, which ought to have been so happy, there was still the tension with Antony, which sooner or later might destroy all our peace. And grief, very close to home. Tiberius Nero was dying.

I tried not to admit it at first, though he grew paler, thinner, and more spectral each time I saw him. He had an ulcer on his leg that would not heal. The doctors lanced it three times, and drained pus from it, but the ulcer worsened. I brought him medicinal drinks, but his sickness was far beyond the reach of any healing skill of mine.

"I'm for it," he said to me one day, as I sat by his bedside.

"No," I said. "It's just a matter of time until you get better."

"We know each other too well for lies."

I bit my lip.

"About my will—"

"Don't talk about that," I said. "Talk about getting well."

"Livia, dear, I'm in very little pain right now. But the pain will come back, and then I'll take a draught for it, and I won't be able to talk. So listen to me now."

I sat in the same bedchamber I had first entered as a girl of fourteen, where I used to gaze at the ceiling, wishing that he would take his hands off me. I thought of never seeing him or hearing his voice again, and my eyes burned with tears. "I am listening," I said.

"Well, I'm freeing a few of my slaves and leaving bequests for them. You'll see that my wishes are honored, I'm sure."

I nodded. His red-haired slave girl now spent her time hovering over his sickbed. I guessed he would provide for her.

"With the exception of those small bequests, everything goes to the boys. I'm happy to be able to leave them fairly well off." For a moment, he did look happy, even self-satisfied. "And I named just the right guardian for them and their property, until they come of age."

I had pushed the thought of this away, because I had not been able to accept that Tiberius Nero was dying. But there had to be a male guardian. The idea of a stranger with authority over my sons disturbed me. What if Tiberius Nero had made the wrong choice?

He read my expression. "Don't you trust me? Of course I chose Caesar. Who else? That's what you'd advise, isn't it?"

I fought to control a sob. "Yes," I said. "Yes. It's what I would advise. Yes. Thank you."

"Caesar promised me once that he would see the boys well placed in the army and public careers. I'm sure I can take his word on that. They'll be important men. I'm leaving quite a legacy behind me. Livia, dear, I beg you, stop crying."

I tried, but I found I could not.

He said with a faint smile, "Really, you've got to do better than this. I'm not even dead yet."

"You never said you forgave me," I said. "You've been so kind. But you never said that."

"Ah well . . ." His face tensed. I saw that he was suffering pain.

"I'll get the girl to bring you a draught," I said.

"Yes, do that, will you?"

I went to the door and gave an order.

When I came back, Tiberius Nero said, "You were fond of me, weren't you? I know you sometimes used to playact in bed. Women do that. But it wasn't all an act, was it?"

I shook my head and took his hand. It felt fleshless now, just bone. "I cared for you. I still do. And in Sparta—in Sparta for a while—well, we were happy in Sparta."

"Sparta," he said. "Well, well." Then his face contorted. "If only Caesar hadn't come along . . . Livia, I do forgive you. Cupid's arrow, right? But curse it, you should have ducked. I'm joking, I'm just joking. Mars, help me, it's bad now, it's very bad. Will you tell Lollia to hurry with that drink?"

If my son Tiberius had been a year or two younger, no one would have expected him to play the part of a man at his father's funeral. Even at his age—nine—he was very young for it, young to deliver his father's eulogy and to light his pyre.

Tavius took his duties as guardian seriously from the first. "People will remember how he acts now," he said to me. "It's important for his future."

Some part of me wanted to cry out that my son was a little boy who had spent the night weeping for his father. He was not up to speechmaking. Though I kept silent, my qualms must have affected Tavius. Before we set out for Tiberius Nero's house, where his body lay in the atrium ready for its final journey, he took my son aside. "If this is too hard for you, you've only to say it. You don't have to give the speech."

"Sir, I'm Father's eldest son. Who else should speak about him? Drusus?"

Quite gently, Tavius said, "What I mean is I can give the eulogy in your place."

Tiberius's eyes blazed. "You? But Father wouldn't want you to do it. He would want me."

Tavius had placed his hand on Tiberius's shoulder. He removed it. But he said in the same gentle voice, "You're right. He would want you to do it."

We walked to the Forum behind the open wagon on which the body lay—Tiberius Nero resting on his side, his limbs arranged as if he were on a dinner couch waiting for a feast to be set before him. In front of the wagon the men in wax portrait masks marched in seemly rows—his ancestors leading him to the afterlife. The hired mourners wailed, and crowds came out to look at us. Many people joined the procession. I held Drusus's hand, and Tavius held Julia's. Tiberius walked a little apart from the rest of the family.

In the Forum, friends of his father escorted Tiberius up to the speakers' platform. He spoke to the assembled multitude. "We come here to honor my father, the former praetor Tiberius Claudius Nero." Tiberius's high-pitched boy's voice was steady and surprisingly strong. "My father was an able senator and a great military commander. Julius Caesar himself praised him for his bravery." He spoke about his father's contribution to Julius Caesar's famous victories in Gaul. The speech had been written for him, of course, but he had memorized every word. "As you all know," he said toward the end, "my father was a steadfast and devoted friend to my dear stepfather, Caesar Octavianus." I had feared his garbling this line or saying it halfheartedly. But no one could have faulted his delivery.

Later, at the Field of Mars, Tiberius took the flaming brand, strode forward and lit his father's pyre, and stood there watching it burn, holding back his tears. I saw his father at that moment—not the uncertain politician but the man who had led raid after raid against the enemy at Perusia though the cause was hopeless. I also saw the courage of his grandsire, my own father. A voice in my heart whispered, *My son will be a great man.*

And yet, afterward, Tiberius lapsed back into being a sad, rather difficult little boy. I had him and Drusus now under my own roof, and that was a thing for which I had never even dared hope. But in small ways Tiberius could irk me as no one else could. Once he saw me when I came home from helping people at a fire. I had a smudge of soot on my cheek. "Mama," he said, "your face is dirty. I don't think you should go to fires. It's unseemly for a lady." I nearly clouted him on the head.

Drusus and little Marcus were easy children to raise. My stepdaughter, like Tiberius, was quite another matter. I don't think she was more than five years old the first time Tavius sighed and said, "I have two spoiled daughters—Rome and Julia." He spent little time with her but was generous with presents. If I scolded her, she complained about me to her father, and he would tell me I expected too much of a child her age. Now that my sons shared my home, Julia and Tiberius decided to warmly dislike each other, and had to be disciplined for quarreling. It grated on my nerves. Meanwhile I was sick every morning, and often later in the day too. This continued even after I felt my baby's first kick.

About that time, one of my informants brought me a tale being told in the marketplace, a little ripple in the river of gossip that engulfed the great in Rome.

People told ugly stories about me because they thought of me as powerful. They certainly never gossiped in the same way about poor, mistreated Octavia.

"Maybe I shouldn't even tell you this, Lady Livia," my informant said. He was a butcher who had a stall in the marketplace, a gregarious man in whom other people confided. He would come to see me in surreptitious ways, never letting anyone know that he had my ear.

We sat in my study. I had a huge pile of work before me that morning. I tapped my stylus impatiently on the edge of my writing table. "Tell me," I said.

"There are people who say you poisoned Tiberius Nero because you wanted your boys back." The butcher rolled his eyes. "They say you are adept with herbs, and you were seen going into his house with a potion."

"What fools some people are," I said. "If I brought Tiberius Nero anything, it was for his good."

"Lady Livia, I'm sure of it."

This story, a mere bubble of conjecture, did not matter. Not then, not ever. And if it made me feel sick inside—well, I was having a difficult pregnancy and felt nauseated a good part of the time anyway.

I put the butcher's tale out of my mind, and concentrated on my work and on the future. I looked forward to two events, one with trepidation, one with great joy: the time when Tavius's alliance with Antony would officially end, and the birth of my child.

Chapter 16

When I felt the first pains, I told one of my maids to summon the midwife, and was struck by the calm sound of my own voice. I wonder sometimes, if the whole world went up in smoke, would I speak in just that steady tone?

Mathematics is a cold art. Numbers are unyielding as stone. You can beg and weep all you want, but that will not change them. The number of soldiers on each side of a battle is a matter of life and death. So, too, the number of months a child is in the womb.

The midwife crouched at my feet. I sat on the birthing chair, my hands gripping its mahogany arms, knowing the time was wrong, that the child should not be born for another three months. I prayed for my labor to stop, for my baby to stay warm and safe within me.

"What will you name him?" I had asked Tavius as we lay in each other's arms after I told him I was pregnant.

"What do you think?"

"Tell me."

"Gaius Julius Caesar." His adoptive father's full name.

"What a name for a little mite," I said.

"He'll grow into it. It will make him strong."

The baby was perfectly formed and male. But tiny. I heard the midwife say, "It's still alive. We should wrap it in something."

It.

"Give me my baby," I said.

"Wait. The afterbirth is coming."

They put me to bed finally and placed the infant in my arms. "Lie down. Rest, please," the midwife said.

I sat up in bed. I did not want to lie down, because if I did perhaps I would go to sleep, and when I awoke, my son would be past needing his mother. I held him close. Tavius's son and mine. Gaius Julius Caesar. He had no weight. His eyes were shut. His skin looked as delicate as flower petals. When he turned his head, I could see tiny blue veins near his temple.

I did not notice when Tavius came into the room. All of a sudden he stood over me. His expression was what I imagined it would be if he ever suffered a mortal wound in battle.

I flinched away from the sight of his face and gazed down at the baby. The child's eyelids kept fluttering, as if he were trying to open his eyes and look at the world.

"Livia," Tavius said.

"Don't try to find comforting words," I said. "There is no comfort."

"The midwife asked me to tell you to rest. You shouldn't be sitting up. You ought to sleep."

I raised my eyes from the baby and looked at Tavius. "Acknowledge him."

He shook his head. "He can't live."

I held the baby out in my arms. Tavius did not want to take him. He stood there, avoiding my gaze. I just kept holding the baby out to him. We remained in those poses, like statues, for what seemed a long time.

Finally, he took the child and said, "Let him be called Gaius." I could hear how close he was to tears. But he never looked down at the baby, just quickly gave him back to me. After that, he went away.

The midwife entered and said I should let her have the baby, so I could rest. "You called him 'it,'" I said. "Go home. I have no need of you."

Later a physician came. "Rest is what you want," he said. "You've been sitting up for hours."

Really? I thought. *Has it been hours?*

"Now, let your maids take the baby, and you go to sleep," the physician said.

I did not pay any attention to him.

When the baby's eyelids stopped fluttering, I slipped my hand inside the blanket and felt his tiny chest. "Breathe," I whispered. I remembered saying that to little Tiberius when we hid from the forest fire in the cave. *Breathe. Live.* I thought of how unappreciative I had been when my other sons were born. I had been young. It had never occurred to me what a blessing it was that life should arise within my womb. I only saw that miracle for what it was, now when it failed.

The midwife entered the room. She had disobeyed me and had not gone home. "Please, give me the child," she said, and I let her take him. When she told me to lie down, I obeyed. I might as well obey. What difference did it make what I did?

I fell into a fever. I remember the heat, and maids wiping my face with cool cloths.

Once Diana came to me, her eyes shining like stars. She stroked my forehead. "Child, you are burning up."

"The baby . . . I want my baby."

"Hush," she said.

"Apollo loves you, doesn't he? Better than anyone. You're his twin. Mother could never give Father a son. She had babies who died too. But Father loved her anyway. I want my baby. You're a goddess. Can't you make them give me back my baby?"

"My poor daughter." Diana looked at me with sadness and went on stroking my brow with her cool hand. "Did you think there was no price to pay?"

I opened my eyes. Tavius sat beside me. "Try to be still," he said.

"Why?"

"You need to sleep."

"Aren't I sleeping?"

"You keep thrashing around. They're afraid you'll throw yourself out of bed."

"I'm thirsty . . . Where are you going?"

"To get you water," Tavius said.

"No, don't go. I have to tell you. We're cursed. Diana as much as told me. This is how we will pay. Through our children."

He said, in a cool, remote voice, "What have we done to deserve a curse?"

"You know. You know as well as I do."

"Listen to me," he said. "You're not well. You have a fever. You're raving."

"Is the baby really dead?"

"Yes." His voice was clotted with grief.

"Why did he die?"

"He was born too soon. Don't you remember?"

"I lost my baby . . . I'll lose you too, won't I? Tavius—"

"Livia, you must hush now, because you don't know what you're saying."

"Help me! The fire is faster than I am. I don't see the cave. Where is my son?"

Tavius's face seemed to fade away. Someone bathed my face with cool water, but it was not my husband.

⋙⋙

Of course I recovered. I have always been strong.

My life continued much as it had been. I was busy with political work, and with my charities and business ventures. Though Tavius spoke gently to me, for a time it was hard for him to look at me. I believed there would never be a child now. I think in his heart Tavius also believed that door had been shut forever.

What is a wife for, I asked myself, *if not to bear children? If not that, first and foremost?*

Tavius had his daughter by Scribonia, but no son, no heir. I had my boys. How strange, we could have beautiful, healthy children by other mates. But our love would be fruitless. So the gods decreed. Are the gods unjust?

One night, before we slept, I whispered to Tavius, "No one will ever love you as much as I do."

"I know that," he said.

Did I only imagine that I heard regret in his voice?

Great affairs did not pause for our private grief. The term of the alliance between Tavius and Antony ended. Tavius, Maecenas, and I crafted the speech that Tavius delivered to the Senate, to explain why the alliance had not been renewed. "You have the best sense of the three of us of what the nobility wants to hear," Tavius said to me. "For that matter, of what the people of Rome want to hear."

I was surprised that he admitted it so baldly. "What they want to hear is that you and Antony are still allies, because that assures peace," I said. "But we can't tell them that, can we?"

"No," he said flatly.

"Then speak with as little personal animus as you can. Talk about how Antony has succumbed to . . . not a woman other than your sister, but foreign influences. He is the puppet of a foreign ruler." There was a carving of a war galley on one of the shelves in Tavius's study, accurate in every detail, a long-ago gift from Agrippa. I found myself staring at it. "Tell them that despite this, you don't want war."

"Truthfully, Antony is hardly Roman anymore," Tavius said.

I thought of how the common people loathed and distrusted anything and anyone that was not Roman. Even the nobility shared much of this feeling.

"Foreign influences." Maecenas nodded. He began scribbling a speech on a waxed tablet.

"If I understand the people, it is because I am like them," I said to Tavius later. "They do not want their sons to die in another civil war."

"Do you know that Antony is building up his navy?"

"If he didn't at this juncture, he would be a fool," I said. *And yet,* I thought, *war is not inevitable.*

Tavius went to the Senate the next day and delivered a fairly moderate speech. "I slipped once," he told me. "I called Antony a drunkard."

I knew he had wanted to call him far worse names. "The point about foreign influence—how did the Senate respond to that?"

Tavius gave me a satisfied smile.

⋙⋙

Antony wrote a savage letter in answer to Tavius's speech, and he made it public. His agents distributed numerous papyrus copies in the Roman streets at the same time that Tavius received the original. In a one-hour period, four of my informants brought me copies of the letter they found in the Forum.

This letter's insults were comparable to those Cicero had once aimed at Antony—insults for which Antony had cut off his head and his hand. Antony called Tavius a "puny, sickly, limping cripple." He said he was a coward, afraid to face the enemy at Philippi, leaving Antony to do his bloody work, then unable to even rise from his bed in Sicily, hiding in fear while Agrippa went to confront Sextus Pompey's fleet.

Antony said Tavius's father had sprung from a line of manual laborers. His father had been able to marry a daughter of the Julii only because he became rich and that noble family was desperate for money. Why, Tavius's great-grandfather had actually been a former slave, a rope maker. Antony traced out Tavius's descent from this slave down three generations. Reading that family tree—noting the detail, the naming of people and places—one sensed that it was probably accurate and that Antony had been investigating Tavius's background for a long time.

Then came the part that made my heart die. "What's come over you?" Antony wrote to Tavius. "Why this hostility? Is it that I'm screwing the queen? What does it matter in whom I insert my prick? And what about you? Is Drusilla the only woman you screw? Good luck to you if, when you read this letter, you haven't also screwed Tertulla or Terentilla or Rufilla or Salvia Titisenia or all of them."

Terentilla, of course, was Maecenas's wife. If I had been a supreme fool, I would have assumed Antony alluded to something long in the past. But I was not such a fool. The other three—I knew them too. I had seen them make eyes at Tavius at dinner parties. I had seen him smile back at them. And I had looked away, as if I had seen nothing.

>>>>>>>

The two of us stood in my study.

"You read it?" he said.

"Of course."

"I never knew my great-grandfather was a slave."

I shrugged.

"What he said . . . about the women . . ."

"Yes?"

Tavius must have known it was pointless to deny what Antony had said on this score—as pointless to deny as the pedigree tracing his bloodline back to a slave. It is difficult to disprove truth.

"If you understood," Tavius said in a low, careful voice, "what a small portion of my life that has been. If you understood how trivial it was—a matter of taking, once in a great while, what was freely offered. It had nothing to do with my life with you."

"Of course," I said, keeping my voice level. "I know that."

I felt that saying anything else would be throwing away all my pride. For who but a fool expected a husband to be faithful? Who? Men of our rank always had other women beside their wives. I had known this. And yet somehow I had refused to believe Tavius could share with someone else what he shared with me. How odd that lack of belief was. It amounted to willful ignorance.

A voice inside my mind cried out: *But he worked so hard, he was so busy! And we were together so much. When in the world did he have time for other women?* But I realized these thoughts were absurd. I would not shame myself by speaking them aloud.

"I never loved any of them," Tavius said. Perhaps he knew me well enough to see through my composure to what lay underneath. He touched my shoulder. "Livia . . ."

"Dearest, you're talking to me about things that are beneath my notice. Really, I prefer not to hear any more about this." Then, because I feared I would cry, or claw his face with my nails, I walked out of the room.

I sat in the garden alone for a time, thinking that whatever else happened, something had been lost to us forever. I had feared his leaving me for a wife who could bear him a child. Now I saw that our marriage would never be what it could have been, whether or not we stayed together.

I watched a bee circle around a long-stemmed iris. Up in a tree, a blackbird sang.

Perhaps I will take a lover, I thought. But I knew I wouldn't. Because there was no other man I wanted. I wondered if that meant I loved Tavius, even now. Maybe. At that moment, I felt absolutely no love for him. How strange, how empty I felt.

⋙⋙

Later that day, I sat with my husband and Maecenas and tried to plot out strategy in light of new events. Maecenas kept darting uneasy glances at me. I ignored that. "Antony is trying to pass off his liaison with Cleopatra as if it were some frivolous love affair," I said. "But Rome will see through that. A foreign queen, and he lets her rule him. That is what Rome will not abide." I looked at Tavius. "Do not even try to answer his slurs. Treat them with cold disdain. That is what Antony deserves. Utter disdain. Denounce him for bowing to Cleopatra, a woman ruler, a foreign queen. You cannot say those two words often enough: *foreign queen*. She wants to rule him, and he, the imbecile, is so blinded—blinded by *lust*—that he will let her do it. That is what you must say."

Tavius nodded, his face looking as if it were carved in stone.

Later, Maecenas sought me out alone. "I want to say I admire you. And you are dealing with this exactly as you should."

A flame of pure rage rose in me. "Oh, am I? Thank you for saying so, Maecenas. You knew it had begun again between him and Terentilla, didn't you? Of course you did. And you just smiled at me."

"Was I supposed to carry tales to you? Please, keep this in perspective. You're the only woman Caesar has ever truly cared for. Isn't that what matters?"

"I don't know," I said. "And I wonder if it's even true. Should I believe it is true, just because you say it? As if you would not willingly lie to smooth his way?"

Maecenas shook his head, wounded.

Of course I knew I was being unfair, venting anger at Tavius on poor Maecenas. I did not care. I patted his cheek. "There, there. We are still friends. But I will know how to value your friendship in the future."

>>>>>>>

Antony also wrote Octavia a letter. Her eyes were dry when she told me about it.

"It was short. I can quote it to you, in case you're curious. 'Octavia, I divorce you. Take what is yours and leave my house.' Not another word, just his seal."

We sat alone in the garden of Antony's house. Inside, slaves were packing Octavia's things.

We heard a boy's loud voice. "My turn!"

"That's Antyllus," Octavia said. "The children are all so noisy. If one is not shouting, another one is crying. What I would give for a little silence. There was nothing about the children in the letter. I suppose I could send his four to Antony, and he'd have to accept them."

I stared at her. Send him her own daughters, Antonia and Antonilla, along with Fulvia's sons?

"I'm joking," she said. "I'll take them all with me when I move, my stepsons too. I hope Antony never remembers them." Her face went stricken. "But they remember *him*. Antyllus especially. He worships his father."

"Tavius will look after them all," I said.

"Yes, I know he will. With a great air of wounded sanctimony." Her expression grew kind. "I've been so full of my own troubles. We never speak of yours."

We had become friends over the last months, a thing I once would never have believed possible.

I patted back a wisp of my hair that had come loose. "That hero statue of Tavius in the Forum—the one with the gold plating—do you know, when they put it up, I thought it was a close likeness of him? Now, I realize it's not. It's good to see things clearly." *Let's change the subject.*

"I still pray there is no war," Octavia said. We could hear Antyllus, his brother, Jullus, and Octavia's son, Marcellus, yelling at each other. "They always argue like that, but in the end they work things out. Really, they're good boys." She paused. "Why do boys grow up to be such beasts? Is it our fault in some way? After all, we raise them."

I had no answers to her questions.

"Can you imagine what it is like to watch the whole world dissolve in war, and realize you could have prevented it if only you'd managed to hold on to your husband?"

I put my arm around Octavia's shoulder. She smelled of floral perfume, a light, clean scent. "I don't think Tavius has decided yet if he will strike if Antony doesn't," I said.

"I believe Tavius will kill Antony in the end," Octavia said. "Or else Antony will kill Tavius, and how is that better?" Her eyes filled with tears. "All the time I was away from Antony, I wrote him letters. I never reproached him. I gave him news of the children, the little things that would strike him funny. I sweated blood over those letters."

And while she labored in the writing, he was in another woman's bed. I whispered, "Did you love him?"

"Not as you love Tavius. More as you love a child. But I will never stop loving him."

She was a good woman. Better than I was in many ways. Looking at her I had a sorrowful sense of the ineffectuality of her sort of goodness in the world.

Tavius and I spoke to each other from a great distance now. And yet a night soon came when he reached for me with anxious need. I did not turn from him, nor did I lay like a cold statue under his caresses.

He began kissing my feet. As I felt his mouth, moving slowly up my body, I closed my eyes. The pleasure came, without my will. But a part of me seemed to hover over the bed, watching with a cynical half-smile.

In the days that followed, I often thought of how for him I had left my first marriage, giving up my sons. Many would say I had abandoned my honor too. What sacrifice had Tavius ever made for me? Would he be willing to give up anything at all for my sake?

When I managed to banish dark thoughts about my marriage, no peaceful musings came to replace them, only fear of what might be coming. Soon Tavius was spending most of his time away from Rome in army camps in Italy, expanding his forces and fortifying their resolve. Agrippa believed in the utility of smaller galleys, which he said could outmaneuver Antony's warships. Tavius began to build these at a frantic pace. Agrippa oversaw the training of the ships' crews. None of this could be hidden. Rome braced for war.

⋙⋙

I did everything I could to bolster Tavius's political position at this time, using the ties I had built up over years with senators and senators' wives. When Tavius was away from Rome, I kept in close touch with my web of informants and guarded his back.

Few senators loved Antony, but some thought he would rule with a looser rein than Tavius did, and preferred that. Others took Antony's bribes.

When the two consuls, who favored Antony, plotted to arrange a Senate vote censuring Tavius—rebuking him for provoking war—I heard of it. I did not hesitate; I knew these men intended Tavius's overthrow, and I immediately sent him warning. He came marching back to Rome, at the head of his legions. Indeed, he marched right into a Senate session. His opponents scattered. There was brawling in the streets, two days of uproar, though the outcome was never in doubt. When the dust cleared, one-third of the Senate had raced off to join Antony.

At first I looked around me in disbelief. The harmony I had helped to cultivate had shattered. Then I felt relieved that at least we had held two-thirds of the Senate.

"I must know who is for me and who is against me," Tavius said. We sat together in his study. His face was set in grim lines.

"Don't you know by who has fled and who has not?" I said, acid in my voice.

"I want my supporters to take a loyalty oath," he said. "They must swear to back me in case of war."

"Dearest, listen to me," I said. "I don't think Cleopatra and Antony have any intention of attacking now. It's too great a risk. If they are looking anywhere for conquest, they are looking east."

He shifted his shoulders. "Sooner or later they will want it all," he said.

"Sooner or later? Sooner or later none of us will be alive!" I caught myself and spoke more calmly. "Why rush into a war that may not be necessary? When no one can say which side will win?"

He looked at me, his eyes guarded and opaque. "I have made no final decision."

Up and down the length of Italy the armies took an oath of allegiance to him. Soon civilians were hustled into town squares, to take the oath too, because Caesar demanded it.

I hid what I thought of this oath-taking business even from my best friends, but not from Tavius. He knew I hated it as he knew I hated the thought of war. I had acted to protect him when the consuls plotted against him, but I could not give him the approval he wanted now.

I saw the horror of civil war coming closer and closer, and it was clear that my beloved husband planned to unleash it. He wished to preempt the possibility of war in the future, when he might be weaker and Antony stronger. He itched to avenge his sister's wrongs. And most fundamentally, he was possessed by a vision. He believed he was meant to hold all of the Roman empire in his hands.

He and I had never been so separate. When we talked of war and peace, my voice became more and more charged with desperation, his replies more and more curt.

If you are afraid, you will snatch eagerly at anything that might promise rescue. When Octavia suddenly received a letter from Antony, my heart leaped with wild hope. I imagined a contrite missive, saying that he had parted from Cleopatra. But no. The letter concerned his children.

He had remembered he had left two sons in Tavius's hands. Plainly he feared that in case of war they could be used against him as hostages, or that Tavius might simply murder them. Antony gave permission for his daughters to remain with Octavia, but he wanted his sons sent to him in Alexandria.

Tavius said, "Put them on the first ship out." But Octavia pleaded that the boys be given a choice.

So, we had another of our grim family gatherings—Tavius, Octavia, and me, in a sitting room in the house in Rome, next to our own, that Tavius had bestowed on his sister. We were joined by Antyllus, then not quite fifteen, and ten-year-old Jullus. They both came from the schoolroom, where they had been at work with their tutor. Jullus had been learning to write Greek letters on papyrus and had ink smeared on his fingers.

Tavius spoke somberly. "You two are not yet men," he told the boys, "but—there's no help for it—you each have to make a man's decision now."

He wanted them to realize that this was a choice of the gravest kind, that it might determine their whole future. The older boy understood. But little Jullus?

"You must either join your father or stay here with us. If you stay, I'll treat you as my sister's sons," Tavius said. "So long as you're loyal to me, you'll be members of my family. It's up to you."

"I want to go to my father!" Antyllus cried.

I saw Octavia shut her eyes in pain. But she said not a word.

Tavius turned to Jullus.

Looking at that boy, seeing his whole body tense, his eyes go wide, I pitied him. He shook and opened his mouth, but no words came out. Then he looked at Octavia, who had been a mother to him for as long as he could remember, and said, "I want to stay with you."

"Traitor!" Antyllus cried.

Jullus flung himself into Octavia's arms, and she held him while he sobbed.

"Miserable traitor! Father will win, and then you'll be sorry! You're siding with the enemy, don't you know it? You're not my brother anymore. You—"

"Enough," Tavius said.

Antyllus clamped his mouth shut.

"Since you are your father's son," Tavius said, "I don't suppose you feel any gratitude toward my sister, who cared for you all these years?"

Antyllus straightened. "I do," he said with a pained dignity. Looking at Octavia, he said, "I will always say you treated me as kindly as if you were my own mother." She nodded to him and tried to smile. She still held his brother in her arms. Antyllus turned back to Tavius. He sneered, and I saw a trace of Fulvia in his features. "When can I take ship for Alexandria? It can't be soon enough."

A former friend of Antony's fled to our side, and whispered in Tavius's ear that something in Antony's will—which he claimed to have seen—was gravely discrediting. Following traditional practice, Antony had placed his will in the protection of the Vestal Virgins. Tavius said he meant to seize it.

"That would violate all custom," I said. I almost added that it would violate all decency too.

"Do you love me?"

We were in our bedchamber when this conversation took place. "What a strange question for you to ask," I said.

I remembered when in the early days of our marriage I had said I liked Sextus Pompey. How warily Tavius had regarded me, and how carefully I had chosen my words to convince him he had my deepest loyalty. He was looking at me now just as he looked at me then.

"Do you love me?" he asked again.

I drew closer to him. I stroked his cheek, and then traced the outline of his lips with my forefinger. He suffered this, an impassive expression on his face. At that moment, I ached with tenderness for him as I had not for a long time. I took his face in my hands and kissed him. "Of course I love you."

"Then why are you seeking to protect my enemy?"

"I'm not. I'm afraid of war."

"I have work still to do. I'll come back and sleep later," he said and walked out of the room.

I lay down on the bed. A candle flickered on the bedside table. When it died and plunged the room into darkness, he had still not returned.

The next day, he demanded Antony's will from the Vestal Virgins. They refused to give it to him, so he led soldiers into their temple to confiscate it. In the will, Antony had directed that wherever he died, even if it were in Rome, his body was to be given to Cleopatra, and laid to rest not in Rome but in Alexandria.

You cannot say the words "foreign queen" often enough, I had told Tavius. In the attack he made on Antony, standing before the Senate and holding up the will, he spoke those words again and again. His following my advice had a certain irony, for he excoriated Antony for being a woman's obedient slave. He had been unmanned by Cleopatra! When Cleopatra ruled Rome, as she clearly meant to do, we would be governed not by consuls and generals but by hairdressers and perfumers, not to mention eunuchs. Antony, Tavius said, was a foreign queen's plaything. He was no man, and he was certainly no patriot if he wanted to be buried away from Rome.

⋙⋙

"Civil war again." I choked on the words.

Tavius was on his feet, leaning back against the writing table in his study. I sat across from him on the couch. We had had so many fruitful discussions in this room, had worked for Rome's good here. "I won't declare war on Antony but on Egypt—on Cleopatra," he said.

As if that mattered. "My love, please don't do this."

Tavius sat down beside me and took my hands in his. "Livia, it has to be one empire. Has to be. How can I share rule with a man like Antony? It is unworkable."

"But what if you lose?"

He looked at me as if he did not understand the language I spoke. He let go of my hands.

"What is all this to you?" I said. "Just another toss of the dice?"

"You know better than that," he said. "I feel the weight of responsibility every moment of the day. But I have a destiny. I know what I can do for Rome, for the whole empire, how well I can govern."

"My beloved, you *can* lose, you know. And even if you don't—think of the slaughter."

"To have a destiny like mine is not always pleasant," he said. "I would not recommend it to anyone who had a free choice. For one thing, it's often lonely."

"Oh, Tavius—" The distance between us seemed so great. It was all mixed together, our differences on the matter of war and peace, our inability to comfort each other after our baby died, the fact that he had lain with other women. All the accumulated discords and hurts of seven years of marriage formed a gulf at this moment.

I wanted to reach out to him, to take his hand again, but I did not. For some reason I could not.

"When I mention my destiny, you look at me as if I'm half-mad. I'm not. I see what is required of me, for Rome's sake." He spoke in a measured voice. I had the feeling he was striving to show me a serene surface. *Look how calm I am as we discuss this,* he was saying. *How can you possibly think I'm half-mad?*

As if I were gazing at a stranger, I was struck by his flawless visage, his blue eyes and golden hair, the fine molding of his features. Even after years of marriage, there were moments when I would catch my breath looking at him, when his beauty still seemed almost godlike to me. I thought, *If he is a god, he is a god of destruction.* No, he was not mad, but he was about to ignite civil war.

Since our marriage, I had thought myself powerful. But now I saw that no real power had been mine. It had always all been his. I had possessed only a knack for wheedling favors.

"You'll see," he said. "I'll win."

"Tavius, please, please, if civil war must come again, let it be on Antony's head. Not yours. Father Jupiter sees what we do. Do you doubt that? We have enough to pay for already, both of us. Beloved—" A well of grief and terror had opened inside me, and tears burned my eyes. Could no words reach him? "We've already been punished with the loss of a child. Do you want Julia and my boys to suffer too?"

His face had become an expressionless mask. "You think the baby's death was the gods' punishment? That's interesting. What do you imagine we deserved punishment for?"

You, for the blood you shed. Me, for betraying my parents' memory and leaving my husband and children for you.

I remained silent, but it was as if he heard my unspoken words. His face tightened, and his eyes seemed to go black. "You choose this moment to succumb to nonsensical guilt and superstitious dread, as if you were a peasant woman?" he said. "At this juncture you lose courage?"

"If this war were right and necessary, I would have courage for it," I said.

"So you're deserting me."

"Am I deserting you by refusing to worship with you at the shrine of your destiny?"

He stood up and as he rose, he was overcome by a paroxysm of coughing and nearly stumbled. He pressed his fist to his mouth, looking infuriated.

"Tavius—"

"You said it didn't matter about the other women," he said. His voice sounded hoarse and raw. "But that was a lie, wasn't it? Is that why you're deserting me?"

I rose and stared at him.

My lack of support was a blow that had sent him reeling. He felt betrayed, and he was deeply shaken or he never would have brought up his liaisons. I thought, *This is the moment to walk back from the edge, before everything good between us is destroyed.* But there was a coil of rage in the center of my chest.

"I thought I could always count on your loyalty," he said. "But I've been watching it erode day by day."

The coil of rage tightened. "And you've been so unfailingly loyal to me."

"What do you mean?"

"You're so loyal to me, as you chase your sluts."

His mouth twisted. "Not many men in my position would keep a wife who was barren."

Pain ripped through me. But rage spoke. "I'm only barren with you," I said.

I knew how deep my knife went in by the way he smiled. I was glad I had hurt him. I wanted to hurt him more.

I felt anger not only at him but at my whole life, how hobbled I had always been, struggling to shape events despite my bonds, and falling, rising to my feet to try again and finally failing when it mattered most, at this terrifying juncture.

"What a pleasure it is," he said, "to have a wife like you, who meddles in my business, and never shuts her mouth, and then when I'm beset by enemies, sides with those who hate me. Are you a traitor or only a coward?" He thrust his face close to mine. "Which are you?"

Our eyes locked. I knew he wanted to intimidate me and make me look away. I stood motionless, returning his gaze. I could give blow for blow. "Do you think it's been a joy to me," I said, "to be married to a monster? The beast who destroyed the Republic?"

He stiffened and took a step back from me.

His worst anger was not hot. It was cold. When he spoke he sounded like an accountant or a schoolmaster who was also an executioner. "You ungrateful, perfidious bitch," he said. "Get out of my sight."

My heart lurched. I stood there for a moment quivering. Then I whirled and walked out of the room.

»»»»»»»

We lived together like strangers as he made final preparations for battle. He declared war on Cleopatra in the ancient way of our ancestors. He went outside the city limits, sacrificed a pig, dipped a spear in its blood, and threw the spear in the direction of Egypt. In this manner, he summoned the gods of Rome to fight Egypt's jackal-headed gods.

The army's departure day came. He entered my study, where I continued to tend to administrative matters, even sorting his mail. I felt our marriage was over. But I numbly performed my usual tasks, and would continue doing so until he told me to stop.

He glanced over a few letters I had set aside for him. Then without looking up, he said, "You ought to have stood by me. You should have realized I'm acting for Rome's sake."

"Every time the Republic was ripped apart, every time murder was done, the assassins said they acted for Rome's sake. And maybe they all believed it. But it came down to this—they wanted power."

"You say that to me? You compare me to assassins?" His eyes glittered. "What kind of wife are you?"

No wife at all, I thought. *No wife at all now.* I did not speak.

His anger ebbed, became something else, perhaps mere indifference. "Tell me," he said, "because I'm curious. If it goes badly for me, and Antony comes here, what will you do?"

I gazed at the winged figure of victory that was etched on his breastplate. "What do you imagine I'll do? I'll twist and turn like an eel to keep the children alive."

Tavius nodded as if he had expected me to say this. "Feel free to spit on my memory if you have to. Rest assured, I will not care." He spoke as though we were discussing something of no account. Then in a different tone, he said, "When you say 'the children,' are you including Julia?"

"I said the children."

"You'll look after her."

I said nothing.

"Tell me you'll look after her."

"Yes. Yes! Are you having misgivings now?"

"Not at all. But one must think of every eventuality."

Yes, I thought. *One must.*

I will remember this conversation. I will remember it always. How he looked. The sound of his voice. If he is killed, this is what I will remember.

"Aren't you going to say some farewell words, Livia? 'With your shield or on it'? Something sweet like that?"

I said one word. It came out harsh and guttural. *"Win."*

"I intend to," he said.

If one of us had made a move toward the other, even held out a hand, what would have happened? But neither of us did. Nor did I weep or scream at him or beg him not to go. I wanted to curse him, and I wanted to cling to him forever. We were both silent.

He walked away. I heard him in the atrium, saying good-bye to the children. Then he was gone.

"Have you received any letters lately from Agrippa?" I asked Caecilia.

"I got one just a few days ago," she said. She was my guest at Prima Porta. We dined one evening alone in the summer dining room, reclining on couches with green silk cushions. She received letters regularly from her husband. I never heard from mine. But if she sensed this and it puzzled her, she did not show it. "We write to each other in cipher, you know. Just in case the messenger gets captured. That way Agrippa can write freely and not worry."

"How is he?" I asked. I knew he and Tavius were with the naval fleet, off the shore of Greece on the Ionian Sea.

"Very well. He says everything is going as planned. The new galleys are all he hoped they'd be." She smiled, her eyes shining bright as the sapphire earrings she wore. She was a devoted wife who had seen her husband off to war with a kiss, and now looked forward to his sure victory. "He is so eager for the fight to get under way," she said, a lilt of eagerness in her own voice.

I motioned for a slave to pour more wine into my goblet.

"It's just like being in a garden here." Caecilia looked around at the murals. On all four sides of us the artist had painted trees and flowering plants. "The details are so exact. You can see that tree is an oak and that one is a cypress."

The two trees at which she pointed looked as if they had grown so close together you could never disentangle the branches. Yet they were distinct. "Yes, the artist is very skilled."

"What I like best are the birds," Caecilia said. "Doves, blackbirds, robins . . ."

"If only we were birds," I said. "Imagine how pleasant it would be, to fly wherever we wanted to. To be so free."

"I would fly to the Ionian today," Caecilia said, her expression wistful. "Just to pay a little visit and see what is happening." She nibbled a pastry. "Cleopatra is with Antony. They say she will go into battle at his side. She even has her own warship. She is hardly like a woman at all, is she?"

What was Cleopatra feeling now? Had she believed it would come to war, or had she miscalculated? Did she regret the provocations she and Antony had offered Tavius? Or was she glad that war had come, believing she was about to win an empire?

"Does Agrippa expect the fighting to begin soon?" I asked Caecilia.

She nodded. "He thinks everything will be settled in a great sea battle. He will command half the fleet, and Caesar will command the other half, and they hope to get Antony in between them." My expression must have changed. Caecilia stared at me and said, "Livia, what's wrong?"

I shook my head, trying to hide what I felt. A wave of fear had engulfed me. Agrippa was a skilled admiral and on shipboard always fortune's darling. But every time in the past when Tavius and Agrippa had split their forces at sea, Tavius had met with disaster.

I imagined Tavius's voice saying what he would have if miles and estrangement had not separated us. *Of course I will command one wing and Agrippa the other. Gods above, Livia, did you imagine I would just go along on his ship for the ride? How would that look?*

Silently I cried out to him, *But you are never fortunate fighting at sea! You almost died three times!*

Caecilia gazed at me with dismay. I raised my wine cup and drank. Finally, I managed to speak in a calm voice. "Did Agrippa write when he thinks this naval battle will take place?"

"He thought he might have good news to send me in early September."

Good news. Of course, Agrippa, staunch and confident, expected the news to be good.

The first of September was only five days away.

»»»»»»»

By the first, I had returned to our house in Rome. That day I dealt in Tavius's stead with the city aediles, who came begging for more funds. I looked over the books of one of my commercial farms and wrote a long, reproving letter to the steward. I attended a senator's dinner party that evening. And inside myself I shivered like a sapling in a thunderstorm.

The second day of September, a little before midday I took lunch with the children, Tiberius, Julia, Drusus, and little Marcus. A simple meal, bread, cheese, grapes. Tiberius had spent the morning drilling at the Field of Mars, then cooled off with a swim. His hair was wet, dark curls plastered to his forehead. Julia, sitting next to him on the same dining couch, said, "I can smell the river. You ought to go and bathe."

Tiberius made a face at her.

"I want to swim in the Tiber too," Julia said to me.

"Don't be silly," Tiberius said. "Girls can't swim."

"Fool, I can swim better than you can. Mama Livia, why can't I swim in the Tiber?"

"Because it would be considered immodest for a girl to do that," I said.

"See?" Tiberius said. He poked her. She poked him back.

"Stop it," I said. "Julia, you're free to swim in the pool at the villa. That's much nicer."

Water. The image came into my mind of green and blue waves under the late summer sky.

"The Tiber is mucky and filthy anyway," Julia said.

"Mucky and filthy, mucky and filthy," Marcus singsonged.

"Mucky and filthy!" Drusus cried. He laughed as if it were the most wonderful joke.

"Enough," I said. The children quieted.

Waves. And ships, galleys. Two fleets. One made up of small ships quick as darting fish. The other fleet's ships were slower but much larger, like ponderous beasts of prey.

"The Tiber isn't filthy," Tiberius said.

"Yes, it is," Julia said. "People pass water in it. And you're named after it, aren't you? After the mucky, filthy Tiber."

"Oh, keep quiet," Tiberius said.

"You're rude. Mama Livia, he's rude to me."

In my mind, the two fleets approached each other. The fleet of darting fish split in two.

It's happening now, I thought. *One great sea battle that will decide everything, just as Agrippa told Caecilia. It's happening now.*

"If my father were home, he wouldn't let him be rude to me." Julia's lower lip trembled.

It's happening now. "Silence," I said. "Julia, that's enough."

Who can say what the heart is capable of knowing? Ships with bronze-armored bows rammed each other. Showers of arrows and javelins and catapult stones fell. Missiles tipped with flaming pitch were hurled. Ships went up in flames. Men shrieked as they leaped into the water, burning.

"Mama, why don't you eat?" Drusus asked.

"I'm not hungry." I rose. "You children finish eating. And behave yourselves."

A drumbeat in my mind: *It's happening now, it's happening now.* Tavius aboard a war galley, a faint smile on his face. His own words came back to him: *My bad luck at sea is a constant in a world in flux.* He remembered three lost naval battles, the sinking ships, the sense of the sea reaching out to drown him. A huge armored galley came sweeping through the water, closer, closer. He watched it approach. Men looked at him, waited for his orders.

I entered the small room off the atrium that held a life-sized statue of Diana. I stood before the marble image, my arms stretched out, palms upward in supplication. "Goddess, the fate of Rome will be decided now," I said. "Don't withhold your aid. Protect your people." My voice had been strong and steady, but all at once I choked. "It must not be Antony who wins. Not Antony and his queen, who doesn't even know you. Tavius loves Rome. He will be a good and just ruler. I beg you—I beg you—make Tavius the victor, not Antony."

I remembered how Tavius and I had said farewell. Were those our last moments together? Not a word of love had been spoken. How had I let him leave without saying that I loved him? Imagining Antony's victory, imagining I would never again hold my beloved in my arms, I sank to my knees and could not restrain my tears.

The eyes of the statue seemed to search my face. *My child, is it Rome you are weeping for?*

No, for him. Tavius. Oh, goddess, please—

I crouched on the floor now, my arms stretched out before me. I wept and knew I would weep forever. I imagined him dead, his eyes open and staring sightlessly, as his body sank into the sea. *Tavius.*

>>>>>>>

The Battle of Actium began on September 2, 722 years after the founding of Rome, at midday. Long before the sun set, all had been decided, though even at midnight men were being rescued from burning ships. The news of what had happened reached Rome with surprising swiftness. The letter I received came later, and confirmed what by then I already knew.

Scrawled on wax stamped with his seal. Just two words. *I won.*

>>>>>>>

Much later, in wintertime, another letter came, a rolled sheet of papyrus, bound in a leather case, but not bearing the impression of his signet ring. There was no salutation either.

> *We will take Alexandria in due time, and then the civil wars will be over. Antony and Cleopatra are within the city walls, and have both been trying to bargain for their lives. Antony sent me a present, the last man alive of those who wielded a knife to kill my father. He had been harboring him for years. I had this murderer decapitated and his body left for the vultures. My father now is fully avenged, just as I swore he would be.*

Antony would like to retire the way Lepidus did. As if I could turn my back on him as long as he breathes. Cleopatra assumes rightly that I cannot leave Antony alive. She deals for her own life, does not care what I do with Antony. Or pretends not to care. In any case, she is prepared to sacrifice him. I wonder, Livia, in similar circumstances, would you be prepared to sacrifice me? I'm a man of few illusions, but until recently I would have said nothing could shake your love for me. In this foul world, it was pleasant to believe in something.

I need a more compliant wife, and I need an heir. I find it amazing that you haven't apologized for the way you spoke to me.

I got too used to you. I know that, because I find myself talking to you in my mind. Arguing. It's good to be rid of you, because I gave you too much power. I think you bewitched me.

After my victory at Actium, you didn't even write to congratulate me.

I'm surrounded by idiots here. The stupidity of soldiers is like no other stupidity on earth. Sometimes I think men are physically brave only because they lack imagination and cannot anticipate what a spear in their guts would feel like.

Why do I waste time writing to you? Probably I won't even send this letter.

You could write and let me know how the children are.

>>>>>>>

How was I to answer such a letter? How, when in my heart I still cared for the man who wrote it; and when he was the most powerful human being on earth, and only a fool would deliberately provoke his enmity?

I composed a long letter in reply. Some fragments of what I wrote remain in my memory.

My dear Tavius, I was not sure you would welcome a letter from me, so I did not write before, but of course I do congratulate you on your

> *magnificent victory. The children are all in excellent health and send their greetings and their love.*
>
> *I would not sacrifice you as Cleopatra would Antony, because compared to her I am foolishly sentimental, so much so that nothing will ever alter my love for you.*
>
> *Nothing matters to me as much as the fact that you are alive and safe. Even your victory pales next to that. No doubt you consider that foolish, but Diana knows it is the truth.*
>
> *You say I am not compliant. Of course that is so. If I promised to change, I doubt if you would believe me. I doubt if it is in my power to change.*
>
> *I fully understand your need for a wife who can give you an heir. We should think of each other with kindness and try to remember past happiness. Happiness is rare.*

I crafted the letter carefully, to blunt his anger, and yet it contained no lies. I could not bring myself to apologize for any words I had spoken to him, though perhaps a wiser woman would have. The sense of loss I felt was intense, but I had been living with that for some time. As for his need for a male heir, I did understand it. He was a monarch now. A monarch who has established rule over a vast empire needs, above all, a son.

⋙⋙⋙

"Now the golden age will come," Maecenas had said, embracing me when first word came of Actium.

A cynic would say that he looked as overjoyed as any man would after learning he had bet on the right horse. But he would have stuck by Tavius to the death. And he did not hold grudges. My past unkind words had been quickly forgotten. Every day we worked together, shouldering the administrative tasks that needed to be done in Tavius's absence.

"The golden age, don't you think that's aiming a bit high?" I said to him once.

Maecenas laughed. "You can call it a golden age, or just the best possible outcome to an extremely nasty political situation. Rome has survived. The energy that civil war drained now will go to better purposes. And the arts will flourish."

Yes, I thought, *I am sure under Tavius the arts will flourish.*

"It will be interesting to see," I said in a distant voice.

A new era would begin. There would be another woman at Tavius's side. And me? I began to think about a separate future, a golden age of my own.

News filtered out of Alexandria and eventually reached us in Rome. Cleopatra had massacred those leading citizens whose loyalty she doubted. Caesarion and Antyllus, seventeen and sixteen years old, had, in a public ceremony, been vested with the rights and duties of men, and enrolled in the Egyptian army, to bolster morale in the city.

"What is the point of all that?" Octavia said. "Of putting those boys in the army? Everyone knows Alexandria will soon fall."

"Cleopatra will hold things together as long as she can," I said.

At Actium, she had been the first of the enemy to flee. It was not cowardice but clear-eyed ruthlessness. She saw how it was going and sought to save what she could. Antony had followed after her, eventually boarding her vessel. They had abandoned their forces, leaving them to flounder and face defeat leaderless. She was as ruthless as ever now, holding on to power in her besieged city.

"If you were Cleopatra or Antony, would you let those boys come of age or bear arms?" Octavia asked me.

We sat in a box at the chariot races. The air was full of the smell of horses and manure. We both felt an obligation to appear in public in Tavius's stead, though neither of us took much interest in what happened on the racing track.

I shook my head. If Caesarion and Antyllus had been my sons, I would already have sent them running, to the ends of the earth. Away from Tavius.

"I like to think my brother has a conscience," Octavia said. "He also has a legalistic turn of mind. I imagine he is relieved that those boys are now of age, bearing arms against him."

"What's the use of talking about this?" I said.

"Would you kill him? Caesarion? Would you be able to do it if you were Tavius?"

I watched the teams of horses parade onto the track and listened to the cheers. The race began. "If he lives—another Caesar—there is every chance there will eventually be another civil war. That would mean the undoing of everything Tavius has fought and labored for. The slaughter would not end."

"And so you would be able to kill him in Tavius's place?"

"I don't know," I said. "And I don't wish to know."

I looked at a team of white horses and another team of blacks, racing neck and neck, straining under their charioteer's whips. They were very close together. Too close. Any moment, they might crash into each other. You would hear screams from the horses, shrieks from the spectators. Drivers might die.

"And Antyllus?" Octavia said. Her voice shook. "What will become of him?"

I said nothing.

"Don't worry, I won't weep out here in public." Octavia let out a slow breath. "I ask myself, can I imagine Antyllus peacefully accepting Tavius's victory, never lifting a hand to strike him down?

Never trying to avenge Antony? If I can't imagine that, then Tavius surely can't."

I saw acceptance mingled with the grief in her face. She had already given up hope for Antyllus, I think, and she talked of Antony as if he were already dead.

I had wanted to be part of the world I had first glimpsed as a girl through my father's eyes, the world of men who wielded power. But had I known I was asking for a front-seat view of butchery? In some way I supposed I had, but the full emotional meaning had eluded me. *No more of this,* I thought.

"Inside myself, I weep for Antyllus, Livia, I weep. And I wonder about the little children Antony has by Cleopatra. It is a risk to leave them alive. Who knows, they might turn into enemies one day. I ask myself if my brother is capable of putting children to death because they could one day threaten him. And I don't know the answer to that question. Do you?"

"No."

In a low voice, Octavia said, "Sometimes I want to run away and hide where no news will ever reach me. Do you ever want to run away and hide?"

"No," I said, "but often lately I picture in my mind a different sort of life. Sometimes a poor girl comes to me, desperate, and I give her a dowry so she can marry some decent fellow, and she comes back to show me the first baby. It makes me happy, as if the gods were smiling down at me. I feel that way when I look at Marcus. It is wonderful, isn't it, that Marcus is an orphan, but he is still safe and loved?"

"Yes," Octavia said. "That is wonderful."

"I think I could have a good life with just my children—I never used to feel that way. Perhaps I'll take in more orphan children. There are so many children left bereft, with no one to care for them. Maybe I will buy special country estates and send them there and have them reared and cared for. And I will visit and be like a mother to them. If I never bear another child, still I could bring up many children—a great many. Don't you think that would be a pleasant way to live?"

Octavia studied me. "And what would Tavius think of you taking in more orphan children?"

I shrugged my shoulders.

I saw knowledge in her eyes at that moment. I expected her to say, *Your marriage to my brother is over, isn't it?* But instead she said, "Livia, is it that you think Tavius will not come back to you? Or that you don't want him back?"

I did not answer. I did not know the answer to this myself.

On the racetrack, one chariot crossed the finish line. Everyone cheered.

\>>>>>>>

My dear Livia,

Your congratulations on my victory were not fulsome. Still, they were appreciated. I also appreciated the lack of rancor in your letter.

In return I will do my best to rise above any rancor toward you, and to put our falling-out into perspective. After all, it is only natural for a woman to fear war, and what would be disloyal and cowardly in a man cannot be judged so harshly in a woman. I have never blamed my sister for her tender heart, so why should I blame you? Certainly we will part friends. To think of you as anything other than a friend would spoil so many good memories.

I am sure you are curious about the situation here. You'll be glad to know I expect Alexandria to capitulate soon without a fight. Meanwhile, Antony writes to me suggesting that he and I fight a single combat to settle matters. What a noble gesture on his part, to suggest we meet personally in battle. After I've already won.

Cleopatra's latest letter is slightly less laughable. She writes that she is willing to abdicate in favor of her children. What she imagines is a pleasant, temporary retirement for herself, and me eventually having to deal with both her and Caesarion.

When I think of Caesarion I feel a heavy weight coming down right on the back of my neck. Is he truly Julius Caesar's son? I would prefer to think he isn't, but I suspect he is. He is certainly Cleopatra's child in every sense. I have spoken to those familiar with this young man's character. They say he is intelligent and ambitious. Too bad. If he were an amiable fool, I could give him some little vassal kingdom and sleep easy.

I see you flinching as you contemplate the decisions before me. Cleopatra would not flinch. You are, as you say, sentimental. The last thing the ruler of an empire needs is a sentimental wife. Maybe after I divorce you, I should marry Cleopatra. She would not annoy me with her qualms. On the other hand, if I married her I would have to employ a food taster.

I shall be merciful to the people of Alexandria. That at least will please you. You see, I still care about pleasing you. Isn't that odd?

\>\>\>\>\>\>\>

My dear Tavius,

The children are in good health and doing nicely in their lessons. They send you their respectful greetings and their love. How happy I am to still be able to count you as a friend. Thank you for your kind and comforting words.

At age thirty-nine, Cleopatra seems unlikely to bear you the brace of fine sons you deserve. She is also, as you suggest, untrustworthy. I think a certain degree of sentimentality may all in all be a good quality in even a ruler's wife. A well-born, virtuous, and sweet-natured Roman girl would be your best choice. It would be ideal if she came from a family line known for fertility. If you wish me to suggest candidates for your hand, you have only to ask, for I want your happiness above all things.

I am glad that you plan to spare the people of Alexandria. I have no right to advise you on great matters, nor do I believe my advice would sway you. I hope you will not take it amiss if I say only this: In all you do, please remember that the gods love mercy.

⋙⋙⋙

When I read his letter to me, it struck me that in the midst of all his great concerns he seemed to be trying to find a way to forgive me for what he had deemed my desertion. He could do it only by seeing me as womanish and soft—"sentimental." And I—I suppose I wished to forgive him too, at the same time that I said farewell to our marriage. I missed him, of course. In the night, I ached with yearning. There were times I would have given my soul to go back in time and be held in his arms, and moments when a memory would make me weep. It was easy to say farewell to the imperator, bitter anguish to give up the man.

For a while, I did not receive any letters from him.

I looked over all my business accounts one day, and then I did a grand tally of my wealth. I would not starve after Tavius divorced me, that was sure. As for my plan to take in little orphans—I had sufficient resources to raise dozens of children.

The news we received from Egypt came slowly and was often unreliable. Inquisitiveness has always been a vice of mine. One day, on impulse, I sent a letter to Tavius with a troop ship that was leaving for Alexandria. *Tell me, please, what is happening,* I begged. I wondered if he would even write back.

⋙⋙⋙

My dear Livia,

Your last letter contained questions, a few stated, some only implied. Why this interest in my affairs? Aren't we finished? After your kind offer to propose future brides for me, I assume your questions arise not from wifely concern but mere curiosity. Nevertheless, I will show my goodwill by answering them.

Yes, Alexandria surrendered peacefully. I made a reassuring speech to the inhabitants, who hailed me for my great benevolence before returning to the corrupt practices and perversions for which this city is famous. Yes, Antony committed suicide. He botched it, as he botched many things in his life. It took him a long time to die, but he was dead before I could get to him and kill him, which I suppose, from his point of view, was the main thing. His death scene was so protracted that his friends had time to carry him a considerable distance to where Cleopatra was hiding—hiding less from me than from him, afraid he would strangle her in revenge for her betrayal and abandonment. They had a moving reconciliation as he bled to death.

I eventually went to see Cleopatra where she was holed up in a huge fortified tomb, guarded by my troops. Yes, she tried to seduce me. No, I wasn't tempted. First of all, she was a bit old for me; second, she wasn't that beautiful by Roman standards; and finally, I will do her the courtesy of saying I didn't see her when she was at her best. (I can see you protesting that you didn't actually ask me about a possible seduction. Will you forgive me if I say I read those questions between the lines of your letter?)

She showed me several love letters she had from my father and read aloud her favorite passages, in a most charming and mellifluous voice. "You remind me of your father in so many ways," she said. "It is an amazing resemblance." I must have looked doubtful. "Truly," she said. "I do not refer to a mere physical resemblance but one of the spirit. And what memories that brings alive in my heart." I took her to mean one Caesar would do as well as another. Who can blame her for wanting to make this one last roll of the dice?

Yes, she killed herself. I let her discover the truth, which was that if she remained alive I would parade her through the streets of Rome in chains. She had a poisonous snake smuggled in and exited the stage gracefully, like the great actress she was. It was exactly what I hoped she would do. She wrote me a last letter in which she asked only that she and Antony be buried in one tomb. This wish I granted.

Antyllus and Caesarion were both speedily executed on my order. Cleopatra had sent Caesarion to hide from me in India. He might have made it there, but he heard a rumor I intended to make him some sort of king and came hotfooting back. Foolish.

I remind you that he and Antyllus had come of age and were grown men by law. If our positions had been reversed I'm sure either of them would have enjoyed eating my heart for dinner. Still, I'm aware of the supreme irony that I began this journey to avenge a man's murder and now end it by killing his only begotten son.

All my decisions were based on cold logic, a calculation of Rome's good. That is my defense, and whether it is valid depends on your point of view. If you kill but take no pleasure in killing, do the gods look on you more kindly? It may be that they smile more on mindless predatory beasts than men like me. I have saved Rome from further civil war, and if I roast in Tartarus for it, so be it. I'll tell you this, though. I hope no one is counting on me fighting any glorious wars to expand the empire. I've smelled all I want to of the stink of battle, and I would prefer never to look at another corpse.

The question of what to do with Cleopatra's young children by Antony has preyed on my mind. I've decided to send them to my sister, who is so motherly I am sure she will delight in raising them. My dear Livia, if not for your pervasive influence, it is possible I would have drowned all three like unwanted puppies. Certainly most of my friends thought that was the safest course. But all the years of your moralistic mewling in my ear have had an effect. Now I have to live with the thought of Mark Antony, in the lowest pit of Hades, laughing his head off at the image of me and my poor sister saddled with no less than six of his brats. I will play loving Uncle Tavius to all of them, and pray every day that they don't take after their father.

Would a monster do that?

I hope you will understand why, with the press of affairs, I have given little thought to personal matters. Should we truly divorce? The desirability of begetting a male heir is undeniable. You and I have had no success there, despite our best efforts. A fecund fifteen-year-old is what most men would recommend to address the difficulty. The other reason I give myself in favor of a divorce is the continual moralistic mewling to which I just referred. On the other side of the question is this—it seems unrealistic to imagine you remaining my closest friend and confidante after the end of our marriage. I ask myself, who will I talk to? Agrippa, you will answer. Maecenas. Yes and yes. And others. Everyone and no one.

Well, the world is full of women, after all.

No doubt after reading all this love talk, you'll want to rush into my arms. I'm afraid you can't, at least not right away. I will be reorganizing the eastern part of my empire for many months. It would not be seemly if I were so uxorious as to insist on having my wife with me. Besides, you wouldn't enjoy living in army camps. You are, we can both happily agree, no Fulvia.

I read the letter at my writing table. I put it down. The table was piled high with correspondence from all over the empire. I looked at it and thought numbly, *Let Tavius divorce me. I will say farewell to all of this. I will not miss it.*

I was no Fulvia. I would never strap on a sword, as she had. Compared to her I was soft and womanish. I pressed my hands to my eyes, as if to shut out the images in my mind. I could see the serpent, coiling to strike. But where had it bitten Cleopatra? On the neck, on the arm? How long had it taken her to die? I found myself imagining the details of her death, and also the deaths of two boys on the cusp of manhood.

Out of this would come . . . what? The golden age Maecenas spoke of? Or a curse on our children and our children's children?

After all the anger, all the betrayal, Antony had exchanged forgiveness with Cleopatra, as he lay bloody in her arms. I visualized her weeping over him. How flawed those two were, how cruel and capable of turning their cruelty even on each other. And yet . . . and yet . . . Did it not mean something that they loved each other, insofar as they were capable of loving? Was that not at least some defense, that, dying, he'd had himself carried through the streets to her? And that she had not turned him away?

I saw myself in Cleopatra's place. The man I held, who bled from a self-inflicted wound, was not Antony but Tavius.

I wept.

>>>>>>>>

Tavius complained that he had no one to talk to. I felt alone too. I had friends, but how could I confide the secrets of my heart when my personal life and matters of state were so intermeshed? If I had had a true confidante I would have told her this: *He misses me. He would not write to me if he did not. If I only say the correct warm and loving words I can perhaps remain his wife. But something in me pulls back. I imagine another life. I imagine no longer being complicit.*

At times I foresaw the future we might have together. How would it be, married to the lord of the empire, and never able to bear him a child? Failing, always failing in what mattered most, even if I succeeded in all else. Seeing the disappointment in his eyes.

I was twenty-eight years old, young enough that I still might have a son who lived. But after all our years of marriage, what were the odds? No. I sensed I had lost the capacity to bring new life into the world.

In the end, with the same calculation of Rome's good that had governed his other decisions, Tavius would cast me off. Or even if he didn't, I would always be waiting for that. Why would I choose that path?

If he knew how to act on the basis of cold logic, so did I. I would choose differently.

Because I was wealthy in my own right, I could be free as almost no woman on earth was free. I would never become Tavius's enemy. That would be unwise. I would maintain a friendship with him, just as I had with Tiberius Nero. A friendship, just cordial enough for safety's sake. Just distant enough that I would never have to hear again about whom he had executed.

I would soar like a bird, solitary, unmated, but untrammeled.

"They are like any other children," Octavia said.

Antony and Cleopatra's three youngsters were in the garden with Octavia's little daughters, their half sisters. They were darker in coloring than Antonia and Antonilla, but one could see a resemblance; every one of Antony's children had his jutting chin. His children by Cleopatra also had their mother's aquiline nose. All the children ran about, shouting and playing, under the eye of a weary-looking nursemaid.

Octavia and I sat on a bench at the edge of the garden, drinking cider out of silver goblets and munching on figs and nuts. "Tavius wrote me that the three of them will have to be exhibited to the people of Rome when he returns in triumph," Octavia said. "I suppose they will ride down the Sacred Way in a wagon, in front of his chariot. But he has promised he will return them to me, right afterward. I wonder if they will have to wear chains."

"Little gold chains, perhaps," I said.

Octavia's face filled with distaste.

"They could have been killed," I said. "They could have been enslaved. Who would dare to object, or would even be surprised, if Tavius chose to destroy those children? Instead, they will wear play chains for an hour and then be kindly reared by you as Roman citizens."

"How quick you are to defend my brother," Octavia said.

I said nothing. I watched Cleopatra's children tossing a ball back and forth with their half sisters, and listened to her little daughter's giggle.

"Whenever I see you, I notice how subdued you are," Octavia said. "You used to have a shine about you. Your eyes were like lanterns, lit from within. Now, even when you talk about your plans, all the orphan children you will save, you seem lifeless to me."

"You are too kind. Please, no more compliments."

Octavia smiled faintly. "A quiet life of good works would suit me. But you?"

"I have devoted a great deal of time to good works already," I said, almost snapping out the words.

"I know you have. Why, that has been one of the props of my brother's rule, hasn't it—you and your good works?"

I tossed my head and did not answer her.

"I know what will happen." Octavia spoke in a low, confidential tone. "When Tavius comes home to you, even covered in all this blood, on that day you'll come alive. You'll mix up remedies for any ache he has, and bathe him in your love, and make him feel he is the son of Apollo. And you'll be his goddess and his queen, won't you?"

I shook my head. How wrong Octavia was. Tavius and I had not written to each other for months. And the thought of washing and kissing his bloody hands repelled me. I saw another shape to my future. *A free woman.* And if I suffered lifelong loneliness, that might balance the scale in the gods' eyes, for my transgressions. "You needn't speak to me with such scorn," I told Octavia.

"But I wasn't speaking to you with scorn," Octavia said. "You misunderstand me. I am telling you what I hope for. I still love my brother, and I want you to sit in the belly of the leviathan with him. If you don't, who could do it? The gods know it would be beyond me. And if he's there alone, I fear for him. Truly, I fear for his sanity with such great and absolute power, if he must carry his burden alone. If you two part, I pity Rome, and I pity Tavius. Most of all, I pity Tavius."

I was silent. Her words surprised me.

"When I search for my brother, the brother I remember, do you know where I see him? With you. In your presence, he becomes human. If he ever were to betray you—"

"Betray me?" I said. "You assume he has not?"

"Oh, the women? You know how little they matter to him. But if he were to abandon you—then I would know that there's nothing left of my brother, that Rome has finally devoured him whole. I swear to you on that day I would rend my garments."

⋙⋙

He was gone for two years. Two years can feel like a century, in certain circumstances.

Before he returned, he wrote me a brief letter. He would not enter Rome proper until it was time to ride through the streets in triumphant parade. That was tradition. *It would be most convenient for me to come to the villa at Prima Porta, since it is just outside of Rome, and a comfortable place to conduct official business. I will stay there until my triumph is organized, if you don't mind.* I imagined his lip curling as he wrote those words: *if you don't mind.*

My response was polite. *Certainly, it makes good sense for you to stay at Prima Porta. Of course I do not mind.*

Runners came with the news, as soon as his ships could be seen off the coast of Italy. I went to my villa, to wait for him. Almost at once houseguests came and filled every available bedchamber. With desperate eagerness, leading senators begged invitations. They must be present to welcome Caesar. As the time for his arrival approached, other senators came, completely uninvited but smiling at me with frantic sycophancy. Soon a good part of the Senate camped in my courtyard. I welcomed them, I gave them food and wine. I wished they would go away.

Everyone seemed to have one or two friends or relatives who—against all advice, for completely incomprehensible reasons—had sided with Antony. Now they wandered like lost sheep on Egyptian sands, or they hid on their relatives' country estates. "Lady Livia, I'm sure Caesar would be moved to mercy, if a plea came from you. My poor nephew is just a harmless idiot. If Caesar would only spare him . . . let him come home . . ."

"This will be part of your role, you know, in the new order," an elderly senator said. "A state is somewhat like a family, when you think of it. A family needs both a father and a mother. Now when I was a boy, my brothers and I constantly got into trouble. My father always wanted to beat us. But in fact we got very few beatings that I remember."

"Oh?" I said.

"Yes. Because our mother was always begging us off." He smiled at me. "You will soften Caesar's heart. And you will help us to love him."

How could I tell this gentle, good man, "I think Caesar will take another wife"?

⋙⋙

"Papa!" Julia's voice rose in a joyous shriek. "Papa!"

I sat reading mail. I got up, smoothed my hair, then walked down a corridor, now filled with Tavius's bodyguard. I found Tavius and the children in the little family sitting room that adjoined the garden.

He stood, wearing a plain soldier's tunic, but no armor, no sword. His hair was clipped short, his face clean-shaven and sunburned. There were lines in the corners of his mouth that I did not remember.

Julia clung to him, her cheek pressed to his chest. He stroked her hair. Drusus and Marcus quivered with excitement. Tiberius stood a little apart, but he was the one Tavius addressed. "I'm not sure the smaller galleys made a difference. Antony's crews all came down with some fever or other. They were easy pickings. There are lucky accidents like that in war."

"But the smaller galleys are better?" Tiberius said.

"If the crews are trained to take advantage of their maneuverability," Tavius replied. Then he saw me. Our eyes met and held. For just a moment by some trick of the light or of my mind, I saw another being, not an imperator but an eighteen-year-old boy. "Tiberius asks very intelligent questions," he said.

"He might have waited for you to sit down before he began asking them," I said. "Welcome home."

"Thank you," he said. "I avoided the courtyard, coming in. It seems packed with people."

"I'm afraid so. Senators. They keep coming. Almost the whole Senate is already here. I'm sure you want peace and quiet, but I couldn't tell them to go away."

"No," he said. "Of course you couldn't." He gently detached himself from Julia and sat down on a couch. I could see he was glad to get off his feet. He looked at me. I saw something in his expression I did not expect to see. Tenderness? Longing?

"You can greet them tomorrow, after you've rested," I said.

He shook his head. "No. That would be discourteous after they've come all the way from Rome. I'll speak to them in a little while."

"Are you hungry?"

"I was seasick through the whole voyage. The thought of food . . ." He grimaced.

"You must be thirsty, though." I clapped my hands to summon a slave, and ordered him to bring water and wine.

"Later I'll tell you stories about Alexandria," Tavius said to Julia. "But run along now. Weren't you having your lessons?"

She did not want to leave and remained motionless.

"Your father is tired," I said. "All of you—go back to your tutor."

Julia shot me an aggrieved look before she and the boys left the room.

I sat beside Tavius. The slave returned. I told him to set down his tray and dismissed him, then poured wine into the goblet. I added water, watched the rich purple of the wine fade to some indeterminate shade. As I did this, I was aware of Tavius watching me. I knew just how he liked his wine mixed. The slave was new and would not have known.

I handed Tavius the goblet. I thought, *A man returns home from making himself master of the Roman empire, and he is tired and thirsty, just like any other man.*

He seemed older. It was not a matter of lines etched into his face, but a subtle alteration in his manner. He raised his goblet to his lips and studied me over the rim as he drank. He paused and said, "The children all look taller and . . . different. It's disconcerting how much they've changed. At least you look the same." He drank some more, and then put down the cup.

The wine left a stain on his lips. I had the impulse to reach out with a finger and wipe it away, as I might have once. I thought of the two trees painted on the walls of the summer dining room, the ones with branches intertwined. Trees that had grown up so close together you could not disentangle them without chopping them to pieces.

How little I knew myself, really. How could I have failed to anticipate what I would feel?

And yet I still believed I could be separate. I had the strength to walk away.

For moments, we looked into each other's eyes. We were very grave. I thought of the burden he carried now. A burden like Atlas's. He had sought it, and now he must endure the unrelenting weight of it. He guessed my thoughts and gave me a wintry smile. "Did you know that after Actium Cleopatra sent me a gold crown and a throne?"

"Did she send you a poisonous snake too?"

He laughed. "I knew you'd say that. The day I get tired of life, I'll put on that crown." His face sobered. "I won't be a king, but I need some kind of title."

I longed to touch him. I seemed to feel that longing in every pore of my skin. "Call yourself First Citizen."

He raised his eyebrows.

"The leading member of the Senate used to have that title. First among equals. Everyone will be pleased."

"First Citizen." He considered. "Why didn't I think of that?"

"You've had other things to think of."

"Yes. And the truth is, traveling doesn't agree with me. It fogs my brain."

Lie down, I thought. *Put your head in my lap. I see how tired you are. I want to watch you sleep.* "You must have seen many interesting sights," I said.

"I saw Alexander the Great's mummy. But that didn't go so well. I touched his nose and it fell off."

I smiled uncertainly, unsure if he was joking.

"His hair was almost the same color as mine, but he wore it long. He was about my height too. No one told me not to touch him."

"The poor Alexandrians were probably too afraid of you to tell you."

"Poor Alexandrians? Poor Alexander, with no nose." Then: "I won it all, Livia. I always knew I would. And I'm going to hold it."

I nodded.

"I won't be satisfied unless I give Rome the best government the world has ever seen. There will be peace, justice, and prosperity. I'll work for those things as long as I have breath in my body."

Yes, I believed that. I also knew how much blood he had shed for the sake of power. There was a fissure at the core of him, a split that ran right through his soul.

"I've been giving a lot of thought to our marriage," he said.

"Oh? I'm surprised." I felt a tightening in the pit of my stomach.

"You know better than to be surprised." He looked away from me for the first time, got up and took a walk around the room, pacing. His limp was more pronounced than it had been before he left. "I like things settled one way or another. Win or lose."

"Not everything comes down to winning or losing," I said.

"Being in some in-between state eats my guts out. Do you know why I stopped writing to you? Because I couldn't make head or tail of the letters you wrote me back. Were you deliberately toying with me?"

"What do you think?"

"I think you couldn't decide if you still wanted to be my wife or not." He shook his head. "You're so contrary. But you wrote that you still loved me."

When I was a girl, I imagined love was a kind of prize for virtuous behavior. That was how the philosophers described it. Love was a tribute that flowed naturally only to those with undivided spirits and pure hearts. It occurred to me now that it was something else, wilder and less comprehensible. An affinity of the soul? Even that did not encompass it.

Stop talking. Come here. I want to hold you. I almost said those words, but I forced myself to keep silent. I imagined myself a free woman with clean hands.

"Well, you'll have to decide now. I want no death of a thousand cuts to our marriage. Either come with me, and greet our guests, and we will begin again." His voice hardened. "Or say no, and I will inform them that you and I have decided on an amicable divorce."

"Amicable," I said. I imagined being his friend and no more than that, and felt a tightening in my throat.

"I pay my debts. But think what you would be throwing away."

"I am thinking of it," I said.

He came and sat beside me again. He said in a low voice, as if he were telling me a secret, "You might want to consider this: I love you. I will love you until the end of my life. If you never bear me a child who lives, I will accept it. I will leave this empire to some other man's son, rather than marry elsewhere and give you up."

I drew in a sharp breath at that. These were words I had not expected to hear. I had thought him unwilling to sacrifice for me. *I will leave this empire to some other man's son.* By his reckoning, he could make no greater sacrifice. I could see in his face how much it would cost him, and also that he was fully resolved to pay the price.

"There is nothing—except your word—that would ever make me give you up," he said. "So put that in the balance. Also put in the balance what you owe Rome."

"Rome," I repeated.

"I will be a better ruler with you than without you. When you think about it you will find you don't doubt that for a moment. Do you?"

I raised my chin. "No."

"See?" He smiled at me. His smile had a practiced charm. I could imagine him using that smile to seduce other women. Oh, I saw him clearly. And if I loved him, it was with knowledge, not with a girl's heart fluttering. "Stay with me, and a hundred years from now, historians will ask this question—how could a man who fought like such a savage for preeminence, in the end become such a great, just, and merciful ruler? And the historians, being men, will never credit you. But who cares about them? What do historians ever accomplish? It will be a wonderful joke. We'll laugh about it together." For just an instant, a stricken look, almost fear, flickered across his face. "We will," he insisted. "We'll laugh." He rose and held out his hand to me.

And so finally, and for always, I chose. Why did I make the choice I did? Because I loved once in my life and forever? Because I desired him still? Or maybe compassion governed me. I imagined him as he would be, alone on that pinnacle. What would loneliness do to him? Yes, perhaps it was compassion. Or perhaps I heard the call of my own destiny.

I think it was all those things.

I rose. I did not take his hand. I kissed him on the lips. He gripped me in his arms and buried his face in the crook of my neck and heaved a sigh like a spent runner. I felt he might fall, and I was propping him up. But only for a moment. He straightened and smiled at me. *I win again,* his eyes said. He kissed me hungrily.

He took a step back and held out his hand again. I laid my hand on his. Then, together, we went to greet the Senate of Rome.

>>>>>>>

He never wore a crown, but for the rest of his life he governed Rome. There was peace at home and by and large in the empire, the Pax Romana—peace such as the world had never seen before. Commerce flourished, and so did poetry. People called it the Golden Age. It wasn't that. It was not even that just Republic of which my father and other good men had dreamed. But it was far better than what had gone before, better than reasonable people even dared hope for, after the decades of blood.

In time, the Senate gave him a new name, Augustus, the revered one. They called him Father of His Country too, and named a month of the year Augustus in his honor.

I was the voice whispering in his ear that mercy could be strength. He more than once pardoned men who had sought to undo him, because I asked him to. I saw to it that no one could ever justly call him a bloody-handed tyrant.

I never bore him a child who lived. His daughter—we do not speak of her; it hurts too much to remember how she broke her father's heart. His grandsons died young. Some whispered that I poisoned them, out of ambition for my own progeny. I shrugged off these tales. People like to tell lies about the great.

There was both happiness and pain in the years Tavius and I shared, but we were married in the fullest sense, and our tie was unbreakable. He had told me that where he grew up people married for life, and so it was with us. I do not look back without regrets. But I have never regretted the choice I made to remain Tavius's wife.

Tiberius and Drusus became the leading generals of their generation. They did not fight other Romans, but battled foreign enemies on our empire's borders. My Marcus, too, had an exemplary if less glorious military career.

Drusus died in Gaul, after a riding accident. It was the greatest sorrow of my life.

In the end, Tiberius was the only man qualified to follow after, take up the reins of government, and hold the empire together. Tavius adopted him, and in due time he inherited all. He rules Rome now—not as gently as I would like.

And that glorious Republic in which my father believed? Even the idea of it recedes. It recedes in memory; it recedes into some unimaginable future time. We were not worthy of it. We lost our way. The gods must judge us.

I began writing down my memories, thinking to sit in judgment on the young woman I was. I find I cannot do it. I am still Livia Drusilla.

The gods must judge me.

My beloved, Rome's revered one, died shortly before what would have been his seventy-seventh birthday. He died in the month of Augustus, peacefully in his bed. During his illness, I was always with him, and as the light waned, I held him in my arms. His last act was to kiss me. His final words were spoken to me. "Keep the memory of our marriage alive," he whispered. I have done that. I hope to do it for eternity.

\>>>>>>>

Livia passed away at the age of eighty-six . . . The Senate . . . voted an arch in her honor—a distinction conferred on no other woman—because she had saved the lives of not a few of them, reared the children of many citizens, and paid the dowries for many girls, in consequence of which some were calling her Mother of Her Country. She was buried in the mausoleum of Augustus.

—Cassius Dio

Author's Note

Livia Drusilla (58 B.C.–29 A.D.) was not only the wife of Caesar Augustus but his political advisor. She is thought to have been the most powerful woman in the history of ancient Rome. Though Augustus himself used the humbler title First Citizen, historians have dubbed him Rome's first emperor. His marriage to Livia lasted fifty-one years, and he was succeeded as emperor by Livia's son Tiberius.

Many of the incidents in this book are based on the historical record. For example, Livia actually survived getting caught in a forest fire, though her hair and clothing were singed; her first husband, Tiberius Nero, gave her away at her wedding to Caesar; and she, along with her sister-in-law, Octavia, received the unusual right (for a woman) to manage her own finances.

Livia has gotten bad press. Rumor has a way even now of attaching to women who break the conventional mold, and it certainly did in ancient Rome. People told stories about her poisoning her husband's potential heirs one by one—and finally him—so that her son Tiberius, at age fifty-five, could assume supreme power. "Poisoner" was not an uncommon charge to be leveled at prominent Roman women. (Even the supremely virtuous Cornelia was accused of poisoning her son-in-law.) Livia's interest in medicinal herbs gave the charges verisimilitude. In recent years, several biographers have argued convincingly that Livia never murdered anyone. Personally, I find the idea laughable that the astute and canny Caesar Augustus misread her character for five decades, stood by while she disposed of his relatives, and then let himself be poisoned by her.

Livia induced her husband to show mercy to at least some of his political opponents. She cared for orphans and, like a good modern First Lady, succored victims of disasters such as fires and earthquakes. If this makes her no saint, it at least does not cast her as a villain.

Her relationship in old age with her son Tiberius was strained, and he saw to it that the arch the Senate wanted constructed in her honor was never built. However, she eventually received a greater distinction. Like Augustus, she was deified—in her case, through the efforts of her grandson, the emperor Claudius. She and her husband were worshipped as gods, and Roman women took oaths by invoking the name of Livia.

The novel's unromantic view of Antony and Cleopatra is, like the portrait of Livia, consistent with facts. The blunt terminology on page 327 is taken from a letter Antony actually wrote, preserved by Suetonius in *The Twelve Caesars*.

I've used the familiar anglicized versions of Mark Antony's and Sextus Pompey's names (rather than calling them Marcus Antonius and Sextus Pompeius). In the case of Caesar Octavianus, later Augustus, I've followed a different course. He never used the name Octavian, and neither have I in this book. In keeping with my desire to take a fresh look at him through Livia's eyes, I've referred to him by his actual Roman name and allowed Livia to call him by a nickname.

Acknowledgments

This book would never have existed without the generous help of extraordinary people. My thanks to:

The friends and fellow writers who were the novel's first readers. Camden McDaris Black, Bruce Bowman, Gina Caulfield, Susan Coventry, Mark Dane, Cynthia Dunn, Mary Hoffman, Barbara Morgan, Vicky Oliver, and Norm Scott all gave me encouragement and support as well as perceptive feedback.

My brilliant literary agent, Elizabeth Winick Rubinstein. Her wise counsel and faith in the book have earned my everlasting gratitude.

The editorial dream team at Amazon Publishing. Terry Goodman has provided a sure guiding hand every step of the way. He, Charlotte Herscher, and Phyllis DeBlanche offered creative insights and expertise that made this a better novel. I'm grateful to all the people at Amazon for their innovative vision and hard work.

About the Author

Phyllis T. Smith was born and currently lives in Brooklyn, New York. After obtaining a bachelor's degree from Brooklyn College and a master's degree from New York University, Phyllis pursued a practical career in computer applications training, yet found herself drawn to literature and art of the ancient world. *I Am Livia* is her first novel. She has another novel set in ancient Rome in the works.